MW01248817

Jerusalem Delivered

Torquato Tasso

Table of Contents

Jerusalem Delivered

Torquato Tasso

Kessinger Publishing reprints thousands of hard–to–find books!

Visit us at http://www.kessinger.net

FIRST BOOK

THE ARGUMENT.
God sends his angel to Tortosa down,
Godfrey unites the Christian Peers and Knights;
And all the Lords and Princes of renown
Choose him their Duke, to rule the wares and fights.
He mustereth all his host, whose number known,
He sends them to the fort that Sion hights;
The aged tyrant Juda's land that guides,
In fear and trouble, to resist provides.

I
The sacred armies, and the godly knight,
That the great sepulchre of Christ did free,
I sing; much wrought his valor and foresight,
And in that glorious war much suffered he;
In vain 'gainst him did Hell oppose her might,
In vain the Turks and Morians armed be:
His soldiers wild, to brawls and mutinies prest,
Reduced he to peace, so Heaven him blest.

II

Jerusalem Delivered

O heavenly Muse, that not with fading bays
Deckest thy brow by the Heliconian spring,
But sittest crowned with stars' immortal rays
In Heaven, where legions of bright angels sing;
Inspire life in my wit, my thoughts upraise,
My verse ennoble, and forgive the thing,
If fictions light I mix with truth divine,
And fill these lines with other praise than thine.

III
Thither thou know'st the world is best inclined
Where luring Parnass most his sweet imparts,
And truth conveyed in verse of gentle kind
To read perhaps will move the dullest hearts:
So we, if children young diseased we find,
Anoint with sweets the vessel's foremost parts
To make them taste the potions sharp we give;
They drink deceived, and so deceived, they live.

IV
Ye noble Princes, that protect and save
The Pilgrim Muses, and their ship defend
From rock of Ignorance and Error's wave,
Your gracious eyes upon this labor bend:
To you these tales of love and conquest brave
I dedicate, to you this work I send:
My Muse hereafter shall perhaps unfold
Your fights, your battles, and your combats bold.

V
For if the Christian Princes ever strive
To win fair Greece out of the tyrants' hands,
And those usurping Ismaelites deprive
Of woful Thrace, which now captived stands,
You must from realms and seas the Turks forth drive,
As Godfrey chased them from Juda's lands,

Jerusalem Delivered

And in this legend, all that glorious deed,
Read, whilst you arm you; arm you, whilst you read.

VI
Six years were run since first in martial guise
The Christian Lords warraid the eastern land;
Nice by assault, and Antioch by surprise,
Both fair, both rich, both won, both conquered stand,
And this defended they in noblest wise
'Gainst Persian knights and many a valiant band;
Tortosa won, lest winter might them shend,
They drew to holds, and coming spring attend.

VII
The sullen season now was come and gone,
That forced them late cease from their noble war,
When God Almighty form his lofty throne,
Set in those parts of Heaven that purest are
(As far above the clear stars every one,
As it is hence up to the highest star),
Looked down, and all at once this world beheld,
Each land, each city, country, town and field.

VIII
All things he viewed, at last in Syria stayed
Upon the Christian Lords his gracious eye,
That wondrous look wherewith he oft surveyed
Men's secret thoughts that most concealed lie
He cast on puissant Godfrey, that assayed
To drive the Turks from Sion's bulwarks high,
And, full of zeal and faith, esteemed light
All worldly honor, empire, treasure, might:
IX
In Baldwin next he spied another thought,
Whom spirits proud to vain ambition move:
Tancred he saw his life's joy set at naught,

So woe–begone was he with pains of love:
Boemond the conquered folk of Antioch brought,
The gentle yoke of Christian rule to prove:
He taught them laws, statutes and customs new,
Arts, crafts, obedience, and religion true;

X

And with such care his busy work he plied,
That to naught else his acting thoughts he bent:
In young Rinaldo fierce desires he spied,
And noble heart of rest impatient;
To wealth or sovereign power he naught applied
His wits, but all to virtue excellent;
Patterns and rules of skill, and courage bold,
He took from Guelpho, and his fathers old.

XI

Thus when the Lord discovered had, and seen
The hidden secrets of each worthy's breast,
Out of the hierarchies of angels sheen
The gentle Gabriel called he from the rest,
'Twixt God and souls of men that righteous been
Ambassador is he, forever blest,
The just commands of Heaven's Eternal King,
'Twixt skies and earth, he up and down doth bring.

XII

To whom the Lord thus spake: "Godfredo find,
And in my name ask him, why doth he rest?
Why be his arms to ease and peace resigned?
Why frees he not Jerusalem distrest?
His peers to counsel call, each baser mind
Let him stir up; for, chieftain of the rest
I choose him here, the earth shall him allow,
His fellows late shall be his subjects now."

Jerusalem Delivered

XIII

This said, the angel swift himself prepared
To execute the charge imposed aright,
In form of airy members fair imbared,
His spirits pure were subject to our sight,
Like to a man in show and shape he fared,
But full of heavenly majesty and might,
A stripling seemed he thrive five winters old,
And radiant beams adorned his locks of gold.

XIV

Of silver wings he took a shining pair,
Fringed with gold, unwearied, nimble, swift;
With these he parts the winds, the clouds, the air,
And over seas and earth himself doth lift,
Thus clad he cut the spheres and circles fair,
And the pure skies with sacred feathers clift;
On Libanon at first his foot he set,
And shook his wings with rory May dews wet.

XV

Then to Tortosa's confines swiftly sped
The sacred messenger, with headlong flight;
Above the eastern wave appeared red
The rising sun, yet scantly half in sight;
Godfrey e'en then his morn–devotions said,
As was his custom, when with Titan bright
Appeared the angel in his shape divine,
Whose glory far obscured Phoebus' shine.

XVI

"Godfrey," quoth he, "behold the season fit
To war, for which thou waited hast so long,
Now serves the time, if thou o'erslip not it,
To free Jerusalem from thrall and wrong:
Thou with thy Lords in council quickly sit;

Comfort the feeble, and confirm the strong,
The Lord of Hosts their general doth make thee,
And for their chieftain they shall gladly take thee.

XVII
"I, messenger from everlasting Jove,
In his great name thus his behests do tell;
Oh, what sure hope of conquest ought thee move,
What zeal, what love should in thy bosom dwell!"
This said, he vanished to those seats above,
In height and clearness which the rest excel,
Down fell the Duke, his joints dissolved asunder,
Blind with the light, and strucken dead with wonder.

XVIII
But when recovered, he considered more,
The man, his manner, and his message said;
If erst he wished, now he longed sore
To end that war, whereof he Lord was made;
Nor swelled his breast with uncouth pride therefore,
That Heaven on him above this charge had laid,
But, for his great Creator would the same,
His will increased: so fire augmenteth flame.

XIX
The captains called forthwith from every tent,
Unto the rendezvous he them invites;
Letter on letter, post on post he sent,
Entreatance fair with counsel he unites,
All, what a noble courage could augment,
The sleeping spark of valor what incites,
He used, that all their thoughts to honor raised,
Some praised, some paid, some counselled, all pleased.

XX
The captains, soldiers, all, save Boemond, came,

And pitched their tents, some in the fields without,
Some of green boughs their slender cabins frame,
Some lodged were Tortosa's streets about,
Of all the host the chief of worth and name
Assembled been, a senate grave and stout;
Then Godfrey, after silence kept a space,
Lift up his voice, and spake with princely grace:

XXI
"Warriors, whom God himself elected hath
His worship true in Sion to restore,
And still preserved from danger, harm and scath,
By many a sea and many an unknown shore,
You have subjected lately to his faith
Some provinces rebellious long before:
And after conquests great, have in the same
Erected trophies to his cross and name.

XXII
"But not for this our homes we first forsook,
And from our native soil have marched so far:
Nor us to dangerous seas have we betook,
Exposed to hazard of so far sought war,
Of glory vain to gain an idle smook,
And lands possess that wild and barbarous are:
That for our conquests were too mean a prey,
To shed our bloods, to work our souls' decay.

XXIII
"But this the scope was of our former thought, —
Of Sion's fort to scale the noble wall,
The Christian folk from bondage to have brought,
Wherein, alas, they long have lived thrall,
In Palestine an empire to have wrought,
Where godliness might reign perpetual,
And none be left, that pilgrims might denay

To see Christ's tomb, and promised vows to pay.

XXIV
"What to this hour successively is done
Was full of peril, to our honor small,
Naught to our first designment, if we shun
The purposed end, or here lie fixed all.
What boots it us there wares to have begun,
Or Europe raised to make proud Asia thrall,
If our beginnings have this ending known,
Not kingdoms raised, but armies overthrown?

XXV
"Not as we list erect we empires new
On frail foundations laid in earthly mould,
Where of our faith and country be but few
Among the thousands stout of Pagans bold,
Where naught behoves us trust to Greece untrue,
And Western aid we far removed behold:
Who buildeth thus, methinks, so buildeth he,
As if his work should his sepulchre be.

XXVI
"Turks, Persians conquered, Antiochia won,
Be glorious acts, and full of glorious praise,
By Heaven's mere grace, not by our prowess done:
Those conquests were achieved by wondrous ways,
If now from that directed course we run
The God of Battles thus before us lays,
His loving kindness shall we lose, I doubt,
And be a byword to the lands about.

XXVII
"Let not these blessings then sent from above
Abused be, or split in profane wise,
But let the issue correspondent prove

8

Jerusalem Delivered

To good beginnings of each enterprise;
The gentle season might our courage move,
Now every passage plain and open lies:
What lets us then the great Jerusalem
With valiant squadrons round about to hem?

XXVIII

"Lords, I protest, and hearken all to it,
Ye times and ages, future, present, past,
Hear all ye blessed in the heavens that sit,
The time for this achievement hasteneth fast:
The longer rest worse will the season fit,
Our sureties shall with doubt be overcast.
If we forslow the siege I well foresee
From Egypt will the Pagans succored be."

XXIX

This said, the hermit Peter rose and spake,
Who sate in counsel those great Lords among:
"At my request this war was undertake,
In private cell, who erst lived closed long,
What Godfrey wills, of that no question make,
There cast no doubts where truth is plain and strong,
Your acts, I trust, will correspond his speech,
Yet one thing more I would you gladly teach.

XXX

"These strifes, unless I far mistake the thing,
And discords raised oft in disordered sort,
Your disobedience and ill managing
Of actions lost, for want of due support,
Refer I justly to a further spring,
Spring of sedition, strife, oppression, tort,
I mean commanding power to sundry given,
In thought, opinion, worth, estate, uneven.

9

XXXI

"Where divers Lords divided empire hold,
Where causes be by gifts, not justice tried,
Where offices be falsely bought and sold,
Needs must the lordship there from virtue slide.
Of friendly parts one body then uphold,
Create one head, the rest to rule and guide:
To one the regal power and sceptre give,
That henceforth may your King and Sovereign live."

XXXII

And therewith stayed his speech. O gracious Muse,
What kindling motions in their breasts do fry?
With grace divine the hermit's talk infuse,
That in their hearts his words may fructify;
By this a virtuous concord they did choose,
And all contentions then began to die;
The Princes with the multitude agree,
That Godfrey ruler of those wars should be.

XXXIII

This power they gave him, by his princely right,
All to command, to judge all, good and ill,
Laws to impose to lands subdued by might,
To maken war both when and where he will,
To hold in due subjection every wight,
Their valors to be guided by his skill;
This done, Report displays her tell-tale wings,
And to each ear the news and tidings brings.

XXXIV

She told the soldiers, who allowed him meet
And well deserving of that sovereign place.
Their first salutes and acclamations sweet
Received he, with love and gentle grace;
After their reverence done with kind regreet

Requited was, with mild and cheerful face,
He bids his armies should the following day
On those fair plains their standards proud display.

XXXV
The golden sun rose from the silver wave,
And with his beams enamelled every green,
When up arose each warrior bold and brave,
Glistering in filed steel and armor sheen,
With jolly plumes their crests adorned they have,
And all tofore their chieftain mustered been:
He from a mountain cast his curious sight
On every footman and on every knight.

XXXVI
My mind, Time's enemy, Oblivion's foe,
Disposer true of each noteworthy thing,
Oh, let thy virtuous might avail me so,
That I each troop and captain great may sing,
That in this glorious war did famous grow,
Forgot till now by Time's evil handling:
This work, derived from my treasures dear,
Let all times hearken, never age outwear.
XXXVII
The French came foremost battailous and bold,
Late led by Hugo, brother to their King,
From France the isle that rivers four infold
With rolling streams descending from their spring,
But Hugo dead, the lily fair of gold,
Their wonted ensign they tofore them bring,
Under Clotharius great, a captain good,
And hardy knight ysprong of princes' blood.

XXXVIII
A thousand were they in strong armors clad,
Next whom there marched forth another band,

That number, nature, and instruction had,
Like them to fight far off or charge at hand,
All valiant Normans by Lord Robert lad,
The native Duke of that renowned land,
Two bishops next their standards proud upbare,
Called Reverend William, and Good Ademare.

XXXIX
Their jolly notes they chanted loud and clear
On merry mornings at the mass divine,
And horrid helms high on their heads they bear
When their fierce courage they to war incline:
The first four hundred horsemen gathered near
To Orange town, and lands that it confine:
But Ademare the Poggian youth brought out,
In number like, in hard assays as stout.

XL
Baldwin, his ensign fair, did next dispread
Among his Bulloigners of noble fame,
His brother gave him all his troops to lead,
When he commander of the field became;
The Count Carinto did him straight succeed,
Grave in advice, well skilled in Mars his game,
Four hundred brought he, but so many thrice
Led Baldwin, clad in gilden arms of price.

XLI
Guelpho next them the land and place possest,
Whose fortunes good with his great acts agree,
By his Italian sire, fro the house of Est,
Well could he bring his noble pedigree,
A German born with rich possessions blest,
A worthy branch sprung from the Guelphian tree.
'Twixt Rhene and Danubie the land contained
He ruled, where Swaves and Rhetians whilom reigned.

XLII

His mother's heritage was this and right,
To which he added more by conquest got,
From thence approved men of passing might
He brought, that death or danger feared not:
It was their wont in feasts to spend the night,
And pass cold days in baths and houses hot.
Five thousand late, of which now scantly are
The third part left, such is the chance of war.

XLIII

The nation then with crisped locks and fair,
That dwell between the seas and Arden Wood,
Where Mosel streams and Rhene the meadows wear,
A battel soil for grain, for pasture good,
Their islanders with them, who oft repair
Their earthen bulwarks 'gainst the ocean flood,
The flood, elsewhere that ships and barks devours,
But there drowns cities, countries, towns and towers;

XLIV

Both in one troop, and but a thousand all,
Under another Robert fierce they run.
Then the English squadron, soldiers stout and tall,
By William led, their sovereign's younger son,
These archers be, and with them come withal,
A people near the Northern Pole that wone,
Whom Ireland sent from loughs and forests hoar,
Divided far by sea from Europe's shore.

XLV

Tancredi next, nor 'mongst them all was one,
Rinald except, a prince of greater might,
With majesty his noble countenance shone,
High were his thoughts, his heart was bold in fight,

No shameful vice his worth had overgone,
His fault was love, by unadvised sight,
Bred in the dangers of adventurous arms,
And nursed with griefs, with sorrows, woes, and harms.

XLVI
Fame tells, that on that ever–blessed day,
When Christian swords with Persian blood were dyed,
The furious Prince Tancredi from that fray
His coward foes chased through forests wide,
Till tired with the fight, the heat, the way,
He sought some place to rest his wearied side,
And drew him near a silver stream that played
Among wild herbs under the greenwood shade.

XLVII
A Pagan damsel there unwares he met,
In shining steel, all save her visage fair,
Her hair unbound she made a wanton net,
To catch sweet breathing from the cooling air.
On her at gaze his longing looks he set,
Sight, wonder; wonder, love; love bred his care;
O love, o wonder; love new born, new bred,
Now groan, now armed, this champion captive led.

XLVIII
Her helm the virgin donned, and but some wight
She feared might come to aid him as they fought,
Her courage earned to have assailed the knight;
Yet thence she fled, uncompanied, unsought,
And left her image in his heart ypight;
Her sweet idea wandered through his thought,
Her shape, her gesture, and her place in mind
He kept, and blew love's fire with that wind.

XLIX

Well might you read his sickness in his eyes,
Their banks were full, their tide was at the flow,
His help far off, his hurt within him lies,
His hopes unstrung, his cares were fit to mow;
Eight hundred horse (from Champain came) he guies,
Champain a land where wealth, ease, pleasure, grow,
Rich Nature's pomp and pride, the Tirrhene main
There woos the hills, hills woo the valleys plain.

L
Two hundred Greeks came next, in fight well tried,
Not surely armed in steel or iron strong,
But each a glaive had pendant by his side,
Their bows and quivers at their shoulders hung,
Their horses well inured to chase and ride,
In diet spare, untired with labor long;
Ready to charge, and to retire at will,
Though broken, scattered, fled, they skirmish still;

LI
Tatine their guide, and except Tatine, none
Of all the Greeks went with the Christian host;
O sin, O shame, O Greece accurst alone!
Did not this fatal war affront thy coast?
Yet safest thou an idle looker—on,
And glad attendest which side won or lost:
Now if thou be a bondslave vile become,
No wrong is that, but God's most righteous doom.

LII
In order last, but first in worth and fame,
Unfeared in fight, untired with hurt or wound,
The noble squadron of adventurers came,
Terrors to all that tread on Asian ground:
Cease Orpheus of thy Minois, Arthur shame
To boast of Lancelot, or thy table round:

For these whom antique times with laurel drest,
These far exceed them, thee, and all the rest.

LIII
Dudon of Consa was their guide and lord,
And for of worth and birth alike they been,
They chose him captain, by their free accord,
For he most acts had done, most battles seen;
Grave was the man in years, in looks, in word,
His locks were gray, yet was his courage green,
Of worth and might the noble badge he bore,
Old scars of grievous wounds received of yore.
LIV
After came Eustace, well esteemed man
For Godfrey's sake his brother, and his own;
The King of Norway's heir Gernando than,
Proud of his father's title, sceptre, crown;
Roger of Balnavill, and Engerlan,
For hardy knights approved were and known;
Besides were numbered in that warlike train
Rambald, Gentonio, and the Gerrards twain.

LV
Ubaldo then, and puissant Rosimond,
Of Lancaster the heir, in rank succeed;
Let none forget Obizo of Tuscain land,
Well worthy praise for many a worthy deed;
Nor those three brethren, Lombards fierce and yond,
Achilles, Sforza, and stern Palamede;
Nor Otton's shield he conquered in those stowres,
In which a snake a naked child devours.

LVI
Guascher and Raiphe in valor like there was.
The one and other Guido, famous both,
Germer and Eberard to overpass,

Jerusalem Delivered

In foul oblivion would my Muse be loth,
With his Gildippes dear, Edward alas,
A loving pair, to war among them go'th
In bond of virtuous love together tied,
Together served they, and together died.

LVII

In school of love are all things taught we see,
There learned this maid of arms the ireful guise,
Still by his side a faithful guard went she,
One true—love knot their lives together ties,
No would to one alone could dangerous be,
But each the smart of other's anguish tries,
If one were hurt, the other felt the sore,
She lost her blood, he spent his life therefore.

LVIII

But these and all, Rinaldo far exceeds,
Star of his sphere, the diamond of this ring,
The nest where courage with sweet mercy breeds:
A comet worthy each eye's wondering,
His years are fewer than his noble deeds,
His fruit is ripe soon as his blossoms spring,
Armed, a Mars, might coyest Venus move,
And if disarmed, then God himself of Love.

LIX

Sophia by Adige's flowery bank him bore,
Sophia the fair, spouse to Bertoldo great,
Fit mother for that pearl, and before
The tender imp was weaned from the teat,
The Princess Maud him took, in Virtue's lore
She brought him up fit for each worthy feat,
Till of these wares the golden trump he hears,
That soundeth glory, fame, praise in his ears.

17

LX

And then, though scantly three times five years old,
He fled alone, by many an unknown coast,
O'er Aegean Seas by many a Greekish hold,
Till he arrived at the Christian host;
A noble flight, adventurous, brave, and bold,
Whereon a valiant prince might justly boast,
Three years he served in field, when scant begin
Few golden hairs to deck his ivory chin.

LXI

The horsemen past, their void–left stations fill
The bands on foot, and Reymond them beforn,
Of Tholouse lord, from lands near Piraene Hill
By Garound streams and salt sea billows worn,
Four thousand foot he brought, well armed, and skill
Had they all pains and travels to have borne,
Stout men of arms and with their guide of power
Like Troy's old town defenced with Ilion's tower.

LXII

Next Stephen of Amboise did five thousand lead,
The men he prest from Tours and Blois but late,
To hard assays unfit, unsure at need,
Yet armed to point in well–attempted plate,
The land did like itself the people breed,
The soil is gentle, smooth, soft, delicate;
Boldly they charge, but soon retire for doubt,
Like fire of straw, soon kindled, soon burnt out.

LXIII

The third Alcasto marched, and with him
The boaster brought six thousand Switzers bold,
Audacious were their looks, their faces grim,
Strong castles on the Alpine clifts they hold,
Their shares and coulters broke, to armors trim

They change that metal, cast in warlike mould,
And with this band late herds and flocks that guide,
Now kings and realms he threatened and defied.

LXIV
The glorious standard last to Heaven they sprad,
With Peter's keys ennobled and his crown,
With it seven thousand stout Camillo had,
Embattailed in walls of iron brown:
In this adventure and occasion, glad
So to revive the Romans' old renown,
Or prove at least to all of wiser thought,
Their hearts were fertile land although unwrought.
LXV
But now was passed every regiment,
Each band, each troop, each person worth regard
When Godfrey with his lords to counsel went,
And thus the Duke his princely will declared:
"I will when day next clears the firmament,
Our ready host in haste be all prepared,
Closely to march to Sion's noble wall,
Unseen, unheard, or undescried at all.

LXVI
"Prepare you then for travel strong and light,
Fierce to the combat, glad to victory."
And with that word and warning soon was dight,
Each soldier, longing for near coming glory,
Impatient be they of the morning bright,
Of honor so them pricked the memory:
But yet their chieftain had conceived a fear
Within his heart, but kept it secret there.

LXVII
For he by faithful spial was assured,
That Egypt's King was forward on his way,

And to arrive at Gaza old procured,
A fort that on the Syrian frontiers lay,
Nor thinks he that a man to wars inured
Will aught forslow, or in his journey stay,
For well he knew him for a dangerous foe:
An herald called he then, and spake him so:

LXVIII
"A pinnace take thee swift as shaft from bow,
And speed thee, Henry, to the Greekish main,
There should arrive, as I by letters know
From one that never aught reports in vain,
A valiant youth in whom all virtues flow,
To help us this great conquest to obtain,
The Prince of Danes he is, and brings to war
A troop with him from under the Arctic star.

LXIX
"And for I doubt the Greekish monarch sly
Will use with him some of his wonted craft,
To stay his passage, or divert awry
Elsewhere his forces, his first journey laft,
My herald good and messenger well try,
See that these succors be not us beraft,
But send him thence with such convenient speed
As with his honor stands and with our need.

LXX
"Return not thou, but Legier stay behind,
And move the Greekish Prince to send us aid,
Tell him his kingly promise doth him bind
To give us succors, by his covenant made."
This said, and thus instruct, his letters signed
The trusty herald took, nor longer stayed,
But sped him thence to done his Lord's behest,
And thus the Duke reduced his thoughts to rest.

Jerusalem Delivered

LXXI

Aurora bright her crystal gates unbarred,
And bridegroom–like forth stept the glorious sun,
When trumpets loud and clarions shrill were heard,
And every one to rouse him fierce begun,
Sweet music to each heart for war prepared,
The soldiers glad by heaps to harness run;
So if with drought endangered be their grain,
Poor ploughmen joy when thunders promise rain.

LXXII

Some shirts of mail, some coats of plate put on,
Some donned a cuirass, some a corslet bright,
And halbert some, and some a habergeon,
So every one in arms was quickly dight,
His wonted guide each soldier tends upon,
Loose in the wind waved their banners light,
Their standard royal toward Heaven they spread,
The cross triumphant on the Pagans dead.

LXXIII

Meanwhile the car that bears the lightning brand
Upon the eastern hill was mounted high,
And smote the glistering armies as they stand,
With quivering beams which dazed the wondering eye,
That Phaeton–like it fired sea and land,
The sparkles seemed up to the skies to fly,
The horses' neigh and clattering armors' sound
Pursue the echo over dale and down.

LXXIV

Their general did with due care provide
To save his men from ambush and from train,
Some troops of horse that lightly armed ride
He sent to scour the woods and forests main,
His pioneers their busy work applied

To even the paths and make the highways plain,
They filled the pits, and smoothed the rougher ground,
And opened every strait they closed found.

LXXV
They meet no forces gathered by their foe,
No towers defenced with rampire, moat, or wall,
No stream, no wood, no mountain could forslow
Their hasty pace, or stop their march at all;
So when his banks the prince of rivers, Po,
Doth overswell, he breaks with hideous fall
The mossy rocks and trees o'ergrown with age,
Nor aught withstands his fury and his rage.

LXXVI
The King of Tripoli in every hold
Shut up his men, munition and his treasure,
The straggling troops sometimes assail he would,
Save that he durst not move them to displeasure;
He stayed their rage with presents, gifts and gold,
And led them through his land at ease and leisure,
To keep his realm in peace and rest he chose,
With what conditions Godfrey list impose.

LXXVII
Those of Mount Seir, that neighboreth by east
The Holy City, faithful folk each one,
Down from the hill descended most and least,
And to the Christian Duke by heaps they gone,
And welcome him and his with joy and feast;
On him they smile, on him they gaze alone,
And were his guides, as faithful from that day
As Hesperus, that leads the sun his way.

LXXVIII
Along the sands his armies safe they guide

Jerusalem Delivered

By ways secure, to them well known before,
Upon the tumbling billows fraughted ride
The armed ships, coasting along the shore,
Which for the camp might every day provide
To bring munition good and victuals store:
The isles of Greece sent in provision meet,
And store of wine from Scios came and Crete.

LXXIX

Great Neptune grieved underneath the load
Of ships, hulks, galleys, barks and brigantines,
In all the mid—earth seas was left no road
Wherein the Pagan his bold sails untwines,
Spread was the huge Armado, wide and broad,
From Venice, Genes, and towns which them confines,
From Holland, England, France and Sicil sent,
And all for Juda ready bound and bent.

LXXX

All these together were combined, and knit
With surest bonds of love and friendship strong,
Together sailed they fraught with all things fit
To service done by land that might belong,
And when occasion served disbarked it,
Then sailed the Asian coasts and isles along;
Thither with speed their hasty course they plied,
Where Christ the Lord for our offences died.

LXXXI

The brazen trump of iron—winged fame,
That mingleth faithful troth with forged lies,
Foretold the heathen how the Christians came,
How thitherward the conquering army hies,
Of every knight it sounds the worth and name,
Each troop, each band, each squadron it descries,
And threat'neth death to those, fire, sword and slaughter,

Who held captived Israel's fairest daughter.

LXXXII

The fear of ill exceeds the evil we fear,
For so our present harms still most annoy us,
Each mind is prest and open every ear
To hear new tidings though they no way joy us,
This secret rumor whispered everywhere
About the town, these Christians will destroy us,
The aged king his coming evil that knew,
Did cursed thoughts in his false heart renew.

LXXXIII

This aged prince ycleped Aladine,
Ruled in care, new sovereign of this state,
A tyrant erst, but now his fell engine
His graver are did somewhat mitigate,
He heard the western lords would undermine
His city's wall, and lay his towers prostrate,
To former fear he adds a new—come doubt,
Treason he fears within, and force without.

LXXXIV

For nations twain inhabit there and dwell
Of sundry faith together in that town,
The lesser part on Christ believed well,
On Termagent the more and on Mahown,
But when this king had made this conquest fell,
And brought that region subject to his crown,
Of burdens all he set the Paynims large,
And on poor Christians laid the double charge.

LXXXV

His native wrath revived with this new thought,
With age and years that weakened was of yore,
Such madness in his cruel bosom wrought,

That now than ever blood he thirsteth more?
So stings a snake that to the fire is brought,
Which harmless lay benumbed with cold before,
A lion so his rage renewed hath,
Though fame before, if he be moved to wrath.

LXXXVI
"I see," quoth he, "some expectation vain,
In these false Christians, and some new content,
Our common loss they trust will be their gain,
They laugh, we weep; they joy while we lament;
And more, perchance, by treason or by train,
To murder us they secretly consent,
Or otherwise to work us harm and woe,
To ope the gates, and so let in our foe.

LXXXVII
"But lest they should effect their cursed will,
Let us destroy this serpent on his nest;
Both young and old, let us this people kill,
The tender infants at their mothers' breast,
Their houses burn, their holy temples fill
With bodies slain of those that loved them best,
And on that tomb they hold so much in price,
Let's offer up their priests in sacrifice."

LXXXVIII
Thus thought the tyrant in his traitorous mind,
But durst not follow what he had decreed,
Yet if the innocents some mercy find,
From cowardice, not truth, did that proceed,
His noble foes durst not his craven kind
Exasperate by such a bloody deed.
For if he need, what grace could then be got,
If thus of peace he broke or loosed the knot?

LXXXIX

His villain heart his cursed rage restrained,
To other thoughts he bent his fierce desire,
The suburbs first flat with the earth he plained,
And burnt their buildings with devouring fire,
Loth was the wretch the Frenchman should have gained
Or help or ease, by finding aught entire,
Cedron, Bethsaida, and each watering else
Empoisoned he, both fountains, springs, and wells.

XC

So wary wise this child of darkness was;
The city's self he strongly fortifies,
Three sides by site it well defenced has,
That's only weak that to the northward lies;
With mighty bars of long enduring brass,
The steel–bound doors and iron gates he ties,
And, lastly, legions armed well provides
Of subjects born, and hired aid besides.

SECOND BOOK

THE ARGUMENT.
Ismeno conjures, but his charms are vain;
Aladine will kill the Christians in his ire:
Sophronia and Olindo would be slain
To save the rest, the King grants their desire;
Clorinda hears their fact and fortunes plain,
Their pardon gets and keeps them from the fire:
Argantes, when Aletes' speeches are
Despised, defies the Duke to mortal war.

Jerusalem Delivered

I

While thus the tyrant bends his thoughts to arms,
Ismeno gan tofore his sight appear,
Ismen dead bones laid in cold graves that warms
And makes them speak, smell, taste, touch, see, and hear;
Ismen with terror of his mighty charms,
That makes great Dis in deepest Hell to fear,
That binds and looses souls condemned to woe,
And sends the devils on errands to and fro.

II

A Christian once, Macon he now adores,
Nor could he quite his wonted faith forsake,
But in his wicked arts both oft implores
Help from the Lord, and aid from Pluto black;
He, from deep caves by Acheron's dark shores,
Where circles vain and spells he used to make,
To advise his king in these extremes is come,
Achitophel so counselled Absalom.

III

"My liege," he says, "the camp fast hither moves,
The axe is laid unto this cedar's root,
But let us work as valiant men behoves,
For boldest hearts good fortune helpeth out;
Your princely care your kingly wisdom proves,
Well have you labored, well foreseen about;
If each perform his charge and duty so,
Nought but his grave here conquer shall your foe.

IV

"From surest castle of my secret cell
I come, partaker of your good and ill,
What counsel sage, or magic's sacred spell
May profit us, all that perform I will:
The sprites impure from bliss that whilom fell

27

Shall to your service bow, constrained by skill;
But how we must begin this enterprise,
I will your Highness thus in brief advise.

V

"Within the Christian's church from light of skies,
An hidden alter stands, far out of sight,
On which the image consecrated lies
Of Christ's dear mother, called a virgin bright,
An hundred lamps aye burn before her eyes,
She in a slender veil of tinsel dight,
On every side great plenty doth behold
Of offerings brought, myrrh, frankincense and gold.

VI

"This idol would I have removed away
From thence, and by your princely hand transport,
In Macon's sacred temple safe it lay,
Which then I will enchant in wondrous sort,
That while the image in that church doth stay,
No strength of arms shall win this noble fort,
Of shake this puissant wall, such passing might
Have spells and charms, if they be said aright."

VII

Advised thus, the king impatient
Flew in his fury to the house of God,
The image took, with words unreverent
Abused the prelates, who that deed forbode,
Swift with his prey, away the tyrant went,
Of God's sharp justice naught he feared the rod,
But in his chapel vile the image laid,
On which the enchanter charms and witchcraft said.

VIII

When Phoebus next unclosed his wakeful eye,

Jerusalem Delivered

Up rose the sexton of that place profane,
And missed the image, where it used to lie,
Each where he sough in grief, in fear, in vain;
Then to the king his loss he gan descry,
Who sore enraged killed him for his pain;
And straight conceived in his malicious wit,
Some Christian bade this great offence commit.

IX

But whether this were act of mortal hand,
Or else the Prince of Heaven's eternal pleasure,
That of his mercy would this wretch withstand,
Nor let so vile a chest hold such a treasure,
As yet conjecture hath not fully scanned;
By godliness let us this action measure,
And truth of purest faith will fitly prove
That this rare grace came down from Heaven above.

X

With busy search the tyrant gan to invade
Each house, each hold, each temple and each tent
To them the fault or faulty one bewrayed
Or hid, he promised gifts or punishment,
His idle charms the false enchanter said,
But in this maze still wandered and miswent,
For Heaven decreed to conceal the same,
To make the miscreant more to feel his shame.

XI

But when the angry king discovered not
What guilty hand this sacrilege had wrought,
His ireful courage boiled in vengeance hot
Against the Christians, whom he faulters thought;
All ruth, compassion, mercy he forgot,
A staff to beat that dog he long had sought,
"Let them all die," quoth he, "kill great and small,

So shall the offender perish sure withal.

XII
"To spill the wine with poison mixed with spares?
Slay then the righteous with the faulty one,
Destroy this field that yieldeth naught but tares,
With thorns this vineyard all is over—gone,
Among these wretches is not one, that cares
For us, our laws, or our religion;
Up, up, dear subjects, fire and weapon take,
Burn, murder, kill these traitors for my sake."
XIII
This Herod thus would Bethlem's infants kill,
The Christians soon this direful news receave,
The trump of death sounds in their hearing shrill,
Their weapon, faith; their fortress, was the grave;
They had no courage, time, device, or will,
To fight, to fly, excuse, or pardon crave,
But stood prepared to die, yet help they find,
Whence least they hope, such knots can Heaven unbind.

XIV
Among them dwelt, her parents' joy and pleasure,
A maid, whose fruit was ripe, not over—yeared,
Her beauty was her not esteemed treasure;
The field of love with plough of virtue eared,
Her labor goodness; godliness her leisure;
Her house the heaven by this full moon aye cleared,
For there, from lovers' eyes withdrawn, alone
With virgin beams this spotless Cynthia shone.

XV
But what availed her resolution chaste,
Whose soberest looks were whetstones to desire?
Nor love consents that beauty's field lie waste,
Her visage set Olindo's heart on fire,

Jerusalem Delivered

O subtle love, a thousand wiles thou hast,
By humble suit, by service, or by hire,
To win a maiden's hold, a thing soon done,
For nature framed all women to be won.

XVI
Sophronia she, Olindo hight the youth,
Both or one town, both in one faith were taught,
She fair, he full of bashfulness and truth,
Loved much, hoped little, and desired nought,
He durst not speak by suit to purchase ruth,
She saw not, marked not, wist not what he sought,
Thus loved, thus served he long, but not regarded,
Unseen, unmarked, unpitied, unrewarded.

XVII
To her came message of the murderment,
Wherein her guiltless friends should hopeless starve,
She that was noble, wise, as fair and gent,
Cast how she might their harmless lives preserve,
Zeal was the spring whence flowed her hardiment,
From maiden shame yet was she loth to swerve:
Yet had her courage ta'en so sure a hold,
That boldness, shamefaced; shame had made her bold.

XVIII
And forth she went, a shop for merchandise
Full of rich stuff, but none for sale exposed,
A veil obscured the sunshine of her eyes,
The rose within herself her sweetness closed,
Each ornament about her seemly lies,
By curious chance, or careless art, composed;
For what the most neglects, most curious prove,
So Beauty's helped by Nature, Heaven, and Love.

XIX

Admired of all, on went this noble maid,
Until the presence of the king she gained,
Nor for he swelled with ire was she afraid,
But his fierce wrath with fearless grace sustained,
"I come," quoth she, "but be thine anger stayed,
And causeless rage 'gainst faultless souls restrained —
I come to show thee, and to bring thee both,
The wight whose fact hath made thy heart so wroth."

XX

Her molest boldness, and that lightning ray
Which her sweet beauty streamed on his face,
Had struck the prince with wonder and dismay,
Changed his cheer, and cleared his moody grace,
That had her eyes disposed their looks to play,
The king had snared been in love's strong lace;
But wayward beauty doth not fancy move,
A frown forbids, a smile engendereth love.

XXI

It was amazement, wonder and delight,
Although not love, that moved his cruel sense;
"Tell on," quoth he, "unfold the chance aright,
Thy people's lives I grant for recompense."
Then she, "Behold the faulter here in sight,
This hand committed that supposed offence,
I took the image, mine that fault, that fact,
Mine be the glory of that virtuous act."

XXII

This spotless lamb thus offered up her blood,
To save the rest of Christ's selected fold,
O noble lie! was ever truth so good?
Blest be the lips that such a leasing told:
Thoughtful awhile remained the tyrant wood,
His native wrath he gan a space withhold,

And said, "That thou discover soon I will,
What aid? what counsel had'st thou in that ill?"

XXIII
"My lofty thoughts," she answered him, "envied
Another's hand should work my high desire,
The thirst of glory can no partner bide,
With mine own self I did alone conspire."
"On thee alone," the tyrant then replied,
"Shall fall the vengeance of my wrath and ire."
" `Tis just and right," quoth she, "I yield consent,
Mine be the honor, mine the punishment."

XXIV
The wretch of new enraged at the same,
Asked where she hid the image so conveyed:
"Not hid," quoth she, "but quite consumed with flame,
The idol is of that eternal maid,
For so at least I have preserved the same,
With hands profane from being eft betrayed.
My Lord, the thing thus stolen demand no more,
Here see the thief that scorneth death therefor.

XXV
"And yet no theft was this, yours was the sin,
I brought again what you unjustly took."
This heard, the tyrant did for rage begin
To whet his teeth, and bend his frowning look,
No pity, youth; fairness, no grace could win;
Joy, comfort, hope, the virgin all forsook;
Wrath killed remorse, vengeance stopped mercy's breath
Love's thrall to hate, and beauty's slave to death.

XXVI
Ta'en was the damsel, and without remorse,
The king condemned her guiltless to the fire,

Her veil and mantle plucked they off by force,
And bound her tender arms in twisted wire:
Dumb was the silver dove, while from her corse
These hungry kites plucked off her rich attire,
And for some deal perplexed was her sprite,
Her damask late, now changed to purest white.

XXVII

The news of this mishap spread far and near,
The people ran, both young and old, to gaze;
Olindo also ran, and gan to fear
His lady was some partner in this case;
But when he found her bound, stript from her gear,
And vile tormentors ready saw in place,
He broke the throng, and into presence brast;
And thus bespake the king in rage and haste:

XXXVIII

"Not so, not so this grief shall bear away
From me the honor of so noble feat,
She durst not, did not, could not so convey
The massy substance of that idol great,
What sleight had she the wardens to betray?
What strength to heave the goddess form her seat?
No, no, my Lord, she sails but with my wind."
Ah, thus he loved, yet was his love unkind!

XXIX

He added further: "Where the shining glass,
Lets in the light amid your temple's side,
By broken by–ways did I inward pass,
And in that window made a postern wide,
Nor shall therefore this ill–advised lass
Usurp the glory should this fact betide,
Mine be these bonds, mine be these flames so pure,
O glorious death, more glorious sepulture!"

XXX

Sophronia raised her modest looks from ground,
And on her lover bent her eyesight mild,
"Tell me, what fury? what conceit unsound
Presenteth here to death so sweet a child?
Is not in me sufficient courage found,
To bear the anger of this tyrant wild?
Or hath fond love thy heart so over–gone?
Wouldst thou not live, nor let me die alone?"

XXXI

Thus spake the nymph, yet spake but to the wind,
She could not alter his well–settled thought;
O miracle! O strife of wondrous kind!
Where love and virtue such contention wrought,
Where death the victor had for meed assigned;
Their own neglect, each other's safety sought;
But thus the king was more provoked to ire,
Their strife for bellows served to anger's fire.

XXXII

He thinks, such thoughts self–guiltiness finds out,
They scorned his power, and therefore scorned the pain,
"Nay, nay," quoth he, "let be your strife and doubt,
You both shall win, and fit reward obtain."
With that the sergeants hent the young man stout,
And bound him likewise in a worthless chain;
Then back to back fast to a stake both ties,
Two harmless turtles dight for sacrifice.

XXXIII

About the pile of fagots, sticks and hay,
The bellows raised the newly–kindled flame,
When thus Olindo, in a doleful lay,
Begun too late his bootless plaints to frame:
"Be these the bonds? Is this the hoped–for day,

Should join me to this long–desired dame?
Is this the fire alike should burn our hearts?
Ah, hard reward for lovers' kind desarts!

XXXIV

"Far other flames and bonds kind lovers prove,
But thus our fortune casts the hapless die,
Death hath exchanged again his shafts with love,
And Cupid thus lets borrowed arrows fly.
O Hymen, say, what fury doth thee move
To lend thy lamps to light a tragedy?
Yet this contents me that I die for thee,
Thy flames, not mine, my death and torment be.

XXXV

"Yet happy were my death, mine ending blest,
My torments easy, full of sweet delight,
It this I could obtain, that breast to breast
Thy bosom might receive my yielded sprite;
And thine with it in heaven's pure clothing drest,
Through clearest skies might take united flight."
Thus he complained, whom gently she reproved,
And sweetly spake him thus, that so her loved:

XXXVI

"Far other plaints, dear friend, tears and laments
The time, the place, and our estates require;
Think on thy sins, which man's old foe presents
Before that judge that quits each soul his hire,
For his name suffer, for no pain torments
Him whose just prayers to his throne aspire:
Behold the heavens, thither thine eyesight bend,
Thy looks, sighs, tears, for intercessors send."

XXXVII

The Pagans loud cried out to God and man,

The Christians mourned in silent lamentation,
The tyrant's self, a thing unused, began
To feel his heart relent, with mere compassion,
But not disposed to ruth or mercy than
He sped him thence home to his habitation:
Sophronia stood not grieved nor discontented,
By all that saw her, but herself, lamented.

XXXVIII
The lovers standing in this doleful wise,
A warrior bold unwares approached near,
In uncouth arms yclad and strange disguise,
From countries far, but new arrived there,
A savage tigress on her helmet lies,
The famous badge Clorinda used to bear;
That wonts in every warlike stowre to win,
By which bright sign well known was that fair inn.

XXXIX
She scorned the arts these silly women use,
Another thought her nobler humor fed,
Her lofty hand would of itself refuse
To touch the dainty needle or nice thread,
She hated chambers, closets, secret news,
And in broad fields preserved her maidenhead:
Proud were her looks, yet sweet, though stern and stout,
Her dam a dove, thus brought an eagle out.

XL
While she was young, she used with tender hand
The foaming steed with froary bit to steer,
To tilt and tourney, wrestle in the sand,
To leave with speed Atlanta swift arear,
Through forests wild, and unfrequented land
To chase the lion, boar, or rugged bear,
The satyrs rough, the fauns and fairies wild,

Jerusalem Delivered

She chased oft, oft took, and oft beguiled.

XLI

This lusty lady came from Persia late,
She with the Christians had encountered eft,
And in their flesh had opened many a gate,
By which their faithful souls their bodies left,
Her eye at first presented her the state
Of these poor souls, of hope and help bereft,
Greedy to know, as is the mind of man,
Their cause of death, swift to the fire she ran.

XLII

The people made her room, and on them twain
Her piercing eyes their fiery weapons dart,
Silent she saw the one, the other 'plain,
The weaker body lodged the nobler heart:
Yet him she saw lament, as if his pain
Were grief and sorrow for another's smart,
And her keep silence so, as if her eyes
Dumb orators were to entreat the skies.

XLIII

Clorinda changed to ruth her warlike mood,
Few silver drops her vermeil cheeks depaint;
Her sorrow was for her that speechless stood,
Her silence more prevailed than his complaint.
She asked an aged man, seemed grave and good,
"Come say me, sir," quoth she, "what hard constraint
Would murder here love's queen and beauty's king?
What fault or fare doth to this death them bring?"

XLIV

Thus she inquired, and answer short he gave,
But such as all the chance at large disclosed,
She wondered at the case, the virgin brave,
That both were guiltless of the fault supposed,

38

Her noble thought cast how she might them save,
The means on suit or battle she reposed.
Quick to the fire she ran, and quenched it out,
And thus bespake the sergeants and the rout:

XLV

"Be there not one among you all that dare
In this your hateful office aught proceed,
Till I return from court, nor take you care
To reap displeasure for not making speed."
To do her will the men themselves prepare,
In their faint hearts her looks such terror breed;
To court she went, their pardon would she get,
But on the way the courteous king she met.

XLVI

"Sir King," quoth she, "my name Clorinda hight,
My fame perchance has pierced your ears ere now,
I come to try my wonted power and might,
And will defend this land, this town, and you,
All hard assays esteem I eath and light,
Great acts I reach to, to small things I bow,
To fight in field, or to defend this wall,
Point what you list, I naught refuse at all."

XLVII

To whom the king, "What land so far remote
From Asia's coasts, or Phoebus' glistering rays,
O glorious virgin, that recordeth not
Thy fame, thine honor, worth, renown, and praise?
Since on my side I have thy succors got,
I need not fear in these my aged days,
For in thine aid more hope, more trust I have,
Than in whole armies of these soldiers brave.

XLVIII

"Now, Godfrey stays too long; he fears, I ween;
Thy courage great keeps all our foes in awe;
For thee all actions far unworthy been,
But such as greatest danger with them draw:
Be you commandress therefore, Princess, Queen
Of all our forces: be thy word a law."
This said, the virgin gan her beaver vail,
And thanked him first, and thus began her tale.

XLIX
"A thing unused, great monarch, may it seem,
To ask reward for service yet to come;
But so your virtuous bounty I esteem,
That I presume for to intreat this groom
And silly maid from danger to redeem,
Condemned to burn by your unpartial doom,
I not excuse, but pity much their youth,
And come to you for mercy and for ruth.

L
"Yet give me leave to tell your Highness this,
You blame the Christians, them my thoughts acquite,
Nor be displeased, I say you judge amiss,
At every shot look not to hit the white,
All what the enchanter did persuade you, is
Against the lore of Macon's sacred rite,
For us commandeth mighty Mahomet
No idols in his temple pure to set.

LI
"To him therefore this wonder done refar,
Give him the praise and honor of the thing,
Of us the gods benign so careful are
Lest customs strange into their church we bring:
Let Ismen with his squares and trigons war,
His weapons be the staff, the glass, the ring;

But let us manage war with blows like knights,
Our praise in arms, our honor lies in fights."

LII

The virgin held her peace when this was said;
And though to pity he never framed his thought,
Yet, for the king admired the noble maid,
His purpose was not to deny her aught:
"I grant them life," quoth he, "your promised aid
Against these Frenchmen hath their pardon bought:
Nor further seek what their offences be,
Guiltless, I quit; guilty, I set them free."

LIII

Thus were they loosed, happiest of humankind,
Olindo, blessed be this act of thine,
True witness of thy great and heavenly mind,
Where sun, moon, stars, of love, faith, virtue, shine.
So forth they went and left pale death behind,
To joy the bliss of marriage rites divine,
With her he would have died, with him content
Was she to live that would with her have brent.

LIV

The king, as wicked thoughts are most suspicious,
Supposed too fast this tree of virtue grew,
O blessed Lord! why should this Pharaoh vicious,
Thus tyrannize upon thy Hebrews true?
Who to perform his will, vile and malicious,
Exiled these, and all the faithful crew,
All that were strong of body, stout of mind,
But kept their wives and children pledge behind.

LV

A hard division, when the harmless sheep
Must leave their lambs to hungry wolves in charge,

But labor's virtues watching, ease her sleep,
Trouble best wind that drives salvation's barge,
The Christians fled, whither they took no keep,
Some strayed wild among the forests large,
Some to Emmaus to the Christian host,
And conquer would again their houses lost.

LVI

Emmaus is a city small, that lies
From Sion's walls distant a little way,
A man that early on the morn doth rise,
May thither walk ere third hour of the day.
Oh, when the Christian lord this town espies
How merry were their hearts? How fresh? How gay?
But for the sun inclined fast to west,
That night there would their chieftain take his rest.

LVII

Their canvas castles up they quickly rear,
And build a city in an hour's space.
When lo, disguised in unusual gear,
Two barons bold approachen gan the place;
Their semblance kind, and mild their gestures were,
Peace in their hands, and friendship in their face,
From Egypt's king ambassadors they come,
Them many a squire attends, and many a groom.

LVIII

The first Aletes, born in lowly shed,
Of parents base, a rose sprung from a brier,
That now his branches over Egypt spread,
No plant in Pharaoh's garden prospered higher;
With pleasing tales his lord's vain ears he fed,
A flatterer, a pick–thank, and a liar:
Cursed be estate got with so many a crime,
Yet this is oft the stair by which men climb.

Jerusalem Delivered

LIX

Argantes called is that other knight,
A stranger came he late to Egypt land,
And there advanced was to honor's height,
For he was stout of courage, strong of hand,
Bold was his heart, and restless was his sprite,
Fierce, stern, outrageous, keen as sharpened brand,
Scorner of God, scant to himself a friend,
And pricked his reason on his weapon's end.

LX

These two entreatance made they might be heard,
Nor was their just petition long denied;
The gallants quickly made their court of guard,
And brought them in where sate their famous guide,
Whose kingly look his princely mind declared,
Where noblesse, virtue, troth, and valor bide.
A slender courtesy made Argantes bold,
So as one prince salute another wold;

LXI

Aletes laid his right hand on his heart,
Bent down his head, and cast his eyes full low,
And reverence made with courtly grace and art,
For all that humble lore to him was know;
His sober lips then did he softly part,
Whence of pure rhetoric, whole streams outflow,
And thus he said, while on the Christian lords
Down fell the mildew of his sugared words:

LXII

"O only worthy, whom the earth all fears,
High God defend thee with his heavenly shield,
And humble so the hearts of all thy peers,
That their stiff necks to thy sweet yoke may yield:

These be the sheaves that honor's harvest bears,
The seed thy valiant acts, the world the field,
Egypt the headland is, where heaped lies
Thy fame, worth, justice, wisdom, victories.

LXIII
"These altogether doth our sovereign hide
In secret store–house of his princely thought,
And prays he may in long accordance bide,
With that great worthy which such wonders wrought,
Nor that oppose against the coming tide
Of proffered love, for that he is not taught
Your Christian faith, for though of divers kind,
The loving vine about her elm is twined.

LXIV
"Receive therefore in that unconquered hand
The precious handle of this cup of love,
If not religion, virtue be the band
'Twixt you to fasten friendship not to move:
But for our mighty king doth understand,
You mean your power 'gainst Juda land to prove,
He would, before this threatened tempest fell,
I should his mind and princely will first tell.

LXV
"His mind is this, he prays thee be contented
To joy in peace the conquests thou hast got,
Be not thy death, or Sion's fall lamented,
Forbear this land, Judea trouble not,
Things done in haste at leisure be repented:
Withdraw thine arms, trust not uncertain lot,
For oft to see what least we think betide;
He is thy friend 'gainst all the world beside.

LXVI

Jerusalem Delivered

"True labour in the vineyard of thy Lord,
Ere prime thou hast the imposed day–work done,
What armies conquered, perished with thy sword?
What cities sacked? what kingdoms hast thou won?
All ears are mazed while tongues thine acts record,
Hands quake for fear, all feet for dread do run,
And though no realms you may to thraldom bring,
No higher can your praise, your glory spring.

LXVII

"Thy sign is in his Apogaeon placed,
And when it moveth next, must needs descend,
Chance in uncertain, fortune double faced,
Smiling at first, she frowneth in the end:
Beware thine honor be not then disgraced,
Take heed thou mar not when thou think'st to mend,
For this the folly is of Fortune's play,
'Gainst doubtful, certain; much, 'gainst small to lay.

LXVIII

"Yet still we sail while prosperous blows the wind,
Till on some secret rock unwares we light,
The sea of glory hath no banks assigned,
They who are wont to win in every fight
Still feed the fire that so inflames thy mind
To bring more nations subject to thy might;
This makes thee blessed peace so light to hold,
Like summer's flies that fear not winter's cold.

LXIX

"They bid thee follow on the path, now made
So plain and easy, enter Fortune's gate,
Nor in thy scabbard sheathe that famous blade,
Till settled by thy kingdom, and estate,
Till Macon's sacred doctrine fall and fade,
Till woeful Asia all lie desolate.
Sweet words I grant, baits and allurements sweet,

But greatest hopes oft greatest crosses meet.

LXX

"For, if thy courage do not blind thine eyes,
If clouds of fury hide not reason's beams,
Then may'st thou see this desperate enterprise.
The field of death, watered with danger's streams;
High state, the bed is where misfortune lies,
Mars most unfriendly, when most kind he seems,
Who climbeth high, on earth he hardest lights,
And lowest falls attend the highest flights.

LXXI

"Tell me if, great in counsel, arms and gold,
The Prince of Egypt war 'gainst you prepare,
What if the valiant Turks and Persians bold,
Unite their forces with Cassanoe's heir?
Oh then, what marble pillar shall uphold
The falling trophies of your conquest fair?
Trust you the monarch of the Greekish land?
That reed will break; and breaking, wound your hand.

LXXII

"The Greekish faith is like that half–cut tree
By which men take wild elephants in Inde,
A thousand times it hath beguiled thee,
As firm as waves in seas, or leaves in wind.
Will they, who erst denied you passage free,
Passage to all men free, by use and kind,
Fight for your sake? Or on them do you trust
To spend their blood, that could scarce spare their dust?

LXXIII

"But all your hope and trust perchance is laid
In these strong troops, which thee environ round;
Yet foes unite are not so soon dismayed

46

As when their strength you erst divided found:
Besides, each hour thy bands are weaker made
With hunger, slaughter, lodging on cold ground,
Meanwhile the Turks seek succors from our king,
Thus fade thy helps, and thus thy cumbers spring.

LXXIV
"Suppose no weapon can thy valor's pride
Subdue, that by no force thou may'st be won,
Admit no steel can hurt or wound thy side,
And be it Heaven hath thee such favor done:
'Gainst Famine yet what shield canst thou provide?
What strength resist? What sleight her wrath can shun?
Go, shake the spear, and draw thy flaming blade,
And try if hunger so be weaker made.
LXXV
"The inhabitants each pasture and each plain
Destroyed have, each field to waste is laid,
In fenced towers bestowed is their grain
Before thou cam'st this kingdom to invade,
These horse and foot, how canst them sustain?
Whence comes thy store? whence thy provision made?
Thy ships to bring it are, perchance, assigned,
Oh, that you live so long as please the wind!

LXXVI
"Perhaps thy fortune doth control the wind,
Doth loose or bind their blasts in secret cave,
The sea, pardie, cruel and deaf by kind,
Will hear thy call, and still her raging wave:
But if our armed galleys be assigned
To aid those ships which Turks and Persians have,
Say then, what hope is left thy slender fleet?
Dare flocks of crows, a flight of eagles meet?

LXXVII

47

"My lord, a double conquest must you make,
If you achieve renown by this emprize:
For if our fleet your navy chase or take,
For want of victuals all your camp then dies;
Of if by land the field you once forsake,
Then vain by sea were hope of victories.
Nor could your ships restore your lost estate:
For steed once stolen, we shut the door too late.

LXXVIII
"In this estate, if thou esteemest light
The proffered kindness of the Egyptian king,
Then give me leave to say, this oversight
Beseems thee not, in whom such virtues spring:
But heavens vouchsafe to guide my mind aright,
To gentle thoughts, that peace and quiet bring,
So that poor Asia her complaints may cease,
And you enjoy your conquests got, in peace.

LXXIX
"Nor ye that part in these adventures have,
Part in his glory, partners in his harms,
Let not blind Fortune so your minds deceive,
To stir him more to try these fierce alarms,
But like the sailor 'scaped from the wave
From further peril that his person arms
By staying safe at home, so stay you all,
Better sit still, men say, than rise to fall."

LXXX
This said Aletes: and a murmur rose
That showed dislike among the Christian peers,
Their angry gestures with mislike disclose
How much his speech offends their noble ears.
Lord Godfrey's eye three times environ goes,
To view what countenance every warrior bears,

And lastly on the Egyptian baron stayed,
To whom the duke thus for his answer said:

LXXXI
"Ambassador, full both of threats and praise,
Thy doubtful message hast thou wisely told,
And if thy sovereign love us as he says,
Tell him he sows to reap an hundred fold,
But where thy talk the coming storm displays
Of threatened warfare from the Pagans bold:
To that I answer, as my cousin is,
In plainest phrase, lest my intent thou miss.

LXXXII
"Know, that till now we suffered have much pain,
By lands and seas, where storms and tempests fall,
To make the passage easy, safe, and plain
That leads us to this venerable wall,
That so we might reward from Heaven obtain,
And free this town from being longer thrall;
Nor is it grievous to so good an end
Our honors, kingdoms, lives and goods to spend.

LXXXIII
"Nor hope of praise, nor thirst of worldly good,
Enticed us to follow this emprise,
The Heavenly Father keep his sacred brood
From foul infection of so great a vice:
But by our zeal aye be that plague withstood,
Let not those pleasures us to sin entice.
His grace, his mercy, and his powerful hand
Will keep us safe from hurt by sea and land.

LXXXIV
"This is the spur that makes our coursers run;
This is our harbor, safe from danger's floods;

49

Jerusalem Delivered

This is our bield, the blustering winds to shun:
This is our guide, through forests, deserts, woods;
This is our summer's shade, our winter's sun:
This is our wealth, our treasure, and our goods:
This is our engine, towers that overthrows,
Our spear that hurts, our sword that wounds our foes.

LXXXV

"Our courage hence, our hope, our valor springs,
Not from the trust we have in shield or spear,
Not from the succors France or Grecia brings,
On such weak posts we list no buildings rear:
He can defend us from the power of kings,
From chance of war, that makes weak hearts to fear;
He can these hungry troops with manna feed,
And make the seas land, if we passage need.

LXXXVI

"But if our sins us of his help deprive,
Of his high justice let no mercy fall;
Yet should our deaths us some contentment give,
To die, where Christ received his burial,
So might we die, not envying them that live;
So would we die, not unrevenged all:
Nor Turks, nor Christians, if we perish such,
Have cause to joy, or to complain too much.

LXXXVII

"Think not that wars we love, and strife affect,
Or that we hate sweet peace, or rest denay,
Think not your sovereign's friendship we reject,
Because we list not in our conquests stay:
But for it seems he would the Jews protect,
Pray him from us that thought aside to lay,
Nor us forbid this town and realm to gain,
And he in peace, rest, joy, long more may reign."

LXXXVIII

This answer given, Argantes wild drew nar,
Trembling for ire, and waxing pale for rage,
Nor could he hold, his wrath increased so far,
But thus inflamed bespake the captain sage:
"Who scorneth peace shall have his fill of war,
I thought my wisdom should thy fury 'suage,
But well you show what joy you take in fight,
Which makes you prize our love and friendship light."

LXXXIX

This said, he took his mantle's foremost part,
And gan the same together fold and wrap;
Then spake again with fell and spiteful heart,
So lions roar enclosed in train or trap,
"Thou proud despiser of inconstant mart,
I bring thee war and peace closed in this lap,
Take quickly one, thou hast no time to muse;
If peace, we rest, we fight, if war thou choose."

XC

His semblance fierce and speechless proud, provoke
The soldiers all, "War, war," at once to cry,
Nor could they tarry till their chieftain spoke,
But for the knight was more inflamed hereby,
His lap he opened and spread forth his cloak:
"To mortal wars," he says, "I you defy;"
And this he uttered with fell rage and hate,
And seemed of Janus' church to undo the gate.

XCI

It seemed fury, discord, madness fell
Flew from his lap, when he unfolds the same;
His glaring eyes with anger's venom swell,
And like the brand of foul Alecto flame,

He looked like huge Tiphoius loosed from hell
Again to shake heaven's everlasting frame,
Or him that built the tower of Shinaar,
Which threat'neth battle 'gainst the morning star.

XCII
Godfredo then: "Depart, and bid your king
Haste hitherward, or else within short while, —
For gladly we accept the war you bring, —
Let him expect us on the banks of Nile."
He entertained them then with banqueting,
And gifts presented to those Pagans vile;
Aletes had a helmet, rich and gay,
Late found at Nice among the conquered prey.

XCIII
Argant a sword, whereof the web was steel,
Pommel, rich stone; hilt gold; approved by touch
With rarest workmanship all forged weel,
The curious art excelled the substance much:
Thus fair, rich, sharp, to see, to have, to feel,
Glad was the Paynim to enjoy it such,
And said, "How I this gift can use and wield,
Soon shall you see, when first we meet in field."

XCIV
Thus took they congee, and the angry knight
Thus to his fellow parleyed on the way,
"Go thou by day, but let me walk by night,
Go thou to Egypt, I at Sion stay,
The answer given thou canst unfold aright,
No need of me, what I can do or say,
Among these arms I will go wreak my spite;
Let Paris court it, Hector loved to fight."

XCV

Thus he who late arrived a messenger
Departs a foe, in act, in word, in thought,
The law of nations or the lore of war,
If he transgresses or no, he recketh naught,
Thus parted they, and ere he wandered far
The friendly star—light to the walls him brought:
Yet his fell heart thought long that little way,
Grieved with each stop, tormented with each stay.

XCVI
Now spread the night her spangled canopy,
And summoned every restless eye to sleep;
On beds of tender grass the beasts down lie,
The fishes slumbered in the silent deep,
Unheard were serpent's hiss and dragon's cry,
Birds left to sing, and Philomen to weep,
Only that noise heaven's rolling circles kest,
Sung lullaby to bring the world to rest.
XCVII
Yet neither sleep, nor ease, nor shadows dark,
Could make the faithful camp or captain rest,
They longed to see the day, to hear the lark
Record her hymns and chant her carols blest,
They yearned to view the walls, the wished mark
To which their journeys long they had addressed;
Each heart attends, each longing eye beholds
What beam the eastern window first unfolds.

THIRD BOOK

THE ARGUMENT.
The camp at great Jerusalem arrives:

Jerusalem Delivered

Clorinda gives them battle, in the breast
Of fair Erminia Tancred's love revives,
He jousts with her unknown whom he loved best;
Argant th' adventurers of their guide deprives,
With stately pomp they lay their Lord in chest:
Godfrey commands to cut the forest down,
And make strong engines to assault the town.

I
The purple morning left her crimson bed,
And donned her robes of pure vermilion hue,
Her amber locks she crowned with roses red,
In Eden's flowery gardens gathered new.
When through the camp a murmur shrill was spread,
Arm, arm, they cried; arm, arm, the trumpets blew,
Their merry noise prevents the joyful blast,
So hum small bees, before their swarms they cast.

II
Their captain rules their courage, guides their heat,
Their forwardness he stayed with gentle rein;
And yet more easy, haply, were the feat
To stop the current near Charybdis main,
Or calm the blustering winds on mountains great,
Than fierce desires of warlike hearts restrain;
He rules them yet, and ranks them in their haste,
For well he knows disordered speed makes waste.

III
Feathered their thoughts, their feet in wings were dight,
Swiftly they marched, yet were not tired thereby,
For willing minds make heaviest burdens light.
But when the gliding sun was mounted high,
Jerusalem, behold, appeared in sight,
Jerusalem they view, they see, they spy,

Jerusalem Delivered

Jerusalem with merry noise they greet,
With joyful shouts, and acclamations sweet.

IV
As when a troop of jolly sailors row
Some new–found land and country to descry,
Through dangerous seas and under stars unknowe,
Thrall to the faithless waves, and trothless sky,
If once the wished shore begun to show,
They all salute it with a joyful cry,
And each to other show the land in haste,
Forgetting quite their pains and perils past.

V
To that delight which their first sight did breed,
That pleased so the secret of their thought
A deep repentance did forthwith succeed
That reverend fear and trembling with it brought,
Scantly they durst their feeble eyes dispreed
Upon that town where Christ was sold and bought,
Where for our sins he faultless suffered pain,
There where he died and where he lived again.

VI
Soft words, low speech, deep sobs, sweet sighs, salt tears
Rose from their hearts, with joy and pleasure mixed;
For thus fares he the Lord aright that fears,
Fear on devotion, joy on faith is fixed:
Such noise their passions make, as when one hears
The hoarse sea waves roar, hollow rocks betwixt;
Or as the wind in holts and shady greaves,
A murmur makes among the boughs and leaves.

VII
Their naked feet trod on the dusty way,
Following the ensample of their zealous guide,

Their scarfs, their crests, their plumes and feathers gay,
They quickly doffed, and willing laid aside,
Their molten hearts their wonted pride allay,
Along their watery cheeks warm tears down slide,
And then such secret speech as this, they used,
While to himself each one himself accused.

VIII
"Flower of goodness, root of lasting bliss,
Thou well of life, whose streams were purple blood
That flowed here, to cleanse the soul amiss
Of sinful men, behold this brutish flood,
That from my melting heart distilled is,
Receive in gree these tears, O Lord so good,
For never wretch with sin so overgone
Had fitter time or greater cause to moan."

IX
This while the wary watchman looked over,
From tops of Sion's towers, the hills and dales,
And saw the dust the fields and pastures cover,
As when thick mists arise from moory vales.
At last the sun−bright shields he gan discover,
And glistering helms for violence none that fails,
The metal shone like lightning bright in skies,
And man and horse amid the dust descries.

X
Then loud he cries, "O what a dust ariseth!
O how it shines with shields and targets clear!
Up, up, to arms, for valiant heart despiseth
The threatened storm of death and danger near.
Behold your foes;" then further thus deviseth,
"Haste, haste, for vain delay increaseth fear,
These horrid clouds of dust that yonder fly,
Your coming foes does hide, and hide the sky."

Jerusalem Delivered

XI

The tender children, and the fathers old,
The aged matrons, and the virgin chaste,
That durst not shake the spear, nor target hold,
Themselves devoutly in their temples placed;
The rest, of members strong and courage bold,
On hardy breasts their harness donned in haste,
Some to the walls, some to the gates them dight,
Their king meanwhile directs them all aright.

XII

All things well ordered, he withdrew with speed
Up to a turret high, two ports between,
That so he might be near at every need,
And overlook the lands and furrows green.
Thither he did the sweet Erminia lead,
That in his court had entertained been
Since Christians Antioch did to bondage bring,
And slew her father, who thereof was king.

XIII

Against their foes Clorinda sallied out,
And many a baron bold was by her side,
Within the postern stood Argantes stout
To rescue her, if ill mote her betide:
With speeches brave she cheered her warlike rout,
And with bold words them heartened as they ride,
"Let us by some brave act," quoth she, "this day
Of Asia's hopes the groundwork found and lay."

XIV

While to her folk thus spake the virgin brave,
Thereby behold forth passed a Christian band
Toward the camp, that herds of cattle drave,
For they that morn had forayed all the land;

The fierce virago would that booty save,
Whom their commander singled hand for hand,
A mighty man at arms, who Guardo hight,
But far too weak to match with her in fight.
XV
They met, and low in dust was Guardo laid,
'Twixt either army, from his sell down kest,
The Pagans shout for joy, and hopeful said,
Those good beginnings would have endings blest:
Against the rest on went the noble maid,
She broke the helm, and pierced the armed breast,
Her men the paths rode through made by her sword,
They pass the stream where she had found the ford.

XVI
Soon was the prey out of their hands recovered,
By step and step the Frenchmen gan retire,
Till on a little hill at last they hovered,
Whose strength preserved them from Clorinda's ire:
When, as a tempest that hath long been covered
In watery clouds breaks out with sparkling fire,
With his strong squadron Lord Tancredi came,
His heart with rage, his eyes with courage flame.

XVII
Mast great the spear was which the gallant bore
That in his warlike pride he made to shake,
As winds tall cedars toss on mountains hoar:
The king, that wondered at his bravery, spake
To her, that near him seated was before,
Who felt her heart with love's hot fever quake,
"Well shouldst thou know," quoth he, "each Christian knight,
By long acquaintance, though in armor dight.

XVIII
"Say, who is he shows so great worthiness,

That rides so rank, and bends his lance so fell?"
To this the princess said nor more nor less,
Her heart with sighs, her eyes with tears, did swell;
But sighs and tears she wisely could suppress,
Her love and passion she dissembled well,
And strove her love and hot desire to cover,
Till heart with sighs, and eyes with tears ran over:

XIX

At last she spoke, and with a crafty sleight
Her secret love disguised in clothes of hate:
"Alas, too well," she says, "I know that knight,
I saw his force and courage proved late,
Too late I viewed him, when his power and might
Shook down the pillar of Cassanoe's state;
Alas what wounds he gives! how fierce, how fell!
No physic helps them cure, nor magic's spell.

XX

"Tancred he hight, O Macon, would he wear
My thrall, ere fates him of this life deprive,
For to his hateful head such spite I bear,
I would him reave his cruel heart on live."
Thus said she, they that her complainings hear
In other sense her wishes credit give.
She sighed withal, they construed all amiss,
And thought she wished to kill, who longed to kiss.
XXI
This while forth pricked Clorinda from the throng
And 'gainst Tancredi set her spear in rest,
Upon their helms they cracked their lances long,
And from her head her gilden casque he kest,
For every lace he broke and every thong,
And in the dust threw down her plumed crest,
About her shoulders shone her golden locks,
Like sunny beams, on alabaster rocks.

XXII

Her looks with fire, her eyes with lightning blaze,
Sweet was her wrath, what then would be her smile?
Tancred, whereon think'st thou? what dost thou gaze?
Hast thou forgot her in so short a while?
The same is she, the shape of whose sweet face
The God of Love did in thy heart compile,
The same that left thee by the cooling stream,
Safe from sun's heat, but scorched with beauty's beam.

XXIII

The prince well knew her, though her painted shield
And golden helm he had not marked before,
She saved her head, and with her axe well steeled
Assailed the knight; but her the knight forbore,
'Gainst other foes he proved him through the field,
Yet she for that refrained ne'er the more,
But following, "Turn thee," cried, in ireful wise;
And so at once she threats to kill him twice.

XXIV

Not once the baron lifts his armed hand
To strike the maid, but gazing on her eyes,
Where lordly Cupid seemed in arms to stand,
No way to ward or shun her blows he tries;
But softly says, "No stroke of thy strong hand
Can vanquish Tancred, but thy conquest lies
In those fair eyes, which fiery weapons dart,
That find no lighting place except this heart."

XXV

At last resolved, although he hoped small grace,
Yet ere he did to tell how much he loved,
For pleasing words in women's ears find place,
And gentle hearts with humble suits are moved:

60

"O thou," quoth he, "withhold thy wrath a space,
For if thou long to see my valor proved,
Were it not better from this warlike rout
Withdrawn, somewhere, alone to fight it out?

XXVI

"So singled, may we both our courage try:"
Clorinda to that motion yielded glad,
And helmless to the forestward gan hie,
Whither the prince right pensive wend and sad,
And there the virgin gan him soon defy.
One blow she strucken, and he warded had,
When he cried, "Hold, and ere we prove our might,
First hear thou some conditions of the fight."

XXVII

She stayed, and desperate love had made him bold;
"Since from the fight thou wilt no respite give,
The covenants be," he said, "that thou unfold
This wretched bosom, and my heart out rive,
Given thee long since, and if thou, cruel, would
I should be dead, let me no longer live,
But pierce this breast, that all the world may say,
The eagle made the turtle–dove her prey.

XXVIII

"Save with thy grace, or let thine anger kill,
Love hath disarmed my life of all defence;
An easy labor harmless blood to spill,
Strike then, and punish where is none offence."
This said the prince, and more perchance had will
To have declared, to move her cruel sense.
But in ill time of Pagans thither came
A troop, and Christians that pursued the same.

XXIX

Jerusalem Delivered

The Pagans fled before their valiant foes,
For dread or craft, it skills not that we know,
A soldier wild, careless to win or lose,
Saw where her locks about the damsel flew,
And at her back he proffereth as he goes
To strike where her he did disarmed view:
But Tancred cried, "Oh stay thy cursed hand,"
And for to ward the blow lift up his brand.

XXX

But yet the cutting steel arrived there,
Where her fair neck adjoined her noble head,
Light was the wound, but through her amber hair
The purple drops down railed bloody red,
So rubies set in flaming gold appear:
But Lord Tancredi, pale with rage as lead,
Flew on the villain, who to flight him bound;
The smart was his, though she received the wound.

XXXI

The villain flies, he, full of rage and ire,
Pursues, she stood and wondered on them both,
But yet to follow them showed no desire,
To stray so far she would perchance be loth,
But quickly turned her, fierce as flaming fire,
And on her foes wreaked her anger wroth,
On every side she kills them down amain,
And now she flies, and now she turns again.

XXXII

As the swift ure by Volga's rolling flood
Chased through the plains the mastiff curs toforn,
Flies to the succor of some neighbor wood,
And often turns again his dreadful horn
Against the dogs imbrued in sweat and blood,
That bite not, till the beast to flight return;

62

Or as the Moors at their strange tennice run,
Defenced, the flying balls unhurt to shun:

XXXIII
So ran Clorinda, so her foes pursued,
Until they both approached the city's wall,
When lo! the Pagans their fierce wrath renewed,
Cast in a ring about they wheeled all,
And 'gainst the Christians' backs and sides they showed
Their courage fierce, and to new combat fall,
When down the hill Argantes came to fight,
Like angry Mars to aid the Trojan knight.

XXXIV
Furious, tofore the foremost of his rank,
In sturdy steel forth stept the warrior bold,
The first he smote down from his saddle sank,
The next under his steel lay on the mould,
Under the Saracen's spear the worthies shrank,
No breastplate could that cursed tree outhold,
When that was broke his precious sword he drew,
And whom he hit, he felled, hurt, or slew.

XXXV
Clorinda slew Ardelio; aged knight,
Whose graver years would for no labor yield,
His age was full of puissance and might
Two sons he had to guard his noble eild,
The first, far from his father's care and sight,
Called Alicandro wounded lay in field,
And Poliphern the younger, by his side,
Had he not nobly fought had surely died.

XXXVI
Tancred by this, that strove to overtake
The villain that had hurt his only dear,

63

From vain pursuit at last returned back,
And his brave troop discomfit saw well near,
Thither he spurred, and gan huge slaughter make,
His shock no steed, his blow no knight could bear,
For dead he strikes him whom he lights upon,
So thunders break high trees on Lebanon.

XXXVII
Dudon his squadron of adventurers brings,
To aid the worthy and his tired crew,
Before the residue young Rinaldo flings
As swift as fiery lightning kindled new,
His argent eagle with her silver wings
In field of azure, fair Erminia knew,
"See there, sir King," she says, "a knight as bold
And brave, as was the son of Peleus old.

XXXVIII
"He wins the prize in joust and tournament,
His acts are numberless, though few his years,
If Europe six likes him to war had sent
Among these thousand strong of Christian peers,
Syria were lost, lost were the Orient,
And all the lands the Southern Ocean wears,
Conquered were all hot Afric's tawny kings,
And all that dwells by Nilus' unknown springs.

XXXIX
"Rinaldo is his name, his armed fist
Breaks down stone walls, when rams and engines fail,
But turn your eyes because I would you wist
What lord that is in green and golden mail,
Dudon he hight who guideth as him list
The adventurers' troop whose prowess seld doth fail,
High birth, grave years, and practise long in war,
And fearless heart, make him renowned far.

XL

"See that big man that all in brown is bound,
Gernando called, the King of Norway's son,
A prouder knight treads not on grass or ground,
His pride hath lost the praise his prowess won;
And that kind pair in white all armed round,
Is Edward and Gildippes, who begun
Through love the hazard of fierce war to prove,
Famous for arms, but famous more for love."

XLI

While thus they tell their foemen's worthiness,
The slaughter rageth in the plain at large.
Tancred and young Rinaldo break the press,
They bruise the helm, and press the sevenfold targe;
The troop by Dudon led performed no less,
But in they come and give a furious charge:
Argantes' self fell at one single blow,
Inglorious, bleeding lay, on earth full low:

XLII

Nor had the boaster ever risen more,
But that Rinaldo's horse e'en then down fell,
And with the fall his leg opprest so sore,
That for a space there must be algates dwell.
Meanwhile the Pagan troops were nigh forlore,
Swiftly they fled, glad they escaped so well,
Argantes and with him Clorinda stout,
For bank and bulwark served to save the rout.

XLIII

These fled the last, and with their force sustained
The Christians' rage, that followed them so near;
Their scattered troops to safety well they trained,
And while the residue fled, the brunt these bear;
Dudon pursued the victory he gained,

And on Tigranes nobly broke his spear,
Then with his sword headless to ground him cast,
So gardeners branches lop that spring too fast.

XLIV
Algazar's breastplate, of fine temper made,
Nor Corban's helmet, forged by magic art,
Could save their owners, for Lord Dudon's blade
Cleft Corban's head, and pierced Algazar's heart,
And their proud souls down to the infernal shade,
From Amurath and Mahomet depart;
Not strong Argantes thought his life was sure,
He could not safely fly, nor fight secure.

XLV
The angry Pagan bit his lips for teen,
He ran, he stayed, he fled, he turned again,
Until at last unmarked, unviewed, unseen,
When Dudon had Almansor newly slain,
Within his side he sheathed his weapon keen,
Down fell the worthy on the dusty plain,
And lifted up his feeble eyes uneath,
Opprest with leaden sleep, of iron death.

XLVI
Three times he strove to view Heaven's golden ray,
And raised him on his feeble elbow thrice,
And thrice he tumbled on the lowly lay,
And three times closed again his dying eyes,
He speaks no word, yet makes his signs to pray;
He sighs, he faints, he groans, and then he dies;
Argantes proud to spoil the corpse disdained,
But shook his sword with blood of Dudon stained.

XLVII
And turning to the Christian knights, he cried:

"Lordlings, behold, this bloody reeking blade
Last night was given me by your noble guide,
Tell him what proof thereof this day is made,
Needs must this please him well that is betide,
That I so well can use this martial trade,
To whom so rare a gift he did present,
Tell him the workman fits the instrument.

XLVIII
"If further proof thereof he long to see,
Say it still thirsts, and would his heart–blood drink;
And if he haste not to encounter me,
Say I will find him when he least doth think."
The Christians at his words enraged be,
But he to shun their ire doth safely shrink
Under the shelter of the neighbor wall,
Well guarded with his troops and soldiers all.

XLIX
Like storms of hail the stones fell down from high,
Cast from their bulwarks, flankers, ports and towers,
The shafts and quarries from their engines fly,
As thick as falling drops in April showers:
The French withdrew, they list not press too nigh,
The Saracens escaped all the powers,
But now Rinaldo from the earth upleapt,
Where by the leg his steed had long him kept;
L
He came and breathed vengeance from his breast
'Gainst him that noble Dudon late had slain;
And being come thus spoke he to the rest,
"Warriors, why stand you gazing here in vain?
Pale death our valiant leader had opprest,
Come wreak his loss, whom bootless you complain.
Those walls are weak, they keep but cowards out
No rampier can withstand a courage stout.

Jerusalem Delivered

LI

"Of double iron, brass or adamant,
Or if this wall were built of flaming fire,
Yet should the Pagan vile a fortress want
To shroud his coward head safe from mine ire;
Come follow then, and bid base fear avaunt,
The harder work deserves the greater hire;"
And with that word close to the walls he starts,
Nor fears he arrows, quarries, stones or darts.

LII

Above the waves as Neptune lift his eyes
To chide the winds, that Trojan ships opprest,
And with his countenance calmed seas, winds and skies;
So looked Rinaldo, when he shook his crest
Before those walls, each Pagan fears and flies
His dreadful sight, or trembling stayed at least:
Such dread his awful visage on them cast.
So seem poor doves at goshawks' sight aghast.

LIII

The herald Ligiere now from Godfrey came,
To will them stay and calm their courage hot;
"Retire," quoth he, "Godfrey commands the same;
To wreak your ire this season fitteth not;"
Though loth, Rinaldo stayed, and stopped the flame,
That boiled in his hardy stomach hot;
His bridled fury grew thereby more fell,
So rivers, stopped, above their banks do swell.

LIV

The hands retire, not dangered by their foes
In their retreat, so wise were they and wary,
To murdered Dudon each lamenting goes,
From wonted use of ruth they list not vary.

Upon their friendly arms they soft impose
The noble burden of his corpse to carry:
Meanwhile Godfredo from a mountain great
Beheld the sacred city and her seat.

LV
Hierusalem is seated on two hills
Of height unlike, and turned side to side,
The space between, a gentle valley fills,
From mount to mount expansed fair and wide.
Three sides are sure imbarred with crags and hills,
The rest is easy, scant to rise espied:
But mighty bulwarks fence that plainer part,
So art helps nature, nature strengtheneth art.

LVI
The town is stored of troughs and cisterns, made
To keep fresh water, but the country seems
Devoid of grass, unfit for ploughmen's trade,
Not fertile, moist with rivers, wells and streams;
There grow few trees to make the summer's shade,
To shield the parched land from scorching beams,
Save that a wood stands six miles from the town,'
With aged cedars dark, and shadows brown.

LVII
By east, among the dusty valleys, glide
The silver streams of Jordan's crystal flood;
By west, the Midland Sea, with bounders tied
Of sandy shores, where Joppa whilom stood;
By north Samaria stands, and on that side
The golden calf was reared in Bethel wood;
Bethlem by south, where Christ incarnate was,
A pearl in steel, a diamond set in brass.

LVIII

Jerusalem Delivered

While thus the Duke on every side descried
The city's strength, the walls and gates about,
And saw where least the same was fortified,
Where weakest seemed the walls to keep him out;
Ermina as he armed rode, him spied,
And thus bespake the heathen tyrant stout,
"See Godfrey there, in purple clad and gold,
His stately port, and princely look behold.

LIX

"Well seems he born to be with honor crowned,
So well the lore he knows of regiment,
Peerless in fight, in counsel grave and sound,
The double gift of glory excellent,
Among these armies is no warrior found
Graver in speech, bolder in tournament.
Raymond pardie in counsel match him might;
Tancred and young Rinaldo like in fight."

LX

To whom the king: "He likes me well therefore,
I knew him whilom in the court of France
When I from Egypt went ambassador,
I saw him there break many a sturdy lance,
And yet his chin no sign of manhood bore;
His youth was forward, but with governance,
His words, his actions, and his portance brave,
Of future virtue, timely tokens gave.

LXI

"Presages, ah too true:" with that a space
He sighed for grief, then said, "Fain would I know
The man in red, with such a knightly grace,
A worthy lord he seemeth by his show,
How like to Godfrey looks he in the face,
How like in person! but some—deal more low."

"Baldwin," quoth she, "that noble baron hight,
By birth his brother, and his match in might.

LXII
"Next look on him that seems for counsel fit,
Whose silver locks betray his store of days,
Raymond he hight, a man of wondrous wit,
Of Toulouse lord, his wisdom is his praise;
What he forethinks doth, as he looks for, hit,
His stratagems have good success always:
With gilded helm beyond him rides the mild
And good Prince William, England's king's dear child.

LXIII
"With him is Guelpho, as his noble mate,
In birth, in acts, in arms alike the rest,
I know him well, since I beheld him late,
By his broad shoulders and his squared breast:
But my proud foe that quite hath ruinate
My high estate, and Antioch opprest,
I see not, Boemond, that to death did bring
Mine aged lord, my father, and my king."

LXIV
Thus talked they; meanwhile Godfredo went
Down to the troops that in the valley stayed,
And for in vain he thought the labor spent,
To assail those parts that to the mountains laid,
Against the northern gate his force he bent,
Gainst it he camped, gainst it his engines played;
All felt the fury of his angry power,
That from those gates lies to the corner tower.

LXV
The town's third part was this, or little less,
Fore which the duke his glorious ensigns spread,

71

For so great compass had that forteress,
That round it could not be environed
With narrow siege — nor Babel's king I guess
That whilom took it, such an army led —
But all the ways he kept, by which his foe
Might to or from the city come or go.

LXVI

His care was next to cast the trenches deep,
So to preserve his resting camp by night,
Lest from the city while his soldiers sleep
They might assail them with untimely flight.
This done he went where lords and princes weep
With dire complaints about the murdered knight,
Where Dudon dead lay slaughtered on the ground.
And all the soldiers sat lamenting round.

LXVII

His wailing friends adorned the mournful bier
With woful pomp, whereon his corpse they laid,
And when they saw the Bulloigne prince draw near,
All felt new grief, and each new sorrow made;
But he, withouten show or change of cheer,
His springing tears within their fountains stayed,
His rueful looks upon the corpse he cast
Awhile, and thus bespake the same at last;

LXVIII

"We need not mourn for thee, here laid to rest,
Earth is thy bed, and not the grave the skies
Are for thy soul the cradle and the nest,
There live, for here thy glory never dies:
For like a Christian knight and champion blest
Thou didst both live and die: now feed thine eyes
With thy Redeemer's sight, where crowned with bliss
Thy faith, zeal, merit, well-deserving is.

72

LXIX

"Our loss, not thine, provokes these plaints and tears:
For when we lost thee, then our ship her mast,
Our chariot lost her wheels, their points our spears,
The bird of conquest her chief feather cast:
But though thy death far from our army hears
Her chiefest earthly aid, in heaven yet placed
Thou wilt procure its help Divine, so reaps
He that sows godly sorrow, joy by heaps.

LXX

"For if our God the Lord Armipotent
Those armed angels in our aid down send
That were at Dothan to his prophet sent,
Thou wilt come down with them, and well defend
Our host, and with thy sacred weapons bent
Gainst Sion's fort, these gates and bulwarks rend,
That so by hand may win this hold, and we
May in these temples praise our Christ for thee."

LXXI

Thus he complained; but now the sable shade
Ycleped night, had thick enveloped
The sun in veil of double darkness made;
Sleep, eased care; rest, brought complaint to bed:
All night the wary duke devising laid
How that high wall should best be battered,
How his strong engines he might aptly frame,
And whence get timber fit to build the same.

LXXII

Up with the lark the sorrowful duke arose,
A mourner chief at Dudon's burial,
Of cypress sad a pile his friends compose
Under a hill o'ergrown with cedars tall,
Beside the hearse a fruitful palm-tree grows,

73

Ennobled since by this great funeral,
Where Dudon's corpse they softly laid in ground,
The priest sung hymns, the soldiers wept around.

LXXIII
Among the boughs, they here and there bestow
Ensigns and arms, as witness of his praise,
Which he from Pagan lords, that did them owe,
Had won in prosperous fights and happy frays:
His shield they fixed on the hole below,
And there this distich under—writ, which says,
"This palm with stretched arms, doth overspread
The champion Dudon's glorious carcase dead."

LXXIV
This work performed with advisement good,
Godfrey his carpenters, and men of skill
In all the camp, sent to an aged wood,
With convoy meet to guard them safe from ill.
Within a valley deep this forest stood,
To Christian eyes unseen, unknown, until
A Syrian told the duke, who thither sent
Those chosen workmen that for timber went.

LXXV
And now the axe raged in the forest wild,
The echo sighed in the groves unseen,
The weeping nymphs fled from their bowers exiled,
Down fell the shady tops of shaking treen,
Down came the sacred palms, the ashes wild,
The funeral cypress, holly ever green,
The weeping fir, thick beech, and sailing pine,
The married elm fell with his fruitful vine.

LXXVI
The shooter grew, the broad—leaved sycamore,

The barren plantain, and the walnut sound,
The myrrh, that her foul sin doth still deplore,
The alder owner of all waterish ground,
Sweet juniper, whose shadow hurteth sore,
Proud cedar, oak, the king of forests crowned;
Thus fell the trees, with noise the deserts roar;
The beasts, their caves, the birds, their nests forlore.

FOURTH BOOK

THE ARGUMENT.
Satan his fiends and spirits assembleth all,
And sends them forth to work the Christians woe,
False Hidraort their aid from hell doth call,
And sends Armida to entrap his foe:
She tells her birth, her fortune, and her fall,
Asks aid, allures and wins the worthies so
That they consent her enterprise to prove;
She wins them with deceit, craft, beauty, love.

I
While thus their work went on with lucky speed,
And reared rams their horned fronts advance,
The Ancient Foe to man, and mortal seed,
His wannish eyes upon them bent askance;
And when he saw their labors well succeed,
He wept for rage, and threatened dire mischance.
He choked his curses, to himself he spake,
Such noise wild bulls that softly bellow make.

II

Jerusalem Delivered

At last resolving in his damned thought
To find some let to stop their warlike feat,
He gave command his princes should be brought
Before the throne of his infernal seat.
O fool! as if it were a thing of naught
God to resist, or change his purpose great,
Who on his foes doth thunder in his ire,
Whose arrows hailstones he and coals of fire.

III

The dreary trumpet blew a dreadful blast,
And rumbled through the lands and kingdoms under,
Through wasteness wide it roared, and hollows vast,
And filled the deep with horror, fear and wonder,
Not half so dreadful noise the tempests cast,
That fall from skies with storms of hail and thunder,
Not half so loud the whistling winds do sing,
Broke from the earthen prisons of their King.

IV

The peers of Pluto's realm assembled been
Amid the palace of their angry King,
In hideous forms and shapes, tofore unseen,
That fear, death, terror and amazement bring,
With ugly paws some trample on the green,
Some gnaw the snakes that on their shoulders hing,
And some their forked tails stretch forth on high,
And tear the twinkling stars from trembling sky.

V

There were Silenus' foul and loathsome route,
There Sphinxes, Centaurs, there were Gorgons fell,
There howling Scillas, yawling round about,
There serpents hiss, there seven-mouthed Hydras yell,
Chimera there spues fire and brimstone out,
And Polyphemus blind supporteth hell,

Jerusalem Delivered

Besides ten thousand monsters therein dwells
Misshaped, unlike themselves, and like naught else.

VI

About their princes each took his wonted seat
On thrones red–hot, ybuilt of burning brass,
Pluto in middest heaved his trident great,
Of rusty iron huge that forged was,
The rocks on which the salt sea billows beat,
And Atlas' tops, the clouds in height that pass,
Compared to his huge person mole–hills be,
So his rough front, his horns so lifted he.

VII

The tyrant proud frowned from his lofty cell,
And with his looks made all his monsters tremble,
His eyes, that full of rage and venom swell,
Two beacons seem, that men to arms assemble,
His feltered locks, that on his bosom fell,
On rugged mountains briars and thorns resemble,
His yawning mouth, that foamed clotted blood,
Gaped like a whirlpool wide in Stygian flood.

VIII

And as Mount Etna vomits sulphur out,
With cliffs of burning crags, and fire and smoke,
So from his mouth flew kindled coals about,
Hot sparks and smells that man and beast would choke,
The gnarring porter durst not whine for doubt;
Still were the Furies, while their sovereign spoke,
And swift Cocytus stayed his murmur shrill,
While thus the murderer thundered out his will:

IX

"Ye powers infernal, worthier far to sit
About the sun, whence you your offspring take,

77

Jerusalem Delivered

With me that whilom, through the welkin flit,
Down tumbled headlong to this empty lake;
Our former glory still remember it,
Our bold attempts and war we once did make
Gainst him, that rules above the starry sphere,
For which like traitors we lie damned here.

X
"And now instead of clear and gladsome sky,
Of Titan's brightness, that so glorious is,
In this deep darkness lo we helpless lie,
Hopeless again to joy our former bliss,
And more, which makes my griefs to multiply,
That sinful creature man, elected is;
And in our place the heavens possess he must,
Vile man, begot of clay, and born of dust.

XI
"Nor this sufficed, but that he also gave
His only Son, his darling to be slain,
To conquer so, hell, death, sin and the grave,
And man condemned to restore again,
He brake our prisons and would algates save
The souls there here should dwell in woe and pain,
And now in heaven with him they live always
With endless glory crowned, and lasting praise.

XII
"But why recount I thus our passed harms?
Remembrance fresh makes weakened sorrows strong,
Expulsed were we with injurious arms
From those due honors, us of right belong.
But let us leave to speak of these alarms,
And bend our forces gainst our present wrong:
Ah! see you not, how he attempted hath
To bring all lands, all nations to his faith?

78

Jerusalem Delivered

XIII
"Then, let us careless spend the day and night,
Without regard what haps, what comes or goes,
Let Asia subject be to Christians' might,
A prey he Sion to her conquering foes,
Let her adore again her Christ aright,
Who her before all nations whilom chose;
In brazen tables he his lore ywrit,
And let all tongues and lands acknowledge it.

XIV
"So shall our sacred altars all be his,
Our holy idols tumbled in the mould,
To him the wretched man that sinful is
Shall pray, and offer incense, myrrh and gold;
Our temples shall their costly deckings miss,
With naked walls and pillars freezing cold,
Tribute of souls shall end, and our estate,
Or Pluto reign in kingdoms desolate.

XV
"Oh, he not then the courage perished clean,
That whilom dwelt within your haughty thought,
When, armed with shining fire and weapons keen,
Against the angels of proud Heaven we fought,
I grant we fell on the Phlegrean green,
Yet good our cause was, though our fortune naught;
For chance assisteth oft the ignobler part,
We lost the field, yet lost we not our heart.

XVI
"Go then, my strength, my hope, my Spirits go,
These western rebels with your power withstand,
Pluck up these weeds, before they overgrow
The gentle garden of the Hebrews' land,

Quench out this spark, before it kindles so
That Asia burn, consumed with the brand.
Use open force, or secret guile unspied;
For craft is virtue gainst a foe defied.

XVII

"Among the knights and worthies of their train,
Let some like outlaws wander uncouth ways,
Let some be slain in field, let some again
Make oracles of women's yeas and nays,
And pine in foolish love, let some complain
On Godfrey's rule, and mutinies gainst him raise,
Turn each one's sword against his fellow's heart,
Thus kill them all or spoil the greatest part."

XVIII

Before his words the tyrant ended had,
The lesser devils arose with ghastly roar,
And thronged forth about the world to gad,
Each land they filled, river, stream and shore,
The goblins, fairies, fiends and furies mad,
Ranged in flowery dales, and mountains hoar,
And under every trembling leaf they sit,
Between the solid earth and welkin flit.

XIX

About the world they spread forth far and wide,
Filling the thoughts of each ungodly heart
With secret mischief, anger, hate and pride,
Wounding lost souls with sin's empoisoned dart.
But say, my Muse, recount whence first they tried
To hurt the Christian lords, and from what part,
Thou knowest of things performed so long agone,
This latter age hears little truth or none.

XX

Jerusalem Delivered

The town Damascus and the lands about
Ruled Hidraort, a wizard grave and sage,
Acquainted well with all the damned rout
Of Pluto's reign, even from his tender age;
Yet of this war he could not figure out
The wished ending, or success presage,
For neither stars above, nor powers of hell,
Nor skill, nor art, nor charm, nor devil could tell.

XXI

And yet he thought, — Oh, vain conceit of man,
Which as thou wishest judgest things to come! —
That the French host to sure destruction ran,
Condemned quite by Heaven's eternal doom:
He thinks no force withstand or vanquish can
The Egyptian strength, and therefore would that some
Both of the prey and glory of the fight
Upon this Syrian folk would haply light.

XXII

But for he held the Frenchmen's worth in prize,
And feared the doubtful gain of bloody war,
He, that was closely false and slyly war,
Cast how he might annoy them most from far:
And as he gan upon this point devise, —
As counsellors in ill still nearest are, —
At hand was Satan, ready ere men need,
If once they think, to make them do, the deed.

XXIII

He counselled him how best to hunt his game,
What dart to cast, what net, what toil to pitch,
A niece he had, a nice and tender dame,
Peerless in wit, in nature's blessings rich,
To all deceit she could her beauty frame,
False, fair and young, a virgin and a witch;
To her he told the sum of this emprise,

And praised her thus, for she was fair and wise:

XXIV

"My dear, who underneath these locks of gold,
And native brightness of thy lovely hue,
Hidest grave thoughts, ripe wit, and wisdom old,
More skill than I, in all mine arts untrue,
To thee my purpose great I must unfold,
This enterprise thy cunning must pursue,
Weave thou to end this web which I begin,
I will the distaff hold, come thou and spin.

XXV

"Go to the Christians' host, and there assay
All subtle sleights that women use in love,
Shed brinish tears, sob, sigh, entreat and pray,
Wring thy fair hands, cast up thine eyes above,
For mourning beauty hath much power, men say,
The stubborn hearts with pity frail to move;
Look pale for dread, and blush sometime for shame,
In seeming truth thy lies will soonest frame.

XXVI

"Take with the bait Lord Godfrey, if thou may'st;
Frame snares of look, strains of alluring speech;
For if he love, the conquest then thou hast,
Thus purposed war thou may'st with ease impeach,
Else lead the other Lords to deserts waste,
And hold them slaves far from their leader's reach:"
Thus taught he her, and for conclusion, saith,
"All things are lawful for our lands and faith."

XXVII

The sweet Armida took this charge on hand,
A tender piece, for beauty, sex and age,
The sun was sunken underneath the land,

Jerusalem Delivered

When she began her wanton pilgrimage,
In silken weeds she trusteth to withstand,
And conquer knights in warlike equipage,
Of their night ambling dame the Syrians prated,
Some good, some bad, as they her loved or hated.

XXVIII

Within few days the nymph arrived there
Where puissant Godfrey had his tents ypight;
Upon her strange attire, and visage clear,
Gazed each soldier, gazed every knight:
As when a comet doth in skies appear,
The people stand amazed at the light;
So wondered they and each at other sought,
What mister wight she was, and whence ybrought.

XXIX

Yet never eye to Cupid's service vowed
Beheld a face of such a lovely pride;
A tinsel veil her amber locks did shroud,
That strove to cover what it could not hide,
The golden sun behind a silver cloud,
So streameth out his beams on every side,
The marble goddess, set at Cnidos, naked
She seemed, were she unclothed, or that awaked.

XXX

The gamesome wind among her tresses plays,
And curleth up those growing riches short;
Her spareful eye to spread his beams denays,
But keeps his shot where Cupid keeps his fort;
The rose and lily on her cheek assays
To paint true fairness out in bravest sort,
Her lips, where blooms naught but the single rose,
Still blush, for still they kiss while still they close.

Jerusalem Delivered

XXXI

Her breasts, two hills o'erspread with purest snow,
Sweet, smooth and supple, soft and gently swelling,
Between them lies a milken dale below,
Where love, youth, gladness, whiteness make their dwelling,
Her breasts half hid, and half were laid to show,
So was the wanton clad, as if this much
Should please the eye, the rest unseen, the touch.

XXXII

As when the sunbeams dive through Tagus' wave,
To spy the store–house of his springtime gold,
Love–piercing thought so through her mantle drave,
And in her gentle bosom wandered bold;
It viewed the wondrous beauty virgins have,
And all to fond desire with vantage told,
Alas! what hope is left, to quench his fire
That kindled is by sight, blown by desire.

XXXIII

Thus passed she, praised, wished, and wondered at,
Among the troops who there encamped lay,
She smiled for joy, but well dissembled that,
Her greedy eye chose out her wished prey;
On all her gestures seeming virtue sat,
Toward the imperial tent she asked the way:
With that she met a bold and lovesome knight,
Lord Godfrey's youngest brother, Eustace hight.

XXXIV

This was the fowl that first fell in the snare,
He saw her fair, and hoped to find her kind;
The throne of Cupid had an easy stair,
His bark is fit to sail with every wind,
The breach he makes no wisdom can repair:
With reverence meet the baron low inclined,
And thus his purpose to the virgin told,

84

For youth, use, nature, all had made him bold.

XXXV

"Lady, if thee beseem a stile so low,
In whose sweet looks such sacred beauty shine, —
For never yet did Heaven such grace bestow
On any daughter born of Adam's line —
Thy name let us, though far unworthy, know,
Unfold thy will, and whence thou art in fine,
Lest my audacious boldness learn too late
What honors due become thy high estate."

XXXVI

"Sir Knight," quoth she, "your praises reach too high
Above her merit you commenden so,
A hapless maid I am, both born to die
And dead to joy, that live in care and woe,
A virgin helpless, fugitive pardie,
My native soil and kingdom thus forego
To seek Duke Godfrey's aid, such store men tell
Of virtuous ruth doth in his bosom dwell.

XXXVII

"Conduct me then that mighty duke before,
If you be courteous, sir, as well you seem."
"Content," quoth he, "since of one womb ybore,
We brothers are, your fortune good esteem
To encounter me whose word prevaileth more
In Godfrey's hearing than you haply deem:
Mine aid I grant, and his I promise too,
All that his sceptre, or my sword, can do."

XXXVIII

He led her easily forth when this was said,
Where Godfrey sat among his lords and peers,
She reverence did, then blushed, as one dismayed

Jerusalem Delivered

To speak, for secret wants and inward fears,
It seemed a bashful shame her speeches stayed,
At last the courteous duke her gently cheers;
Silence was made, and she began her tale,
They sit to hear, thus sung this nightingale:

XXXIX
"Victorious prince, whose honorable name
Is held so great among our Pagan kings,
That to those lands thou dost by conquest tame
That thou hast won them some content it brings;
Well known to all is thy immortal fame,
The earth, thy worth, thy foe, thy praises sings,
And Paynims wronged come to seek thine aid,
So doth thy virtue, so thy power persuade.

XL
"And I though bred in Macon's heathenish lore,
Which thou oppressest with thy puissant might,
Yet trust thou wilt an helpless maid restore,
And repossess her in her father's right:
Others in their distress do aid implore
Of kin and friends; but I in this sad plight
Invoke thy help, my kingdom to invade,
So doth thy virtue, so my need persuade.

XLI
"In thee I hope, thy succors I invoke,
To win the crown whence I am dispossest;
For like renown awaiteth on the stroke
To cast the haughty down or raise the opprest;
Nor greater glory brings a sceptre broke,
Than doth deliverance of a maid distrest;
And since thou canst at will perform the thing,
More is thy praise to make, than kill a king.

XLII

86

"But if thou would'st thy succors due excuse,
Because in Christ I have no hope nor trust,
Ah yet for virtue's sake, thy virtue use!
Who scorneth gold because it lies in dust?
Be witness Heaven, if thou to grant refuse,
Thou dost forsake a maid in cause most just,
And for thou shalt at large my fortunes know,
I will my wrongs and their great treasons show.

XLIII
"Prince Arbilan that reigned in his life
On fair Damascus, was my noble sire,
Born of mean race he was, yet got to wife
The Queen Chariclia, such was the fire
Of her hot love, but soon the fatal knife
Had cut the thread that kept their joys entire,
For so mishap her cruel lot had cast,
My birth, her death; my first day, was her last.
XLIV
"And ere five years were fully come and gone
Since his dear spouse to hasty death did yield,
My father also died, consumed with moan,
And sought his love amid the Elysian fields,
His crown and me, poor orphan, left alone,
Mine uncle governed in my tender eild;
For well he thought, if mortal men have faith,
In brother's breast true love his mansion hath.

XLV
"He took the charge of me and of the crown,
And with kind shows of love so brought to pass
That through Damascus great report was blown
How good, how just, how kind mine uncle was;
Whether he kept his wicked hate unknown
And hid the serpent in the flowering grass,
On that true faith did in his bosom won,

Because he meant to match me with his son.

XLVI

"Which son, within short while, did undertake
Degree of knighthood, as beseemed him well,
Yet never durst he for his lady's sake
Break sword or lance, advance in lofty sell;
As fair he was, as Citherea's make,
As proud as he that signoriseth hell,
In fashions wayward, and in love unkind,
For Cupid deigns not wound a currish mind.

XLVII

"This paragon should Queen Armida wed,
A goodly swain to be a princess' fere,
A lovely partner of a lady's bed,
A noble head a golden crown to wear:
His glosing sire his errand daily said,
And sugared speeches whispered in mine ear
To make me take this darling in mine arms,
But still the adder stopt her ears from charms.

XLVIII

"At last he left me with a troubled grace,
Through which transparent was his inward spite,
Methought I read the story in his face
Of these mishaps that on me since have light,
Since that foul spirits haunt my resting–place,
And ghastly visions break any sleep by night,
Grief, horror, fear my fainting soul did kill,
For so my mind foreshowed my coming ill.

XLIX

"Three times the shape of my dear mother came,
Pale, sad, dismayed, to warn me in my dream,
Alas, how far transformed from the same

Whose eyes shone erst like Titan's glorious beam:
`Daughter,' she says, `fly, fly, behold thy dame
Foreshows the treasons of thy wretched eame,
Who poison gainst thy harmless life provides:'
This said, to shapeless air unseen she glides.

L
"But what avail high walls or bulwarks strong,
Where fainting cowards have the piece to guard?
My sex too weak, mine age was all to young,
To undertake alone a work so hard,
To wander wild the desert woods among,
A banished maid, of wonted ease debarred,
So grievous seemed, that liefer were my death,
And there to expire where first I drew my breath.
LI
"I feared deadly evil if long I stayed,
And yet to fly had neither will nor power,
Nor durst my heart declare it waxed afraid,
Lest so I hasten might my dying hour:
Thus restless waited I, unhappy maid,
What hand should first pluck up my springing flower,
Even as the wretch condemned to lose his life
Awaits the falling of the murdering knife.

LII
"In these extremes, for so my fortune would
Perchance preserve me to my further ill,
One of my noble father's servants old,
That for his goodness bore his child good will,
With store of tears this treason gan unfold,
And said; my guardian would his pupil kill,
And that himself, if promise made be kept,
Should give me poison dire ere next I slept.

LIII

89

"And further told me, if I wished to live,
I must convey myself by secret flight,
And offered then all succours he could give
To aid his mistress, banished from her right.
His words of comfort, fear to exile drive,
The dread of death, made lesser dangers light:
So we concluded, when the shadows dim
Obscured the earth I should depart with him.

LIV
"Of close escapes the aged patroness,
Blacker than erst, her sable mantle spread,
When with two trusty maids, in great distress,
Both from mine uncle and my realm I fled;
Oft looked I back, but hardly could suppress
Those streams of tears, mine eyes uncessant shed,
For when I looked on my kingdom lost,
It was a grief, a death, an hell almost.

LV
"My steeds drew on the burden of my limbs,
But still my locks, my thoughts, drew back as fast,
So fare the men, that from the heaven's brims,
Far out to sea, by sudden storm are cast;
Swift o'er the grass the rolling chariot swims,
Through ways unknown, all night, all day we haste,
At last, nigh tired, a castle strong we fand,
The utmost border of my native land.

LVI
"The fort Arontes was, for so the knight
Was called, that my deliverance thus had wrought,
But when the tyrant saw, by mature flight
I had escaped the treasons of his thought,
The rage increased in the cursed wight
Gainst me, and him, that me to safety brought,

90

And us accused, we would have poisoned
Him, but descried, to save our lives we fled.

LVII
"And that in lieu of his approved truth,
To poison him I hired had my guide,
That he despatched, mine unbridled youth
Might rage at will, in no subjection tied,
And that each night I slept — O foul untruth! —
Mine honor lost, by this Arontes' side:
But Heaven I pray send down revenging fire,
When so base love shall change my chaste desire.

LVIII
"Not that he sitteth on my regal throne,
Nor that he thirst to drink my lukewarm blood,
So grieveth me, as this despite alone,
That my renown, which ever blameless stood,
Hath lost the light wherewith it always shone:
With forged lies he makes his tale so good,
And holds my subjects' hearts in such suspense,
That none take armor for their queen's defence.

LIX
"And though he do my regal throne possess,
Clothed in purple, crowned with burnished gold;
Yet is his hate, his rancor, ne'er the less,
Since naught assuageth malice when 'tis old:
He threats to burn Arontes' forteress,
And murder him unless he yield the hold,
And me and mine threats not with war, but death,
Thus causeless hatred, endless is uneath.

LX
"And so he trusts to wash away the stain,
And hide his shameful fact with mine offence,

And saith he will restore the throne again
To his late honor and due excellence,
And therefore would I should be algates slain,
For while I live, his right is in suspense,
This is the cause my guiltless life is sought,
For on my ruin is his safety wrought.

LXI

"And let the tyrant have his heart's desire,
Let him perform the cruelty he meant,
My guiltless blood must quench the ceaseless fire
On which my endless tears were bootless spent,
Unless thou help; to thee, renowned Sire,
I fly, a virgin, orphan, innocent,
And let these tears that on thy feet distil,
Redeem the drops of blood, he thirsts to spill.

LXII

"By these thy glorious feet, that tread secure
On necks of tyrants, by thy conquests brave,
By that right hand, and by those temples pure
Thou seek'st to free from Macon's lore, I crave
Help for this sickness none but thou canst cure,
My life and kingdom let thy mercy save
From death and ruin: but in vain I prove thee,
If right, if truth, if justice cannot move thee.

LXIII

"Thou who dost all thou wishest, at thy will,
And never willest aught but what is right,
Preserve this guiltless blood they seek to spill;
Thine be my kingdom, save it with thy might:
Among these captains, lords, and knights of skill,
Appoint me ten, approved most in fight,
Who with assistance of my friends and kin,
May serve my kingdom lost again to win.

LXIV

"For lo a knight, that had a gate to ward,
A man of chiefest trust about his king,
Hath promised so to beguile the guard
That me and mine he undertakes to bring
Safe, where the tyrant haply sleepeth hard
He counselled me to undertake this thing,
Of these some little succor to intreat,
Whose name alone accomplish can the feat."

LXV

This said, his answer did the nymph attend,
Her looks, her sighs, her gestures all did pray him:
But Godfrey wisely did his grant suspend,
He doubts the worst, and that awhile did stay him,
He knows, who fears no God, he loves no friend,
He fears the heathen false would thus betray him:
But yet such ruth dwelt in his princely mind,
That gainst his wisdom, pity made him kind.

LXVI

Besides the kindness of his gentle thought,
Ready to comfort each distressed wight,
The maiden's offer profit with it brought;
For if the Syrian kingdom were her right,
That won, the way were easy, which he sought,
To bring all Asia subject to his might:
There might he raise munition, arms and treasure
To work the Egyptian king and his displeasure.

LXVII

Thus was his noble heart long time betwixt
Fear and remorse, not granting nor denying,
Upon his eyes the dame her lookings fixed,
As if her life and death lay on his saying,

Some tears she shed, with sighs and sobbings mixed,
As if her hopes were dead through his delaying;
At last her earnest suit the duke denayed,
But with sweet words thus would content the maid:

LXVIII
"If not in service of our God we fought,
In meaner quarrel if this sword were shaken,
Well might thou gather in thy gentle thought,
So fair a princess should not be forsaken;
But since these armies, from the world's end brought,
To free this sacred town have undertaken,
It were unfit we turned our strength away,
And victory, even in her coming, stay.

LXIX
"I promise thee, and on my princely word
The burden of thy wish and hope repose,
That when this chosen temple of the Lord,
Her holy doors shall to his saints unclose
In rest and peace; then this victorious sword
Shall execute due vengeance on thy foes;
But if for pity of a worldly dame
I left this work, such pity were my shame."

LXX
At this the princess bent her eyes to ground,
And stood unmoved, though not unmarked, a space,
The secret bleeding of her inward wound
Shed heavenly dew upon her angel's face,
"Poor wretch," quoth she, "in tears and sorrows drowned,
Death be thy peace, the grave thy resting–place,
Since such thy hap, that lest thou mercy find
The gentlest heart on earth is proved unkind.

LXXI

"Where none attends, what boots it to complain?
Men's froward hearts are moved with women's tears
As marble stones are pierced with drops of rain,
No plaints find passage through unwilling ears:
The tyrant, haply, would his wraith restrain
Heard he these prayers ruthless Godfrey hears,
Yet not thy fault is this, my chance, I see,
Hath made even pity, pitiless in thee.
LXXII
"So both thy goodness, and good hap, denayed me,
Grief, sorrow, mischief, care, hath overthrown me,
The star that ruled my birthday hath betrayed me,
My genius sees his charge, but dares not own me,
Of queen–like state, my flight hath disarrayed me,
My father died, ere he five years had known me,
My kingdom lost, and lastly resteth now,
Down with the tree sith broke is every bough.

LXXIII
"And for the modest lore of maidenhood,
Bids me not sojourn with these armed men,
O whither shall I fly, what secret wood
Shall hide me from the tyrant? or what den,
What rock, what vault, what cave can do me good?
No, no, where death is sure, it resteth then
To scorn his power and be it therefore seen,
Armida lived, and died, both like a queen."
LXXIV
With that she looked as if a proud disdain
Kindled displeasure in her noble mind,
The way she came she turned her steps again,
With gesture sad but in disdainful kind,
A tempest railed down her cheeks amain,
With tears of woe, and sighs of anger's wind;
The drops her footsteps wash, whereon she treads,
And seems to step on pearls, or crystal beads.

LXXV

Her cheeks on which this streaming nectar fell,
Stilled through the limbeck of her diamond eyes,
The roses white and red resembled well,
Whereon the rory May–dew sprinkled lies
When the fair morn first blusheth from her cell,
And breatheth balm from opened paradise;
Thus sighed, thus mourned, thus wept this lovely queen,
And in each drop bathed a grace unseen.

LXXVI

Thrice twenty Cupids unperceived flew
To gather up this liquor, ere it fall,
And of each drop an arrow forged new,
Else, as it came, snatched up the crystal ball,
And at rebellious hearts for wildfire threw.
O wondrous love! thou makest gain of all;
For if she weeping sit, or smiling stand,
She bends thy bow, or kindleth else thy brand.

LXXVII

This forged plaint drew forth unfeigned tears
From many eyes, and pierced each worthy's heart;
Each one condoleth with her that her hears,
And of her grief would help her bear the smart:
If Godfrey aid her not, not one but swears
Some tigress gave him suck on roughest part
Midst the rude crags, on Alpine cliffs aloft:
Hard is that heart which beauty makes not soft.

LXXVIII

But jolly Eustace, in whose breast the brand
Of love and pity kindled had the flame,
While others softly whispered underhand,
Before the duke with comely boldness came:

96

"Brother and lord," quoth he, "too long you stand
In your first purpose, yet vouchsafe to frame
Your thoughts to ours, and lend this virgin aid:
Thanks are half lost when good turns are delayed.

LXXIX

"And think not that Eustace's talk assays
To turn these forces from this present war,
Or that I wish you should your armies raise
From Sion's walls, my speech tends not so far:
But we that venture all for fame and praise,
That to no charge nor service bounden are,
Forth of our troop may ten well spared be
To succor her, which naught can weaken thee.

LXXX

"And know, they shall in God's high service fight,
That virgins innocent save and defend:
Dear will the spoils be in the Heaven's sight,
That from a tyrant's hateful head we rend:
Nor seemed I forward in this lady's right,
With hope of gain or profit in the end;
But for I know he arms unworthy bears,
To help a maiden's cause that shuns or fears.

LXXXI

"Ah! be it not pardie declared in France,
Or elsewhere told where courtesy is in prize,
That we forsook so fair a chevisance,
For doubt or fear that might from fight arise;
Else, here surrender I both sword and lance,
And swear no more to use this martial guise;
For ill deserves he to be termed a knight,
That bears a blunt sword in a lady's right."

LXXXII

Thus parleyed he, and with confused sound,
The rest approved what the gallant said,
Their general their knights encompassed round,
With humble grace, and earnest suit they prayed:
"I yield," quoth he, "and it be happy found,
What I have granted, let her have your aid:
Yours be the thanks, for yours the danger is,
If aught succeed, as much I fear, amiss.

LXXXIII
"But if with you my words may credit find,
Oh temper then this heat misguides you so!"
Thus much he said, but they with fancy blind,
Accept his grant, and let his counsel go.
What works not beauty, man's relenting mind
Is eath to move with plaints and shows of woe:
Her lips cast forth a chain of sugared words,
That captive led most of the Christian lords.
LXXXIV
Eustace recalled her, and bespake her thus:
"Beauty's chief darling, let those sorrows be,
For such assistance shall you find in us
As with your need, or will, may best agree:"
With that she cheered her forehead dolorous,
And smiled for joy, that Phoebus blushed to see,
And had she deigned her veil for to remove,
The God himself once more had fallen in love.

LXXXV
With that she broke the silence once again,
And gave the knight great thanks in little speech,
She said she would his handmaid poor remain,
So far as honor's laws received no breach.
Her humble gestures made the residue plain,
Dumb eloquence, persuading more than speech:
Thus women know, and thus they use the guise,

Jerusalem Delivered

To enchant the valiant, and beguile the wise.

LXXXVI
And when she saw her enterprise had got
Some wished mean of quick and good proceeding,
She thought to strike the iron that was hot,
For every action hath his hour of speeding:
Medea or false Circe changed not
So far the shapes of men, as her eyes spreading
Altered their hearts, and with her syren's sound
In lust, their minds, their hearts, in love she drowned.

LXXXVII
All wily sleights that subtle women know,
Hourly she used, to catch some lover new.
None kenned the bent of her unsteadfast bow,
For with the time her thoughts her looks renew,
From some she cast her modest eyes below,
At some her gazing glances roving flew,
And while she thus pursued her wanton sport,
She spurred the slow, and reined the forward short.

LXXXVIII
If some, as hopeless that she would be won,
Forebore to love, because they durst not move her,
On them her gentle looks to smile begun,
As who say she is kind if you dare prove her
On every heart thus shone this lustful sun,
All strove to serve, to please, to woo, to love her,
And in their hearts that chaste and bashful were,
Her eye's hot glance dissolved the frost of fear.

LXXXIX
On them who durst with fingering bold assay
To touch the softness of her tender skin,
She looked as coy, as if she list not play,

And made as things of worth were hard to win;
Yet tempered so her deignful looks alway,
That outward scorn showed store of grace within:
Thus with false hope their longing hearts she fired,
For hardest gotten things are most desired.

XC

Alone sometimes she walked in secret where,
To ruminate upon her discontent,
Within her eyelids sate the swelling tear,
Not poured forth, though sprung from sad lament,
And with this craft a thousand souls well near
In snares of foolish ruth and love she hent,
And kept as slaves, by which we fitly prove
That witless pity breedeth fruitless love.

XCI

Sometimes, as if her hope unloosed had
The chains of grief, wherein her thoughts lay fettered,
Upon her minions looked she blithe and glad,
In that deceitful lore so was she lettered;
Not glorious Titan, in his brightness clad,
The sunshine of her face in lustre bettered:
For when she list to cheer her beauties so,
She smiled away the clouds of grief and woe.

XCII

Her double charm of smiles and sugared words,
Lulled on sleep the virtue of their senses,
Reason shall aid gainst those assaults affords,
Wisdom no warrant from those sweet offences;
Cupid's deep rivers have their shallow fords,
His griefs, bring joys; his losses, recompenses;
He breeds the sore, and cures us of the pain:
Achilles' lance that wounds and heals again.

Jerusalem Delivered

XCIII

While thus she them torments twixt frost and fire,
Twixt joy and grief, twixt hope and restless fear,
The sly enchantress felt her gain the nigher,
These were her flocks that golden fleeces bear:
But if someone durst utter his desire,
And by complaining make his griefs appear,
He labored hard rocks with plaints to move,
She had not learned the gamut then of love.

XCIV

For down she bet her bashful eyes to ground,
And donned the weed of women's modest grace,
Down from her eyes welled the pearls round,
Upon the bright enamel of her face;
Such honey drops on springing flowers are found
When Phoebus holds the crimson morn in chase;
Full seemed her looks of anger, and of shame;
Yet pity shone transparent through the same.

XCV

If she perceived by his outward cheer,
That any would his love by talk bewray,
Sometimes she heard him, sometimes stopped her ear,
And played fast and loose the livelong day:
Thus all her lovers kind deluded were,
Their earnest suit got neither yea nor nay;
But like the sort of weary huntsmen fare,
That hunt all day, and lose at night the hare.

XCVI

These were the arts by which she captived
A thousand souls of young and lusty knights;
These were the arms wherewith love conquered
Their feeble hearts subdued in wanton fights:
What wonder if Achilles were misled,
Of great Alcides at their ladies' sights,

Since these true champions of the Lord above
Were thralls to beauty, yielden slaves to lore.

FIFTH BOOK

THE ARGUMENT.
Gernando scorns Rinaldo should aspire
To rule that charge for which he seeks and strives,
And slanders him so far, that in his ire
The wronged knight his foe of life deprives:
Far from the camp the slayer doth retire,
Nor lets himself be bound in chains or gyves:
Armide departs content, and from the seas
Godfrey hears news which him and his displease.

I
While thus Armida false the knights misled
In wandering errors of deceitful love,
And thought, besides the champions promised,
The other lordlings in her aid to move,
In Godfrey's thought a strong contention bred
Who fittest were this hazard great to prove;
For all the worthies of the adventures' band
Were like in birth, in power, in strength of hand.

II
But first the prince, by grave advice, decreed
They should some knight choose at their own election,
That in his charge Lord Dudon might succeed,
And of that glorious troop should take protection;
So none should grieve, displeased with the deed,

Nor blame the causer of their new subjection:
Besides, Godfredo showed by this device,
How much he held that regiment in price.

III
He called the worthies then, and spake them so:
"Lordlings, you know I yielded to your will,
And gave you license with this dame to go,
To win her kingdom and that tyrant kill:
But now again I let you further know,
In following her it may betide yon ill;
Refrain therefore, and change this forward thought
For death unsent for, danger comes unsought.

IV
"But if to shun these perils, sought so far,
May seem disgraceful to the place yon hold;
If grave advice and prudent counsel are
Esteemed detractors from your courage bold;
Then know, I none against his will debar,
Nor what I granted erst I now withhold;
But he mine empire, as it ought of right,
Sweet, easy, pleasant, gentle, meek and light.

V
"Go then or tarry, each as likes him best,
Free power I grant you on this enterprise;
But first in Dudon's place, now laid in chest,
Choose you some other captain stout and wise;
Then ten appoint among the worthiest,
But let no more attempt this hard emprise,
In this my will content you that I have,
For power constrained is but a glorious slave."

VI
Thus Godfrey said, and thus his brother spake,

And answered for himself and all his peers:
"My lord, as well it fitteth thee to make
These wise delays and cast these doubts and fears,
So 'tis our part at first to undertake;
Courage and haste beseems our might and years;
And this proceeding with so grave advice,
Wisdom, in you, in us were cowardice.

VII

"Since then the feat is easy, danger none,
All set in battle and in hardy fight,
Do thou permit the chosen ten to gone
And aid the damsel:" thus devised the knight,
To make men think the sun of honor shone
There where the lamp of Cupid gave the light:
The rest perceive his guile, and it approve,
And call that knighthood which was childish love.

VIII

But loving Eustace, that with jealous eye
Beheld the worth of Sophia's noble child,
And his fair shape did secretly envy,
Besides the virtues in his breast compiled,
And, for in love he would no company,
He stored his mouth with speeches smoothly filed,
Drawing his rival to attend his word;
Thus with fair sleight he laid the knight abord:

IX

"Of great Bertoldo thou far greater heir,
Thou star of knighthood, flower of chivalry,
Tell me, who now shall lead this squadron fair,
Since our late guide in marble cold doth lie?
I, that with famous Dudon might compare
In all, but years, hoar locks, and gravity,
To whom should I, Duke Godfrey's brother, yield,

Unless to thee, the Christian army's shield?

X

"Thee whom high birth makes equal with the best
Thine acts prefer both me and all beforn;
Nor that in fight thou both surpass the rest,
And Godfrey's worthy self, I hold in scorn;
Thee to obey then am I only pressed;
Before these worthies be thine eagle borne;
This honor haply thou esteemest light,
Whose day of glory never yet found night.

XI

"Yet mayest thou further by this means display
The spreading wings of thy immortal fame;
I will procure it, if thou sayest not nay,
And all their wills to thine election frame:
But for I scantly am resolved which way
To bend my force, or where employ the same,
Leave me, I pray, at my discretion free
To help Armida, or serve here with thee."

XII

This last request, for love is evil to hide,
Empurpled both his cheeks with scarlet red;
Rinaldo soon his passions had descried,
And gently smiling turned aside his head,
And, for weak Cupid was too feeble eyed
To strike him sure, the fire in him was dead;
So that of rivals was he naught afraid,
Nor cared he for the journey or the maid.

XIII

But in his noble thought revolved he oft
Dudon's high prowess, death and burial,
And how Argantes bore his plumes aloft,

Praising his fortunes for that worthy's fall;
Besides, the knight's sweet words and praises soft
To his due honor did him fitly call,
And made his heart rejoice, for well he knew,
Though much he praised him, all his words were true.

XIV

"Degrees," quoth he, "of honors high to hold,
I would them first deserve, and the desire;
And were my valor such as you have told,
Would I for that to higher place aspire:
But if to honors due raise me you would,
I will not of my works refuse the hire;
And much it glads me, that my power and might
Ypraised is by such a valiant knight.

XV

"I neither seek it nor refuse the place,
Which if I get, the praise and thanks be thine."
Eustace, this spoken, hied thence apace
To know which way his fellows' hearts incline:
But Prince Gernando coveted the place,
Whom though Armida sought to undermine,
Gainst him yet vain did all her engines prove,
His pride was such, there was no place for love.

XVI

Gernando was the King of Norway's son,
That many a realm and region had to guide,
And for his elders lands and crowns had won.
His heart was puffed up with endless pride:
The other boasts more what himself had done
Than all his ancestors' great acts beside;
Yet his forefathers old before him were
Famous in war and peace five hundred years.

XVII

This barbarous prince, who only vainly thought
That bliss in wealth and kingly power doth lie,
And in respect esteemed all virtue naught
Unless it were adorned with titles high,
Could not endure, that to the place he sought
A simple knight should dare to press so nigh;
And in his breast so boiled fell despite,
That ire and wrath exiled reason quite.

XVIII

The hidden devil, that lies in close await
To win the fort of unbelieving man,
Found entry there, where ire undid the gate,
And in his bosom unperceived ran;
It filled his heart with malice, strife and hate,
It made him rage, blaspheme, swear, curse and ban,
Invisible it still attends him near,
And thus each minute whispereth in his ear.

XIX

What, shall Rinaldo match thee? dares he tell
Those idle names of his vain pedigree?
Then let him say, if thee he would excel,
What lands, what realms his tributaries be:
If his forefathers in the graves that dwell,
Were honored like thine that live, let see:
Oh how dares one so mean aspire so high,
Born in that servile country Italy?

XX

Now, if he win, or if he lose the day,
Yet is his praise and glory hence derived,
For that the world will, to his credit, say,
Lo, this is he that with Gernando strived.
The charge some deal thee haply honor may,

That noble Dudon had while here he lived;
But laid on him he would the office shame,
Let it suffice, he durst desire the same.

XXI

If when this breath from man's frail body flies
The soul take keep, or know the things done here,
Oh, how looks Dudon from the glorious skies?
What wrath, what anger in his face appear,
On this proud youngling while he bends his eyes,
Marking how high he doth his feathers rear?
Seeing his rash attempt, how soon he dare,
Though but a boy, with his great worth compare.

XXII

He dares not only, but he strives and proves,
Where chastisement were fit there wins he praise:
One counsels him, his speech him forward moves;
Another fool approveth all he says:
If Godfrey favor him more than behoves,
Why then he wrongeth thee an hundred ways;
Nor let thy state so far disgraced be,
Now what thou art and canst, let Godfrey see.

XXIII

With such false words the kindled fire began
To every vein his poisoned heart to reach,
It swelled his scornful heart, and forth it ran
At his proud looks, and too audacious speech;
All that he thought blameworthy in the man,
To his disgrace that would be each where preach;
He termed him proud and vain, his worth in fight
He called fool–hardise, rashness, madness right.

XXIV

All that in him was rare or excellent,

Jerusalem Delivered

All that was good, all that was princely found,
With such sharp words as malice could invent,
He blamed, such power has wicked tongue to wound.
The youth, for everywhere those rumors went,
Of these reproaches heard sometimes the sound;
Nor did for that his tongue the fault amend,
Until it brought him to his woful end.

XXV

The cursed fiend that set his tongue at large,
Still bred more fancies in his idle brain,
His heart with slanders new did overcharge,
And soothed him still in his angry vein;
Amid the camp a place was broad and large,
Where one fair regiment might easily train;
And there in tilt and harmless tournament
Their days of rest the youths and gallants spent.

XXVI

There, as his fortune would it should betide,
Amid the press Gernando gan retire,
To vomit out his venom unespied,
Wherewith foul envy did his heart inspire.
Rinaldo heard him as he stood beside,
And as he could not bridle wrath and ire,
"Thou liest," cried he loud, and with that word
About his head he tossed his flaming sword.

XXVII

Thunder his voice, and lightning seemed his brand,
So fell his look, and furious was his cheer,
Gernando trembled, for he saw at hand
Pale death, and neither help nor comfort near,
Yet for the soldiers all to witness stand
He made proud sign, as though he naught did fear,
But bravely drew his little–helping blade,

And valiant show of strong resistance made.

XXVIII

With that a thousand blades of burnished steel
Glistered on heaps like flames of fire in sight,
Hundreds, that knew not yet the quarrel weel,
Ran thither, some to gaze and some to fight:
The empty air a sound confused did feel
Of murmurs low, and outcries loud on height,
Like rolling waves and Boreas' angry blasts
When roaring seas against the rocks he casts.

XXIX

But not for this the wronged warrior stayed
His just displeasure and incensed ire,
He cared not what the vulgar did or said,
To vengeance did his courage fierce aspire:
Among the thickest weapons way he made,
His thundering sword made all on heaps retire,
So that of near a thousand stayed not one,
But Prince Gernando bore the brunt alone.

XXX

His hand, too quick to execute his wrath,
Performed all, as pleased his eye and heart,
At head and breast oft times he strucken hath,
Now at the right, now at the other part:
On every side thus did he harm and scath,
And oft beguile his sight with nimble art,
That no defence the prince of wounds acquits,
Where least he thinks, or fears, there most he hits.

XXXI

Nor ceased be, till in Gernando's breast
He sheathed once or twice his furious blade;
Down fell the hapless prince with death oppressed,

A double way to his weak soul was made;
His bloody sword the victor wiped and dressed,
Nor longer by the slaughtered body stayed,
But sped him thence, and soon appeased hath
His hate, his ire, his rancor and his wrath.

XXXII
Called by the tumult, Godfrey drew him near,
And there beheld a sad and rueful sight,
The signs of death upon his face appear,
With dust and blood his locks were loathly dight,
Sighs and complaints on each side might he hear,
Made for the sudden death of that great knight:
Amazed, he asked who durst and did so much;
For yet he knew not whom the fault would touch.

XXXIII
Arnoldo, minion of the Prince thus slain,
Augments the fault in telling it, and saith,
This Prince murdered, for a quarrel vain,
By young Rinaldo in his desperate wrath,
And with that sword that should Christ's law maintain,
One of Christ's champions bold he killed hath,
And this he did in such a place and hour,
As if he scorned your rule, despised your power.

XXXIV
And further adds, that he deserved death
By law, and law should inviolate,
That none offence could greater be uneath,
And yet the place the fault did aggravate:
If he escapes, that mischief would take breath,
And flourish bold in spite of rule and state;
And that Gernando's friends would venge the wrong,
Although to justice that did first belong,

Jerusalem Delivered

XXXV

And by that means, should discord, hate and strife
Raise mutinies, and what therefore ensueth:
Lastly he praised the dead, and still had rife
All words he thought could vengeance move or rut
Against him Tancred argued for life,
With honest reasons to excuse the youth:
The Duke heard all, but with such sober cheer,
As banished hope, and still increased fear.

XXXVI

"Great Prince," quoth Tancred; "set before thine eyes
Rinaldo's worth and courage what it is,
How much our hope of conquest in him lies;
Regard that princely house and race of his;
He that correcteth every fault he spies,
And judgeth all alike, doth all amiss;
For faults, you know, are greater thought or less,
As is the person's self that doth transgress."

XXXVII

Godfredo answered him; "If high and low
Of sovereign power alike should feel the stroke,
Then, Tancred, ill you counsel us, I trow;
If lords should know no law, as erst you spoke,
How vile and base our empire were you know,
If none but slaves and peasants bear the yoke;
Weak is the sceptre and the power is small
That such provisos bring annexed withal.

XXXVIII

"But mine was freely given ere 'twas sought,
Nor that it lessened be I now consent;
Right well know I both when and where I ought
To give condign reward and punishment,
Since you are all in like subjection brought,

112

Both high and low obey, and be content."
This heard, Tancredi wisely stayed his words,
Such weight the sayings have of kings and lords.

XXXIX
Old Raymond praised his speech, for old men think
They ever wisest seem when most severe,
" 'Tis best," quoth he, "to make these great ones shrink,
The people love him whom the nobles fear:
There must the rule to all disorders sink,
Where pardons more than punishments appear;
For feeble is each kingdom, frail and weak,
Unless his basis be this fear I speak."

XL
These words Tancredi heard and pondered well,
And by them wist how Godfrey's thoughts were bent,
Nor list he longer with these old men dwell,
But turned his horse and to Rinaldo went,
Who, when his noble foe death–wounded fell,
Withdrew him softly to his gorgeous tent;
There Tancred found him, and at large declared
The words and speeches sharp which late you heard.

XLI
And said, "Although I wot the outward show
Is not true witness of the secret thought,
For that some men so subtle are, I trow,
That what they purpose most appeareth naught;
Yet dare I say Godfredo means, I know,
Such knowledge hath his looks and speeches wrought,
You shall first prisoner be, and then be tried
As he shall deem it good and law provide."

XLII
With that a bitter smile well might you see

Jerusalem Delivered

Rinaldo cast, with scorn and high disdain,
"Let them in fetters plead their cause," quoth he,
"That are base peasants, born of servile stain,
I was free born, I live and will die free
Before these feet be fettered in a chain:
These hands were made to shake sharp spears and swords,
Not to be tied in gyves and twisted cords.

XLIII

"If my good service reap this recompense,
To be clapt up in close and secret mew,
And as a thief be after dragged from thence,
To suffer punishment as law finds due;
Let Godfrey come or send, I will not hence
Until we know who shall this bargain rue,
That of our tragedy the late done fact
May be the first, and this the second, act.

XLIV

"Give me mine arms," he cried; his squire them brings,
And clad his head, and dressed in iron strong,
About his neck his silver shield he flings,
Down by his side a cutting sword there hung;
Among this earth's brave lords and mighty kings,
Was none so stout, so fierce, so fair, so young,
God Mars he seemed descending from his sphere,
Or one whose looks could make great Mars to fear.

XLV

Tancredi labored with some pleasing speech
His spirits fierce and courage to appease;
"Young Prince, thy valor," thus he gan to preach,
"Can chastise all that do thee wrong, at ease,
I know your virtue can your enemies teach,
That you can venge you when and where you please:
But God forbid this day you lift your arm

To do this camp and us your friends such harm.

XLVI

"Tell me what will you do? why would you stain
Your noble hands in our unguilty blood?
By wounding Christians, will you again
Pierce Christ, whose parts they are and members good?
Will you destroy us for your glory vain,
Unstayed as rolling waves in ocean flood?
Far be it from you so to prove your strength,
And let your zeal appease your rage at length.

XLVII

"For God's love stay your heat, and just displeasure,
Appease your wrath, your courage fierce assuage,
Patience, a praise; forbearance, is a treasure;
Suffrance, an angel's is; a monster, rage;
At least you actions by example measure,
And think how I in mine unbridled age
Was wronged, yet I would not revengement take
On all this camp, for one offender's sake.

XLVIII

"Cilicia conquered I, as all men wot,
And there the glorious cross on high I reared,
But Baldwin came, and what I nobly got
Bereft me falsely when I least him feared;
He seemed my friend, and I discovered not
His secret covetise which since appeared;
Yet strive I not to get mine own by fight,
Or civil war, although perchance I might.

XLIX

"If then you scorn to be in prison pent,
If bonds, as high disgrace, your hands refuse;
Or if your thoughts still to maintain are bent

115

Jerusalem Delivered

Your liberty, as men of honor use:
To Antioch what if forthwith you went?
And leave me here your absence to excuse,
There with Prince Boemond live in ease and peace,
Until this storm of Godfrey's anger cease.

L

"For soon, if forces come from Egypt land,
Or other nations that us here confine,
Godfrey will beaten be with his own wand,
And feel he wants that valor great of thine,
Our camp may seem an arm without a hand,
Amid our troops unless thy eagle shine:"
With that came Guelpho and those words approved,
And prayed him go, if him he feared or loved.

LI

Their speeches soften much the warrior's heart,
And make his wilful thoughts at last relent,
So that he yields, and saith he will depart,
And leave the Christian camp incontinent.
His friends, whose love did never shrink or start,
Preferred their aid, what way soe'er he went:
He thanked them all, but left them all, besides
Two bold and trusty squires, and so he rides.

LII

He rides, revolving in his noble spright
Such haughty thoughts as fill the glorious mind;
On hard adventures was his whole delight,
And now to wondrous acts his will inclined;
Alone against the Pagans would he fight,
And kill their kings from Egypt unto Inde,
From Cynthia's hills and Nilus' unknown spring
He would fetch praise and glorious conquest bring.

LIII

But Guelpho, when the prince his leave had take
And now had spurred his courser on his way,
No longer tarriance with the rest would make,
But tastes to find Godfredo, if he may:
Who seeing him approaching, forthwith spake,
"Guelpho," quoth he, "for thee I only stay,
For thee I sent my heralds all about,
In every tent to seek and find thee out."

LIV

This said, he softly drew the knight aside
Where none might hear, and then bespake him thus:
"How chanceth it thy nephew's rage and pride,
Makes him so far forget himself and us?
Hardly could I believe what is betide,
A murder done for cause so frivolous,
How I have loved him, thou and all can tell;
But Godfrey loved him but whilst he did well.

LV

"I must provide that every one have right,
That all be heard, each cause be well discussed,
As far from partial love as free from spite,
I hear complaints, yet naught but proves I trust:
Now if Rinaldo weigh our rule too light,
And have the sacred lore of war so brust,
Take you the charge that he before us come
To clear himself and hear our upright dome.

LVI

"But let him come withouten bond or chain,
For still my thoughts to do him grace are framed;
But if our power he haply shall disdain,
As well I know his courage yet untamed,
To bring him by persuasion take some pain:

117

Else, if I prove severe, both you be blamed,
That forced my gentle nature gainst my thought
To rigor, lest our laws return to naught."

LVII

Lord Guelpho answered thus: "What heart can bear
Such slanders false, devised by hate and spite?
Or with stayed patience, reproaches hear,
And not revenge by battle or by fight?
The Norway Prince hath bought his folly dear,
But who with words could stay the angry knight?
A fool is he that comes to preach or prate
When men with swords their right and wrong debate.

LVIII

"And where you wish he should himself submit
To hear the censure of your upright laws;
Alas, that cannot be, for he is flit
Out if this camp, withouten stay or pause,
There take my gage, behold I offer it
To him that first accused him in this cause,
Or any else that dare, and will maintain
That for his pride the prince was justly slain.

LIX

"I say with reason Lord Gernando's pride
He hath abated, if he have offended
Gainst your commands, who are his lord and guide,
Oh pardon him, that fault shall be amended."
"If he be gone," quoth Godfrey, "let him ride
And brawl elsewhere, here let all strife be ended:
And you, Lord Guelpho, for your nephew's sake,
Breed us no new, nor quarrels old awake."

LX

This while, the fair and false Armida strived

To get her promised aid in sure possession,
The day to end, with endless plaint she derived;
Wit, beauty, craft for her made intercession:
But when the earth was once of light deprived,
And western seas felt Titan's hot impression,
'Twixt two old knights, and matrons twain she went,
Where pitched was her fair and curious tent.

LXI
But this false queen of craft and sly invention, —
Whose looks, love's arrows were; whose eyes his quivers;
Whose beauty matchless, free from reprehension,
A wonder left by Heaven to after–livers, —
Among the Christian lord had bred contention
Who first should quench his flames in Cupid's rivers,
While all her weapons and her darts rehearsed,
Had not Godfredo's constant bosom pierced.

LXII
To change his modest thought the dame procureth,
And proffereth heaps of love's enticing treasure:
But as the falcon newly gorged endureth
Her keeper lure her oft, but comes at leisure;
So he, whom fulness of delight assureth
What long repentance comes of love's short pleasure,
Her crafts, her arts, herself and all despiseth,
So base affections fall, when virtue riseth.

LXIII
And not one foot his steadfast foot was moved
Out of that heavenly path, wherein he paced,
Yet thousand wiles and thousand ways she proved,
To have that castle fair of goodness raised:
She used those looks and smiles that most behoved
To melt the frost which his hard heart embraced,
And gainst his breast a thousand shot she ventured,

Yet was the fort so strong it was not entered.

LXIV

The dame who thought that one blink of her eye
Could make the chastest heart feel love's sweet pain,
Oh, how her pride abated was hereby!
When all her sleights were void, her crafts were vain,
Some other where she would her forces try,
Where at more ease she might more vantage gain,
As tired soldiers whom some fort keeps out,
Thence raise their siege, and spoil the towns about.

LXV

But yet all ways the wily witch could find
Could not Tancredi's heart to loveward move,
His sails were filled with another wind,
He list no blast of new affection prove;
For, as one poison doth exclude by kind
Another's force, so love excludeth love:
These two alone nor more nor less the dame
Could win, the rest all burnt in her sweet flame.

LXVI

The princess, though her purpose would not frame,
As late she hoped, and as still she would,
Yet, for the lords and knights of greatest name
Became her prey, as erst you heard it told,
She thought, ere truth–revealing time or frame
Bewrayed her act, to lead them to some hold,
Where chains and band she meant to make them prove,
Composed by Vulcan not by gentle love.

LXVII

The time prefixed at length was come and past,
Which Godfrey had set down to lend her aid,
When at his feet herself to earth she cast,

"The hour is come, my Lord," she humbly said,
"And if the tyrant haply hear at last,
His banished niece hath your assistance prayed,
He will in arms to save his kingdom rise,
So shall we harder make this enterprise.

LXVIII
"Before report can bring the tyrant news,
Or his espials certify their king,
Oh let thy goodness these few champions choose,
That to her kingdom should thy handmaid bring;
Who, except Heaven to aid the right refuse,
Recover shall her crown, from whence shall spring
Thy profit; for betide thee peace or war,
Thine all her cities, all her subjects are."

LXIX
The captain sage the damsel fair assured,
His word was passed and should not be recanted,
And she with sweet and humble grace endured
To let him point those ten, which late he granted:
But to be one, each one fought and procured,
No suit, no entreaty, intercession wanted;
There envy each at others' love exceeded,
And all importunate made, more than needed.

LXX
She that well saw the secret of their hearts,
And knew how best to warm them in their blood,
Against them threw the cursed poisoned darts
Of jealousy, and grief at others' good,
For love she wist was weak without those arts,
And slow; for jealousy is Cupid's food;
For the swift steed runs not so fast alone,
As when some strain, some strive him to outgone.

Jerusalem Delivered

LXXI

Her words in such alluring sort she framed,
Her looks enticing, and her wooing smiles,
That every one his fellows' favors blamed,
That of their mistress he received erewhiles:
This foolish crew of lovers unashamed,
Mad with the poison of her secret wiles,
Ran forward still, in this disordered sort,
Nor could Godfredo's bridle rein them short.

LXXII

He that would satisfy each good desire,
Withouten partial love, of every knight,
Although he swelled with shame, with grief and ire
To see these fellows and these fashions light;
Yet since by no advice they would retire,
Another way he sought to set them right:
"Write all your names," quoth he, "and see whom chance
Of lot, to this exploit will first advance."

LXXIII

Their names were writ, and in an helmet shaken,
While each did fortune's grace and aid implore;
At last they drew them, and the foremost taken
The Earl of Pembroke was, Artemidore,
Doubtless the county thought his bread well baken;
Next Gerrard followed, then with tresses hoar
Old Wenceslaus, that felt Cupid's rage
Now in his doating and his dying age.

LXXIV

Oh how contentment in their foreheads shined!
Their looks with joy; thoughts swelled with secret pleasure,
These three it seemed good success designed
To make the lords of love and beauty's treasure:
Their doubtful fellows at their hap repined,

Jerusalem Delivered

And with small patience wait Fortune's leisure,
Upon his lips that read the scrolls attending,
As if their lives were on his words depending.

LXXV

Guasco the fourth, Ridolpho him succeeds,
Then Ulderick whom love list so advance,
Lord William of Ronciglion next he reads,
Then Eberard, and Henry born in France,
Rambaldo last, whom wicked lust so leads
That he forsook his Saviour with mischance;
This wretch the tenth was who was thus deluded,
The rest to their huge grief were all excluded.

LXXVI

O'ercome with envy, wrath and jealousy,
The rest blind Fortune curse, and all her laws,
And mad with love, yet out on love they cry,
That in his kingdom let her judge their cause:
And for man's mind is such, that oft we try
Things most forbidden, without stay or pause,
In spite of fortune purposed many a knight
To follow fair Armida when 'twas night.

LXXVII

To follow her, by night or else by day,
And in her quarrel venture life and limb.
With sighs and tears she gan them softly pray
To keep that promise, when the skies were dim,
To this and that knight did she plain and say,
What grief she felt to part withouten him:
Meanwhile the ten had donned their armor best,
And taken leave of Godfrey and the rest.

LXXVIII

The duke advised them every one apart,

How light, how trustless was the Pagan's faith,
And told what policy, what wit, what art,
Avoids deceit, which heedless men betray'th;
His speeches pierce their ear, but not their heart,
Love calls it folly, whatso wisdom saith:
Thus warned he leaves them to their wanton guide,
Who parts that night; such haste had she to ride.

LXXIX

The conqueress departs, and with her led
These prisoners, whom love would captive keep,
The hearts of those she left behind her bled,
With point of sorrow's arrow pierced deep.
But when the night her drowsy mantle spread,
And filled the earth with silence, shade and sleep,
In secret sort then each forsook his tent,
And as blind Cupid led them blind they went.

LXXX

Eustatio first, who scantly could forbear,
Till friendly night might hide his haste and shame,
He rode in post, and let his breast him bear
As his blind fancy would his journey frame,
All night he wandered and he wist not where;
But with the morning he espied the dame,
That with her guard up from a village rode
Where she and they that night had made abode.

LXXXI

Thither he galloped fast, and drawing near
Rambaldo knew the knight, and loudly cried,
"Whence comes young Eustace, and what seeks he here?"
"I come," quoth he, "to serve the Queen Armide,
If she accept me, would we all were there
Where my good–will and faith might best be tried."
"Who," quoth the other, "choseth thee to prove

This high exploit of hers?" He answered, "Love."

LXXXII
"Love hath Eustatio chosen, Fortune thee,
In thy conceit which is the best election?"
"Nay, then, these shifts are vain," replied he,
"These titles false serve thee for no protection,
Thou canst not here for this admitted be
Our fellow–servant, in this sweet subjection."
"And who," quoth Eustace, angry, "dares deny
My fellowship?" Rambaldo answered, "I."

LXXXIII
And with that word his cutting sword he drew,
That glittered bright, and sparkled flaming fire;
Upon his foe the other champion flew,
With equal courage, and with equal ire.
The gentle princess, who the danger knew,
Between them stepped, and prayed them both retire.
"Rambald," quoth she, "why should you grudge or plain,
If I a champion, you an helper gain?

LXXXIV
"If me you love, why wish you me deprived
In so great need of such a puissant knight?
But welcome Eustace, in good time arrived,
Defender of my state, my life, my right.
I wish my hapless self no longer lived,
When I esteem such good assistance light."
Thus talked they on, and travelled on their way
Their fellowship increasing every day.

LXXXV
From every side they come, yet wist there none
Of others coming or of others' mind,
She welcomes all, and telleth every one,

What joy her thoughts in his arrival find.
But when Duke Godfrey wist his knights were gone,
Within his breast his wiser soul divined
Some hard mishap upon his friends should light,
For which he sighed all day, and wept all night.

LXXXVI
A messenger, while thus he mused, drew near,
All soiled with dust and sweat, quite out of breath,
It seemed the man did heavy tidings bear,
Upon his looks sate news of loss and death:
"My lord," quoth he, "so many ships appear
At sea, that Neptune bears the load uneath,
From Egypt come they all, this lets thee weet
William Lord Admiral of the Genoa fleet,

LXXXVII
"Besides a convoy coming from the shore
With victual for this noble camp of thine
Surprised was, and lost is all that store,
Mules, horses, camels laden, corn and wine;
Thy servants fought till they could fight no more,
For all were slain or captives made in fine:
The Arabian outlaws them assailed by night,
When least they feared, and least they looked for fight.

LXXXVIII
"Their frantic boldness doth presume so far,
That many Christians have they falsely slain,
And like a raging flood they spared are,
And overflow each country, field and plain;
Send therefore some strong troops of men of war,
To force them hence, and drive them home again,
And keep the ways between these tents of thine
And those broad seas, the seas of Palestine."

126

LXXXIX

From mouth to mouth the heavy rumor spread
Of these misfortunes, which dispersed wide
Among the soldiers, great amazement bred;
Famine they doubt, and new come foes beside:
The duke, that saw their wonted courage fled,
And in the place thereof weak fear espied,
With merry looks these cheerful words he spake,
To make them heart again and courage take.

XC

"You champions bold, with me that 'scaped have
So many dangers, and such hard assays,
Whom still your God did keep, defend and save
In all your battles, combats, fights and frays,
You that subdued the Turks and Persians brave,
That thirst and hunger held in scorn always,
And vanquished hills, and seas, with heat and cold,
Shall vain reports appal your courage bold?

XCI

"That Lord who helped you out at every need,
When aught befell this glorious camp amiss,
Shall fortune all your actions well to speed,
On whom his mercy large extended is;
Tofore his tomb, when conquering hands you spreed,
With what delight will you remember this?
Be strong therefore, and keep your valors high
To honor, conquest, fame and victory."

XCII

Their hopes half dead and courage well–nigh lost,
Revived with these brave speeches of their guide;
But in his breast a thousand cares he tost,
Although his sorrows he could wisely hide;
He studied how to feed that mighty host,

In so great scarceness, and what force provide
He should against the Egyptian warriors sly,
And how subdue those thieves of Araby.

SIXTH BOOK

THE ARGUMENT.
Argantes calls the Christians out to just:
Otho not chosen doth his strength assay,
But from his saddle tumbleth in the dust,
And captive to the town is sent away:
Tancred begins new fight, and when both trust
To win the praise and palm, night ends the fray:
Erminia hopes to cure her wounded knight,
And from the city armed rides by night.

I
But better hopes had them recomforted
That lay besieged in the sacred town;
With new supply late were they victualled,
When night obscured the earth with shadows brown;
Their armies and engines on the walls they spread,
Their slings to cast, and stones to tumble down;
And all that side which to the northward lies,
High rampiers and strong bulwarks fortifies.

II
Their wary king commands now here now there,
To build this tower, to make that bulwark strong,
Whether the sun, the moon, or stars appear,
To give them time to work, no time comes wrong:

Jerusalem Delivered

In every street new weapons forged were,
By cunning smiths, sweating with labor long;
While thus the careful prince provision made,
To him Argantes came, and boasting said:

III
"How long shall we, like prisoners in chains,
Captived lie inclosed within this wall?
I see your workmen taking endless pains
To make new weapons for no use at all;
Meanwhile these eastern thieves destroy the plains,
Your towns are burnt, your forts and castles fall,
Yet none of us dares at these gates out–peep,
Or sound one trumpet shrill to break their sleep.

IV
"Their time in feasting and good cheer they spend,
Nor dare we once their banquets sweet molest,
The days and night likewise they bring to end,
In peace, assurance, quiet, ease and rest;
But we must yield whom hunger soon will shend,
And make for peace, to save our lives, request,
Else, if th' Egyptian army stay too long,
Like cowards die within this fortress strong.
V
"Yet never shall my courage great consent
So vile a death should end my noble days,
Nor on mine arms within these walls ypent
To–morrow's sun shall spread his timely rays:
Let sacred Heavens dispose as they are bent
Of this frail like, yet not withouten praise
Of valor, prowess, might, Argantes shall
Inglorious die, or unrevenged fall.

VI
"But if the roots of wonted chivalry

Be not quite dead your princely breast within,
Devise not how with frame and praise to die,
But how to live, to conquer and to win;
Let us together at these gates outfly,
And skirmish bold and bloody fight begin;
For when last need to desperation driveth,
Who dareth most he wisest counsel giveth.

VII
"But if in field your wisdom dare not venture
To hazard all your troops to doubtful fight,
Then bind yourself to Godfrey by indenture,
To end your quarrels by one single knight:
And for the Christian this accord shall enter
With better will, say such you know your right
That he the weapons, place and time shall choose,
And let him for his best, that vantage use.

VIII
"For though your foe had hands, like Hector strong,
With heart unfeared, and courage stern and stout,
Yet no misfortune can your justice wrong,
And what that wanteth, shall this arm help out,
In spite of fate shall this right hand ere long,
Return victorious: if hereof you doubt,
Take it for pledge, wherein if trust you have,
It shall yourself defend and kingdom save."

IX
"Bold youth," the tyrant thus began to speak,
"Although I withered seem with age and years,
Yet are not these old arms so faint and weak,
Nor this hoar head so full of doubts and fears
But whenas death this vital thread shall break,
He shall my courage hear, my death who hears:
And Aladine that lived a king and knight,

130

To his fair morn will have an evening bright.

X

"But that which yet I would have further blazed,
To thee in secret shall be told and spoken,
Great Soliman of Nice, so far ypraised,
To be revenged for his sceptre broken,
The men of arms of Araby hath raised,
From Inde to Africk, and, when we give token,
Attends the favor of the friendly night
To victual us, and with our foes to fight.

XI

"Now though Godfredo hold by warlike feat
Some castles poor and forts in vile oppression,
Care not for that; for still our princely seat,
This stately town, we keep in our possession,
But thou appease and calm that courage great,
Which in thy bosom make so hot impression;
And stay fit time, which will betide are long,
To increase thy glory, and revenge our wrong."

XII

The Saracen at this was inly spited,
Who Soliman's great worth had long envied,
To hear him praised thus he naught delighted,
Nor that the king upon his aid relied:
"Within your power, sir king," he says, "united
Are peace and war, nor shall that be denied;
But for the Turk and his Arabian band,
He lost his own, shall he defend your land?

XIII

"Perchance he comes some heavenly messenger,
Sent down to set the Pagan people free,
Then let Argantes for himself take care,

This sword, I trust, shall well safe–conduct me:
But while you rest and all your forces spare,
That I go forth to war at least agree;
Though not your champion, yet a private knight,
I will some Christian prove in single fight."

XIV

The king replied, "Though thy force and might
Should be reserved to better time and use;
Yet that thou challenge some renowned knight,
Among the Christians bold I not refuse."
The warrior breathing out desire of fight,
An herald called, and said, "Go tell those news
To Godfrey's self, and to the western lords,
And in their hearings boldly say these words:

XV

"Say that a knight, who holds in great disdain
To be thus closed up in secret new,
Will with his sword in open field maintain,
If any dare deny his words for true,
That no devotion, as they falsely feign,
Hath moved the French these countries to subdue;
But vile ambition, and pride's hateful vice,
Desire of rule, and spoil, and covetice.

XVI

"And that to fight I am not only prest
With one or two that dare defend the cause,
But come the fourth or fifth, come all the rest,
Come all that will, and all that weapon draws,
Let him that yields obey the victor's hest,
As wills the lore of mighty Mars his laws:"
This was the challenge that fierce Pagan sent,
The herald donned his coat–of–arms, and went.

XVII

And when the man before the presence came
Of princely Godfrey, and his captains bold:
"My Lord," quoth he, "may I withouten blame
Before your Grace, my message brave unfold?"
"Thou mayest," he answered, "we approve the same;
Withouten fear, be thine ambassage told."
"Then," quoth the herald, "shall your highness see,
If this ambassage sharp or pleasing be."

XVIII

The challenge gan he then at large expose,
With mighty threats, high terms and glorious words;
On every side an angry murmur rose,
To wrath so moved were the knights and lords.
Then Godfrey spake, and said, "The man hath chose
An hard exploit, but when he feels our swords,
I trust we shall so far entreat the knight,
As to excuse the fourth or fifth of fight.

XIX

"But let him come and prove, the field I grant,
Nor wrong nor treason let him doubt or fear,
Some here shall pay him for his glorious vaunt,
Without or guile, or vantage, that I swear.
The herald turned when he had ended scant,
And hasted back the way he came whileare,
Nor stayed he aught, nor once forslowed his pace,
Till he bespake Argantes face to face.

XX

"Arm you, my lord," he said, "your bold defies
By your brave foes accepted boldly been,
This combat neither high nor low denies,
Ten thousand wish to meet you on the green;
A thousand frowned with angry flaming eyes,

133

And shaked for rage their swords and weapons keen;
The field is safely granted by their guide,"
This said, the champion for his armor cried.
XXI
While he was armed, his heart for ire nigh brake,
So yearned his courage hot his foes to find:
The King to fair Clorinda present spake;
"If he go forth, remain not you behind,
But of our soldiers best a thousand take,
To guard his person and your own assigned;
Yet let him meet alone the Christian knight,
And stand yourself aloof, while they two fight."

XXII
Thus spake the King, and soon without abode
The troop went forth in shining armor clad,
Before the rest the Pagan champion rode,
His wonted arms and ensigns all he had:
A goodly plan displayed wide and broad,
Between the city and the camp was spread,
A place like that wherein proud Rome beheld
The forward young men manage spear and shield.

XXIII
There all alone Argantes took his stand,
Defying Christ and all his servants true,
In stature, stomach, and in strength of hand,
In pride, presumption, and in dreadful show,
Encelade like, on the Phlegrean strand,
Of that huge giant Jesse's infant slew;
But his fierce semblant they esteemed light,
For most not knew, or else not feared his might.

XXIV
As yet not one had Godfrey singled out
To undertake this hardy enterprise,

Jerusalem Delivered

But on Prince Tancred saw he all the rout
Had fixed their wishes, and had cast their eyes,
On him he spied them gazing round about,
As though their honor on his prowess lies,
And now they whispered louder what they meant,
Which Godfrey heard and saw, and was content.

XXV

The rest gave place; for every one descried
To whom their chieftain's will did most incline,
"Tancred," quoth he, "I pray thee calm the pride,
Abate the rage of yonder Saracine:"
No longer would the chosen champion bide,
His face with joy, his eyes with gladness shine,
His helm he took, and ready steed bestrode,
And guarded with his trusty friends forth rode.

XXVI

But scantly had he spurred his courser swift
Near to the plain, where proud Argantes stayed,
When unawares his eyes he chanced to lift,
And on the hill beheld the warlike maid,
As white as snow upon the Alpine clift
The virgin shone in silver arms arrayed,
Her vental up so high, that he descried
Her goodly visage, and her beauty's pride.

XXVII

He saw not where the Pagan stood, and stared,
As if with looks he would his foeman kill,
But full of other thoughts he forward fared,
And sent his looks before him up the hill,
His gesture such his troubled soul declared,
At last as marble rock he standeth still,
Stone cold without; within, burnt with love's flame,
And quite forgot himself, and why he came.

XXVIII

The challenger, that yet saw none appear
That made or sign or show came to just,
"How long," cried he, "shall I attend you here?
Dares none come forth? dares none his fortune trust?"
The other stood amazed, love stopped his ear,
He thinks on Cupid, think of Mars who lust;
But forth stert Otho bold, and took the field,
A gentle knight whom God from danger shield.

XXIX

This youth was one of those, who late desired
With that vain–glorious boaster to have fought,
But Tancred chosen, he and all retired;
Now when his slackness he awhile admired,
And saw elsewhere employed was his thought,
Nor that to just, though chosen, once he proffered,
He boldly took that fit occasion offered.

XXX

No tiger, panther, spotted leopard,
Runs half so swift, the forests wild among,
As this young champion hasted thitherward,
Where he attending saw the Pagan strong:
Tancredi started with the noise he heard,
As waked from sleep, where he had dreamed long,
"Oh stay," he cried, "to me belongs this war!"
But cried too late, Otho was gone too far.

XXXI

Then full of fury, anger and despite,
He stayed his horse, and waxed red for shame,
The fight was his, but now disgraced quite
Himself he thought, another played his game;
Meanwhile the Saracen did hugely smite
On Otho's helm, who to requite the same,

His foe quite through his sevenfold targe did bear,
And in his breastplate stuck and broke his spear.

XXXII
The encounter such, upon the tender grass,
Down from his steed the Christian backward fell;
Yet his proud foe so strong and sturdy was,
That he nor shook, nor staggered in his sell,
But to the knight that lay full low, alas,
In high disdain his will thus gan he tell,
"Yield thee my slave, and this thine honor be,
Thou may'st report thou hast encountered me."

XXXIII
"Not so," quoth he, "pardy it's not the guise
Of Christian knights, though fall'n, so soon to yield;
I can my fall excuse in better wise,
And will revenge this shame, or die in field."
The great Circassian bent his frowning eyes,
Like that grim visage in Minerva's shield,
"Then learn," quoth he, "what force Argantes useth
Against that fool that proffered grace refuseth."

XXXIV
With that he spurred his horse with speed and haste,
Forgetting what good knights to virtue owe,
Otho his fury shunned, and, as he passed,
At his right side he reached a noble blow,
Wide was the wound, the blood outstreamed fast,
And from his side fell to his stirrup low:
But what avails to hurt, if wounds augment
Our foe's fierce courage, strength and hardiment?

XXXV
Argantes nimbly turned his ready steed,
And ere his foe was wist or well aware,

Against his side he drove his courser's head,
What force could he gainst so great might prepare?
Weak were his feeble joints, his courage dead,
His heart amazed, his paleness showed his care,
His tender side gainst the hard earth he cast,
Shamed, with the first fall; bruised, with the last.

XXXVI

The victor spurred again his light–foot steed,
And made his passage over Otho's heart,
And cried, "These fools thus under foot I tread,
This dare contend with me in equal mart."
Tancred for anger shook his noble head,
So was he grieved with that unknightly part;
The fault was his, he was so slow before,
With double valor would he salve that sore.

XXXVII

Forward he galloped fast, and loudly cried:
"Villain," quoth he, "thy conquest is thy shame,
What praise? what honor shall this fact betide?
What gain? what guerdon shall befall the same?
Among the Arabian thieves thy face go hide,
Far from resort of men of worth and fame,
Or else in woods and mountains wild, by night,
On savage beasts employ thy savage might."

XXXVIII

The Pagan patience never knew, nor used,
Trembling for ire, his sandy locks he tore,
Our from his lips flew such a sound confused,
As lions make in deserts thick, which roar;
Or as when clouds together crushed and bruised,
Pour down a tempest by the Caspian shore;
So was his speech imperfect, stopped, and broken,
He roared and thundered when he should have spoken.

Jerusalem Delivered

XXXIX

But when with threats they both had whetted keen
Their eager rage, their fury, spite and ire,
They turned their steeds and left large space between
To make their forces greater, 'proaching nigher,
With terms that warlike and that worthy been:
O sacred Muse, my haughty thoughts inspire,
And make a trumpet of my slender quill
To thunder out this furious combat shrill.

XL

These sons of Mayors bore, instead of spears,
Two knotty masts, which none but they could lift,
Each foaming steed so fast his master bears,
That never beast, bird, shaft flew half so swift;
Such was their fury, as when Boreas tears
The shattered crags from Taurus' northern clift,
Upon their helms their lances long they broke,
And up to heaven flew splinters, spark and smoke.

XLI

The shock made all the towers and turrets quake,
And woods and mountains all nigh hand resound;
Yet could not all that force and fury shake
The valiant champions, nor their persons wound;
Together hurtled both their steeds, and brake
Each other's neck, the riders lay on ground:
But they, great masters of war's dreadful art,
Plucked forth their swords and soon from earth up start.

XLII

Close at his surest ward each warrior lieth,
He wisely guides his hand, his foot, his eye,
This blow he proveth, that defence he trieth,
He traverseth, retireth, presseth nigh,

Now strikes he out, and now he falsifieth,
This blow he wardeth, that he lets slip by,
And for advantage oft he lets some part
Discovered seem; thus art deludeth art.

XLIII
The Pagan ill defenced with sword or targe,
Tancredi's thigh, as he supposed, espied
And reaching forth gainst it his weapon large,
Quite naked to his foe leaves his left–side;
Tancred avoideth quick his furious charge,
And gave him eke a wound deep, sore and wide;
That done, himself safe to his ward retired,
His courage praised by all, his skill admired.

XLIV
The proud Circassian saw his streaming blood,
Down from his wound, as from a fountain, running,
He sighed for rage, and trembled as he stood,
He blamed his fortune, folly, want of cunning;
He lift his sword aloft, for ire nigh wood,
And forward rushed: Tancred his fury shunning,
With a sharp thrust once more the Pagan hit,
To his broad shoulder where his arm is knit.

XLV
Like as a bear through pierced with a dart
Within the secret woods, no further flieth,
But bites the senseless weapon mad with smart,
Seeking revenge till unrevenged she dieth;
So mad Argantes fared, when his proud heart
Wound upon wound, and shame on shame espieth,
Desire of vengeance so o'ercame his senses,
That he forgot all dangers, all defences.

XLVI

Uniting force extreme, with endless wrath,
Supporting both with youth and strength untired,
His thundering blows so fast about he layeth,
That skies and earth the flying sparkles fired;
His foe to strike one blow no leisure hath,
Scantly he breathed, though he oft desired,
His warlike skill and cunning all was waste,
Such was Argantes' force, and such his haste.

XLVII
Long time Tancredi had in vain attended
When this huge storm should overblow and pass,
Some blows his mighty target well defended,
Some fell beside, and wounded deep the grass;
But when he saw the tempest never ended,
Nor that the Paynim's force aught weaker was,
He high advanced his cutting sword at length,
And rage to rage opposed, and strength to strength.

XLVIII
Wrath bore the sway, both art and reason fail,
Fury new force, and courage new supplies,
Their armors forged were of metal frail,
On every side thereof, huge cantels flies,
The land was strewed all with plate and mail.
That, on the earth; on that, their warm blood lies.
And at each rush and every blow they smote
Thunder the noise, the sparks, seemed lightning hot.

XLIX
The Christian people and the Pagans gazed,
On this fierce combat wishing oft the end,
Twixt hope and fear they stood long time amazed,
To see the knights assail, and eke defend,
Yet neither sign they made, nor noise they raised,
But for the issue of the fight attend,

And stood as still, as life and sense they wanted,
Save that their hearts within their bosoms panted.
L
Now were they tired both, and well—nigh spent,
Their blows show greater will than power to wound;
But Night her gentle daughter Darkness, sent,
With friendly shade to overspread the ground,
Two heralds to the fighting champions went,
To part the fray, as laws of arms them bound
Aridens born in France, and wise Pindore,
The man that brought the challenge proud before.
LI
These men their sceptres interpose, between
The doubtful hazards of uncertain fight;
For such their privilege hath ever been,
The law of nations doth defend their right;
Pindore began, "Stay, stay, you warriors keen,
Equal your honor, equal is your might;
Forbear this combat, so we deem it best,
Give night her due, and grant your persons rest.

LII
"Man goeth forth to labor with the sun,
But with the night, all creatures draw to sleep,
Nor yet of hidden praise in darkness won
The valiant heart of noble knight takes keep:"
Argantes answered him, "The fight begun
Now to forbear, doth wound my heart right deep:
Yet will I stay, so that this Christian swear,
Before you both, again to meet me here."

LIII
"I swear," quoth Tancred, "but swear thou likewise
To make return thy prisoner eke with thee;
Else for achievement of this enterprise,
None other time but this expect of me;"

142

Thus swore they both; the heralds both devise,
What time for this exploit should fittest be:
And for their wounds of rest and cure had need,
To meet again the sixth day was decreed.

LIV
This fight was deep imprinted in their hearts
That saw this bloody fray to ending brought,
An horror great possessed their weaker parts,
Which made them shrink who on their combat thought:
Much speech was of the praise and high desarts
Of these brave champions that so nobly fought;
But which for knightly worth was most ypraised,
Of that was doubt and disputation raised.

LV
All long to see them end this doubtful fray,
And as they favor, so they wish success,
These hope true virtue shall obtain the day,
Those trust on fury, strength and hardiness;
But on Erminia most this burden lay,
Whose looks her trouble and her fear express;
For on this dangerous combat's doubtful end
Her joy, her comfort, hope and life depend.

LVI
Her the sole daughter of that hapless king,
That of proud Antioch late wore the crown,
The Christian soldiers to Tancredi bring,
When they had sacked and spoiled that glorious town;
But he, in whom all good and virtue spring,
The virgin's honor saved, and her renown;
And when her city and her state was lost,
Then was her person loved and honored most.

LVII

He honored her, served her, and leave her gave,
And willed her go whither and when she list,
Her gold and jewels had he care to save,
And them restored all, she nothing missed,
She, that beheld this youth and person brave,
When, by this deed, his noble mind she wist,
Laid ope her heart for Cupid's shaft to hit,
Who never knots of love more surer knit.

LVIII
Her body free, captivated was her heart,
And love the keys did of that prison bear,
Prepared to go, it was a death to part
From that kind Lord, and from that prison dear,
But thou, O honor, which esteemed art
The chiefest virtue noble ladies wear,
Enforcest her against her will, to wend
To Aladine, her mother's dearest friend.

LIX
At Sion was this princess entertained,
By that old tyrant and her mother dear,
Whose loss too soon the woful damsel plained,
Her grief was such, she lived not half the year,
Yet banishment, nor loss of friends constrained
The hapless maid her passions to forbear,
For though exceeding were her woe and grief,
Of all her sorrows yet her love was chief.

LX
The silly maid in secret longing pined,
Her hope a mote drawn up by Phoebus' rays,
Her love a mountain seemed, whereon bright shined
Fresh memory of Tancred's worth and praise,
Within her closet if her self she shrined,
A hotter fire her tender heart assays:

Tancred at last, to raise her hope nigh dead,
Before those walls did his broad ensign spread.

LXI

The rest to view the Christian army feared,
Such seemed their number, such their power and might,
But she alone her troubled forehead cleared,
And on them spread her beauty shining bright;
In every squadron when it first appeared,
Her curious eye sought out her chosen knight;
And every gallant that the rest excels,
The same seems him, so love and fancy tells.

LXII

Within the kingly palace builded high,
A turret standeth near the city's wall,
From which Erminia might at ease descry
The western host, the plains and mountains all,
And there she stood all the long day to spy,
From Phoebus' rising to his evening fall,
And with her thoughts disputed of his praise,
And every thought a scalding sigh did raise.

LXIII

From hence the furious combat she surveyed,
And felt her heart tremble with fear and pain,
Her secret thoughts thus to her fancy said,
Behold thy dear in danger to be slain;
So with suspect, with fear and grief dismayed,
Attended she her darling's loss or gain,
And ever when the Pagan lift his blade,
The stroke a wound in her weak bosom made.

LXIV

But when she saw the end, and wist withal
Their strong contention should eftsoons begin,

Amazement strange her courage did appal,
Her vital blood was icy cold within;
Sometimes she sighed, sometimes tears let fall,
To witness what distress her heart was in;
Hopeless, dismayed, pale, sad, astonished,
Her love, her fear; her fear, her torment bred.

LXV

Her idle brain unto her soul presented
Death in an hundred ugly fashions painted,
And if she slept, then was her grief augmented,
With such sad visions were her thoughts acquainted;
She saw her lord with wounds and hurts tormented,
How he complained, called for her help, and fainted,
And found, awaked from that unquiet sleeping,
Her heart with panting sore; eyes, red with weeping.

LXVI

Yet these presages of his coming ill,
Not greatest cause of her discomfort were,
She saw his blood from his deep wounds distil,
Nor what he suffered could she bide or bear:
Besides, report her longing ear did fill,
Doubling his danger, doubling so her fear,
That she concludes, so was her courage lost,
Her wounded lord was weak, faint, dead almost.

LXVII

And for her mother had her taught before
The secret virtue of each herb that springs,
Besides fit charms for every wound or sore
Corruption breedeth or misfortune brings, —
An art esteemed in those times of yore,
Beseeming daughters of great lords and kings —
She would herself be surgeon to her knight,
And heal him with her skill, or with her sight.

LXVIII

Thus would she cure her love, and cure her foe
She must, that had her friends and kinsfolk slain:
Some cursed weeds her cunning hand did know,
That could augment his harm, increase his pain;
But she abhorred to be revenged so,
No treason should her spotless person stain,
And virtueless she wished all herbs and charms
Wherewith false men increase their patients' harms.

LXIX

Nor feared she among the bands to stray
Of armed men, for often had she seen
The tragic end of many a bloody fray;
Her life had full of haps and hazards been,
This made her bold in every hard assay,
More than her feeble sex became, I ween;
She feared not the shake of every reed,
So cowards are courageous made through need.

LXX

Love, fearless, hardy, and audacious love,
Emboldened had this tender damsel so,
That where wild beasts and serpents glide and move
Through Afric's deserts durst she ride or go,
Save that her honor, she esteemed above
Her life and body's safety, told her no;
For in the secret of her troubled thought,
A doubtful combat, love and honor fought.

LXXI

"O spotless virgin," Honor thus began,
"That my true lore observed firmly hast,
When with thy foes thou didst in bondage won,
Remember then I kept thee pure and chaste,

147

At liberty now, where wouldest thou run,
To lay that field of princely virtue waste,
Or lost that jewel ladies hold so dear?
Is maidenhood so great a load to bear?

LXXII

"Or deem'st thou it a praise of little prize,
The glorious title of a virgin's name?
That thou will gad by night in giglot wise,
Amid thine armed foes, to seek thy shame.
O fool, a woman conquers when she flies,
Refusal kindleth, proffers quench the flame.
Thy lord will judge thou sinnest beyond measure,
If vainly thus thou waste so rich a treasure."

LXXIII

The sly deceiver Cupid thus beguiled
The simple damsel, with his filed tongue:
"Thou wert not born," quoth he, "in desert wild
The cruel bears and savage beasts among,
That you shouldest scorn fair Citherea's child,
Or hate those pleasures that to youth belong,
Nor did the gods thy heart of iron frame;
To be in love is neither sin nor shame.

LXXIV

"Go then, go, whither sweet desire inviteth,
How can thy gentle knight so cruel be?
Love in his heart thy grief and sorrows writeth,
For thy laments how he complaineth, see.
Oh cruel woman, whom no care exciteth
To save his life, that saved and honored thee!
He languished, one foot thou wilt not move
To succor him, yet say'st thou art in love.

LXXV

"No, no, stay here Argantes' wounds to cure,
And make him strong to shed thy darling's blood,
Of such reward he may himself assure,
That doth a thankless woman so much good:
Ah, may it be thy patience can endure
To see the strength of this Circassian wood,
And not with horror and amazement shrink,
When on their future fight thou hap'st to think?

LXXVI
"Besides the thanks and praises for the deed,
Suppose what joy, what comfort shalt thou win,
When thy soft hand doth wholesome plaisters speed,
Upon the breaches in his ivory skin,
Thence to thy dearest lord may health succeed,
Strength to his limbs, blood to his cheeks so thin,
And his rare beauties, now half dead and more,
Thou may'st to him, him to thyself restore.

LXXVII
"So shall some part of his adventures bold
And valiant acts henceforth be held as thine;
His dear embracements shall thee straight enfold,
Together joined in marriage rites divine:
Lastly high place of honor shalt thou hold
Among the matrons sage and dames Latine,
In Italy, a land, as each one tells,
Where valor true, and true religion dwells."
LXXVIII
With such vain hopes the silly maid abused,
Promised herself mountains and hills of gold;
Yet were her thoughts with doubts and fears confused
How to escape unseen out of that hold,
Because the watchman every minute used
To guard the walls against the Christians bold,
And in such fury and such heat of war,

Jerusalem Delivered

The gates or seld or never opened are.

LXXIX
With strong Clorinda was Erminia sweet
In surest links of dearest friendship bound,
With her she used the rising sun to greet,
And her, when Phoebus glided under ground,
She made the lovely partner of her sheet;
In both their hearts one will, one thought was found;
Nor aught she hid from that virago bold,
Except her love, that tale to none she told.

LXXX
That kept she secret, if Clorinda heard
Her make complaints, or secretly lament,
To other cause her sorrow she referred:
Matter enough she had of discontent,
Like as the bird that having close imbarred
Her tender young ones in the springing bent,
To draw the searcher further from her nest,
Cries and complains most where she needeth least.

LXXXI
Alone, within her chamber's secret part,
Sitting one day upon her heavy thought,
Devising by what means, what sleight, what art,
Her close departure should be safest wrought,
Assembled in her unresolved heart
An hundred passions strove and ceaseless fought;
At last she saw high hanging on the wall
Clorinda's silver arms, and sighed withal:

LXXXII
And sighing, softly to herself she said,
"How blessed is this virgin in her might?
How I envy the glory of the maid,

150

Yet envy not her shape, or beauty's light;
Her steps are not with trailing garments stayed,
Nor chambers hide her valor shining bright;
But armed she rides, and breaketh sword and spear,
Nor is her strength restrained by shame or fear.

LXXXIII
"Alas, why did not Heaven these members frail
With lively force and vigor strengthen so
That I this silken gown and slender veil
Might for a breastplate and an helm forego?
Then should not heat, nor cold, nor rain, nor hail,
Nor storms that fall, nor blustering winds that blow
Withhold me, but I would both day and night,
In pitched field, or private combat fight.

LXXXIV
"Nor haddest thou, Argantes, first begun
With my dear lord that fierce and cruel fight,
But I to that encounter would have run,
And haply ta'en him captive by my might;
Yet should he find, our furious combat done,
His thraldom easy, and his bondage light;
For fetters, mine embracements should he prove;
For diet, kisses sweet; for keeper, love.

LXXXV
"Or else my tender bosom opened wide,
And heart though pierced with his cruel blade,
The bloody weapon in my wounded side
Might cure the wound which love before had made;
Then should my soul in rest and quiet slide
Down to the valleys of the Elysian shade,
And my mishap the knight perchance would move,
To shed some tears upon his murdered love.

Jerusalem Delivered

LXXXVI
"Alas! impossible are all these things,
Such wishes vain afflict my woful sprite,
Why yield I thus to plaints and sorrowings,
As if all hope and help were perished quite?
My heart dares much, it soars with Cupid's wings,
Why use I not for once these armors bright?
I may sustain awhile this shield aloft,
Though I be tender, feeble, weak and soft.

LXXXVII
"Love, strong, bold, mighty never–tired love,
Supplieth force to all his servants true;
The fearful stags he doth to battle move,
Till each his horns in others' blood imbrue;
Yet mean not I the haps of war to prove,
A stratagem I have devised new,
Clorinda–like in this fair harness dight,
I will escape out of the town this night.

LXXXVIII
"I know the men that have the gate to ward,
If she command are not her will deny,
In what sort else could I beguile the guard?
This way is only left, this will I try:
O gentle love, in this adventure hard
Thine handmaid guide, assist and fortify!
The time, the hour now fitteth best the thing,
While stout Clorinda talketh with the king."

LXXXIX
Resolved thus, without delay she went,
As her strong passion did her rashly guide,
And those bright arms, down from the rafter hent,
Within her closet did she closely hide;
That might she do unseen, for she had sent

The rest, on sleeveless errands from her side,
And night her stealths brought to their wished end,
Night, patroness of thieves, and lovers' friend.

XC

Some sparkling fires on heaven's bright visage shone;
His azure robe the orient blueness lost,
When she, whose wit and reason both were gone,
Called for a squire she loved and trusted most,
To whom and to a maid, a faithful one,
Part of her will she told, how that in post
She would depart from Juda's king, and feigned
That other cause her sudden flight constrained.

XCI

The trusty squire provided needments meet,
As for their journey fitting most should be;
Meanwhile her vesture, pendant to her feet,
Erminia doft, as erst determined she,
Stripped to her petticoat the virgin sweet
So slender was, that wonder was to see;
Her handmaid ready at her mistress' will,
To arm her helped, though simple were her skill.

XCII

The rugged steel oppressed and offended
Her dainty neck, and locks of shining gold;
Her tender arm so feeble was, it bended
When that huge target it presumed to hold,
The burnished steel bright rays far off extended,
She feigned courage, and appeared bold;
Fast by her side unseen smiled Venus' son,
As erst he laughed when Alcides spun.

XCIII

Oh, with what labor did her shoulders bear
That heavy burthen, and how slow she went!

Her maid, to see that all the coasts were clear,
Before her mistress, through the streets was sent;
Love gave her courage, love exiled fear,
Love to her tired limbs new vigor lent,
Till she approached where the squire abode,
There took they horse forthwith and forward rode.

XCIV
Disguised they went, and by unused ways,
And secret paths they strove unseen to gone,
Until the watch they meet, which sore affrays
Their soldiers new, when swords and weapons shone
Yet none to stop their journey once essays,
But place and passage yielded every one;
For that while armor, and that helmet bright,
Were known and feared, in the darkest night.

XCV
Erminia, though some deal she were dismayed,
Yet went she on, and goodly countenance bore,
She doubted lest her purpose were bewrayed,
Her too much boldness she repented sore;
But now the gate her fear and passage stayed,
The heedless porter she beguiled therefore,
"I am Clorinda, ope the gate," she cried,
"Where as the king commands, this late I ride."

XCVI
Her woman's voice and terms all framed been,
Most like the speeches of the princess stout,
Who would have thought on horseback to have seen
That feeble damsel armed round about?
The porter her obeyed, and she, between
Her trusty squire and maiden, sallied out,
And through the secret dales they silent pass,
Where danger least, least fear, least peril was.

XCVII
But when these fair adventurers entered were
Deep in a vale, Erminia stayed her haste,
To be recalled she had no cause to fear,
This foremost hazard had she trimly past;
But dangers new, tofore unseen, appear,
New perils she descried, new doubts she cast.
The way that her desire to quiet brought,
More difficult now seemed than erst she thought.

XCVIII
Armed to ride among her angry foes,
She now perceived it were great oversight,
Yet would she not, she thought, herself disclose,
Until she came before her chosen knight,
To him she purposed to present the rose
Pure, spotless, clean, untouched of mortal wight,
She stayed therefore, and in her thoughts more wise,
She called her squire, whom thus she gan advise.

XCIX
"Thou must," quoth she, "be mine ambassador,
Be wise, be careful, true, and diligent,
Go to the camp, present thyself before
The Prince Tancredi, wounded in his tent;
Tell him thy mistress comes to care his sore,
If he to grant her peace and rest consent
Gainst whom fierce love such cruel war hath raised,
So shall his wounds be cured, her torments eased.

C
"And say, in him such hope and trust she hath,
That in his powers she fears no shame nor scorn,
Tell him thus much, and whatso'er he saith,
Unfold no more, but make a quick return,

I, for this place is free from harm and scath,
Within this valley will meanwhile sojourn."
Thus spake the princess: and her servant true
To execute the charge imposed, flew;

CI

And was received, he so discreetly wrought,
First of the watch that guarded in their place,
Before the wounded prince then was he brought,
Who heard his message kind, with gentle grace,
Which told, he left him tossing in his thought
A thousand doubts, and turned his speedy pace
To bring his lady and his mistress word,
She might be welcome to that courteous lord.

CII

But she, impatient, to whose desire
Grievous and harmful seemed each little stay,
Recounts his steps, and thinks, now draws he nigher,
Now enters in, now speaks, now comes his way;
And that which grieved her most, the careful squire
Less speedy seemed than e'er before that day;
Lastly she forward rode with love to guide,
Until the Christian tents at hand she spied.

CIII

Invested in her starry veil, the night
In her kind arms embraced all this round,
The silver moon form sea uprising bright
Spread frosty pearl upon the candid ground:
And Cynthia–like for beauty's glorious light
The love–sick nymph threw glittering beams around,
And counsellors of her old love she made
Those valleys dumb, that silence, and that shade.

CIV

Beholding then the camp, quoth she, "O fair
And castle–like pavilions, richly wrought!
From you how sweet methinketh blows the air,
How comforts it my heart, my soul, my thought?
Through heaven's fair face from gulf of sad despair
My tossed bark to port well–nigh is brought:
In you I seek redress for all my harms,
Rest, midst your weapons; peace, amongst your arms.

CV
"Receive me, then, and let me mercy find,
As gentle love assureth me I shall,
Among you had I entertainment kind
When first I was the Prince Tancredi's thrall:
I covet not, led by ambition blind
You should me in my father's throne install,
Might I but serve in you my lord so dear,
That my content, my joy, my comfort were."

CVI
Thus parleyed she, poor soul, and never feared
The sudden blow of Fortune's cruel spite,
She stood where Phoebe's splendent beam appeared
Upon her silver armor double bright,
The place about her round she shining cleared
With that pure white wherein the nymph was dight:
The tigress great, that on her helmet laid,
Bore witness where she went, and where she stayed.

CVII
So as her fortune would, a Christian band
Their secret ambush there had closely framed,
Led by two brothers of Italia land,
Young Poliphern and Alicandro named,
These with their forces watched to withstand
Those that brought victuals to their foes untamed,
And kept that passage; them Erminia spied,

157

And fled as fast as her swift steed could ride.

CVIII
But Poliphern, before whose watery eyes,
His aged father strong Clorinda slew,
When that bright shield and silver helm he spies,
The championess he thought he saw and knew;
Upon his hidden mates for aid he cries
Gainst his supposed foe, and forth he flew,
As he was rash, and heedless in his wrath,
Bending his lance, "Thou art but dead," he saith.

CIX
As when a chased hind her course doth bend
To seek by soil to find some ease or goad;
Whether from craggy rock the spring descend,
Or softly glide within the shady wood;
If there the dogs she meet, where late she wend
To comfort her weak limbs in cooling flood,
Again she flies swift as she fled at first,
Forgetting weakness, weariness and thirst.

CX
So she, that thought to rest her weary sprite,
And quench the endless thirst of ardent love
With dear embracements of her lord and knight,
But such as marriage rites should first approve,
When she beheld her foe, with weapon bright
Threatening her death, his trusty courser move,
Her love, her lord, herself abandoned,
She spurred her speedy steed, and swift she fled.

CXI
Erminia fled, scantly the tender grass
Her Pegasus with his light footsteps bent,
Her maiden's beast for speed did likewise pass;

158

Yet divers ways, such was their fear, they went:
The squire who all too late returned, alas.
With tardy news from Prince Tancredi's tent,
Fled likewise, when he saw his mistress gone,
It booted not to sojourn there alone.

CXII
But Alicandro wiser than the rest,
Who this supposed Clorinda saw likewise,
To follow her yet was he nothing pressed,
But in his ambush still and close he lies,
A messenger to Godfrey he addressed,
That should him of this accident advise,
How that his brother chased with naked blade
Clorinda's self, or else Clorinda's shade.

CXIII
Yet that it was, or that it could be she,
He had small cause or reason to suppose,
Occasion great and weighty must it be
Should make her ride by night among her foes:
What Godfrey willed that observed he,
And with his soldiers lay in ambush close:
These news through all the Christian army went,
In every cabin talked, in every tent.

CXIV
Tancred, whose thoughts the squire had filled with doubt
By his sweet words, supposed now hearing this,
Alas! the virgin came to seek me out,
And for my sake her life in danger is;
Himself forthwith he singled from the rout,
And rode in haste, though half his arms he miss;
Among those sandy fields and valleys green,
To seek his love, he galloped fast unseen.

SEVENTH BOOK

THE ARGUMENT.
A shepherd fair Erminia entertains,
Whom whilst Tancredi seeks in vain to find,
He is entrapped in Armida's trains:
Raymond with strong Argantes is assigned
To fight, an angel to his aid he gains:
Satan that sees the Pagan's fury blind,
And hasty wrath turn to his loss and harm,
Doth raise new tempest, uproar and alarm.

I
Erminia's steed this while his mistress bore
Through forests thick among the shady treen,
Her feeble hand the bridle reins forlore,
Half in a swoon she was, for fear I ween;
But her fleet courser spared ne'er the more,
To bear her through the desert woods unseen
Of her strong foes, that chased her through the plain,
And still pursued, but still pursued in vain.

II
Like as the weary hounds at last retire,
Windless, displeased, from the fruitless chase,
When the sly beast tapished in bush and brier,
No art nor pains can rouse out of his place:
The Christian knights so full of shame and ire
Returned back, with faint and weary pace:
Yet still the fearful dame fled swift as wind,
Nor ever stayed, nor ever looked behind.

Jerusalem Delivered

III

Through thick and thin, all night, all day, she drived,
Withouten comfort, company, or guide,
Her plaints and tears with every thought revived,
She heard and saw her griefs, but naught beside:
But when the sun his burning chariot dived
In Thetis' wave, and weary team untied,
On Jordan's sandy banks her course she stayed
At last, there down she light, and down she laid.

IV

Her tears, her drink; her food, her sorrowings,
This was her diet that unhappy night:
But sleep, that sweet repose and quiet brings,
To ease the griefs of discontented wight,
Spread forth his tender, soft, and nimble wings,
In his dull arms folding the virgin bright;
And Love, his mother, and the Graces kept
Strong watch and ward, while this fair lady slept.

V

The birds awoke her with their morning song,
Their warbling music pierced her tender ear,
The murmuring brooks and whistling winds among
The rattling boughs and leaves, their parts did bear;
Her eyes unclosed beheld the groves along
Of swains and shepherd grooms that dwellings were;
And that sweet noise, birds, winds and waters sent,
Provoked again the virgin to lament.

VI

Her plaints were interrupted with a sound,
That seemed from thickest bushes to proceed,
Some jolly shepherd sung a lusty round,
And to his voice he tuned his oaten reed;

Thither she went, an old man there she found,
At whose right hand his little flock did feed,
Sat making baskets, his three sons among,
That learned their father's art, and learned his song.

VIII
"But, father, since this land, these towns and towers
Destroyed are with sword, with fire and spoil,
How many it be unhurt that you and yours
In safety thus apply your harmless toil?"
"My son," quoth he, "this poor estate of ours
Is ever safe from storm of warlike broil;
This wilderness doth us in safety keep,
No thundering drum, no trumpet breaks our sleep.

IX
"Haply just Heaven's defence and shield of right
Doth love the innocence of simple swains,
The thunderbolts on highest mountains light,
And seld or never strike the lower plains;
So kings have cause to fear Bellona's might,
Not they whose sweat and toil their dinner gains,
Nor ever greedy soldier was enticed
By poverty, neglected and despised.

X
"O poverty, chief of the heavenly brood,
Dearer to me than wealth or kingly crown:
No wish for honor, thirst of others' good,
Can move my heart, contented with mine own:
We quench our thirst with water of this flood,
Nor fear we poison should therein be thrown;
These little flocks of sheep and tender goats
Give milk for food, and wool to make us coats.

XI

"We little wish, we need but little wealth,
From cold and hunger us to clothe and feed;
These are my sons, their care preserves form stealth
Their father's flocks, nor servants more I need:
Amid these groves I walk oft for my health,
And to the fishes, birds, and beasts give heed,
How they are fed, in forest, spring and lake,
And their contentment for example take.

XII
"Time was, for each one hath his doating time,
These silver locks were golden tresses then,
That country life I hated as a crime,
And from the forest's sweet contentment ran,
To Memphis's stately palace would I climb,
And there I but a simple gardener were,
Yet could I mark abuses, see and hear.

XIII
"Enticed on with hope of future gain,
I suffered long what did my soul displease;
But when my youth was spent, my hope was vain.
I felt my native strength at last decrease;
I gan my loss of lusty years complain,
And wished I had enjoyed the country's peace;
I bade the court farewell, and with content
My latter age here have I quiet spent."
XIV
While thus he spake, Erminia hushed and still
His wise discourses heard, with great attention,
His speeches grave those idle fancies kill
Which in her troubled soul bred such dissension;
After much thought reformed was her will,
Within those woods to dwell was her intention,
Till Fortune should occasion new afford,
To turn her home to her desired lord.

Jerusalem Delivered

XV
She said therefore, "O shepherd fortunate!
That troubles some didst whilom feel and prove,
Yet livest now in this contented state,
Let my mishap thy thoughts to pity move,
To entertain me as a willing mate
In shepherd's life which I admire and love;
Within these pleasant groves perchance my heart,
Of her discomforts, may unload some part.
XVI
"If gold or wealth, of most esteemed dear,
If jewels rich thou diddest hold in prize,
Such store thereof, such plenty have I here,
As to a greedy mind might well suffice:"
With that down trickled many a silver tear,
Two crystal streams fell from her watery eyes;
Part of her sad misfortunes then she told,
And wept, and with her wept that shepherd old.

XVII
With speeches kind, he gan the virgin dear
Toward his cottage gently home to guide;
His aged wife there made her homely cheer,
Yet welcomed her, and placed her by her side.
The princess donned a poor pastoral's gear,
A kerchief coarse upon her head she tied;
But yet her gestures and her looks, I guess,
Were such as ill beseemed a shepherdess.

XVIII
Not those rude garments could obscure and hide
The heavenly beauty of her angel's face,
Nor was her princely offspring damnified
Or aught disparaged by those labors base;
Her little flocks to pasture would she guide,

And milk her goats, and in their folds them place,
Both cheese and butter could she make, and frame
Herself to please the shepherd and his dame.

XIX
But oft, when underneath the greenwood shade
Her flocks lay hid from Phoebus' scorching rays,
Unto her knight she songs and sonnets made,
And them engraved in bark of beech and bays;
She told how Cupid did her first invade,
How conquered her, and ends with Tancred's praise:
And when her passion's writ she over read,
Again she mourned, again salt tears she shed.

XX
"You happy trees forever keep," quoth she,
"This woful story in your tender rind,
Another day under your shade maybe
Will come to rest again some lover kind;
Who if these trophies of my griefs he see,
Shall feel dear pity pierce his gentle mind;"
With that she sighed and said, "Too late I prove
There is no troth in fortune, trust in love.

XXI
"Yet may it be, if gracious heavens attend
The earnest suit of a distressed wight,
At my entreat they will vouchsafe to send
To these huge deserts that unthankful knight,
That when to earth the man his eyes shall bend,
And sees my grave, my tomb, and ashes light,
My woful death his stubborn heart may move,
With tears and sorrows to reward my love.

XXII
"So, though my life hath most unhappy been,

Jerusalem Delivered

At least yet shall my spirit dead be blest,
My ashes cold shall, buried on this green,
Enjoy that good this body ne'er possessed."
Thus she complained to the senseless treen,
Floods in her eyes, and fires were in her breast;
But he for whom these streams of tears she shed,
Wandered far off, alas, as chance him led.

XXIII
He followed on the footsteps he had traced,
Till in high woods and forests old he came,
Where bushes, thorns and trees so thick were placed,
And so obscure the shadows of the same,
That soon he lost the tract wherein he paced;
Yet went he on, which way he could not aim,
But still attentive was his longing ear
If noise of horse or noise of arms he hear.

XXIV
If with the breathing of the gentle wind,
An aspen leaf but shaked on the tree,
If bird or beast stirred in the bushes blind,
Thither he spurred, thither he rode to see:
Out of the wood by Cynthia's favor kind,
At last, with travel great and pains, got he,
And following on a little path, he heard
A rumbling sound, and hasted thitherward.

XXV
It was a fountain from the living stone,
That poured down clear streams in noble store,
Whose conduit pipes, united all in one,
Throughout a rocky channel ghastly roar;
Here Tancred stayed, and called, yet answered none,
Save babbling echo, from the crooked shore;
And there the weary knight at last espies

The springing daylight red and white arise.

XXVI

He sighed sore, and guiltless heaven gan blame,
That wished success to his desire denied,
And sharp revenge protested for the same,
If aught but good his mistress fair betide;
Then wished he to return the way he came,
Although he wist not by what path to ride,
And time drew near when he again must fight
With proud Argantes, that vain–glorious knight.

XXVII

His stalwart steed the champion stout bestrode
And pricked fast to find the way he lost,
But through a valley as he musing rode,
He saw a man that seemed for haste a post,
His horn was hung between his shoulders broad,
As is the guise with us: Tancredi crossed
His way, and gently prayed the man to say,
To Godfrey's camp how he should find the way.

XXVIII

"Sir," in the Italian language answered he,
"I ride where noble Boemond hath me sent:"
The prince thought this his uncle's man should be,
And after him his course with speed he bent,
A fortress stately built at last they see,
Bout which a muddy stinking lake there went,
There they arrived when Titan went to rest
His weary limbs in night's untroubled nest.

XXIX

The courier gave the fort a warning blast;
The drawbridge was let down by them within:
"If thou a Christian be," quoth he, "thou mayest

167

Till Phoebus shine again, here take thine inn,
The County of Cosenza, three days past,
This castle from the Turks did nobly win."
The prince beheld the piece, which site and art
Impregnable had made on every part.

XXX

He feared within a pile so fortified
Some secret treason or enchantment lay,
But had he known even there he should have died,
Yet should his looks no sign of fear betray;
For wheresoever will or chance him guide,
His strong victorious hand still made him way:
Yet for the combat he must shortly make,
No new adventures list he undertake.

XXXI

Before the castle, in a meadow plain
Beside the bridge's end, he stayed and stood,
Nor was entreated by the speeches vain
Of his false guide, to pass beyond the flood.
Upon the bridge appeared a warlike swain,
From top to toe all clad in armor good,
Who brandishing a broad and cutting sword,
Thus threatened death with many an idle word.

XXXII

"O thou, whom chance or will brings to the soil,
Where fair Armida doth the sceptre guide,
Thou canst not fly, of arms thyself despoil,
And let thy hands with iron chains be tied;
Enter and rest thee from thy weary toil.
Within this dungeon shalt thou safe abide,
And never hope again to see the day,
Or that thy hair for age shall turn to gray;

Jerusalem Delivered

XXXIII

"Except thou swear her valiant knights to aid
Against those traitors of the Christian crew."
Tancred at this discourse a little stayed,
His arms, his gesture, and his voice he knew:
It was Rambaldo, who for that false maid
Forsook his country and religion true,
And of that fort defender chief became,
And those vile creatures stablished in the same.

XXXIV

The warrior answered, blushing red for shame,
"Cursed apostate, and ungracious wight,
I am that Tancred who defend the name
Of Christ, and have been aye his faithful knight;
His rebel foes can I subdue and tame,
As thou shalt find before we end this fight;
And thy false heart cleft with this vengeful sword,
Shall feel the ire of thy forsaken Lord."

XXXV

When that great name Rambaldo's ears did fill,
He shook for fear and looked pale for dread,
Yet proudly said, "Tancred, thy hap was ill
To wander hither where thou art but dead,
Where naught can help, thy courage, strength and skill;
To Godfrey will I send thy cursed head,
That he may see, how for Armida's sake,
Of him and of his Christ a scorn I make."

XXXVI

This said, the day to sable night was turned,
That scant one could another's arms descry,
But soon an hundred lamps and torches burned,
That cleared all the earth and all the sky;
The castle seemed a stage with lights adorned,

169

On which men play some pompous tragedy;
Within a terrace sat on high the queen,
And heard, and saw, and kept herself unseen.

XXXVII

The noble baron whet his courage hot,
And busked him boldly to the dreadful fight;
Upon his horse long while he tarried not,
Because on foot he saw the Pagan knight,
Who underneath his trusty shield was got,
His sword was drawn, closed was his helmet bright,
Gainst whom the prince marched on a stately pace,
Wrath in his voice, rage in his eyes and face.

XXXVIII

His foe, his furious charge not well abiding,
Traversed his ground, and stated here and there,
But he, though faint and weary both with riding,
Yet followed fast and still oppressed him near,
And on what side he felt Rambaldo sliding,
On that his forces most employed were;
Now at his helm, not at his hauberk bright,
He thundered blows, now at his face and sight.

XXXIX

Against those numbers battery chief he maketh,
Wherein man's life keeps chiefest residence;
At his proud threats the Gascoign warrior quaketh,
And uncouth fear appalled every sense,
To nimble shifts the knight himself betaketh,
And skippeth here and there for his defence:
Now with his rage, now with his trusty blade,
Against his blows he good resistance made.

XL

Yet no such quickness for defence he used,

As did the prince to work him harm and scathe;
His shield was cleft in twain, his helmet bruised,
And in his blood is other arms did bathe;
On him he heaped blows, with thrusts confused,
And more or less each stroke annoyed him hath;
He feared, and in his troubled bosom strove
Remorse of conscience, shame, disdain and love.

XLI
At last so careless foul despair him made,
He meant to prove his fortune ill or good,
His shield cast down, he took his helpless blade
In both his hands, which yet had drawn no blood,
And with such force upon the prince he laid,
That neither plate nor mail the blow withstood,
The wicked steel seized deep in his right side,
And with his streaming blood his bases dyed:
XLII
Another stroke he lent him on the brow,
So great that loudly rung the sounding steel;
Yet pierced he not the helmet with the blow,
Although the owner twice or thrice did reel.
The prince, whose looks disdainful anger show,
Now meant to use his puissance every deal,
He shaked his head and crashed his teeth for ire,
His lips breathed wrath, eyes sparkled shining fire.

XLIII
The Pagan wretch no longer could sustain
The dreadful terror of his fierce aspect,
Against the threatened blow he saw right plain
No tempered armor could his life protect,
He leapt aside, the stroke fell down in vain,
Against a pillar near a bridge erect.
Thence flaming fire and thousand sparks outstart,
And kill with fear the coward Pagan's heart.

171

Jerusalem Delivered

XLIV

Toward the bridge the fearful Paynim fled,
And in swift flight, his hope of life reposed;
Himself fast after Lord Tancredi sped,
And now in equal pace almost they closed,
When all the burning lamps extinguished
The shining fort his goodly splendor losed,
And all those stars on heaven's blue face that shone
With Cynthia's self, dispeared were and gone.

XLV

Amid those witchcrafts and that ugly shade,
No further could the prince pursue the chase,
Nothing he saw, yet forward still he made,
With doubtful steps, and ill assured pace;
At last his foot upon a threshold trad,
And ere he wist, he entered had the place;
With ghastly noise the door–leaves shut behind,
And closed him fast in prison dark and blind.

XLVI

As in our seas in the Commachian Bay,
A silly fish, with streams enclosed, striveth,
To shun the fury and avoid the sway
Wherewith the current in that whirlpool driveth,
Yet seeketh all in vain, but finds no way
Out of that watery prison, where she diveth:
For with such force there be the tides in brought,
There entereth all that will, thence issueth naught:

XLVII

This prison so entrapped that valiant knight;
Of which the gate was framed by subtle train,
To close without the help of human wight,
So sure none could undo the leaves again;

Against the doors he bended all his might,
But all his forces were employed in vain,
At last a voice gan to him loudly call,
"Yield thee," quoth it, "thou art Armida's thrall."

XLVIII
"Within this dungeon buried shalt thou spend
The res'due of thy woful days and years;"
The champions list not more with words contend,
But in his heart kept close his griefs and fears,
He blamed love, chance gan he reprehend,
And gainst enchantment huge complaints he rears.
"It were small loss," softly he thus begun,
"To lose the brightness of the shining sun;
XLIX
"But I. alas, the golden beam forego
Of my far brighter sun; nor can I say
If these poor eyes shall e'er be blessed so,
As once again to view that shining ray:"
Then thought he on his proud Circassian foe,
And said, "Ah! how shall I perform that fray?
He, and the world with him, will Tancred blame,
This is my grief, my fault, mine endless shame."

L
While those high spirits of this champion good,
With love and honor's care are thus oppressed,
While he torments himself, Argantes wood,
Waxed weary of his bed and of his rest,
Such hate of peace, and such desire of blood,
Such thirst of glory, boiled in his breast;
That though he scant could stir or stand upright,
Yet longed he for the appointed day to fight.

LI
The night which that expected day forewent,

173

Scantly the Pagan closed his eyes to sleep,
He told how night her sliding hours spent,
And rose ere springing day began to peep;
He called for armor, which incontinent
Was brought by him that used the same to keep,
That harness rich old Aladine him gave,
A worthy present for a champion brave.

LII

He donned them on, not long their riches eyed,
Nor did he aught with so great weight incline,
His wonted sword upon his thigh he tied,
The blade was old and tough, of temper fine.
As when a comet far and wide descried,
In scorn of Phoebus midst bright heaven doth shine,
And tidings sad of death and mischief brings
To mighty lords, to monarchs, and to kings.

LIII

So shone the Pagan in bright armor clad,
And rolled his eyes great swollen with ire and blood,
His dreadful gestures threatened horror sad,
And ugly death upon his forehead stood;
Not one of all his squires the courage had
To approach their master in his angry mood,
Above his head he shook his naked blade,
And gainst the subtle air vain battle made.

LIV

"The Christian thief," quoth he, "that was so bold
To combat me in hard and single fight,
Shall wounded fall inglorious on the mould,
His locks with clods of blood and dust bedight,
And living shall with watery eyes behold
How from his back I tear his harness bright,
Nor shall his dying words me so entreat,

174

But that I'll give his flesh to dogs for meat."

LV
Like as a bull when, pricked with jealousy,
He spies the rival of his hot desire,
Through all the fields doth bellow, roar and cry,
And with his thundering voice augments his ire,
And threatening battle to the empty sky,
Tears with his horn each tree, plant, bush and brier,
And with his foot casts up the sand on height,
Defying his strong foe to deadly fight:

LVI
Such was the Pagan's fury, such his cry.
A herald called he then, and thus he spoke;
"Go to the camp, and in my name, defy
The man that combats for his Jesus' sake;"
This said, upon his steed he mounted high,
And with him did his noble prisoner take,
The town he thus forsook, and on the green
He ran, as mad or frantic he had been.

LVII
A bugle small he winded loud and shrill,
That made resound the fields and valleys near,
Louder than thunder from Olympus hill
Seemed that dreadful blast to all that hear;
The Christian lords of prowess, strength and skill,
Within the imperial tent assembled were,
The herald there in boasting terms defied
Tancredi first, and all that durst beside.

LVIII
With sober those ten which chosen were by lot,
And viewed at leisure every lord and knight;
But yet for all his looks not one stepped out,

With courage bold, to undertake the fight:
Absent were all the Christian champions stout,
No news of Tancred since his secret flight;
Boemond far off, and banished from the crew
Was that strong prince who proud Gernando slew:

LIX

And eke those ten which chosen were by lot,
And all the worthies of the camp beside,
After Armida false were followed hot,
When night were come their fight to hide;
The rest their hands and hearts that trusted not,
Blushed for shame, yet silent still abide;
For none there was that sought to purchase fame
In so great peril, fear exiled shame.

LX

The angry duke their fear discovered plain,
By their pale looks and silence from each part,
And as he moved was with just disdain,
These words he said, and from his seat upstart:
"Unworthy life I judge that coward swain
To hazard it even now that wants the heart,
When this vile Pagan with his glorious boast
Dishonors and defies Christ's sacred host.

LXI

"But let my camp sit still in peace and rest,
And my life's hazard at their ease behold.
Come bring me here my fairest arms and best;"
And they were brought sooner than could be told.
But gentle Raymond in his aged breast,
Who had mature advice, and counsel old,
Than whom in all the camp were none or few
Of greater might, before Godfredo drew,

LXII

And gravely said, "Ah, let it not betide,
On one man's hand to venture all his host!
No private soldier thou, thou are our guide,
If thou miscarry, all our hope were lost,
By thee must Babel fell, and all her pride;
Of our true faith thou art the prop and post,
Rule with thy sceptre, conquer with thy word,
Let others combat make with spear and sword.

LXIII
"Let me this Pagan's glorious pride assuage,
These aged arms can yet their weapons use,
Let others shun Bellona's dreadful rage,
These silver locks shall not Raymondo scuse:
Oh that I were in prime of lusty age,
Like you that this adventure brave refuse,
And dare not once lift up your coward eyes,
Gainst him that you and Christ himself defies!

LXIV
"Or as I was when all the lords of fame
And Germain princes great stood by to view,
In Conrad's court, the second of that name,
When Leopold in single fight I slew;
A greater praise I reaped by the same,
So strong a foe in combat to subdue,
Than he should do who all alone should chase
Or kill a thousand of these Pagans base.

LXV
"Within these arms, bad I that strength again,
This boasting Paynim had not lived now,
Yet in this breast doth courage still remain;
For age or years these members shall not bow;
And if I be in this encounter slain,
Scotfree Argantes shall not scape, I vow;

Give me mine arms, this battle shall with praise
Augment mine honor, got in younger days."

LXVI

The jolly baron old thus bravely spake,
His words are spurs to virtue; every knight
That seemed before to tremble and to quake,
Now talked bold, example hath such might;
Each one the battle fierce would undertake,
Now strove they all who should begin the fight;
Baldwin and Roger both, would combat fain,
Stephen, Guelpho, Gernier and the Gerrards twain;

LXVII

And Pyrrhus, who with help of Boemond's sword
Proud Antioch by cunning sleight opprest;
The battle eke with many a lowly word,
Ralph, Rosimond, and Eberard request,
A Scottish, an Irish, and an English lord,
Whose lands the seas divide far from the rest,
And for the fight did likewise humbly sue,
Edward and his Gildippes, lovers true.

LXVIII

But Raymond more than all the rest doth sue
Upon that Pagan fierce to wreak his ire,
Now wants he naught of all his armors due
Except his helm that shone like flaming fire.
To whom Godfredo thus; "O mirror true
Of antique worth! thy courage doth inspire
New strength in us, of Mars in thee doth shine
The art, the honor and the discipline.

LXIX

"If ten like thee of valor and of age,
Among these legions I could haply find,

I should the best of Babel's pride assuage,
And spread our faith from Thule to furthest Inde;
But now I pray thee calm thy valiant rage,
Reserve thyself till greater need us bind,
And let the rest each one write down his name,
And see whom Fortune chooseth to this game, —
LXX
"Or rather see whom God's high judgement taketh,
To whom is chance, and fate, and fortune slave."
Raymond his earnest suit not yet forsaketh,
His name writ with the residue would he have,
Godfrey himself in his bright helmet shaketh
The scrolls, with names of all the champions brave:
They drew, and read the first whereon they hit,
Wherein was "Raymond, Earl of Tholouse," writ.

LXXI
His name with joy and mighty shouts they bless;
The rest allow his choice, and fortune praise,
New vigor blushed through those looks of his;
It seemed he now resumed his youthful days,
Like to a snake whose slough new changed is,
That shines like gold against the sunny rays:
But Godfrey most approved his fortune high,
And wished him honor, conquest, victory.

LXXII
Then from his side he took his noble brand,
And giving it to Raymond, thus he spake:
"This is the sword wherewith in Saxon land,
The great Rubello battle used to make,
From him I took it, fighting hand to hand,
And took his life with it, and many a lake
Of blood with it I have shed since that day,
With thee God grant it proves as happy may."

LXXIII

Of these delays meanwhile impatient,
Argantes threateneth loud and sternly cries,
"O glorious people of the Occident!
Behold him here that all your host defies:
Why comes not Tancred, whose great hardiment,
With you is prized so dear? Pardie he lies
Still on his pillow, and presumes the night
Again may shield him from my power and might.

LXXIV

"Why then some other come, by hand and hand,
Come all, come forth on horseback, come on foot, ·
If not one man dares combat hand to hand,
In all the thousands of so great a rout:
See where the tomb of Mary's Son doth stand,
March thither, warriors hold, what makes you doubt?
Why run you not, there for your sins to weep
Or to what greater need these forces keep?"

LXXV

Thus scorned by that heathen Saracine
Were all the soldiers of Christ's sacred name:
Raymond, while others at his words repine,
Burst forth in rage, he could not bear this shame:
For fire of courage brighter far doth shine
If challenges and threats augment the same;
So that, upon his steed he mounted light,
Which Aquilino for his swiftness hight.

LXXVI

This jennet was by Tagus bred; for oft
The breeder of these beasts to war assigned,
When first on trees burgeon the blossoms soft
Pricked forward with the sting of fertile kind,
Against the air casts up her head aloft

And gathereth seed so from the fruitful wind
And thus conceiving of the gentle blast,
A wonder strange and rare, she foals at last.

LXXVII

And had you seen the beast, you would have said
The light and subtile wind his father was;
For if his course upon the sands he made
No sign was left what way the beast did pass;
Or if he menaged were, or if he played,
He scantly bended down the tender grass:
Thus mounted rode the Earl, and as he went,
Thus prayed, to Heaven his zealous looks upbent.

LXXVIII

"O Lord, that diddest save, keep and defend
Thy servant David from Goliath's rage,
And broughtest that huge giant to his end,
Slain by a faithful child of tender age;
Like grace, O Lord, like mercy now extend!
Let me this vile blasphemous pride assuage,
That all the world may to thy glory know,
Old men and babes thy foes can overthrow!"

LXXIX

Thus prayed the County, and his prayers dear
Strengthened with zeal, with godliness and faith,
Before the throne of that great Lord appear,
In whose sweet grace is life, death in his wrath,
Among his armies bright and legions clear,
The Lord an angel good selected hath,
To whom the charge was given to guard the knight,
And keep him safe from that fierce Pagan's might.

LXXX

The angel good, appointed for the guard

Of noble Raymond from his tender eild,
That kept him then, and kept him afterward,
When spear and sword he able was to wield,
Now when his great Creator's will he heard,
That in this fight he should him chiefly shield,
Up to a tower set on a rock he flies,
Where all the heavenly arms and weapons lies:

LXXXI

There stands the lance wherewith great Michael slew
The aged dragon in a bloody fight,
There are the dreadful thunders forged new,
With storms and plagues that on poor sinners light;
The massy trident mayest thou pendant view
There on a golden pin hung up on height,
Wherewith sometimes he smites this solid land,
And throws down towns and towers thereon which stand.

LXXXII

Among the blessed weapons there which stands
Upon a diamond shield his looks he bended,
So great that it might cover all the lands,
Twixt Caucasus and Atlas hills extended;
With it the lord's dear flocks and faithful bands,
The holy kings and cities are defended,
The sacred angel took his target sheen,
And by the Christian champion stood unseen.

LXXXIII

But now the walls and turrets round about,
Both young and old with many thousands fill;
The king Clorinda sent and her brave rout,
To keep the field, she stayed upon the hill:
Godfrey likewise some Christian bands sent out
Which armed, and ranked in good array stood still,
And to their champions empty let remain

Twixt either troop a large and spacious plain.

LXXXIV

Argantes looked for Tancredi bold,
But saw an uncouth foe at last appear,
Raymond rode on, and what he asked him, told,
Better by chance, "Tancred is now elsewhere,
Yet glory not of that, myself behold
Am come prepared, and bid thee battle here,
And in his place, or for myself to fight,
Lo, here I am, who scorn thy heathenish might."

LXXXV

The Pagan cast a scornful smile and said,
"But where is Tancred, is he still in bed?
His looks late seemed to make high heaven afraid;
But now for dread he is or dead or fled;
But whe'er earth's centre or the deep sea made
His lurking hole, it should not save his head."
"Thou liest," he says, "to say so brave a knight
Is fled from thee, who thee exceeds in might."

LXXXVI

The angry Pagan said, "I have not spilt
My labor then, if thou his place supply,
Go take the field, and let's see how thou wilt
Maintain thy foolish words and that brave lie;"
Thus parleyed they to meet in equal tilt,
Each took his aim at other's helm on high,
Even in the fight his foe good Raymond hit,
But shaked him not, he did so firmly sit.

LXXXVII

The fierce Circassian missed of his blow,
A thing which seld befell the man before,
The angel, by unseen, his force did know,

183

And far awry the poignant weapon bore,
He burst his lance against the sand below,
And bit his lips for rage, and cursed and swore,
Against his foe returned he swift as wind,
Half mad in arms a second match to find.

LXXXVIII

Like to a ram that butts with horned head,
So spurred he forth his horse with desperate race:
Raymond at his right hand let slide his steed,
And as he passed struck at the Pagan's face;
He turned again, the earl was nothing dread,
Yet stept aside, and to his rage gave place,
And on his helm with all his strength gan smite,
Which was so hard his courtlax could not bite.

LXXXIX

The Saracen employed his art and force
To grip his foe within his mighty arms,
But he avoided nimbly with his horse,
He was no prentice in those fierce alarms,
About him made he many a winding course,
No strength, nor sleight the subtle warrior harms,
His nimble steed obeyed his ready hand,
And where he stept no print left in the sand.

XC

As when a captain doth besiege some hold,
Set in a marsh or high up on a hill,
And trieth ways and wiles a thousandfold,
To bring the piece subjected to his will;
So fared the County with the Pagan bold;
And when he did his head and breast none ill,
His weaker parts he wisely gan assail,
And entrance searched oft 'twixt mail and mail.

Jerusalem Delivered

XCI

At last he hit him on a place or twain,
That on his arms the red blood trickled down,
And yet himself untouched did remain,
No nail was broke, no plume cut from his crown;
Argantes raging spent his strength in vain,
Waste were his strokes, his thrusts were idle thrown,
Yet pressed he on, and doubled still his blows,
And where he hits he neither cares nor knows.

XCII

Among a thousand blows the Saracine
At last struck one, when Raymond was so near,
That not the swiftness of his Aquiline
Could his dear lord from that huge danger bear:
But lo, at hand unseen was help divine,
Which saves when worldly comforts none appear,
The angel on his targe received that stroke,
And on that shield Argantes' sword was broke.

XCIII

The sword was broke, therein no wonder lies
If earthly tempered metal could not hold
Against that target forged above the skies,
Down fell the blade in pieces on the mould;
The proud Circassian scant believed his eyes,
Though naught were left him but the hilts of gold,
And full of thoughts amazed awhile he stood,
Wondering the Christian's armor was so good.

XCIV

The brittle web of that rich sword he thought,
Was broke through hardness of the County's shield;
And so thought Raymond, who discovered naught
What succor Heaven did for his safety yield:
But when he saw the man gainst whom he fought

185

Unweaponed, still stood he in the field;
His noble heart esteemed the glory light,
At such advantage if he slew the knight.

XCV

"Go fetch," he would have said, "another blade,"
When in his heart a better thought arose,
How for Christ's glory he was champion made,
How Godfrey had him to this combat chose,
The army's honor on his shoulder laid
To hazards new he list not that expose;
While thus his thoughts debated on the case,
The hilts Argantes hurled at his face.

XCVI

And forward spurred his mounture fierce withal,
Within his arms longing his foe to strain,
Upon whose helm the heavy blow did fall,
And bent well–nigh the metal to his brain:
But he, whose courage was heroical,
Leapt by, and makes the Pagan's onset vain,
And wounds his hand, which he outstretched saw,
Fiercer than eagles' talon, lions' paw.

XCVII

Now here, now there, on every side he rode,
With nimble speed, and spurred now out, now in,
And as he went and came still laid on load
Where Lord Argantes' arms were weak and thin;
All that huge force which in his arms abode,
His wrath, his ire, his great desire to win,
Against his foe together all he bent,
And heaven and fortune furthered his intent.
XCVIII

But he, whose courage for no peril fails,
Well armed, and better hearted, scorns his power.

Jerusalem Delivered

Like a tall ship when spent are all her sails,
Which still resists the rage of storm and shower,
Whose mighty ribs fast bound with bands and nails,
Withstands fierce Neptune's wrath, for many an hour,
And yields not up her bruised keel to winds,
In whose stern blast no ruth nor grace she finds:

XCIX

Argantes such thy present danger was,
When Satan stirred to aid thee at thy need,
In human shape he forged an airy mass,
And made the shade a body seem indeed;
Well might the spirit of Clorinda pass,
Like her it was, in armor and in weed,
In stature, beauty, countenance and face,
In looks, in speech, in gesture, and in pace.

C

And for the spirit should seem the same indeed,
From where she was whose show and shape it had,
Toward the wall it rode with feigned speed,
Where stood the people all dismayed and sad,
To see their knight of help have so great need,
And yet the law of arms all help forbad.
There in a turret sat a soldier stout
To watch, and at a loop–hole peeped out;

CI

The spirit spake to him, called Oradine,
The noblest archer then that handled bow,
"O Oradine," quoth she, "who straight as line
Can'st shoot, and hit each mark set high or low,
If yonder knight, alas! be slain in fine,
As likest is, great ruth it were you know,
And greater shame, if his victorious foe
Should with his spoils triumphant homeward go.

187

CII

"Now prove thy skill, thine arrow's sharp head dip
In yonder thievish Frenchman's guilty blood,
I promise thee thy sovereign shall not slip
To give thee large rewards for such a good;"
Thus said the spirit; the man did laugh and skip
For hope of future gain, nor longer stood,
But from his quiver huge a shaft he hent,
And set it in his mighty bow new bent,

CIII

Twanged the string, out flew the quarrel long,
And through the subtle air did singing pass,
It hit the knight the buckles rich among,
Wherewith his precious girdle fastened was,
It bruised them and pierced his hauberk strong,
Some little blood down trickled on the grass;
Light was the wound; the angel by unseen,
The sharp head blunted of the weapon keen.

CIV

Raymond drew forth the shaft, as much behoved,
And with the steel, his blood out streaming came,
With bitter words his foe he then reproved,
For breaking faith, to his eternal shame.
Godfrey, whose careful eyes from his beloved
Were never turned, saw and marked the same,
And when he viewed the wounded County bleed,
He sighed, and feared, more perchance than need;

CV

And with his words, and with his threatening eyes,
He stirred his captains to revenge that wrong;
Forthwith the spurred courser forward hies,
Within their rests put were their lances long,

Jerusalem Delivered

From either side a squadron brave out flies,
And boldly made a fierce encounter strong,
The raised dust to overspread begun
Their shining arms, and far more shining sun.
CVI
Of breaking spears, of ringing helm and shield,
A dreadful rumor roared on every side,
There lay a horse, another through the field
Ran masterless, dismounted was his guide;
Here one lay dead, there did another yield,
Some sighed, some sobbed, some prayed, and some cried;
Fierce was the fight, and longer still it lasted,
Fiercer and fewer, still themselves they wasted.

CVII
Argantes nimbly leapt amid the throng,
And from a soldier wrung an iron mace,
And breaking through the ranks and ranges long,
Therewith he passage made himself and place,
Raymond he sought, the thickest press among.
To take revenge for !ate received disgrace,
A greedy wolf he seemed, and would assuage
With Raymond's blood his hunger and his rage.

CVIII
The way he found not easy as he would,
But fierce encounters put him oft to pain,
He met Ormanno and Rogero bold,
Of Balnavile, Guy, and the Gerrards twain;
Yet nothing might his rage and haste withhold,
These worthies strove to stop him, but in vain,
With these strong lets increased still his ire,
Like rivers stopped, or closely smouldered fire.

CIX
He slew Ormanno, and wounded Guy, and laid

Rogero low, among the people slain,
On every side new troops the man invade,
Yet all their blows were waste, their onsets vain,
But while Argantes thus his prizes played,
And seemed alone this skirmish to sustain,
The duke his brother called and thus he spake,
"Go with thy troop, fight for thy Saviour's sake;

CX

"There enter in where hottest is the fight,
Thy force against the left wing strongly bend."
This said, so brave an onset gave the knight,
That many a Paynim bold there made his end:
The Turks too weak seemed to sustain his might,
And could not from his power their lives defend,
Their ensigns rent, and broke was their array,
And men and horse on heaps together lay.

CXI

O'erthrown likewise away the right wing ran,
Nor was there one again that turned his face,
Save bold Argantes, else fled every man,
Fear drove them thence on heaps, with headlong chase:
He stayed alone, and battle new began,
Five hundred men, weaponed with sword and mace,
So great resistance never could have made,
As did Argantes with his single blade:

CXII

The strokes of swords and thrusts of many a spear,
The shock of many a joust he long sustained,
He seemed of strength enough this charge to bear,
And time to strike, now here, now there, he gained
His armors broke, his members bruised were,
He sweat and bled, yet courage still he feigned;
But now his foes upon him pressed so fast,

That with their weight they bore him back at last.

CXIII

His back against this storm at length he turned,
Whose headlong fury bore him backward still,
Not like to one that fled, but one that mourned
Because he did his foes no greater ill,
His threatening eyes like flaming torches burned,
His courage thirsted yet more blood to spill,
And every way and every mean he sought,
To stay his flying mates, but all for naught.

CXIV

This good he did, while thus he played his part,
His bands and troops at ease, and safe, retired;
Yet coward dread lacks order, fear wants art,
Deaf to attend, commanded or desired.
But Godfrey that perceived in his wise heart,
How his bold knights to victory aspired,
Fresh soldiers sent, to make more quick pursuit,
And help to gather conquest's precious fruit.

CXV

But this, alas, was not the appointed day,
Set down by Heaven to end this mortal war:
The western lords this time had borne away
The prize, for which they travelled had so far,
Had not the devils, that saw the sure decay
Of their false kingdom by this bloody war,
At once made heaven and earth with darkness blind,
And stirred up tempests, storms, and blustering wind.

CXVI

Heaven's glorious lamp, wrapped in an ugly veil
Of shadows dark, was hid from mortal eye,
And hell's grim blackness did bright skies assail;

On every side the fiery lightnings fly,
The thunders roar, the streaming rain and hail
Pour down and make that sea which erst was dry.
The tempests rend the oaks and cedars brake,
And make not trees but rocks and mountains shake.

CXVII
The rain, the lightning, and the raging wind,
Beat in the Frenchmen's eyes with hideous force,
The soldiers stayed amazed in heart and mind,
The terror such that stopped both man and horse.
Surprised with this evil no way they find,
Whither for succor to direct their course,
But wise Clorinda soon the advantage spied,
And spurring forth thus to her soldiers cried:

CXVIII
"You hardy men at arms behold," quoth she,
"How Heaven, how Justice in our aid doth fight,
Our visages are from this tempest free,
Our hands at will may wield our weapons bright,
The fury of this friendly storm you see
Upon the foreheads of our foes doth light,
And blinds their eyes, then let us take the tide,
Come, follow me, good fortune be our guide."

CXIX
This said, against her foes on rode the dame,
And turned their backs against the wind and rain;
Upon the French with furious rage she came,
And scorned those idle blows they struck in vain;
Argantes at the instant did the same,
And them who chased him now chased again,
Naught but his fearful back each Christian shows
Against the tempest, and against their blows.

Jerusalem Delivered

CXX

The cruel hail, and deadly wounding blade,
Upon their shoulders smote them as they fled,
The blood new spilt while thus they slaughter made,
The water fallen from skies had dyed red,
Among the murdered bodies Pyrrhus laid,
And valiant Raiphe his heart blood there out bled,
The first subdued by strong Argantes' might,
The second conquered by that virgin knight.

CXXI

Thus fled the French, and then pursued in chase
The wicked sprites and all the Syrian train:
But gainst their force and gainst their fell menace
Of hail and wind, of tempest and of rain,
Godfrey alone turned his audacious face,
Blaming his barons for their fear so vain,
Himself the camp gate boldly stood to keep,
And saved his men within his trenches deep.

CXXII

And twice upon Argantes proud he flew,
And beat him backward, maugre all his might,
And twice his thirsty sword he did imbrue,
In Pagan's blood where thickest was the fight;
At last himself with all his folk withdrew,
And that day's conquest gave the virgin bright,
Which got, she home retired and all her men,
And thus she chased this lion to his den.

CXXIII

Yet ceased not the fury and the ire
Of these huge storms, of wind, of rain and hail,
Now was it dark, now shone the lightning fire,
The wind and water every place assail,
No bank was safe, no rampire left entire,
No tent could stand, when beam and cordage fail,

Wind, thunder, rain, all gave a dreadful sound,
And with that music deafed the trembling ground.

EIGHTH BOOK

THE ARGUMENT.
A messenger to Godfrey sage doth tell
The Prince of Denmark's valour, death and end:
The Italians, trusting signs untrue too well,
Think their Rinaldo slain: the wicked fiend
Breeds fury in their breasts, their bosoms swell
With ire and hate, and war and strife forth send:
They threaten Godfrey; he prays to the Lord,
And calms their fury with his look and word.

I
Now were the skies of storms and tempests cleared,
Lord Aeolus shut up his winds in hold,
The silver–mantled morning fresh appeared,
With roses crowned, and buskined high with gold;
The spirits yet which had these tempests reared,
Their malice would still more and more unfold;
And one of them that Astragor was named,
His speeches thus to foul Alecto framed.

II
"Alecto, see, we could not stop nor stay
The knight that to our foes new tidings brings,
Who from the hands escaped, with life away,
Of that great prince, chief of all Pagan kings:
He comes, the fall of his slain lord to say,

194

Of death and loss he tells, and such sad things,
Great news he brings, and greatest dangers is,
Bertoldo's son shall be called home for this.

III
"Thou knowest what would befall, bestir thee than;
Prevent with craft, what force could not withstand,
Turn to their evil the speeches of the man,
With his own weapon wound Godfredo's hand;
Kindle debate, infect with poison wan
The English, Switzer, and Italian band,
Great tumult move, make brawls and quarrels rife,
Set all the camp on uproar and at strife.
IV
"This act beseems thee well, and of the deed
Much may'st thou boast before our lord and king."
Thus said the sprite. Persuasion small did need,
The monster grants to undertake the thing.
Meanwhile the knight, whose coming thus they dread,
Before the camp his weary limbs doth bring,
And well−nigh breathless, "Warriors bold," he cried,
"Who shall conduct me to your famous guide?"

V
An hundred strove the stranger's guide to be,
To hearken news the knights by heaps assemble,
The man fell lowly down upon his knee,
And kissed the hand that made proud Babel tremble;
"Right puissant lord, whose valiant acts," quoth he,
"The sands and stars in number best resemble,
Would God some gladder news I might unfold,"
And there he paused, and sighed; then thus he told:

VI
"Sweno, the King of Denmark's only heir,
The stay and staff of his declining eild,

195

Longed to be among these squadrons fair
Who for Christ's faith here serve with spear and shield;
No weariness, no storms of sea or air,
No such contents as crowns and sceptres yield,
No dear entreaties of so kind a sire,
Could in his bosom quench that glorious fire.

VII

"He thirsted sore to learn this warlike art
Of thee, great lord and master of the same;
And was ashamed in his noble heart,
That never act he did deserved fame;
Besides, the news and tidings from each part
Of young Rinaldo's worth and praises came:
But that which most his courage stirred hath,
Is zeal, religion, godliness, and faith.

VIII

"He hasted forward, then without delay,
And with him took of knights a chosen band,
Directly toward Thrace we took the way,
To Byzance old, chief fortress of that land,
There the Greek monarch gently prayed him stay,
And there an herald sent from you we fand,
How Antioch was won, who first declared,
And how defended nobly afterward.

IX

"Defended gainst Corbana, valiant knight,
That all the Persian armies had to guide,
And brought so many soldiers bold to fight,
That void of men he left that kingdom wide;
He told thine acts, thy wisdom and thy might,
And told the deeds of many a lord beside,
His speech at length to young Rinaldo passed,
And told his great achievements, first and last:

Jerusalem Delivered

X
"And how this noble camp of yours, of late
Besieged had this town, and in what sort,
And how you prayed him to participate
Of the last conquest of this noble fort.
In hardy Sweno opened was the gate
Of worthy anger by this brave report,
So that each hour seemed five years long,
Till he were fighting with these Pagans strong.

XI
"And while the herald told your fights and frays,
Himself of cowardice reproved he thought,
And him to stay that counsels him, or prays,
He hears not, or, else heard, regardeth naught,
He fears no perils but whilst he delays,
Lest this last work without his help be wrought:
In this his doubt, in this his danger lies,
No hazard else he fears, no peril spies.

XII
"Thus hasting on, he hasted on his death,
Death that to him and us was fatal guide.
The rising morn appeared yet aneath,
When he and we were armed, and fit to ride,
The nearest way seemed best, o'er hold and heath
We went, through deserts waste, and forests wide,
The streets and ways he openeth as he goes,
And sets each land free from intruding foes.

XIII
"Now want of food, now dangerous ways we find,
Now open war, now ambush closely laid;
Yet passed we forth, all perils left behind,
Our foes or dead or run away afraid,

197

Jerusalem Delivered

Of victory so happy blew the wind,
That careless all the heedless to it made:
Until one day his tents he happed to rear,
To Palestine when we approached near.

XIV

"There did our scouts return and bring us news,
That dreadful noise of horse and arms they hear,
And that they deemed by sundry signs and shows
There was some mighty host of Pagans near.
At these sad tidings many changed their hues,
Some looked pale for dread, some shook for fear,
Only our noble lord was altered naught,
In look, in face, in gesture, or in thought.

XV

"But said, `A crown prepare you to possess
Of martyrdom, or happy victory;
For this I hope, for that I wish no less,
Of greater merit and of greater glory.
Brethren, this camp will shortly be, I guess,
A temple, sacred to our memory,
To which the holy men of future age,
To view our graves shall come in pilgrimage.'

XVI

"This said, he set the watch in order right
To guard the camp, along the trenches deep,
And as he armed was, so every knight
He willed on his back his arms to keep.
Now had the stillness of the quiet night
Drowned all the world in silence and in sleep,
When suddenly we heard a dreadful sound,
Which deafed the earth, and tremble made the ground.

XVII

Jerusalem Delivered

" `Arm, arm,' they cried; Prince Sweno at the same,
Glistering in shining steel leaped foremost out,
His visage shone, his noble looks did flame,
With kindled brand of courage bold and stout,
When lo, the Pagans to assault us came,
And with huge numbers hemmed us round about,
A forest thick of spears about us grew,
And over us a cloud of arrows flew:

XVIII
"Uneven the fight, unequal was the fray,
Our enemies were twenty men to one,
On every side the slain and wounded lay
Unseen, where naught but glistering weapons shone:
The number of the dead could no man say,
So was the place with darkness overgone,
The night her mantle black upon its spreads,
Hiding our losses and our valiant deeds.

XIX
"But hardy Sweno midst the other train,
By his great acts was well descried I wot,
No darkness could his valor's daylight stain,
Such wondrous blows on every side he smote;
A stream of blood, a bank of bodies slain,
About him made a bulwark of bodies slain,
And when soe'er he turned his fatal brand,
Dread in his looks and death sate in his hand.

XX
"Thus fought we till the morning bright appeared,
And strewed roses on the azure sky,
But when her lamp had night's thick darkness cleared,
Wherein the bodies dead did buried lie,
Then our sad cries to heaven for grief we reared,
Our loss apparent was, for we descry

How all our camp destroyed was almost,
And all our people well–nigh slain and lost;

XXI

"Of thousands twain an hundred scant survived.
When Sweno murdered saw each valiant knight,
I know not if his heart in sunder rived
For dear compassion of that woful sight;
He showed no change, but said: `Since so deprived
We are of all our friends by chance of fight,
Come follow them, the path to heaven their blood
Marks out, now angels made, of martyrs good.'

XXII

"This said, and glad I think of death at hand,
The signs of heavenly joy shone through his eyes,
Of Saracens against a mighty band,
With fearless heart and constant breast he flies;
No steel could shield them from his cutting bran
But whom he hits without recure he dies,
He never struck but felled or killed his foe
And wounded was himself from top to toe.

XXIII

"Not strength, but courage now, preserved on live
This hardy champion, fortress of our faith,
Strucken he strikes, still stronger more they strive,
The more they hurt him, more he doth them scathe,
When toward him a furious knight gan drive,
Of members huge, fierce looks, and full of wrath,
That with the aid of many a Pagan crew,
After long fight, at last Prince Sweno slew.

XXIV

"Ah, heavy chance! Down fell the valiant youth,
Nor mongst us all did one so strong appear
As to revenge his death: that this is truth,
By his dear blood and noble bones I swear,

Jerusalem Delivered

That of my life I had not care nor ruth,
No wounds I shunned, no blows I would off bear,
And had not Heaven my wished end denied,
Even there I should, and willing should, have died.

XXV

"Alive I fell among my fellows slain,
Yet wounded so that each one thought me dead,
Nor what our foes did since can I explain,
So sore amazed was my heart and head;
But when I opened first mine eyes again,
Night's curtain black upon the earth was spread,
And through the darkness to my feeble sight,
Appeared the twinkling of a slender light.

XXVI

"Not so much force or judgement in me lies
As to discern things seen and not mistake,
I saw like them who ope and shut their eyes
By turns, now half asleep, now half awake;
My body eke another torment tries,
My wounds began to smart, my hurts to ache;
For every sore each member pinched was
With night's sharp air, heaven's frost and earth's cold grass.

XXVII

"But still the light approached near and near,
And with the same a whispering murmur run,
Till at my side arrived both they were,
When I to spread my feeble eyes begun:
Two men behold in vestures long appear,
With each a lamp in hand, who said, `O son
In that dear Lord who helps his servants, trust,
Who ere they ask, grants all things to the just.'

XXVIII

"This said, each one his sacred blessings flings
Upon my corse, with broad our–stretched hand,
And mumbled hymns and psalms and holy things,
Which I could neither hear nor understand;
`Arise,' quoth they, with that as I had wings,
All whole and sound I leaped up from the land.
Oh miracle, sweet, gentle, strange and true!
My limbs new strength received, and vigor new.

XXIX

"I gazed on them like one whose heart denieth
To think that done, he sees so strangely wrought;
Till one said thus, `O thou of little faith,
What doubts perplex thy unbelieving thought?
Each one of us a living body hath,
We are Christ's chosen servants, fear us naught,
Who to avoid the world's allurements vain,
In wilful penance, hermits poor remain.

XXX

" `Us messengers to comfort thee elect
That Lord hath sent that rules both heaven and hell;
Who often doth his blessed will effect,
By such weak means, as wonder is to tell;
He will not that this body lie neglect,
Wherein so noble soul did lately dwell
To which again when it uprisen is
It shall united be in lasting bliss.

XXXI

" `I say Lord Sweno's corpse, for which prepared
A tomb there is according to his worth,
By which his honor shall be far declared,
And his just praises spread from south to north:"
But lift thine eyes up to the heavens ward,
Mark yonder light that like the sun shines forth

202

Jerusalem Delivered

That shall direct thee with those beams so clear,
To find the body of thy master dear.'

XXXII
"With that I saw from Cynthia's silver face,
Like to a falling star a beam down slide,
That bright as golden line marked out the place,
And lightened with clear streams the forest wide;
So Latmos shone when Phoebe left the chase,
And laid her down by her Endymion's side,
Such was the light that well discern I could,
His shape, his wounds, his face, though dead, yet bold.

XXXIII
"He lay not grovelling now, but as a knight
That ever had to heavenly things desire,
So toward heaven the prince lay bolt upright,
Like him that upward still sought to aspire,
His right hand closed held his weapon bright,
Ready to strike and execute his ire,
His left upon his breast was humbly laid,
That men might know, that while he died he prayed.

XXXIV
"Whilst on his wounds with bootless tears I wept,
That neither helped him, nor eased my care,
One of those aged fathers to him stepped,
And forced his hand that needless weapon spare:
`This sword,' quoth he, `hath yet good token kept,
That of the Pagans' blood he drunk his share,
And blusheth still he could not save his lord,
Rich, strong and sharp, was never better sword.

XXXV
" `Heaven, therefore, will not, though the prince be slain,
Who used erst to wield this precious brand

That so brave blade unused should remain;
But that it pass from strong to stronger hand,
Who with like force can wield the same again,
And longer shall in grace of fortune stand,
And with the same shall bitter vengeance take
On him that Sweno slew, for Sweno's sake.

XXXVI
" `Great Solyman killed Sweno, Solyman
For Sweno's sake, upon this sword must die.
Here, take the blade, and with it haste thee than
Thither where Godfrey doth encamped lie,
And fear not thou that any shall or can
Or stop thy way, or lead thy steps awry;
For He that doth thee on this message send,
Thee with His hand shall guide, keep and defend.

XXXVII
" `Arrived there it is His blessed will,
With true report that thou declare and tell
The zeal, the strength, the courage and the skill
In thy beloved lord that late did dwell,
How for Christ's sake he came his blood to spill,
And sample left to all of doing well,
That future ages may admire his deed,
And courage take when his brave end they read.

XXXVIII
" `It resteth now, thou know that gentle knight
That of this sword shall be thy master's heir,
It is Rinaldo young, with whom in might
And martial skill no champion may compare,
Give it to him and say, "The Heavens bright
Of this revenge to him commit the care."
While thus I listened what this old man said,
A wonder new from further speech us stayed;

XXXIX

"For there whereas the wounded body lay,
A stately tomb with curious work, behold,
And wondrous art was built out of the clay,
Which, rising round, the carcass did enfold;
With words engraven in the marble gray,
The warrior's name, his worth and praise that told,
On which I gazing stood, and often read
That epitaph of my dear master dead.

XL

" `Among his soldiers,' quoth the hermit, `here
Must Sweno's corpse remain in marble chest,
While up to heaven are flown their spirits dear,
To live in endless joy forever blest,
His funeral thou hast with many a tear
Accompanied, it's now high time to rest,
Come be my guest, until the morning ray
Shall light the world again, then take thy way.'

XLI

"This said, he led me over holts and hags,
Through thorns and bushes scant my legs I drew
Till underneath a heap of stones and crags
At last he brought me to a secret mew;
Among the bears, wild boars, the wolves and stags,
There dwelt he safe with his disciple true,
And feared no treason, force, nor hurt at all,
His guiltless conscience was his castle's wall.

XLII

"My supper roots; my bed was moss and leaves;
But weariness in little rest found ease:
But when the purple morning night bereaves
Of late usurped rule on lands and seas,

205

Jerusalem Delivered

His loathed couch each wakeful hermit leaves,
To pray rose they, and I, for so they please,
I congee took when ended was the same,
And hitherward, as they advised me, came."

XLIII
The Dane his woful tale had done, when thus
The good Prince Godfrey answered him, "Sir knight,
Thou bringest tidings sad and dolorous,
For which our heavy camp laments of right,
Since so brave troops and so dear friends to us,
One hour hath spent, in one unlucky fight;
And so appeared hath thy master stout,
As lightning doth, now kindled, now quenched out.

XLIV
"But such a death and end exceedeth all
The conquests vain of realms, or spoils of gold,
Nor aged Rome's proud stately capital,
Did ever triumph yet like theirs behold;
They sit in heaven on thrones celestial,
Crowned with glory, for their conquest bold,
Where each his hurts I think to other shows,
And glory in those bloody wounds and blows.

XLV
"But thou who hast part of thy race to run,
With haps and hazards of this world ytost,
rejoice, for those high honors they have won,
Which cannot be by chance or fortune crossed:
But for thou askest for Bertoldo's son,
Know, that he wandereth, banished from this host,
And till of him new tidings some man tell,
Within this camp I deem it best thou dwell."

XLVI

206

Jerusalem Delivered

These words of theirs in many a soul renewed
The sweet remembrance of fair Sophia's child,
Some with salt tears for him their cheeks bedewed,
Lest evil betide him mongst the Pagans wild,
And every one his valiant prowess showed,
And of his battles stories long compiled,
Telling the Dane his acts and conquests past,
Which made his ears amazed, his heart aghast.

XLVII
Now when remembrance of the youth had wrought
A tender pity in each softened mind,
Behold returned home with all they caught
The bands that were to forage late assigned,
And with them in abundance great they brought
Both flocks and herds of every sort and kind.
And corn, although not much, and hay to feed
Their noble steeds and coursers when they need.

XLVIII
They also brought of misadventure sad
Tokens and signs, seemed too apparent true,
Rinaldo's armor, frushed and hacked they had,
Oft pierced through, with blood besmeared new;
About the camp, for always rumors bad
Are farthest spread, these woful tidings flew.
Longing to see what they were loth to know.

XLIX
His heavy hauberk was both seen and known,
And his brand shield, wherein displayed flies
The bird that proves her chickens for their own
By looking against the sun with open eyes;
That shield was to the Pagans often shown,
In many a hard and hardy enterprise,
But now with many a gash and many a stroke

They see, and sigh to see it, frushed and broke.

L
While all his soldiers whispered under hand,
And here and there the fault and cause do lay,
Godfrey before him called Aliprand
Captain of those that brought of late this prey,
A man who did on points of virtue stand,
Blameless in words, and true whate'er he say,
"Say," quoth the duke, "where you this armor had,
Hide not the truth, but tell it good or bad."

LI
He answered him, "As far from hence think I
As on two days a speedy post well rideth,
To Gaza–ward a little plain doth lie,
Itself among the steepy hills which hideth,
Through it slow falling from the mountains high,
A rolling brook twixt bush and bramble glideth,
Clad with thick shade of boughs of broad–leaved treen,
Fit place for men to lie in wait unseen.

LII
"Thither, to seek some flocks or herds, we went
Perchance close hid under the green–wood shaw,
And found the springing grass with blood besprent,
A warrior tumbled in his blood we saw,
His arms though dusty, bloody, hacked and rent,
Yet well we knew, when near the corse we draw;
To which, to view his face, in vain I started,
For from his body his fair head was parted;

LIII
"His right hand wanted eke, with many a wound
The trunk through pierced was from back to breast,
A little by, his empty helm we found

208

The silver eagle shining on his crest;
To spy at whom to ask we gazed round,
A child then toward us his steps addressed,
But when us armed by the corse he spied,
He ran away his fearful face to hide:

LIV
"But we pursued him, took him, spake him fair,
Till comforted at last he answer made,
How that, the day before, he saw repair
A band of soldiers from that forest shade,
Of whom one carried by the golden hair
A head but late cut off with murdering blade,
The face was fair and young, and on the chin
No sign of heard to bud did yet begin.

LV
"And how in sindal wrapt away he bore
That head with him hung at his saddle–bow.
And how the murtherers by the arms they wore,
For soldiers of our camp he well did know;
The carcass I disarmed and weeping sore,
Because I guessed who should that harness owe,
Away I brought it, but first order gave,
That noble body should be laid in grave.

LVI
"But if it be his trunk whom I believe,
A nobler tomb his worth deserveth well."
This said, good Aliprando took his leave,
Of certain troth he had no more to tell,
Sore sighed the duke, so did these news him grieve,
Fears in his heart, doubts in his bosom dwell,
He yearned to know, to find and learns the truth,
And punish would them that had slain the youth.

LVII

But now the night dispread her lazy wings
O'er the broad fields of heaven's bright wilderness,
Sleep, the soul's rest, and ease of careful things,
Buried in happy peace both more and less,
Thou Argillan alone, whom sorrow stings,
Still wakest, musing on great deeds I guess,
Nor sufferest in thy watchful eyes to creep
The sweet repose of mild and gentle sleep.

LVIII

This man was strong of limb, and all his 'says
Were bold, of ready tongue, and working sprite,
Near Trento born, bred up in brawls and frays,
In jars, in quarrels, and in civil fight,
Which exiled, the hills and public ways
He filled with blood, and robberies day and night
Until to Asia's wars at last he came,
And boldly there he served, and purchased fame.

LIX

He closed his eyes at last when day drew near.
Yet slept he not, but senseless lay opprest
With strange amazedness and sudden fear
Which false Alecto breathed in his breast,
His working powers within deluded were,
Stone still he quiet lay, yet took no rest,
For to his thought the fiend herself presented,
And with strange visions his weak brain tormented.

LX

A murdered body huge beside him stood,
Of head and right hand both but lately spoiled,
His left hand bore the head, whose visage good,
Both pale and wan, with dust and gore defoiled,
Yet spake, though dead, with whose sad words the blood

Forth at his lips in huge abundance boiled,
"Fly, Argillan, from this false camp fly far,
Whose guide, a traitor; captains, murderers are.

LXI

"Godfrey hath murdered me by treason vile,
What favor then hope you my trusty friends?
His villain heart is full of fraud and guile,
To your destruction all his thoughts he bends,
Yet if thou thirst of praise for noble stile,
If in thy strength thou trust, thy strength that ends
All hard assays, fly not, first with his blood
Appease my ghost wandering by Lethe flood;

LXII

"I will thy weapon whet, inflame thine ire,
Arm thy right hand, and strengthen every part."
This said; even while she spake she did inspire
With fury, rage, and wrath his troubled heart:
The man awaked, and from his eyes like fire
The poisoned sparks of headstrong madness start,
And armed as he was, forth is he gone,
And gathered all the Italian bands in one.

LXIII

He gathered them where lay the arms that late
Were good Rinaldo's; then with semblance stout
And furious words his fore–conceived hate
In bitter speeches thus he vomits out;
"Is not this people barbarous and ingrate,
In whom truth finds no place, faith takes no rout?
Whose thirst unquenched is of blood and gold,
Whom no yoke boweth, bridle none can hold.

LXIV

"So much we suffered have these seven years long,

Under this servile and unworthy yoke,
That thorough Rome and Italy our wrong
A thousand years hereafter shall be spoke:
I count not how Cilicia's kingdom strong,
Subdued was by Prince Tancredi's stroke,
Nor how false Baldwin him that land bereaves
Of virtue's harvest, fraud there reaped the sheaves:
LXV
"Nor speak I how each hour, at every need,
Quick, ready, resolute at all assays,
With fire and sword we hasted forth with speed,
And bore the brunt of all their fights and frays;
But when we had performed and done the deed,
At ease and leisure they divide the preys,
We reaped naught but travel for our toil,
Theirs was the praise, the realms, the gold, the spoil.
LXVI
"Yet all this season were we willing blind,
Offended unrevenged, wronged but unwroken,
Light griefs could not provoke our quiet mind,
But now, alas! the mortal blow is stroken,
Rinaldo have they slain, and law of kind,
Of arms, of nations, and of high heaven broken,
Why doth not heaven kill them with fire and thunder?
To swallow them why cleaves not earth asunder?

LXVII
"They have Rinaldo slain, the sword and shield
Of Christ's true faith, and unrevenged he lies;
Still unrevenged lieth in the field
His noble corpse to feed the crows and pies:
Who murdered him? who shall us certain yield?
Who sees not that, although he wanted eyes?
Who knows not how the Italian chivalry
Proud Godfrey and false Baldwin both envy

LXVIII

"What need we further proof? Heaven, heaven, I swear,
Will not consent herein we be beguiled,
This night I saw his murdered sprite appear,
Pale, sad and wan, with wounds and blood defiled,
A spectacle full both of grief and fear;
Godfrey, for murdering him, the ghost reviled.
I saw it was no dream, before mine eyes,
Howe'er I look, still, still methinks it flies.

LXIX

"What shall we do? shall we be governed still
By this false hand, contaminate with blood?
Or else depart and travel forth, until
To Euphrates we come, that sacred flood,
Where dwells a people void of martial skill,
Whose cities rich, whose land is fat and good,
Where kingdoms great we may at ease provide,
Far from these Frenchmen's malice, from their pride;

LXX

"Then let us go, and no revengement take
For this brave knight, though it lie in our power:
No, no, that courage rather newly wake,
Which never sleeps in fear and dread one hour,
And this pestiferous serpent, poisoned snake,
Of all our knights that hath destroyed the flower,
First let us slay, and his deserved end
Example make to him that kills his friend.

LXXI

"I will, I will, if your courageous force,
Dareth so much as it can well perform,
Tear out his cursed heart without remorse,
The nest of treason false and guile enorm."
Thus spake the angry knight with headlong course;

The rest him followed with a furious storm,
"Arm, arm." they cried, to arms the soldiers ran.
And as they run, "Arm, arm," cried every man.

LXXII
Mongst them Alecto strowed wasteful fire,
Envenoming the hearts of most and least,
Folly, disdain, madness, strife, rancor, ire,
Thirst to shed blood, in every breast increased,
This ill spread far, and till it set on fire
With rage the Italian lodgings, never ceased,
From thence unto the Switzers' camp it went,
And last infected every English tent.

LXXIII
Not public loss of their beloved knight,
Alone stirred up their rage and wrath untamed,
But fore–conceived griefs, and quarrels light,
The ire still nourished, and still inflamed,
Awaked was each former cause of spite,
The Frenchmen cruel and unjust they named,
And with bold threats they made their hatred known,
Hate seld kept close, and oft unwisely shown:

LXXIV
Like boiling liquor in a seething pot,
That fumeth, swelleth high, and bubbleth fast,
Till o'er the brims among the embers hot,
Part of the broth and of the scum is cast,
Their rage and wrath those few appeased not
In whom of wisdom yet remained some taste,
Camillo, William, Tancred were away,
And all whose greatness might their madness stay.

LXXV
Now headlong ran to harness in this heat

These furious people, all on heaps confused,
The roaring trumpets battle gan to threat,
As it in time of mortal war is used,
The messengers ran to Godfredo great,
And bade him arm, while on this noise he mused,
And Baldwin first well clad in iron hard,
Stepped to his side, a sure and faithful guard.

LXXVI
Their murmurs heard, to heaven he lift his een,
As was his wont, to God for aid he fled;
"O Lord, thou knowest this right hand of mine
Abhorred ever civil blood to shed,
Illumine their dark souls with light divine,
Repress their rage, by hellish fury bred,
The innocency of my guiltless mind
Thou knowest, and make these know, with fury blind."

LXXVII
Tis said he felt infused in each vein,
A sacred heat from heaven above distilled,
A heat in man that courage could constrain
That his brave look with awful boldness filled.
Well guarded forth he went to meet the train
Of those that would revenge Rinaldo killed;
And though their threats he heard, and saw them bent
To arms on every side, yet on he went.

LXXVIII
Above his hauberk strong a coat he ware,
Embroidered fair with pearl and rich stone,
His hands were naked, and his face was bare,
Wherein a lamp of majesty bright shone;
He shook his golden mace, wherewith he dare
Resist the force of his rebellious foe:
Thus he appeared, and thus he gan them teach,

In shape an angel, and a God in speech:

LXXIX

"What foolish words? what threats be these I hear?
What noise of arms? who dares these tumults move?
Am I so honored? stand you so in fear?
Where is your late obedience? where your love?
Of Godfrey's falsehood who can witness bear?
Who dare or will these accusations prove?
Perchance you look I should entreaties bring,
Sue for your favors, or excuse the thing.

LXXX

"Ah, God forbid these lands should hear or see
Him so disgraced at whose great name they quake;
This sceptre and my noble acts for me
A true defence before the world can make:
Yet for sharp justice governed shall be
With clemency, I will no vengeance take
For this offence, but for Rinaldo's love,
I pardon you, hereafter wiser prove.

LXXXI

"But Argillano's guilty blood shall wash
This stain away, who kindled this debate,
And led by hasty rage and fury rash,
To these disorders first undid the gate;"
While thus he spoke, the lightning beams did flash
Out of his eyes of majesty and state,
That Argillan, — who would have thought it? — shook
For fear and terror, conquered with his look.

LXXXII

The rest with indiscreet and foolish wrath
Who threatened late with words of shame and pride,
Whose hands so ready were to harm and scath,

And brandished bright swords on every side;
Now hushed and still attend what Godfrey saith,
With shame and fear their bashful looks they hide,
And Argillan they let in chains be bound,
Although their weapons him environed round.

LXXXIII
So when a lion shakes his dreadful mane,
And beats his tail with courage proud and wroth,
If his commander come, who first took pain
To tame his youth, his lofty crest down goeth,
His threats he feareth, and obeys the rein
Of thralldom base, and serviceage, though loth,
Nor can his sharp teeth nor his armed paws,
Force him rebel against his ruler's laws.

LXXXIV
Fame as a winged warrior they beheld,
With semblant fierce and furious look that stood,
And in his left hand had a splendent shield
Wherewith he covered safe their chieftain good,
His other hand a naked sword did wield,
From which distilling fell the lukewarm blood,
The blood pardie of many a realm and town,
Whereon the Lord his wrath had poured down.

LXXXV
Thus was the tumult, without bloodshed, ended.
Their arms laid down, strife into exile sent.
Godfrey his thoughts to greater actions bended.
And homeward to his rich pavilion went,
For to assault the fortress he intended
Before the second or third day were spent;
Meanwhile his timber wrought he oft surveyed
Whereof his ram and engines great he made.

NINTH BOOK

THE ARGUMENT.
Alecto false great Solyman doth move
By night the Christians in their tents to kill:
But God who their intents saw from above,
Sends Michael down from his sacred hill:
The spirits foul to hell the angels drove;
The knights delivered from the witch, at will
Destroy the Pagans, scatter all their host:
The Soldan flies when all his bands are lost.

I
The grisly child of Erebus the grim,
Who saw these tumults done and tempest spent,
Gainst stream of grace who ever strove to swim
And all her thoughts against Heaven's wisdom bent,
Departed now, bright Titan's beams were dim
And fruitful lands waxed barren as she went.
She sought the rest of her infernal crew,
New storms to raise, new broils, and tumults new.

II
She, that well wist her sisters had enticed,
By their false arts, far from the Christian host,
Tancred, Rinaldo, and the rest, best prized
For martial skill, for might esteemed most,
Said, of these discords and these strifes advised,
"Great Solyman, when day his light hath lost,
These Christians shall assail with sudden war,
And kill them all while thus they strive and jar."

Jerusalem Delivered

III

With that where Solyman remained she flew,
And found him out with his Arabian bands,
Great Solyman, of all Christ's foes untrue,
Boldest of courage, mightiest of his hands,
Like him was none of all that earth–bred crew
That heaped mountains on the Aemonian sands,
Of Turks he sovereign was, and Nice his seat,
Where late he dwelt, and ruled that kingdom great.

IV

The lands forenenst the Greekish shore he held,
From Sangar's mouth to crooked Meander's fall,
Where they of Phrygia, Mysia, Lydia dwelled,
Bithynia's towns, and Pontus' cities all:
But when the hearts of Christian princes swelled,
And rose in arms to make proud Asia thrall,
Those lands were won where he did sceptre wield
And he twice beaten was in pitched field.

V

When Fortune oft he had in vain assayed,
And spent his forces, which availed him naught,
To Egypt's king himself he close conveyed,
Who welcomed him as he could best have thought,
Glad in his heart, and inly well apayed,
That to his court so great a lord was brought:
For he decreed his armies huge to bring
To succor Juda land and Juda's king.

VI

But, ere he open war proclaimed, he would
That Solyman should kindle first the fire,
And with huge sums of false enticing gold
The Arabian thieves he sent him forth to hire,

Jerusalem Delivered

While he the Asian lords and Morians hold
Unites; the Soldan won to his desire
Those outlaws, ready aye for gold to fight,
The hope of gain hath such alluring might.

VII

Thus made their captain to destroy and burn,
In Juda land he entered is so far,
That all the ways whereby he should return
By Godfrey's people kept and stopped are,
And now he gan his former losses mourn,
This wound had hit him on an elder scar,
On great adventures ran his hardy thought,
But naught assured, he yet resolved on naught.

VIII

To him Alecto came, and semblant bore
Of one whose age was great, whose looks were grave,
Whose cheeks were bloodless, and whose locks were hoar
Mustaches strouting long and chin close shave,
A steepled turban on her head she wore,
Her garment wide, and by her side, her glaive,
Her gilden quiver at her shoulders hung,
And in her hand a bow was, stiff and strong.

IX

"We have." Quoth she,."through wildernesses gone,
Through sterile sands, strange paths, and uncouth ways,
Yet spoil or booty have we gotten none,
Nor victory deserving fame or praise,
Godfrey meanwhile to ruin stick and stone
Of this fair town, with battery sore assays;
And if awhile we rest, we shall behold
This glorious city smoking lie in mould.

X

Jerusalem Delivered

"Are sheep–cotes burnt, or preys of sheep or kine,
The cause why Solyman these bands did arm?
Canst thou that kingdom lately lost of thine
Recover thus, or thus redress thy harm?
No, no, when heaven's small candles next shall shine,
Within their tents give them a bold alarm;
Believe Araspes old, whose grave advice
Thou hast in exile proved, and proved in Nice.

XI
"He feareth naught, he doubts no sudden broil
From these ill–armed and worse–hearted bands,
He thinks this people, used to rob and spoil,
To such exploit dares not lift up their hands;
Up then and with thy courage put to foil
This fearless camp, while thus secure it stands."
This said, her poison in his breast she hides,
And then to shapeless air unseen she glides.

XII
The Soldan cried, "O thou which in my thought
Increased hast my rage and fury so,
Nor seem'st a wight of mortal metal wrought,
I follow thee, whereso thee list to go,
Mountains of men by dint of sword down brought
Thou shalt behold, and seas of red blood flow
Where'er I go; only be thou my guide
When sable night the azure skies shall hide."

XIII
When this was said, he mustered all his crew,
Reproved the cowards, and allowed the bold:
His forward camp, inspired with courage new,
Was ready dight to follow where he would:
Alecto's self the warning trumpet blew
And to the wind his standard great unrolled,

221

Jerusalem Delivered

Thus on they marched, and thus on they went,
Of their approach their speed the news prevent.

XIV
Alecto left them, and her person dight
Like one that came some tidings new to tell:
It was the time, when first the rising night
Her sparkling diamonds poureth forth to sell,
When, into Sion come, she marched right
Where Juda's aged tyrant used to dwell,
To whom of Solyman's designment bold,
The place, the manner, and the time she told.
XV
Their mantle dark, the grisly shadows spread,
Stained with spots of deepest sanguine hue,
Warm drops of blood, on earth's black visage shed,
Supplied the place of pure and precious dew,
The moon and stars for fear of sprites were fled,
The shrieking goblins eachwhere howling flew,
The furies roar, the ghosts and fairies yell,
The earth was filled with devils, and empty hell.

XVI
The Soldan fierce, through all this horror, went
Toward the camp of his redoubted foes,
The night was more than half consumed and spent;
Now headlong down the western hill she goes,
When distant scant a mile from Godfrey's tent
He let his people there awhile repose,
And victualled them, and then he boldly spoke
These words which rage and courage might provoke:

XVII
"See there a camp, full stuffed of spoils and preys,
Not half so strong as false report recordeth;
See there the storehouse, where their captain lays

Our treasures stolen, where Asia's wealth he hoardeth;
Now chance the ball unto our racket plays,
Take then the vantage which good luck affordeth;
For all their arms, their horses, gold and treasure
Are ours, ours without loss, harm or displeasure.

XVIII
"Nor is this camp that great victorious host
That slew the Persian lords, and Nice hath won:
For those in this long war are spent and lost,
These are the dregs, the wine is all outrun,
And these few left, are drowned and dead almost
In heavy sleep, the labor half is done
To send them headlong to Avernus deep,
For little differs death and heavy sleep.

XIX
"Come, come, this sword the passage open shall
Into their camp, and on their bodies slain
We will pass o'er their rampire and their wall;
This blade, as scythes cut down the fields of grain,
Shall cut them so, Christ's kingdom now shall fall,
Asia her freedom, you shall praise obtain."
Thus he inflamed his soldiers to the fight,
And led them on through silence of the night.

XX
The sentinel by starlight, lo, descried
This mighty Soldan and his host draw near,
Who found not as he hoped the Christians' guide
Unware, ne yet unready was his gear:
The scouts, when this huge army they descried,
Ran back, and gan with shouts the 'larum rear;
The watch stert up and drew their weapons bright,
And busked them bold to battle and to fight.

Jerusalem Delivered

XXI

The Arabians wist they could not come unseen,
And therefore loud their jarring trumpets sound,
Their yelling cries to heaven upheaved been,
The horses thundered on the solid ground,
The mountains roared, and the valley green,
The echoes sighed from the caves around,
Alecto with her brand, kindled in hell,
Tokened to them in David's tower that dwell.

XXII

Before the rest forth pricked the Soldan fast,
Against the watch, not yet in order just,
As swift as hideous Boreas' hasty blast
From hollow rocks when first his storms outburst,
The raging floods, that trees and rocks down cast,
Thunders, that towns and towers drive to dust:
Earthquakes, to tear the world in twain that threat,
Are naught, compared to his fury great.

XXIII

He struck no blow, but that his foe he hit;
And never hit, but made a grievous wound:
And never wounded, but death followed it;
And yet no peril, hurt or harm he found,
No weapon on his hardened helmet bit,
No puissant stroke his senses once astound,
Yet like a bell his tinkling helmet rung,
And thence flew flames of fire and sparks among.

XXIV

Himself well nigh had put the watch to flight,
A jolly troop of Frenchmen strong and stout,
When his Arabians came by heaps to fight,
Covering, like raging floods, the fields about;
The beaten Christians run away full light,

Jerusalem Delivered

The Pagans, mingled with the flying rout,
Entered their camp, and filled, as they stood,
Their tents with ruin, slaughter, death and blood.

XXV

High on the Soldan's helm enamelled laid
An hideous dragon, armed with many a scale,
With iron paws, and leathern wings displayed,
Which twisted on a knot her forked tail,
With triple tongue it seemed she hissed and brayed,
About her jaws the froth and venom trail,
And as he stirred, and as his foes him hit,
So flames to cast and fire she seemed to spit.

XXVI

With this strange light, the Soldan fierce appeared
Dreadful to those that round about him been,
As to poor sailors, when huge storms are reared,
With lightning flash the rafting seas are seen;
Some fled away, because his strength they feared,
Some bolder gainst him bent their weapons keen,
And forward night, in evils and mischiefs pleased,
Their dangers hid, and dangers still increased.

XXVII

Among the rest that strove to merit praise,
Was old Latinus, born by Tiber's bank,
To whose stout heart in fights and bloody frays,
For all his eild, base fear yet never sank;
Five sons he had, the comforts of his days,
That from his side in no adventure shrank,
But long before their time, in iron strong
They clad their members, tender, soft and young.

XXVIII

The bold ensample of their father's might

225

Their weapons whetted and their wrath increased,
"Come let us go," quoth he, "where yonder knight
Upon our soldiers makes his bloody feast,
Let not their slaughter once your hearts affright,
Where danger most appears, there fear it least,
For honor dwells in hard attempts, my sons,
And greatest praise, in greatest peril, wons."
XXIX
Her tender brood the forest's savage queen,
Ere on their crests their rugged manes appear,
Before their mouths by nature armed been,
Or paws have strength a silly lamb to tear,
So leadeth forth to prey, and makes them keen,
And learns by her ensample naught to fear
The hunter, in those desert woods that takes
The lesser beasts whereon his feast he makes.

XXX
The noble father and his hardy crew
Fierce Solyman on every side invade,
At once all six upon the Soldan flew,
With lances sharp, and strong encounters made,
His broken spear the eldest boy down threw,
And boldly, over–boldly, drew his blade,
Wherewith he strove, but strove therewith in vain,
The Pagan's steed, unmarked, to have slain.

XXXI
But as a mountain or a cape of land
Assailed with storms and seas on every side,
Doth unremoved, steadfast, still withstand
Storm, thunder, lightning, tempest, wind, and tide:
The Soldan so withstood Latinus' band,
And unremoved did all their justs abide,
And of that hapless youth, who hurt his steed,
Down to the chin he cleft in twain the head.

XXXII

Kind Aramante, who saw his brother slain,
To hold him up stretched forth his friendly arm,
Oh foolish kindness, and oh pity vain,
To add our proper loss, to other's harm!
The prince let fall his sword, and cut in twain
About his brother twined, the child's weak arm.
Down from their saddles both together slide,
Together mourned they, and together died.

XXXIII

That done, Sabino's lance with nimble force
He cut in twain, and 'gainst the stripling bold
He spurred his steed, that underneath his horse
The hardy infant tumbled on the mould,
Whose soul, out squeezed from his bruised corpse,
With ugly painfulness forsook her hold,
And deeply mourned that of so sweet a cage
She left the bliss, and joys of youthful age.

XXXIV

But Picus yet and Lawrence were on live,
Whom at one birth their mother fair brought out,
A pair whose likeness made the parents strive
Oft which was which, and joyed in their doubt:
But what their birth did undistinguished give,
The Soldan's rage made known, for Picus stout
Headless at one huge blow he laid in dust,
And through the breast his gentle brother thrust.

XXXV

Their father, but no father now, alas!
When all his noble sons at once were slain,
In their five deaths so often murdered was,
I know not how his life could him sustain,

Except his heart were forged of steel or brass,
Yet still he lived, pardie, he saw not plain
Their dying looks, although their deaths he knows,
It is some ease not to behold our woes.

XXXVI

He wept not, for the night her curtain spread
Between his cause of weeping and his eyes,
But still he mourned and on sharp vengeance fed,
And thinks he conquers, if revenged he dies;
He thirsts the Soldan's heathenish blood to shed,
And yet his own at less than naught doth prize,
Nor can he tell whether he liefer would,
Or die himself, or kill the Pagan bold.

XXXVII

At last, "Is this right hand," quoth he, "so weak,
That thou disdain'st gainst me to use thy might?
Can it naught do? can this tongue nothing speak
That may provoke thine ire, thy wrath and spite?"
With that he struck, his anger great to wreak,
A blow, that pierced the mail and metal bright,
And in his flank set ope a floodgate wide,
Whereat the blood out streamed from his side.

XXXVIII

Provoked with his cry, and with that blow,
The Turk upon him gan his blade discharge,
He cleft his breastplate, having first pierced through,
Lined with seven bulls' hides, his mighty targe,
And sheathed his weapons in his guts below;
Wretched Latinus at that issue large,
And at his mouth, poured out his vital blood,
And sprinkled with the same his murdered brood.

XXXIX

Jerusalem Delivered

On Apennine like as a sturdy tree,
Against the winds that makes resistance stout,
If with a storm it overturned be,
Falls down and breaks the trees and plants about;
So Latine fell, and with him felled he
And slew the nearest of the Pagans' rout,
A worthy end, fit for a man of fame,
That dying, slew; and conquered, overcame.

XL
Meanwhile the Soldan strove his rage
To satisfy with blood of Christian spilled,
The Arabians heartened by their captain stern,
With murder every tent and cabin filled,
Henry the English knight, and Olipherne,
O fierce Draguto, by thy hands were killed!
Gilbert and Philip were by Ariadene
Both slain, both born upon the banks of Rhone.

XLI
Albazar with his mace Ernesto slew,
Under Algazel Engerlan down fell,
But the huge murder of the meaner crew,
Or manner of their deaths, what tongue can tell?
Godfrey, when first the heathen trumpets blew,
Awaked, which heard, no fear could make him dwell,
But he and his were up and armed ere long,
And marched forward with a squadron strong.

XLII
He that well heard the rumor and the cry,
And marked the tumult still grow more and more,
The Arabian thieves he judged by and by
Against his soldiers made this battle sore;
For that they forayed all the countries nigh,
And spoiled the fields, the duke knew well before,

Yet thought he not they had the hardiment
So to assail him in his armed tent.
XLIII
All suddenly he heard, while on he went,
How to the city–ward, "Arm, arm!" they cried,
The noise upreared to the firmament,
With dreadful howling filled the valleys wlde:
This was Clorinda, whom the king forth sent
To battle, and Argantes by her side.
The duke, this heard, to Guelpho turned, and prayed
Him his lieutenant be, and to him said:

XLIV
"You hear this new alarm from yonder part,
That from the town breaks out with so much rage,
Us needeth much your valor and your art
To calm their fury, and their heat to 'suage;
Go thither then, and with you take some part
Of these brave soldiers of mine equipage,
While with the residue of my champions bold
I drive these wolves again out of our fold."

XLV
They parted, this agreed on them between,
By divers paths, Lord Guelpho to the hill,
And Godfrey hasted where the Arabians keen
His men like silly sheep destroy and kill;
But as he went his troops increased been,
From every part the people flocked still,
That now grown strong enough, he 'proached nigh
Where the fierce Turk caused many a Christian die.

XLVI
So from the top of Vesulus the cold,
Down to the sandy valleys, tumbleth Po,
Whose streams the further from the fountain rolled

Still stronger wax, and with more puissance go;
And horned like a bull his forehead bold
He lifts, and o'er his broken banks doth flow,
And with his horns to pierce the sea assays,
To which he proffereth war, not tribute pays.

XLVII

The duke his men fast flying did espy,
And thither ran, and thus, displeased, spake,
"What fear is this? Oh, whither do you fly?
See who they be that this pursuit do make,
A heartless band, that dare no battle try,
Who wounds before dare neither give nor take,
Against them turn your stern eye's threatening sight,
An angry look will put them all to flight."

XLVIII

This said, he spurred forth where Solyman
Destroyed Christ's vineyard like a savage boar,
Through streams of blood, through dust and dirt he ran,
O'er heaps of bodies wallowing in their gore,
The squadrons close his sword to ope began,
He broke their ranks, behind, beside, before,
And, where he goes, under his feet he treads
The armed Saracens, and barbed steeds.

XLIX

This slaughter–house of angry Mars he passed,
Where thousands dead, half–dead, and dying were.
The hardy Soldan saw him come in haste,
Yet neither stepped aside nor shrunk for fear,
But busked him bold to fight, aloft he cast
His blade, prepared to strike, and stepped near,
These noble princes twain, so Fortune wrought
From the world's end here met, and here they fought:

L

With virtue, fury; strength with courage strove,
For Asia's mighty empire, who can tell
With how strange force their cruel blows they drove?
How sore their combat was? how fierce, how fell?
Great deeds they wrought, each other's harness clove;
Yet still in darkness, more the ruth, they dwell.
The night their acts her black veil covered under,
Their acts whereat the sun, the world might wonder.

LI

The Christians by their guide's ensample hearted,
Of their best armed made a squadron strong,
And to defend their chieftain forth they started:
The Pagans also saved their knight from wrong,
Fortune her favors twixt them evenly parted,
Fierce was the encounter, bloody, doubtful, long;
These won, those lost; these lost, those won again;
The loss was equal, even the numbers slain.

LII

With equal rage, as when the southern wind,
Meeteth in battle strong the northern blast,
The sea and air to neither is resigned,
But cloud gainst cloud, and wave gainst wave they cast:
So from this skirmish neither part declined,
But fought it out, and kept their footings fast,
And oft with furious shock together rush,
And shield gainst shield, and helm gainst helm they crush.

LIII

The battle eke to Sionward grew hot,
The soldiers slain, the hardy knights were killed,
Legions of sprites from Limbo's prisons got,
The empty air, the hills and valleys filled,
Hearting the Pagans that they shrinked not,
Till where they stood their dearest blood they spilled;

Jerusalem Delivered

And with new rage Argantes they inspire,
Whose heat no flames, whose burning need no fire.

LIV

Where he came in he put to shameful flight
The fearful watch, and o'er the trenches leaped,
Even with the ground he made the rampire's height,
And murdered bodies in the ditch unheaped,
So that his greedy mates with labor light,
Amid the tents, a bloody harvest reaped:
Clorinda went the proud Circassian by,
So from a piece two chained bullets fly.

LV

Now fled the Frenchmen, when in lucky hour
Arrived Guelpho, and his helping band,
He made them turn against this stormy shower,
And with bold face their wicked foes withstand.
Sternly they fought, that from their wounds downpour
The streams of blood and run on either hand:
The Lord of heaven meanwhile upon this fight,
From his high throne bent down his gracious sight.

LVI

From whence with grace and goodness compassed round,
He ruleth, blesseth, keepeth all he wrought,
Above the air, the fire, the sea and ground,
Our sense, our wit, our reason and our thought,
Where persons three, with power and glory crowned,
Are all one God, who made all things of naught,
Under whose feet, subjected to his grace,
Sit nature, fortune, motion, time and place.

LVII

This is the place, from whence like smoke and dust
Of this frail world the wealth, the pomp and power,

He tosseth, tumbleth, turneth as he lust,
And guides our life, our death, our end and hour:
No eye, however virtuous, pure and just,
Can view the brightness of that glorious bower,
On every side the blessed spirits be,
Equal in joys, though differing in degree.

LVIII
With harmony of their celestial song
The palace echoed from the chambers pure,
At last he Michael called, in harness strong
Of never yielding diamonds armed sure,
"Behold," quoth he, "to do despite and wrong
To that dear flock my mercy hath in cure,
How Satan from hell's loathsome prison sends
His ghosts, his sprites, his furies and his fiends.

LIX
"Go bid them all depart, and leave the care
Of war to soldiers, as doth best pertain:
Bid them forbear to infect the earth and air;
To darken heaven's fair light, bid them refrain;
Bid them to Acheron's black flood repair,
Fit house for them, the house of grief and pain:
There let their king himself and them torment,
So I command, go tell them mine intent."

LX
This said, the winged warrior low inclined
At his Creator's feet with reverence due;
Then spread his golden feathers to the wind,
And swift as thought away the angel flew,
He passed the light, and shining fire assigned
The glorious seat of his selected crew,
The mover first, and circle crystalline,
The firmament, where fixed stars all shine;

Jerusalem Delivered

LXI

Unlike in working then, in shape and show,
At his left hand, Saturn he left and Jove,
And those untruly errant called I trow,
Since he errs not, who them doth guide and move:
The fields he passed then, whence hail and snow,
Thunder and rain fall down from clouds above,
Where heat and cold, dryness and moisture strive,
Whose wars all creatures kill, and slain, revive.

LXII

The horrid darkness, and the shadows dun
Dispersed he with his eternal wings,
The flames which from his heavenly eyes outrun
Beguiled the earth and all her sable things;
After a storm so spreadeth forth the sun
His rays and binds the clouds in golden strings,
Or in the stillness of a moonshine even
A falling star so glideth down from Heaven.

LXIII

But when the infernal troop he 'proached near,
That still the Pagans' ire and rage provoke,
The angel on his wings himself did bear,
And shook his lance, and thus at last he spoke:
"Have you not learned yet to know and fear
The Lord's just wrath, and thunder's dreadful stroke?
Or in the torments of your endless ill,
Are you still fierce, still proud, rebellious still?

LXIV

"The Lord hath sworn to break the iron bands
The brazen gates of Sion's fort which close,
Who is it that his sacred will withstands?
Against his wrath who dares himself oppose?
Go hence, you cursed, to your appointed lands,

The realms of death, of torments, and of woes,
And in the deeps of that infernal lake
Your battles fight, and there your triumphs make.

LXV

"There tyrannize upon the souls you find
Condemned to woe, and double still their pains;
Where some complain, where some their teeth do grind,
Some howl, and weep, some clank their iron chains:"
This said they fled, and those that stayed behind,
With his sharp lance he driveth and constrains;
They sighing left the lands, his silver sheep
Where Hesperus doth lead, doth feed, and keep.

LXVI

And toward hell their lazy wings display,
To wreak their malice on the damned ghosts;
The birds that follow Titan's hottest ray,
Pass not in so great flocks to warmer coasts,
Nor leaves in so great numbers fall away
When winter nips them with his new—come frosts;
The earth delivered from so foul annoy,
Recalled her beauty, and resumed her joy.

LXVII

But not for this in fierce Argantes' breast
Lessened the rancor and decreased the ire,
Although Alecto left him to infest
With the hot brands of her infernal fire,
Round his armed head his trenchant blade he blest,
And those thick ranks that seemed moist entire
He breaks; the strong, the high, the weak, the low,
Were equalized by his murdering blow.

LXVIII

Not far from him amid the blood and dust,

Heads, arms, and legs, Clorinda strewed wide
Her sword through Berengarius' breast she thrust,
Quite through the heart, where life doth chiefly bide,
And that fell blow she struck so sure and just,
That at his back his life and blood forth glide;
Even in the mouth she smote Albinus then,
And cut in twain the visage of the man.

LXIX

Gernier's right hand she from his arm divided,
Whereof but late she had received a wound;
The hand his sword still held, although not guided,
The fingers half alive stirred on the ground;
So from a serpent slain the tail divided
Moves in the grass, rolleth and tumbleth round,
The championess so wounded left the knight,
And gainst Achilles turned her weapon bright.

LXX

Upon his neck light that unhappy blow,
And cut the sinews and the throat in twain,
The head fell down upon the earth below,
And soiled with dust the visage on the plain;
The headless trunk, a woful thing to know,
Still in the saddle seated did remain;
Until his steed, that felt the reins at large,
With leaps and flings that burden did discharge.
LXXI
While thus this fair and fierce Bellona slew
The western lords, and put their troops to flight,
Gildippes raged mongst the Pagan crew,
And low in dust laid many a worthy knight:
Like was their sex, their beauty and their hue,
Like was their youth, their courage and their might;
Yet fortune would they should the battle try
Of mightier foes, for both were framed to die.

LXXII

Yet wished they oft, and strove in vain to meet,
So great betwixt them was the press and throng,
But hardy Guelpho gainst Clorinda sweet
Ventured his sword to work her harm and wrong,
And with a cutting blow so did her greet,
That from her side the blood streamed down along;
But with a thrust an answer sharp she made,
And 'twixt his ribs colored somedeal her blade.

LXXIII

Lord Guelpho struck again, but hit her not,
For strong Osmida haply passed by,
And not meant him, another's wound he got,
That cleft his front in twain above his eye:
Near Guelpho now the battle waxed hot,
For all the troops he led gan thither hie,
And thither drew eke many a Paynim knight,
That fierce, stern, bloody, deadly waxed the fight.

LXXIV

Meanwhile the purple morning peeped o'er
The eastern threshold to our half of land,
And Argillano in this great uproar
From prison loosed was, and what he fand,
Those arms he hent, and to the field them bore,
Resolved to take his chance what came to hand,
And with great acts amid the Pagan host
Would win again his reputation lost.

LXXV

As a fierce steed 'scaped from his stall at large,
Where he had long been kept for warlike need,
Runs through the fields unto the flowery marge
Of some green forest where he used to feed,

His curled mane his shoulders broad doth charge
And from his lofty crest doth spring and spreed,
Thunder his feet, his nostrils fire breathe out,
And with his neigh the world resounds about.

LXXVI
So Argillan rushed forth, sparkled his eyes,
His front high lifted was, no fear therein,
Lightly he leaps and skips, it seems he flies,
He left no sign in dust imprinted thin,
And coming near his foes, he sternly cries,
As one that forced not all their strength a pin,
"You outcasts of the world, you men of naught
What hath in you this boldness newly wrought?

LXXVII
"Too weak are you to bear a helm or shield
Unfit to arm your breast in iron bright,
You run half—naked trembling through the field,
Your blows are feeble, and your hope in flight,
Your facts and all the actions that you wield,
The darkness hides, your bulwark is the night,
Now she is gone, how will your fights succeed?
Now better arms and better hearts you need."

LXXVIII
While thus he spoke, he gave a cruel stroke
Against Algazel's throat with might and main;
And as he would have answered him, and spoke,
He stopped his words, and cut his jaws in twain;
Upon his eyes death spread his misty cloak,
A chilling frost congealed every vein,
He fell, and with his teeth the earth he tore,
Raging in death, and full of rage before.

LXXIX

Then by his puissance mighty Saladine,
Proud Agricalt and Muleasses died,
And at one wondrous blow his weapon fine,
Did Adiazel in two parts divide,
Then through the breast he wounded Ariadine,
Whom dying with sharp taunts he gan deride,
He lifting up uneath his feeble eyes,
To his proud scorns thus answereth, ere he dies:

LXXX

"Not thou, whoe'er thou art, shall glory long
Thy happy conquest in my death, I trow,
Like chance awaits thee from a hand more strong,
Which by my side will shortly lay thee low:"
He smiled, and said, "Of mine hour short or long
Let heaven take care; but here meanwhile die thou,
Pasture for wolves and crows," on him his foot
He set, and drew his sword and life both out.

LXXXI

Among this squadron rode a gentle page,
The Soldan's minion, darling, and delight,
On whose fair chin the spring–time of his age
Yet blossomed out her flowers, small or light;
The sweat spread on his cheeks with heat and rage
Seemed pearls or morning dews on lilies white,
The dust therein uprolled adorned his hair,
His face seemed fierce and sweet, wrathful and fair.

LXXXII

His steed was white, and white as purest snow
That falls on tops of aged Apennine,
Lightning and storm are not so 'swift I trow
As he, to run, to stop, to turn and twine;
A dart his right hand shaked, prest to throw;
His cutlass by his thigh, short, hooked, fine,

Jerusalem Delivered

And braving in his Turkish pomp he shone,
In purple robe, o'erfret with gold and stone.

LXXXIII
The hardy boy, while thirst of warlike praise
Bewitched so his unadvised thought,
Gainst every band his childish strength assays,
And little danger found, though much he sought,
Till Argillan, that watched fit time always
In his swift turns to strike him as he fought,
Did unawares his snow–white courser slay,
And under him his master tumbling lay:

LXXXIV
And gainst his face, where love and pity stand,
To pray him that rich throne of beauty spare,
The cruel man stretched forth his murdering hand,
To spoil those gifts, whereof he had no share:
It seemed remorse and sense was in his brand
Which, lighting flat, to hurt the lad forbare;
But all for naught, gainst him the point he bent
That, what the edge had spared, pierced and rent.

LXXXV
Fierce Solyman that with Godfredo strived
Who first should enter conquest's glorious gate,
Left off the fray and thither headlong drived,
When first he saw the lad in such estate;
He brake the press, and soon enough arrived
To take revenge, but to his aid too late,
Because he saw his Lesbine slain and lost,
Like a sweet flower nipped with untimely frost.

LXXXVI
He saw wax dim the starlight of his eyes,
His ivory neck upon his shoulders fell,

241

In his pale looks kind pity's image lies,
That death even mourned, to hear his passing bell.
His marble heart such soft impression tries,
That midst his wrath his manly tears outwell,
Thou weepest, Solyman, thou that beheld
Thy kingdoms lost, and not one tear could yield.

LXXXVII
But when the murderer's sword he hapt to view
Dropping with blood of his Lesbino dead,
His pity vanished, ire and rage renew,
He had no leisure bootless tears to shed;
But with his blade on Argillano flew,
And cleft his shield, his helmet, and his head,
Down to his throat; and worthy was that blow
Of Solyman, his strength and wrath to show:

LXXXVIII
And not content with this, down from his horse
He lights, and that dead carcass rent and tore,
Like a fierce dog that takes his angry course
To bite the stone which had him hit before.
Oh comfort vain for grief of so great force,
To wound the senseless earth that feels no sore!
But mighty Godfrey 'gainst the Soldan's train
Spent not, this while, his force and blows in vain.

LXXXIX
A thousand hardy Turks affront he had
In sturdy iron armed from head to foot,
Resolved in all adventures good or bad,
In actions wise, in execution stout,
Whom Solyman into Arabia lad,
When from his kingdom he was first cast out,
Where living wild with their exiled guide
To him in all extremes they faithful bide;

Jerusalem Delivered

XC

All these in thickest order sure unite,
For Godfrey's valor small or nothing shrank,
Corcutes first he on the face did smite,
Then wounded strong Rosteno in the flank,
At one blow Selim's head he stroke off quite,
Then both Rossano's arms, in every rank
The boldest knights, of all that chosen crew,
He felled, maimed, wounded, hurt and slew.

XCI

While thus he killed many a Saracine
And all their fierce assaults unhurt sustained,
Ere fortune wholly from the Turks decline,
While still they hoped much, though small they gained,
Behold a cloud of dust, wherein doth shine
Lightning of war in midst thereof contained,
Whence unawares burst forth a storm of swords,
Which tremble made the Pagan knights and lords.

XCII

These fifty champions were, mongst whom there stands,
In silver field, the ensign of Christ's death,
If I had mouths and tongues as Briareus hands,
If voice as iron tough, if iron breath,
What harm this troop wrought to the heathen bands,
What knights they slew, I could recount uneath
In vain the Turks resist, the Arabians fly;
If they fly, they are slain; if fight, they die.

XCIII

Fear, cruelty, grief, horror, sorrow, pain,
Run through the field, disguised in divers shapes,
Death might you see triumphant on the plain,
Drowning in blood him that from blows escapes.
The king meanwhile with parcel of his train

243

Comes hastily out, and for sure conquest gapes,
And from a bank whereon he stood, beheld
The doubtful hazard of that bloody field.

XCIV

But when he saw the Pagans shrink away,
He sounded the retreat, and gan desire
His messengers in his behalf to pray
Argantes and Clorinda to retire;
The furious couple both at once said nay,
Even drunk with shedding blood, and mad with ire,
At last they went, and to recomfort thought
And stay their troops from flight, but all for nought.

XCV

For who can govern cowardice or fear?
Their host already was begun to fly,
They cast their shields and cutting swords arrear,
As not defended but made slow thereby,
A hollow dale the city's bulwarks near
From west to south outstretched long doth lie,
Thither they fled, and in a mist of dust,
Toward the walls they run, they throng, they thrust.

XCVI

While down the bank disordered thus they ran,
The Christian knights huge slaughter on them made;
But when to climb the other hill they gan,
Old Aladine came fiercely to their aid:
On that steep brae Lord Guelpho would not than
Hazard his folk, but there his soldiers stayed,
And safe within the city's walls the king .
The relics small of that sharp fight did bring:

XCVII

Meanwhile the Soldan in this latest charge

Had done as much as human force was able,
All sweat and blood appeared his members large,
His breath was short, his courage waxed unstable,
His arm grew weak to bear his mighty targe,
His hand to rule his heavy sword unable,
Which bruised, not cut, so blunted was the blade
It lost the use for which a sword was made.

XCVIII
Feeling his weakness, he gan musing stand,
And in his troubled thought this question tossed,
If he himself should murder with his hand,
Because none else should of his conquest boast,
Or he should save his life, when on the land
Lay slain the pride of his subdued host,
"At last to fortune's power," quoth he, "I yield,
And on my flight let her her trophies build.
XCIX
"Let Godfrey view my flight, and smile to see
This mine unworthy second banishment,
For armed again soon shall he hear of me,
From his proud head the unsettled crown to rent,
For, as my wrongs, my wrath etern shall be,
At every hour the bow of war new bent,
I will rise again, a foe, fierce, bold,
Though dead, though slain, though burnt to ashes cold."

TENTH BOOK

THE ARGUMENT.
Ismen from sleep awakes the Soldan great,
And into Sion brings the Prince by night

Jerusalem Delivered

Where the sad king sits fearful on his seat,
Whom he emboldeneth and excites to fight;
Godfredo hears his lords and knights repeat
How they escaped Armida's wrath and spite:
Rinaldo known to live, Peter foresays
His Offspring's virtue, good deserts, and praise.

I
A gallant steed, while thus the Soldan said,
Came trotting by him, without lord or guide,
Quickly his hand upon the reins he laid,
And weak and weary climbed up to ride;
The snake that on his crest hot fire out−braid
Was quite cut off, his helm had lost the pride,
His coat was rent, his harness hacked and cleft,
And of his kingly pomp no sign was left.

II
As when a savage wolf chased from the fold,
To hide his head runs to some holt or wood,
Who, though he filled have while it might hold
His greedy paunch, yet hungreth after food,
With sanguine tongue forth of his lips out−rolled
About his jaws that licks up foam and blood;
So from this bloody fray the Soldan hied,
His rage unquenched, his wrath unsatisfied.

III
And, as his fortune would, he scaped free
From thousand arrows which about him flew,
From swords and lances, instruments that be
Of certain death, himself he safe withdrew,
Unknown, unseen, disguised, travelled he,
By desert paths and ways but used by few,
And rode revolving in his troubled thought
What course to take, and yet resolved on naught.

Jerusalem Delivered

IV

Thither at last he meant to take his way,
Where Egypt's king assembled all his host,
To join with him, and once again assay
To win by fight, by which so oft he lost:
Determined thus, he made no longer stay,
But thitherward spurred forth his steed in post,
Nor need he guide, the way right well he could,
That leads to sandy plains of Gaza old.

V

Nor though his smarting wounds torment him oft,
His body weak and wounded back and side,
Yet rested he, nor once his armor doffed,
But all day long o'er hills and dales doth ride:
But when the night cast up her shade aloft
And all earth's colors strange in sables dyed,
He light, and as he could his wounds upbound,
And shook ripe dates down from a palm he found.

VI

On them he supped, and amid the field
To rest his weary limbs awhile he sought,
He made his pillow of his broken shield
To ease the griefs of his distempered thought,
But little ease could so hard lodging yield,
His wounds so smarted that he slept right naught,
And, in his breast, his proud heart rent in twain,
Two inward vultures, Sorrow and Disdain.

VII

At length when midnight with her silence deep
Did heaven and earth hushed, still, and quiet make,
Sore watched and weary, he began to steep
His cares and sorrows in oblivion's lake,

And in a little, short, unquiet sleep
Some small repose his fainting spirits take;
But, while he slept, a voice grave and severe
At unawares thus thundered in his ear:

VIII

"O Solyman! thou far—renowned king,
Till better season serve, forbear thy rest;
A stranger doth thy lands in thraldom bring,
Nice is a slave, by Christian yoke oppressed;
Sleepest thou here, forgetful of this thing,
That here thy friends lie slain, not laid in chest,
Whose bones bear witness of thy shame and scorn!
And wilt thou idly here attend the morn?"

IX

The king awoke, and saw before his eyes
A man whose presence seemed grave and old,
A writhen staff his steps unstable guies,
Which served his feeble members to uphold.
"And what art thou?" the prince in scorn replies,
"What sprite to vex poor passengers so bold,
To break their sleep? or what to thee belongs
My shame, my loss, my vengeance or my wrongs."

X

"I am the man of thine intent," quoth he,
"And purpose new that sure conjecture hath,
And better than thou weenest know I thee:
I proffer thee my service and my faith.
My speeches therefore sharp and biting be,
Because quick words the whetstones are of wrath, —
Accept in gree, my lord, the words I spoke,
As spurs thine ire and courage to provoke.

XI

"But now to visit Egypt's mighty king,
Unless my judgment fall, you are prepared,
I prophesy, about a needless thing
You suffer shall a voyage long and hard:
For though you stay, the monarch great will bring
His new assembled host to Juda–ward,
No place of service there, no cause of fight,
Nor gainst our foes to use your force and might.

XII

"But if you follow me, within this wall
With Christian arms hemmed in on every side,
Withouten battle, fight, or stroke at all,
Even at noonday, I will you safely guide,
Where you delight, rejoice, and glory shall
In perils great to see your prowess tried.
That noble town you may preserve and shield,
Till Egypt's host come to renew the field."
XIII
While thus he parleyed, of this aged guest
The Turk the words and looks did both admire,
And from his haughty eyes and furious breast
He laid apart his pride, his rage and ire,
And humbly said, "I willing am and prest
To follow where thou leadest, reverend sire,
And that advice best fits my angry vein
That tells of greatest peril, greatest pain."

XIV

The old man praised his words, and for the air
His late received wounds to worse disposes,
A quintessence therein he poured fair,
That stops the bleeding, and incision closes:
Beholding then before Apollo's chair
How fresh Aurora violets strewed and roses,
"It's time," he says, "to wend, for Titan bright

249

To wonted labor summons every wight."

XV
And to a chariot, that beside did stand,
Ascended he, and with him Solyman,
He took the reins, and with a mastering hand
Ruled his steeds, and whipped them now and than,
The wheels or horses' feet upon the land
Had left no sign nor token where they ran,
The coursers pant and smoke with lukewarm sweat
And, foaming cream, their iron mouthfuls eat.

XVI
The air about them round, a wondrous thing,
Itself on heaps in solid thickness drew,
The chariot hiding and environing,
The subtle mist no mortal eye could view;
And yet no stone from engine cast or sling
Could pierce the cloud, it was of proof so true;
Yet seen it was to them within which ride,
And heaven and earth without, all clear beside.

XVII
His beetle brows the Turk amazed bent,
He wrinkled up his front, and wildly stared
Upon the cloud and chariot as it went,
For speed to Cynthia's car right well compared:
The other seeing his astonishment
How he bewondered was, and how he fared,
All suddenly by name the prince gan call,
By which awaked thus he spoke withal:

XVIII
"Whoe'er thou art above all worldly wit
That hast these high and wondrous marvels brought,
And know'st the deep intents which hidden sit

]n secret closet of man's private thought,
If in thy skilful heart this lot be writ,
To tell the event of things to end unbrought;
Then say, what issue and what ends the stars
Allot to Asia's troubles, broils and wars.

XIX
"But tell me first thy name, and by what art
Thou dost these wonders strange, above our skill;
For full of marvel is my troubled heart,
Tell then and leave me not amazed still."
The wizard smiled and answered, "In some part
Easy it is to satisfy thy will,
Ismen I hight, called an enchanter great,
Such skill have I in magic's secret feat;

XX
"But that I should the sure events unfold
Of things to come, or destinies foretell,
Too rash is your desire, your wish too bold,
To mortal heart such knowledge never fell;
Our wit and strength on us bestowed I hold,
To shun the evils and harms, mongst which we dwell,
They make their fortune who are stout and wise,
Wit rules the heavens, discretion guides the skies.
XXI
"That puissant arm of thine that well can rend
From Godfrey's brow the new usurped crown,
And not alone protect, save and defend
From his fierce people, this besieged town,
Gainst fire and sword with strength and courage bend,
Adventure, suffer, trust, tread perils down,
And to content, and to encourage thee,
Know this, which as I in a cloud foresee:

XXII

"I guess, before the over–gliding sun
Shall many years mete out by weeks and days,
A prince that shall in fertile Egypt won,
Shall fill all Asia with his prosperous frays,
I speak not of his acts in quiet done,
His policy, his rule, his wisdom's praise,
Let this suffice, by him these Christians shall
In fight subdued fly, and conquered fall.

XXIII
"And their great empire and usurped state
Shall overthrown in dust and ashes lie,
Their woful remnant in an angle strait
Compassed with sea themselves shall fortify,
From thee shall spring this lord of war and fate."
Whereto great Solyman gan thus reply:
"0 happy man to so great praise ybore!"
Thus he rejoiced, but yet envied more;

XXIV
And said, "Let chance with good or bad aspect
Upon me look as sacred Heaven's decree,
This heart to her I never will subject,
Nor ever conquered shall she look on me;
The moon her chariot shall awry direct
Ere from this course I will diverted be."
While thus he spake, it seemed he breathed fire,
So fierce his courage was, so hot his ire.

XXV
Thus talked they, till they arrived been
Nigh to the place where Godfrey's tents were reared,
There was a woful spectacle yseen,
Death in a thousand ugly forms appeared,
The Soldan changed hue for grief and teen,
On that sad book his shame and loss he lead,

Ah, with what grief his men, his friends he found;
And standards proud, inglorious lie on ground!

XXVI
And saw one visage of some well–known friend.
In foul despite, a rascal Frenchman tread,
And there another ragged peasant rend
The arms and garments from some champion dead,
And there with stately pomp by heaps they wend,
And Christians slain roll up in webs of lead;
Lastly the Turks and slain Arabians, brought
On heaps, he saw them burn with fire to naught.

XXVII
Deeply he sighed, and with naked sword
Out of the coach he leaped in the mire,
But Ismen called again the angry lord,
And with grave words appeased his foolish ire.
The prince content remounted at his sword,
Toward a hill on drove the aged sire,
And hasting forward up the bank they pass,
Till far behind the Christian leaguer was.

XXVIII
There they alight and took their way on foot,
The empty chariot vanished out of sight,
Yet still the cloud environed them about.
At their left hand down went they from the height
Of Sion's Hill, till they approached the route
On that side where to west he looketh right,
There Ismen stayed, and his eyesight bent
Upon the bushy rocks, and thither went.

XXIX
A hollow cave was in the craggy stone,
Wrought out by hand a number years tofore,

And for of long that way had walked none,
The vault was hid with plants and bushes hoar,
The wizard stooping in thereat to gone,
The thorns aside and scratching brambles bore,
His right hand sought the passage through the cleft,
And for his guide he gave the prince his left:

XXX

"What," quoth the Soldan, "by what privy mine,
What hidden vault behoves it me to creep?
This sword can find a better way than thine,
Although our foes the passage guard and keep."
"Let not," quoth he, "thy princely foot repine
To tread this secret path, though dark and deep;
For great King Herod used to tread the same,
He that in arms had whilom so great fame.

XXXI

"This passage made he, when he would suppress
His subjects' pride, and them in bondage hold;
By this he could from that small forteress
Antonia called, of Antony the bold,
Convey his folk unseen of more and less
Even to the middest of the temple old,
Thence, hither; where these privy ways begin,
And bring unseen whole armies out and in.

XXXII

"But now saye I in all this world lives none
That knows the secret of this darksome place,
Come then where Aladine sits on his throne,
With lords and princes set about his grace;
He feareth more than fitteth such an one,
Such signs of doubt show in his cheer and face;
Fitly you come, hear, see, and keep you still,
Till time and season serve, then speak your fill."

XXXIII

This said, that narrow entrance passed the knight,
So creeps a camel through a needle's eye,
And through the ways as black as darkest night
He followed him that did him rule and guie;
Strait was the way at first, withouten light,
But further in, did further amplify;
So that upright walked at ease the men
Ere they had passed half that secret den,

XXXIV

A privy door Ismen unlocked at last,
And up they clomb a little–used stair,
Thereat the day a feeble beam in cast,
Dim was the light, and nothing clear the air;
Out of the hollow cave at length they passed
Into a goodly hall, high, broad and fair,
Where crowned with gold, and all in purple clad
Sate the sad king, among his nobles sad.

XXXV

The Turk, close in his hollow cloud imbarred,
Unseen, at will did all the prease behold,
These heavy speeches of the king he heard,
Who thus from lofty siege his pleasure told;
"My lords, last day our state was much impaired,
Our friends were slain, killed were our soldiers bold,
Great helps and greater hopes are us bereft,
Nor aught but aid from Egypt land is left:

XXXVI

"And well you see far distant is that aid,
Upon our heels our danger treadeth still,
For your advice was this assembly made,
Each what he thinketh speak, and what he will."

A whisper soft arose when this was said,
As gentle winds the groves with murmur fill,
But with bold face, high looks and merry cheer,
Argantes rose, the rest their talk forbear.

XXXVII

"0 worthy sovereign," thus began to say
The hardy young man to the tyrant wise,
"What words be these? what fears do you dismay?
Who knows not this, you need not our advice!
But on your hand your hope of conquest lay,
And, for no loss true virtue damnifies,
Make her our shield, pray her us succors give,
And without her let us not wish to live.

XXXVIII

"Nor say I this for that I aught misdeem
That Egypt's promised succors fail us might,
Doubtful of my great master's words to seem
To me were neither lawful, just, nor right!
I speak these words, for spurs I them esteem
To waken up each dull and fearful sprite,
And make our hearts resolved to all assays,
To win with honor, or to die with praise."

XXXIX

Thus much Argantes said, and said no more,
As if the case were clear of which he spoke.
Orcano rose, of princely stem ybore,
Whose presence 'mongst them bore a mighty stroke,
A man esteemed well in arms of yore,
But now was coupled new in marriage yoke;
Young babes he had, to fight which made him loth,
He was a husband and a father both.

XL

Jerusalem Delivered

"My lord," quoth he, "I will not reprehend
The earnest zeal of this audacious speech,
From courage sprung, which seld is close ypend
In swelling stomach without violent breach:
And though to you our good Circassian friend
In terms too bold and fervent oft doth preach,
Yet hold I that for good, in warlike feat
For his great deeds respond his speeches great.

XLI

"But if it you beseem, whom graver age
And long experience hath made wise and sly,
To rule the heat of youth and hardy rage,
Which somewhat have misled this knight awry,
In equal balance ponder then and gauge
Your hopes far distant, with your perils nigh;
This town's old walls and rampires new compare
With Godfrey's forces and his engines rare.

XLII

"But, if I may say what I think unblamed,
This town is strong, by nature, site and art,
But engines huge and instruments are framed
Gainst these defences by our adverse part,
Who thinks him most secure is eathest shamed;
I hope the best, yet fear unconstant mart,
And with this siege if we be long up pent,
Famine I doubt, our store will all be spent.

XLIII

"For all that store of cattle and of grain
Which yesterday within these walls you brought,
While your proud foes triumphant through the plain
On naught but shedding blood, and conquest thought,
Too little is this city to sustain,
To raise the siege unless some means be sought;

257

And it must last till the prefixed hour
That it be raised by Egypt's aid and power.

XLIV
"But what if that appointed day they miss?
Or else, ere we expect, what if they came?
The victory yet is not ours for this,
Oh save this town from ruin, us from shame!
With that same Godfrey still our warfare is,
These armies, soldiers, captains are the same
Who have so oft amid the dusty plain
Turks, Persians, Syrians and Arabians slain.

XLV
"And thou Argantes wotest what they be;
Oft hast thou fled from that victorious host,
Thy shoulders often hast thou let them see,
And in thy feet hath been thy safeguard most;
Clorinda bright and I fled eke with thee,
None than his fellows had more cause to boast,
Nor blame I any; for in every fight
We showed courage, valor, strength and might.

XLVI
"And though this hardy knight the certain threat
Of near–approaching death to hear disdain;
Yet to this state of loss and danger great,
From this strong foe I see the tokens plain;
No fort how strong soe'er by art or seat,
Can hinder Godfrey why he should not reign:
This makes me say, — to witness heaven I bring,
Zeal to this state, love to my lord and king —

XLVII
"The king of Tripoli was well advised
To purchase peace, and so preserve his crown:

258

But Solyman, who Godfrey's love despised,
Is either dead or deep in prison thrown;
Else fearful is he run away disguised,
And scant his life is left him for his own,
And yet with gifts, with tribute, and with gold,
He might in peace his empire still have hold."

XLVIII
Thus spake Orcanes, and some inkling gave
In doubtful words of that he would have said;
To sue for peace or yield himself a slave
He durst not openly his king persuade:
But at those words the Soldan gan to rave,
And gainst his will wrapt in the cloud he stayed,
Whom Ismen thus bespake, "How can you bear
These words, my lord? or these reproaches hear?"
XLIX
"Oh, let me speak," quoth he, "with ire and scorn
I burn, and gains, my will thus hid I stay!"
This said. the smoky cloud was cleft and torn,
Which like a veil upon them stretched lay,
And up to open heaven forthwith was borne,
And left the prince in view of lightsome day,
With princely look amid the press he shined,
And on a sudden, thus declared his mind.

L
"Of whom you speak behold the Soldan here,
Neither afraid nor run away for dread,
And that these slanders, lies and fables were,
This hand shall prove upon that coward's head,
I, who have shed a sea of blood well near,
And heaped up mountains high of Christians dead,
I in their camp who still maintained the fray,
My men all murdered, I that run away.

259

LI

"If this, or any coward vile beside,
False to his faith and country, dares reply;
And speak of concord with yon men of pride,
By your good leave, Sir King, here shall he die,
The lambs and wolves shall in one fold abide,
The doves and serpents in one nest shall lie,
Before one town us and these Christians shall
In peace and love unite within one wall."

LII

While thus he spoke, his broad and trenchant sword
His hand held high aloft in threatening guise;
Dumb stood the knights, so dreadful was his word;
A storm was in his front, fire in his eyes,
He turned at last to Sion's aged lord,
And calmed his visage stern in humbler wise:
"Behold," quoth he, "good prince, what aid I bring,
Since 5olyman is joined with Juda's king."

LIII

King Aladine from his rich throne upstart
And said, "Oh how I joy thy face to view,
My noble friend! it lesseneth in some part
My grief, for slaughter of my subjects true;
My weak estate to stablish come thou art,
And mayest thine own again in time renew,
If Heavens consent:" with that the Soldan bold
In dear embracements did he long enfold.

LIV

Their greetings done, the king resigned his throne
To Solyman, and set himself beside,
In a rich seat adorned with gold and stone,
And Ismen sage did at his elbow bide,
Of whom he asked what way they two had gone,

And he declared all what had them betide:
Clorinda bright to Solyman addressed
Her salutations first, then all the rest.

LV

Among them rose Ormusses' valiant knight,
Whom late the Soldan with a convoy sent,
And when most hot and bloody was the fight,
By secret paths and blind byways he went,
Till aided by the silence and the night
Safe in the city's walls himself he pent,
And there refreshed with corn and cattle store
The pined soldiers famished nigh before.

LVI

With surly countenance and disdainful grace,
Sullen and sad, sat the Circassian stout,
Like a fierce lion grumbling in his place,
His fiery eyes that turns and rolls about;
Nor durst Orcanes view the Soldan's face,
But still upon the floor did pore and tout:
Thus with his lords and peers in counselling,
The Turkish monarch sat with Juda's king.

LVII

Godfrey this while gave victory the rein,
And following her the straits he opened all;
Then for his soldiers and his captains slain,
He celebrates a stately funeral,
And told his camp within a day or twain
He would assault the city's mighty wall,
And all the heathen there enclosed doth threat,
With fire and sword, with death and danger great.

LVIII

And for he had that noble squadron known,
In the last fight which brought him so great aid,

Jerusalem Delivered

To be the lords and princes of his own
Who followed late the sly enticing maid,
And with them Tancred, who had late been thrown
In prison deep, by that false witch betrayed,
Before the hermit and some private friends,
For all those worthies, lords and knights, he sends;

LIX

And thus he said, "Some one of you declare
Your fortunes, whether good or to be blamed,
And to assist us with your valors rare
In so great need, how was your coming framed?"
They blush, and on the ground amazed stare,
For virtue is of little guilt ashamed,
At last the English prince with countenance bold,
The silence broke, and thus their errors told:

LX

"We, not elect to that exploit by lot,
With secret flight from hence ourselves withdrew,
Following false Cupid, I deny it not,
Enticed forth by love and beauty's hue;
A jealous fire burnt in our stomachs hot,
And by close ways we passed least in view,
Her words, her looks, alas I know too late,
Nursed our love, our jealousy, our hate.

LXI

"At last we gan approach that woful clime,
Where fire and brimstone down from Heaven was sent
To take revenge for sin and shameful crime
Gainst kind commit, by those who nould repent;
A loathsome lake of brimstone, pitch and lime,
O'ergoes that land, erst sweet and redolent,
And when it moves, thence stench and smoke up flies
Which dim the welkin and infect the skies.

Jerusalem Delivered

LXII

"This is the lake in which yet never might
Aught that hath weight sink to the bottom down,
But like to cork or leaves or feathers light,
Stones, iron, men, there fleet and never drown;
Therein a castle stands, to which by sight
But o'er a narrow bridge no way is known,
Hither us brought, here welcomed us the witch,
The house within was stately, pleasant, rich.

LXIII

"The heavens were clear, and wholsome was the air,
High trees, sweet meadows, waters pure and good;
For there in thickest shade of myrtles fair
A crystal spring poured out a silver flood;
Amid the herbs, the grass and flowers rare,
The falling leaves down pattered from the wood,
The birds sung hymns of love; yet speak I naught
Of gold and marble rich, and richly wrought.

LXIV

"Under the curtain of the greenwood shade,
Beside the brook upon the velvet grass,
In massy vessel of pure silver made,
A banquet rich and costly furnished was,
All beasts, all birds beguiled by fowler's trade,
All fish were there in floods or seas that pass,
All dainties made by art, and at the table
An hundred virgins served, for husbands able.

LXV

"She with sweet words and false enticing smiles,
Infused love among the dainties set,
And with empoisoned cups our souls beguiles,
And made each knight himself and God forget:

She rose and turned again within short whiles,
With changed looks where wrath and anger met,
A charming rod, a book with her she brings,
On which she mumbled strange and secret things.

LXVI
"She read, and change I felt my will and thought,
I longed to change my life, and place of biding,
That virtue strange in me no pleasure wrought,
I leapt into the flood myself there hiding,
My legs and feet both into one were brought,
Mine arms and hands into my shoulders sliding,
My skin was full of scales, like shields of brass,
Now made a fish, where late a knight I was.

LXVII
"The rest with me like shape, like garments wore,
And dived with me in that quicksilver stream,
Such mind, to my remembrance, then I bore,
As when on vain and foolish things men dream;
At last our shade it pleased her to restore,
Then full of wonder and of fear we seem,
And with an ireful look the angry maid
Thus threatened us, and made us thus afraid.

LXVIII
" `You see,' quoth she, `my sacred might and skill,
How you are subject to my rule and power,
In endless thraldom damned if I will
I can torment and keep you in this tower,
Or make you birds, or trees on craggy hill,
To bide the bitter blasts of storm and shower;
Or harden you to rocks on mountains old,
Or melt your flesh and bones to rivers cold:

LXIX

" `Yet may you well avoid mine ire and wrath,
If to my will your yielding hearts you bend,
You must forsake your Christendom and faith,
And gainst Godfredo false my crown defend.'
We all refused, for speedy death each prayeth,
Save false Rambaldo, he became her friend,
We in a dungeon deep were helpless cast,
In misery and iron chained fast.

LXX
"Then, for alone they say falls no mishap,
Within short while Prince Tancred thither came,
And was unwares surprised in the trap:
But there short while we stayed, the wily dame
In other folds our mischiefs would upwrap.
From Hidraort an hundred horsemen came,
Whose guide, a baron bold to Egypt's king,
Should us disarmed and bound in fetters bring.

LXXI
"Now on our way, the way to death we ride,
But Providence Divine thus for us wrought,
Rinaldo, whose high virtue is his guide
To great exploits, exceeding human thought,
Met us, and all at once our guard defied,
And ere he left the fight to earth them brought.
And in their harness armed us in the place,
Which late were ours, before our late disgrace.

LXXII
"I and all these the hardy champion knew,
We saw his valor, and his voice we heard;
Then is the rumor of his death untrue,
His life is safe, good fortune long it guard,
Three times the golden sun hath risen new,
Since us he left and rode to Antioch−ward;

But first his armors, broken, hacked and cleft,
Unfit for service, there he doft and left."

LXXIII

Thus spake the Briton prince, with humble cheer
The hermit sage to heaven cast up his eyne,
His color and his countenance changed were,
With heavenly grace his looks and visage shine,
Ravished with zeal his soul approached near
The seat of angels pure, and saints divine,
And there he learned of things and haps to come,
To give foreknowledge true, and certain doom.

LXXIV

At last he spoke, in more than human sound,
And told what things his wisdom great foresaw,
And at his thundering voice the folk around
Attentive stood, with trembling and with awe:
"Rinaldo lives," he said, "the tokens found
From women's craft their false beginnings draw,
He lives, and heaven will long preserve his days,
To greater glory, and to greater praise.

LXXV

"These are but trifles yet, though Asia's kings
Shrink at his name, and tremble at his view,
I well foresee he shall do greater things,
And wicked emperors conquer and subdue;
Under the shadow of his eagle's wings
Shall holy Church preserve her sacred crew,
From Caesar's bird he shall the sable train
Pluck off, and break her talons sharp in twain.

LXXVI

"His children's children at his hardiness
And great attempts shall take example fair,
From emperors unjust in all distress

They shall defend the state of Peter's chair,
To raise the humble up, pride to suppress,
To help the innocents shall be their care.
This bird of east shall fly with conquest great,
As far as moon gives light or sun gives heat;
LXXVII
"Her eyes behold the truth and purest light,
And thunders down in Peter's aid she brings,
And where for Christ and Christian faith men fight,
There forth she spreadeth her victorious wings,
This virtue nature gives her and this might;
Then lure her home, for on her presence hings
The happy end of this great enterprise,
So Heaven decrees, and so command the skies."

LXXVIII
These words of his of Prince Rinaldo's death
Out of their troubled hearts, the fear had rased;
In all this joy yet Godfrey smiled uneath.
In his wise thought such care and heed was placed.
But now from deeps of regions underneath
Night's veil arose, and sun's bright lustre chased,
When all full sweetly in their cabins slept,
Save he, whose thoughts his eyes still open kept.

ELEVENTH BOOK

THE ARGUMENT.
With grave procession, songs and psalms devout
Heaven's sacred aid the Christian lords invoke;
That done, they scale the wall which kept them out:
The fort is almost won, the gates nigh broke:

Jerusalem Delivered

Godfrey is wounded by Clorinda stout,
And lost is that day's conquest by the stroke;
The angel cures him, he returns to fight,
But lost his labor, for day lost his light.

I
The Christian army's great and puissant guide,
To assault the town that all his thoughts had bent,
Did ladders, rams, and engines huge provide,
When reverend Peter to him gravely went,
And drawing him with sober grace aside,
With words severe thus told his high intent;
"Right well, my lord, these earthly strengths you move,
But let us first begin from Heaven above:

II
"With public prayer, zeal and faith devout,
The aid, assistance, and the help obtain
Of all the blessed of the heavenly rout,
With whose support you conquest sure may gain;
First let the priests before thine armies stout
With sacred hymns their holy voices strain.
And thou and all thy lords and peers with thee,
Of godliness and faith examples be."

III
Thus spake the hermit grave in words severe:
Godfrey allowed his counsel, sage, and wise,
"Of Christ the Lord," quoth he, "thou servant dear,
I yield to follow thy divine advice,
And while the princes I assemble here,
The great procession, songs and sacrifice,
With Bishop William, thou and Ademare,
With sacred and with solemn pomp prepare."

Jerusalem Delivered

IV

Next morn the bishops twain, the heremite,
And all the clerks and priests of less estate,
Did in the middest of the camp unite
Within a place for prayer consecrate,
Each priest adorned was in a surplice white,
The bishops donned their albes and copes of state,
Above their rochets buttoned fair before,
And mitres on their heads like crowns they wore.

V

Peter alone, before, spread to the wind
The glorious sign of our salvation great,
With easy pace the choir come all behind,
And hymns and psalms in order true repeat,
With sweet respondence in harmonious kind
Their humble song the yielding air doth beat,
"Lastly, together went the reverend pair
Of prelates sage, William and Ademare,

VI

The mighty duke came next, as princes do,
Without companion, marching all alone,
The lords and captains then came two and two,
With easy pace thus ordered, passing through
The trench and rampire, to the fields they gone,
No thundering drum, no trumpet shrill they hear,
Their godly music psalms and prayers were.

VII

To thee, O Father, Son, and sacred Sprite,
One true, eternal, everlasting King;
To Christ's dear mother, Mary, vIrgin bright,
Psalms of thanksgiving and of praise they sing;
To them that angels down from heaven to fight
Gainst the blasphemous beast and dragon bring;

Jerusalem Delivered

To him also that of our Saviour good,
Washed the sacred font in Jordan's flood.

VIII
Him likewise they invoke, called the Rock
Whereon the Lord, they say, his Church did rear,
Whose true successors close or else unlock
The blessed gates of grace and mercy dear;
And all the elected twelve the chosen flock,
Of his triumphant death who witness bear;
And them by torment, slaughter, fire and sword
Who martyrs died to confirm his word;

IX
And them also whose books and writings tell
What certain path to heavenly bliss us leads;
And hermits good, and ancresses that dwell
Mewed up in walls, and mumble on their beads,
And virgin nuns in close and private cell,
Where, but shrift fathers, never mankind treads:
On these they called, and on all the rout
Of angels, martyrs, and of saints devout.

X
Singing and saying thus, the camp devout
Spread forth her zealous squadrons broad and wide';
Toward mount Olivet went all this route,
So called of olive trees the hills which hide,
A mountain known by fame the world throughout,
Which riseth on the city's eastern side,
From it divided by the valley green
Of Josaphat, that fills the space between.

XI
Hither the armies went, and chanted shrill,
That all the deep and hollow dales resound;

270

Jerusalem Delivered

From hollow mounts and caves in every hill,
A thousand echoes also sung around,
It seemed some clever, that sung with art and skill,
Dwelt in those savage dens and shady ground,
For oft resounds from the banks they hear,
The name of Christ and of his mother dear.

XII

Upon the walls the Pagans old and young
Stood hushed and still, amated and amazed,
At their grave order and their humble song,
At their strange pomp and customs new they gazed:
But when the show they had beholden long,
An hideous yell the wicked miscreants raised,
That with vile blasphemies the mountain hoar,
The woods, the waters, and the valleys roar.

XIII

But yet with sacred notes the hosts proceed,
Though blasphemies they hear and cursed things;
So with Apollo's harp Pan tunes his reed,
So adders hiss where Philomela sings;
Nor flying darts nor stones the Christians dreed,
Nor arrows shot, nor quarries cast from slings;
But with assured faith, as dreading naught,
The holy work begun to end they brought.

XIV

A table set they on the mountain's height
To minister thereon the sacrament,
In golden candlesticks a hallowed light
At either end of virgin wax there brent;
In costly vestments sacred William dight,
With fear and trembling to the altar went,
And prayer there and service loud begins,
Both for his own and all the army's sins.

Jerusalem Delivered

XV

Humbly they heard his words that stood him nigh,
The rest far off upon him bent their eyes,
But when he ended had the service high,
"You servants of the Lord depart," he cries:
His hands he lifted then up to the sky,
And blessed all those warlike companies;
And they dismissed returned the way they came,
Their order as before, their pomp the same.

XVI

Within their camp arrived, this voyage ended,
Toward his tent the duke himself withdrew,
Upon their guide by heaps the bands attended,
Till his pavilion's stately door they view,
There to the Lord his welfare they commended,
And with him left the worthies of the crew,
Whom at a costly and rich feast he placed,
And with the highest room old Raymond graced.

XVII

Now when the hungry knights sufficed are
With meat, with drink, with spices of the best,
Quoth he, "When next you see the morning star,
To assault the town be ready all and prest:
To—morrow is a day of pains and war,
This of repose, of quiet, peace, and rest;
Go, take your ease this evening, and this night,
And make you strong against to—morrow's fight."
XVIII

They took their leave, and Godfrey's heralds rode
To intimate his will on every side,
And published it through all the lodgings broad,
That gainst the morn each should himself provide;
Meanwhile they might their hearts of cares unload,

And rest their tired limbs that eveningtide;
Thus fared they till night their eyes did close,
Night friend to gentle rest and sweet repose.

XIX
With little sign as yet of springing day
Out peeped, not well appeared the rising morn,
The plough yet tore not up the fertile lay,
Nor to their feed the sheep from folds return,
The birds sate silent on the greenwood spray
Amid the groves unheard was hound and horn,
When trumpets shrill, true signs of hardy fights,
Called up to arms the soldiers, called the knights:
XX
"Arm, arm at once!" an hundred squadrons cried,
And with their cry to arm them all begin.
Godfrey arose, that day he laid aside
His hauberk strong he wonts to combat in,
And donned a breastplate fair, of proof untried,
Such one as footmen use, light, easy, thin.
Scantly the warlord thus clothed had his gromes,
When aged Raymond to his presence comes.

XXI
And furnished to us when he the man beheld,
By his attire his secret thought he guessed,
"Where is," quoth he, "your sure and trusty shield?
Your helm, your hauberk strong? where all the rest?
Why be you half disarmed? why to the field
Approach you in these weak defences dressed?
I see this day you mean a course to run,
Wherein may peril much, small praise be won.

XXII
"Alas, do you that idle prise expect,
To set first foot this conquered wall above?

Of less account some knight thereto object
Whose loss so great and harmful cannot prove;
My lord, your life with greater care protect,
And love yourself because all us you love,
Your happy life is spirit, soul, and breath
Of all this camp, preserve it then from death."

XXIII

To this he answered thus, "You know," he said,
"In Clarimont by mighty Urban's hand
When I was girded with this noble blade,
For Christ's true faith to fight in every land,
To God even then a secret vow I made,
Not as a captain here this day to stand
And give directions, but with shield and sword
To fight, to win, or die for Christ my Lord.

XXIV

"When all this camp in battle strong shall be
Ordained and ordered, well disposed all,
And all things done which to the high degree
And sacred place I hold belongen shall;
Then reason is it, nor dissuade thou me,
That I likewise assault this sacred wall,
Lest from my vow to God late made I swerve:
He shall this life defend, keep and preserve."

XXV

Thus he concludes, and every hardy knight
His sample followed, and his brethren twain,
The other princes put on harness light,
As footmen use: but all the Pagan train
Toward that side bent their defensive might
Which lies exposed to view of Charles's wain
And Zephyrus' sweet blasts, for on that part
The town was weakest, both by side and art.

XXVI

On all parts else the fort was strong by site,
With mighty hills defenced from foreign rage,
And to this part the tyrant gan unite
His subjects born and bands that serve for wage,
From this exploit he spared nor great nor lite,
The aged men, and boys of tender age,
To fire of angry war still brought new fuel,
Stones, darts, lime, brimstone and bitumen cruel.

XXVII

All full of arms and weapons was the wall,
Under whose basis that fair plain doth run,
There stood the Soldan like a giant tall,
So stood at Rhodes the Coloss of the sun,
Waist high, Argantes showed himself withal,
At whose stern looks the French to quake begun,
Clorinda on the corner tower alone,
In silver arms like rising Cynthia shone.

XXVIII

Her rattling quiver at her shoulders hung,
Therein a flash of arrows feathered weel.
In her left hand her bow was bended strong,
Therein a shaft headed with mortal steel,
So fit to shoot she singled forth among
Her foes who first her quarries' strength should feel,
So fit to shoot Latona's daughter stood
When Niobe she killed and all her brood.

XXIX

The aged tyrant tottered on his feet
From gate to gate, from wall to wall he flew,
He comforts all his bands with speeches sweet,
And every fort and bastion doth review,

For every need prepared in every street
New regiments he placed and weapons new.
The matrons grave within their temples high
To idols false for succors call and cry,

XXX

"O Macon, break in twain the steeled lance
On wicked Godfrey with thy righteous hands,
Against thy name he doth his arm advance,
His rebel blood pour out upon these sands;"
These cries within his ears no enterance
Could find, for naught he hears, naught understands.
While thus the town for her defence ordains,
His armies Godfrey ordereth on the plains;

XXXI

His forces first on foot he forward brought,
With goodly order, providence and art,
And gainst these towers which to assail he thought,
In battles twain his strength he doth depart,
Between them crossbows stood, and engines wrought
To cast a stone, a quarry, or a dart,
From whence like thunder's dint or lightnings new
Against the bulwark stones and lances flew.

XXXII

His men at arms did back his bands on foot,
The light horse ride far off and serve for wings,
He gave the sign, so mighty was the rout
Of those that shot with bows and cast with slings,
Such storms of shafts and stones flew all about,
That many a Pagan proud to death it brings,
Some died, some at their loops durst scant outpeep,
Some fled and left the place they took to keep.

XXXIII

The hardy Frenchmen, full of heat and haste,

Ran boldly forward to the ditches large,
And o'er their heads an iron pentice vast
They built, by joining many a shield and targe,
Some with their engines ceaseless shot and cast,
And volleys huge of arrows sharp discharge,
Upon the ditches some employed their pain
To fill the moat and even it with the plain.

XXXIV
With slime or mud the ditches were not soft,
But dry and sandy, void of waters clear,
Though large and deep the Christians fill them oft,
With rubbish, fagots, stones, and trees they bear:
Adrastus first advanced his crest aloft,
And boldly gan a strong scalado rear,
And through the falling storm did upward climb
Of stones, darts, arrows, fire, pitch and lime:
XXXV
The hardy Switzer now so far was gone
That half way up with mickle pain he got,
A thousand weapons he sustained alone,
And his audacious climbing ceased not;
At last upon him fell a mighty stone,
As from some engine great it had been shot,
It broke his helm, he tumbled from the height,
The strong Circassian cast that wondrous weight;

XXXVI
Not mortal was the blow, yet with the fall
On earth sore bruised the man lay in a swoon.
Argantes gan with boasting words to call,
"Who cometh next? this first is tumbled down,
Come, hardy soldiers, come, assault this wall,
I will not shrink, nor fly, nor hide my crown,
If in your trench yourselves for dread you hold,
There shall you die like sheep killed in their fold."

XXXVII

Thus boasted he; but in their trenches deep,
The hidden squadrons kept themselves from scath,
The curtain made of shields did well off keep
Both darts and shot, and scorned all their wrath.
But now the ram upon the rampiers steep,
On mighty beams his head advanced hath,
With dreadful horns of iron tough tree great,
The walls and bulwarks trembled at his threat.

XXXVIII

An hundred able men meanwhile let fall
The weights behind, the engine tumbled down
And battered flat the battlements and wall:
So fell Taigetus hill on Sparta town,
It crushed the steeled shield in pieces small,
And beat the helmet to the wearers' crown,
And on the ruins of the walls and stones,
Dispersed left their blood their brains and bones.

XXXIX

The fierce assailants kept no longer close
Under the shelter of their target fine,
But their bold fronts to chance of war expose,
And gainst those towers let their virtue shine,
The scaling ladders up to skies arose,
The ground—works deep some closely undermine,
The walls before the Frenchmen shrink and shake,
And gaping sign of headlong falling make:

XL

And fallen they had, so far the strength extends
Of that fierce ram and his redoubted stroke,
But that the Pagan's care the place defends
And saved by warlike skill the wall nigh broke:

For to what part soe'er the engine bends,
Their sacks of wool they place the blow to choke,
Whose yielding breaks the strokes thereon which light,
So weakness oft subdues the greatest might.

XLI
While thus the worthies of the western crew
Maintained their brave assault and skirmish hot,
Her mighty bow Clorinda often drew,
And many a sharp and deadly arrow shot;
And from her bow no steeled shaft there flew
But that some blood the cursed engine got,
Blood of some valiant knight or man of fame,
For that proud shootress scorned weaker game.

XLII
The first she hit among the Christian peers
Was the bold son of England's noble king,
Above the trench himself he scantly rears,
But she an arrow loosed from the string,
The wicked steel his gauntlet breaks and tears,
And through his right hand thrust the piercing sting;
Disabled thus from fight, he gan retire,
Groaning for pain, but fretting more for ire.

XLIII
Lord Stephen of Amboise on the ditch's brim,
And on a ladder high, Clotharius died,
From back to breast an arrow pierced him,
The other was shot through from side to side:
Then as he managed brave his courser trim,
On his left arm he hit the Flemings' guide,
He stopped, and from the wound the reed out-twined,
But left the iron in his flesh behind.

XLIV

As Ademare stood to behold the fight
High on the bank, withdrawn to breathe a space,
A fatal shaft upon his forehead light,
His hand he lifted up to feel the place,
Whereon a second arrow chanced right,
And nailed his hand unto his wounded face,
He fell, and with his blood distained the land,
His holy blood shed by a virgin's hand.

XLV

While Palamede stood near the battlement,
Despising perils all, and all mishap,
And upward still his hardy footings bent,
On his right eye he caught a deadly clap,
Through his right eye Clorinda's seventh shaft went,
And in his neck broke forth a bloody gap;
He underneath that bulwark dying fell,
Which late to scale and win he trusted well.

XLVI

Thus shot the maid: the duke with hard assay
And sharp assault, meanwhile the town oppressed,
Against that part which to his campward lay
An engine huge and wondrous he addressed,
A tower of wood built for the town's decay
As high as were the walls and bulwarks best,
A turret full of men and weapons pent,
And yet on wheels it rolled, moved, and went.

XLVII

This rolling fort his nigh approaches made,
And darts and arrows spit against his foes,
As ships are wont in fight, so it assayed
With the strong wall to grapple and to close,
The Pagans on each side the piece invade,
And all their force against this mass oppose,

Jerusalem Delivered

Sometimes the wheels, sometimes the battlement
With timber, logs and stones, they broke and rent,
XLVIII
So thick flew stones and darts, that no man sees
The azure heavens, the sun his brightness lost,
The clouds of weapons, like to swarms of bees,
Move the air, and there each other crossed:
And look how falling leaves drop down from trees,
When the moist sap is nipped with timely frost,
Or apples in strong winds from branches fall;
The Saracens so tumbled from the wall.

XLIX
For on their part the greatest slaughter light,
They had no shelter gainst so sharp a shower,
Some left on live betook themselves to flight,
So feared they this deadly thundering tower:
But Solyman stayed like a valiant knight,
And some with him, that trusted in his power,
Argantes with a long beech tree in hand,
Ran thither, this huge engine to withstand:

L
With this he pushed the tower, and back it drives
The length of all his tree, a wondrous way,
The hardy virgin by his side arrives,
To help Argantes in this hard assay:
The band that used the ram, this season strives
To cut the cords, wherein the woolpacks lay,
Which done, the sacks down in the trenches fall,
And to the battery naked left the wall.

LI
The tower above, the ram beneath doth thunder,
What lime and stone such puissance could abide?
The wall began, new bruised and crushed asunder,

281

Her wounded lap to open broad and wide,
Godfrey himself and his brought safely under
The shattered wall, where greatest breach he spied,
Himself he saves behind his mighty targe,
A shield not used but in some desperate charge.

LII

From hence he sees where Solyman descends,
Down to the threshold of the gaping breach,
And there it seems the mighty prince intends
Godfredo's hoped entrance to impeach:
Argantes, and with him the maid, defends
The walls above, to which the tower doth reach,
His noble heart, when Godfrey this beheld,
With courage new with wrath and valor swelled.

LIII

He turned about and to good Sigiere spake,
Who bare his greatest shield and mighty bow,
"That sure and trusty target let me take,
Impenetrable is that shield I know,
Over these ruins will I passage make,
And enter first, the way is eath and low,
And time requires that by some noble feat
I should make known my strength and puissance great."

LIV

He scant had spoken, scant received the charge,
When on his leg a sudden shaft him hit,
And through that part a hole made wide and large,
Where his strong sinews fastened were and knit.
Clorinda, thou this arrow didst discharge,
And let the Pagans bless thy hand for it,
For by that shot thou savedst them that day
From bondage vile, from death and sure decay.

Jerusalem Delivered

282

LV

The wounded duke, as though he felt no pain,
Still forward went, and mounted up the breach
His high attempt at first he nould refrain,
And after called his lords with cheerful speech;
But when his leg could not his weight sustain,
He saw his will did far his power outreach,
And more he strove his grief increased the more,
The bold assault he left at length therefore:

LVI

And with his hand he beckoned Guelpho near,
And said, "I must withdraw me to my tent,
My place and person in mine absence bear,
Supply my want, let not the fight relent,
I go, and will ere long again be here;
I go and straight return: "this said, he went,
On a light steed he leaped, and o'er the green
He rode, but rode not, as he thought, unseen.

LVII

When Godfrey parted, parted eke the heart, .
The strength and fortune of the Christian bands,.
Courage increased in their adverse part,
Wrath in their hearts, and vigor in their hands:
Valor, success, strength, hardiness and art,
Failed in the princes of the western lands,
Their swords were blunt, faint was their trumpet's blast,
Their sun was set, or else with clouds o'ercast.

LVIII

Upon the bulwarks now appeared bold
That fearful band that late for dread was fled!
The women that Clorinda's strength behold,
Their country's love to war encouraged,
They weapons got, and fight like men they would,

Their gowns tucked up, their locks were loose and spread,
Sharp darts they cast, and without dread or fear,
Exposed their breasts to save their fortress dear.
LIX
But that which most dismayed the Christian knights,
And added courage to the Pagans most,
Was Guelpho's sudden fall in all men's sights,
Who tumbled headlong down, his footing lost,
A mighty stone upon the worthy lights,
But whence it came none wist, nor from what coast;
And with like blow, which more their hearts dismayed,
Beside him low in dust old Raymond laid:

LX
And Eustace eke within the ditches large,
To narrow shifts and last extremes they drive,
Upon their foes so fierce the Pagans charge,
And with good—fortune so their blows they give,
That whom they hit, in spite of helm or targe,
They deeply wound, or else of life deprive.
At this their good success Argantes proud,
Waxing more fell, thus roared and cried aloud:

LXI
"This is not Antioch, nor the evening dark
Can help your privy sleights with friendly shade,
The sun yet shines, your falsehood can we mark,
In other wise this bold assault is made;
Of praise and glory quenched is the spark
That made you first these eastern lands invade,
Why cease you now? why take you not this fort?
What! are you weary for a charge so short?"

LXII
Thus raged he, and in such hellish sort
Increased the fury in the brain—sick knight,

That he esteemed that large and ample fort
Too strait a field, wherein to prove his might,
There where the breach had framed a new–made port,
Himself he placed, with nimble skips and light,
He cleared the passage out, and thus he cried
To Solyman, that fought close by his side:

LXIII
"Come, Solyman, the time and place behold,
That of our valors well may judge the doubt,
What sayest thou? amongst these Christians bold,
First leap he forth that holds himself most stout:"
While thus his will the mighty champion told,
Both Solyman and he at once leaped out,
Fury the first provoked, disdain the last,
Who scorned the challenge ere his lips it passed.

LXIV
Upon their foes unlooked–for they flew,
Each spited other for his virtue's sake,
So many soldiers this fierce couple slew,
So many shields they cleft and helms they break,
So many ladders to the earth they threw,
That well they seemed a mount thereof to make,
Or else some vamure fit to save the town,
Instead of that the Christians late beat down.

LXV
The folk that strove with rage and haste before
Who first the wall and rampire should ascend,
Retire, and for that honor strive no more,
Scantly they could their limbs and lives defend,
They fled, their engines lost the Pagans tore
In pieces small, their rams to naught they rend,
And all unfit for further service make
With so great force and rage their beams they brake.

LXVI

The Pagans ran transported with their ire,
Now here, now there, and woful slaughters wrought,
At last they called for devouring fire,
Two burning pines against the tower they brought,
So from the palace of their hellish sire,
When all this world they would consume to naught,
The fury sisters come with fire in hands,
Shaking their snaky locks and sparkling brands:

LXVII

But noble Tancred, who this while applied
Grave exhortations to his bold Latines,
When of these knights the wondrous acts he spied,
And saw the champions with their burning pines,
He left his talk, and thither forthwith hied,
To stop the rage of those fell Saracines.
And with such force the fight he there renewed,
That now they fled and lost who late pursued.

LXVIII

Thus changed the state and fortune of the fray,
Meanwhile the wounded duke, in grief and teen,
Within his great pavilion rich and gay,
Good Sigiere and Baldwin stood between;
His other friends whom his mishap dismay,
With grief and tears about assembled been:
He strove in haste the weapon out to wind,
And broke the reed, but left the head behind.

LXIX

He bade them take the speediest way they might,
Of that unlucky hurt to make him sound,
And to lay ope the depth thereof to sight,
He willed them open, search and lance the wound,

"Send me again," quoth he, "to end this fight,
Before the sun be sunken under ground;"
And leaning on a broken spear, he thrust
His leg straight out, to him that cure it must.

LXX

Erotimus, born on the banks of Po,
Was he that undertook to cure the knight,
All what green herbs or waters pure could do,
He knew their power, their virtue, and their might,
A noble poet was the man also,
But in this science had a more delight,
He could restore to health death–wounded men,
And make their names immortal with his pen.

LXXI

The mighty duke yet never changed cheer,
But grieved to see his friends lamenting stand;
The leech prepared his cloths and cleansing gear,
And with a belt his gown about him band,
Now with his herbs the steely head to tear
Out of the flesh he proved, now with his hand,
Now with his hand, now with his instrument
He shaked and plucked it, yet not forth it went.

LXXII

His labor vain, his art prevailed naught,
His luck was ill, although his skill were good,
To such extremes the wounded prince he brought,
That with fell pain he swooned as he stood:
But the angel pure, that kept him, went and sought
Divine dictamnum, out of Ida wood,
This herb is rough, and bears a purple flower,
And in his budding leaves lies all his power.

LXXIII

Kind nature first upon the craggy clift
Bewrayed this herb unto the mountain goat,
That when her sides a cruel shaft hath rift,
With it she shakes the reed out of her coat;
This in a moment fetched the angel swift,
And brought from Ida hill, though far remote,
The juice whereof in a prepared bath
Unseen the blessed spirit poured hath.

LXXIV
Pure nectar from that spring of Lydia than,
And panaces divine therein he threw,
The cunning leech to bathe the wound began,
And of itself the steely head outflew;
The bleeding stanched, no vermile drop outran,
The leg again waxed strong with vigor new:
Erotimus cried out, "This hurt and wound
No human art or hand so soon makes sound:

LXXV
"Some angel good I think come down from skies
Thy surgeon is, for here plain tokens are
Of grace divine which to thy help applies,
Thy weapon take and haste again to war."
In precious cloths his leg the chieftain ties,
Naught could the man from blood and fight debar;
A sturdy lance in his right hand he braced,
His shield he took, and on his helmet laced:
LXXVI
And with a thousand knights and barons bold,
Toward the town he hasted from his camp,
In clouds of dust was Titan's face enrolled,
Trembled the earth whereon the worthies stamp,
His foes far off his dreadful looks behold,
Which in their hearts of courage quenched the lamp,
A chilling fear ran cold through every vein,

Jerusalem Delivered

Lord Godfrey shouted thrice and all his train:

LXXVII

Their sovereign's voice his hardy people knew,
And his loud cries that cheered each fearful heart;
Thereat new strength they took and courage new,
And to the fierce assault again they start.
The Pagans twain this while themselves withdrew
Within the breach to save that battered part,
And with great loss a skirmish hot they hold
Against Tancredi and his squadron bold.

LXXVIII

Thither came Godfrey armed round about
In trusty plate, with fierce and dreadful look;
At first approach against Argantes stout
Headed with poignant steel a lance he shook,
No casting engine with such force throws out
A knotty spear, and as the way it took,
It whistled in the air, the fearless knight
Opposed his shield against that weapon's might.

LXXIX

The dreadful blow quite through his target drove,
And bored through his breastplate strong and thick,
The tender skin it in his bosom rove,
The purple–blood out–streamed from the quick;
To wrest it out the wounded Pagan strove
And little leisure gave it there to stick;
At Godfrey's head the lance again he cast,
And said, "Lo, there again thy dart thou hast."

LXXX

The spear flew back the way it lately came,
And would revenge the harm itself had done,
But missed the mark whereat the man did aim,
He stepped aside the furious blow to shun:

But Sigiere in his throat received the same,
The murdering weapon at his neck out–run,
Nor aught it grieved the man to lose his breath,
Since in his prince's stead he suffered death.

LXXXI

Even then the Soldan struck with monstrous main
The noble leader of the Norman band,
He reeled awhile and staggered with the pain,
And wheeling round fell grovelling on the sand:
Godfrey no longer could the grief sustain
Of these displeasures, but with flaming brand,
Up to the breach in heat and haste he goes,
And hand to hand there combats with his foes;

LXXXII

And there great wonders surely wrought he had,
Mortal the fight, and fierce had been the fray,
But that dark night, from her pavilion sad,
Her cloudy wings did on the earth display,
Her quiet shades she interposed glad
To cause the knights their arms aside to lay;
Godfrey withdrew, and to their tents they wend,
And thus this bloody day was brought to end.

LXXXIII

The weak and wounded ere he left the field,
The godly duke to safety thence conveyed,
Nor to his foes his engines would he yield,
In them his hope to win the fortress laid;
Then to the tower he went, and it beheeld,
The tower that late the Pagan lords dismayed
But now stood bruised, broken, cracked and shivered,
From some sharp storm as it were late delivered.

LXXXIV

From dangers great escaped, but late it was,
And now to safety brought well–nigh it seems,
But as a ship that under sail doth pass
The roaring billows and the raging streams,
And drawing nigh the wished port, alas,
Breaks on some hidden rocks her ribs and beams;
Or as a steed rough ways that well hath passed,
Before his inn stumbleth and falls at last:

LXXXV
Such hap befell that tower, for on that side
Gainst which the Pagans' force and battery bend,
Two wheels were broke whereon the piece should ride,
The maimed engine could no further wend,
The troop that guarded it that part provide
To underprop with posts, and it defend
Till carpenters and cunning workmen came
Whose skill should help and rear again the same.

LXXXVI
Thus Godfrey bids, and that ere springing–day,
The cracks and bruises all amend they should,
Each open passage, and each privy way
About the piece, he kept with soldiers bold:
But the loud rumor, both of that they say,
And that they do, is heard within the hold,
A thousand lights about the tower they view,
And what they wrought all night both saw and knew.

TWELFTH BOOK

THE ARGUMENT.

Jerusalem Delivered

Clorinda hears her eunuch old report
Her birth, her offspring, and her native land;
Disguised she fireth Godfrey's rolling fort.
The burned piece falls smoking on the sand:
With Tancred long unknown in desperate sort
She fights, and falls through pierced with his brand:
Christened she dies; with sighs, with plaints and tears.
He wails her death; Argant revengement swears.

I

Now in dark night was all the world embarred;
But yet the tired armies took no rest,
The careful French kept heedful watch and ward,
While their high tower the workmen newly dressed,
The Pagan crew to reinforce prepared
The weakened bulwarks, late to earth down kest,
Their rampiers broke and bruised walls to mend,
Lastly their hurts the wounded knights attend.

II

Their wounds were dressed, part of the work was brought
To wished end, part left to other days,
A dull desire to rest deep midnight wrought,
His heavy rod sleep on their eyelids lays:
Yet rested not Clorinda's working thought,
Which thirsted still for fame and warlike praise,
Argantes eke accompanied the maid
From place to place, which to herself thus said:

III

"This day Argantes strong, and Solyman,
Strange things have done, and purchased great renown,
Among our foes out of the walls they ran,
Their rams they broke and rent their engines down:
I used my bow, of naught else boast I can,

292

My self stood safe meanwhile within this town,
And happy was my shot, and prosperous too,
But that was all a woman's hand could do.

IV
"On birds and beasts in forests wild that feed
It were more fit mine arrows to bestow,
Than for a feeble maid in warlike deed
With strong and hardy knights herself to show.
Why take I not again my virgin's weed,
And spend my days in secret cell unknow?"
Thus thought, thus mused, thus devised the maid,
And turning to the knight, at last thus said:

V
"My thoughts are full, my lord, of strange desire
Some high attempt of war to undertake,
Whether high God my mind therewith inspire
Or of his will his God mankind doth make,
Among our foes behold the light and fire,
I will among them wend, and burn or break
The tower, God grant therein I have my will
And that performed, betide me good or ill.

VI
"But if it fortune such my chance should be,
That to this town I never turn again,
Mine eunuch, whom I dearly love, with thee
I leave my faithful maids, and all my train,
To Egypt then conducted safely see
Those woful damsels and that aged swain,
Help them, my lord, in that distressed case,
Their feeble sex, his age, deserveth grace."

VII
Argantes wondering stood, and felt the effect

Of true renown pierce through his glorious mind,
"And wilt thou go," quoth he, "and me neglect,
Disgraced, despised, leave in this fort behind?
Shall I while these strong walls my life protect
Behold thy flames and fires tossed in the wind,
No, no, thy fellow have I been in arms,
And will be still, in praise, in death, in harms.

VIII
"This heart of mine death's bitter stroke despiseth,
For praise this life, for glory take this breath."
"My soul and more," quoth she, "thy friendship prizeth,
For this thy proffered aid required uneath,
I but a woman am, no loss ariseth
To this besieged city by my death,
But if, as God forbid, this night thou fall,
Ah! who shall then, who can, defend this wall!"

IX
"Too late these 'scuses vain," the knight replied,
"You bring; my will is firm, my mind is set,
! follow you whereso you list me guide,
Or go before if you my purpose let."
This said, they hasted to the palace wide
About their prince where all his lords were met,
Clorinda spoke for both, and said, "Sir king,
Attend my words, hear, and allow the thing:

X
"Argantes here, this bold and hardy knight,
Will undertake to burn the wondrous tower,
And I with him, only we stay till night
Bury in sleep our foes at deadest hour."
The king with that cast up his hands on height,
The tears for joy upon his cheeks down pour.
"Praised," quoth he, "be Macon whom we serve,

Jerusalem Delivered

This land I see he keeps and will preserve:

XI

"Nor shall so soon this shaken kingdom fall,
While such unconquered hearts my state defend:
But for this act what praise or guerdon shall
I give your virtues, which so far extend?
Let fame your praises sound through nations all,
And fill the world therewith to either end,
Take half my wealth and kingdom for your meed?
You are rewarded half even with the deed."

XII

Thus spake the prince, and gently 'gan distrain,
Now him, now her, between his friendly arms:
The Soldan by, no longer could refrain
That noble envy which his bosom warms,
"Nor I," quoth he, "bear this broad sword in vain,
Nor yet am unexpert in night alarms,
Take me with you: ah." Quoth Clorinda, "no!
Whom leave we here of prowess if you go?"

XIII

This spoken, ready with a proud refuse
Argantes was his proffered aid to scorn,
Whom Aladine prevents, and with excuse
To Solyman thus gan his speeches torn:
"Right noble prince, as aye hath been your use
Your self so still you bear and long have borne,
Bold in all acts, no danger can affright
Your heart, nor tired is your strength with fight.

XIV

"If you went forth great things perform you would,
In my conceit yet far unfit it seems
That you, who most excel in courage bold,

At once should leave this town in these extremes,
Nor would I that these twain should leave this hold,
My heart their noble lives far worthier deems,
If this attempt of less importance were,
Or weaker posts so great a weight could bear.
XV
"But for well—guarded is the mighty tower
With hardy troops and squadrons round about,
And cannot harmed be with little power,
Nor fit the time to send whole armies out,
This pair who passed have many a dreadful stowre,
And proffer now to prove this venture stout,
Alone to this attempt let them go forth,
Alone than thousands of more price and worth.

XVI
"Thou, as it best beseems a mighty king,
With ready bands besides the gate attend,
That when this couple have performed the thing,
And shall again their footsteps homeward bend,
From their strong foes upon them following
Thou may'st them keep, preserve, save and defend:"
Thus said the king, "The Soldan must consent,"
Silent remained the Turk, and discontent.

XVII
Then Ismen said, "You twain that undertake
This hard attempt, awhile I pray you stay,
Till I a wildfire of fine temper make,
That this great engine burn to ashes may;
Haply the guard that now doth watch and wake,
Will then lie tumbled sleeping on the lay;"
Thus they conclude, and in their chambers sit,
To wait the time for this adventure fit.

XVIII

Clorinda there her silver arms off rent,
Her helm, her shield, her hauberk shining bright,
An armor black as jet or coal she hent,
Wherein withouten plume herself she dight;
For thus disguised amid her foes she meant
To pass unseen, by help of friendly night,
To whom her eunuch, old Arsetes, came,
That from her cradle nursed and kept the dame.

XIX

This aged sire had followed far and near,
Through lands and seas, the strong and hardy maid,
He saw her leave her arms and wonted gear,
Her danger nigh that sudden change foresaid:
By his white locks from black that changed were
In following her, the woful man her prayed,
By all his service and his taken pain,
To leave that fond attempt, but prayed in vain.

XX

"At last," quoth he, "since hardened to thine ill,
Thy cruel heart is to thy loss prepared,
That my weak age, nor tears that down distil,
Not humble suit, nor plaint, thou list regard;
Attend awhile, strange things unfold I will,
Hear both thy birth and high estate declared;
Follow my counsel, or thy will that done,"
She sat to hear, the eunuch thus begun:

XXI

"Senapus ruled, and yet perchance doth reign
In mighty Ethiop, and her deserts waste,
The lore of Christ both he and all his train
Of people black, hath kept and long embraced,
To him a Pagan was I sold for gain,
And with his queen, as her chief eunuch, placed;

Jerusalem Delivered

Black was this queen as jet, yet on her eyes
Sweet loveliness, in black attired, lies.

XXII

"The fire of love and frost of jealousy,
Her husband's troubled soul alike torment,
The tide of fond suspicion flowed high,
The foe to love and plague to sweet content,
He mewed her up from sight of mortal eye,
Nor day he would his beams on her had bent:
She, wise and lowly, by her husband's pleasure,
Her joy, her peace, her will, her wish did measure.

XXIII

"Her prison was a chamber, painted round
With goodly portraits and with stories old,
As white as snow there stood a virgin bound,
Besides a dragon fierce, a champion bold
The monster did with poignant spear through wound,
The gored beast lay dead upon the mould;
The gentle queen before this image laid.
She plained, she mourned, she wept, she sighed, she prayed:

XXIV

"At last with child she proved, and forth she brought,
And thou art she, a daughter fair and bright,
In her thy color white new terror wrought,
She wondered on thy face with strange affright,
But yet she purposed in her fearful thought
To hide thee from the king, thy father's sight,
Lest thy bright hue should his suspect approve,
For seld a crow begets a silver dove.

XXV

"And to her spouse to show she was disposed
A negro's babe late born, in room of thee,

And for the tower wherein she lay enclosed,
Was with her damsels only wond and me,
To me, on whose true faith she most reposed,
She gave thee, ere thou couldest christened be,
Nor could I since find means thee to baptize,
In Pagan lands thou knowest it's not the guise.

XXVI

"To me she gave thee, and she wept withal,
To foster thee in some far distant place.
Who can her griefs and plaints to reckoning call,
How oft she swooned at the last embrace:
Her streaming tears amid her kisses fall,
Her sighs, her dire complaints did interlace?
And looking up at last, ` O God,' quoth she,
`Who dost my heart and inward mourning see,

XXVII

"`If mind and body spotless to this day,
If I have kept my bed still undefiled,
Not for myself a sinful wretch I pray,
That in thy presence am an abject vilde,
Preserve this babe, whose mother must denay
To nourish it, preserve this harmless child,
Oh let it live, and chaste like me it make,
But for good fortune elsewhere sample take.

XXVIII

"'Thou heavenly soldier which delivered hast
That sacred virgin from the serpent old,
If on thine altars I have offerings placed,
And sacrificed myrrh, frankincense and gold,
On this poor child thy heavenly looks down cast,
With gracious eye this silly babe behold;'
This said, her strength and living sprite was fled,
She sighed, she groaned, she swooned in her bed.

Jerusalem Delivered

XXIX

"Weeping I took thee, in a little chest,
Covered with herbs and leaves, I brought thee out
So secretly, that none of all the rest
Of such an act suspicion had or doubt,
To wilderness my steps I first addressed,
Where horrid shades enclosed me round about,
A tigress there I met, in whose fierce eyes
Fury and wrath, rage, death and terror lies:

XXX

"Up to a tree I leaped, and on the grass,
Such was my sudden fear, I left thee lying,
To thee the beast with furious course did pass,
With curious looks upon thy visage prying,
All suddenly both meek and mild she was,
With friendly cheer thy tender body eying:
At last she licked thee, and with gesture mild
About thee played, and thou upon her smiled.

XXXI

"Her fearful muzzle full of dreadful threat,
In thy weak hand thou took'st withouten dread;
The gentle beast with milk–outstretched teat,
As nurses' custom, proffered thee to feed.
As one that wondereth on some marvel great,
I stood this while amazed at the deed.
When thee she saw well filled and satisfied,
Unto the woods again the tigress hied.

XXXII

"She gone, down from the tree I came in haste,
And took thee up, and on my journey wend,
Within a little thorp I stayed at last,
And to a nurse the charge of thee commend,

Jerusalem Delivered

And sporting with thee there long time I passed,
Till term of sixteen months were brought to end,
And thou begun, as little children do,
With half clipped words to prattle, and to go.

XXXIII
"But having passed the August of mine age,
When more than half my tap of life was run,
Rich by rewards given by your mother sage,
For merits past, and service yet undone,
I longed to leave this wandering pilgrimage,
And in my native soil again to won,
To get some seely home I had desire,
Loth still to warm me at another's fire.

XXXIV
"To Egypt–ward, where I was born, I went,
And bore thee with me, by a rolling flood,
Till I with savage thieves well–nigh was hent;
Before the brook, the thieves behind me stood:
Thee to forsake I never could consent,
And gladly would I 'scape those outlaws wood,
Into the flood I leaped far from the brim,
My left hand bore thee, with the right I swim.

XXXV
"Swift was the current, in the middle stream
A whirlpool gaped with devouring jaws,
The gulf, on such mishap ere I could dream,
Into his deep abyss my carcass draws,
There I forsook thee, the wild waters seem
To pity thee, a gentle wind there blows
Whose friendly puffs safe to the shore thee drive,
Where wet and weary I at last arrive:

XXXVI

301

"I took thee up, and in my dream that night,
When buried was the world in sleep and shade,
I saw a champion clad in armor bright
That o'er my head shaked a flaming blade,
He said, 'I charge thee execute aright,
That charge this infant's mother on thee laid,
Baptize the child, high Heaven esteems her dear,
And I her keeper will attend her near:

XXXVII

"'I will her keep, defend, save and protect,
I made the waters mild, the tigress tame,
O wretch that heavenly warnings dost reject!'
The warrior vanished having said the same.
I rose and journeyed on my way direct
When blushing morn from Tithon's bed forth came,
But for my faith is true and sure I ween,
And dreams are false, you still unchristened been.

XXXVIII

"A Pagan therefore thee I fostered have,
Nor of thy birth the truth did ever tell,
Since you increased are in courage brave,
Your sex and nature's—self you both excel,
Full many a realm have you made bond and slave,
Your fortunes last yourself remember well,
And how in peace and war, in joy and teen,
I have your servant, and your tutor been.

XXXIX

"Last morn, from skies ere stars exiled were,
In deep and deathlike sleep my senses drowned,
The self—same vision did again appear,
With stormy wrathful looks, and thundering sound,
`Villain,' quoth he, `within short while thy dear
Must change her life, and leave this sinful ground,
Thine be the loss, the torment, and the care,'

This said, he fled through skies, through clouds and air.

XL

"Hear then my joy, my hope, my darling, hear,
High Heaven some dire misfortune threatened hath,
Displeased pardie, because I did thee lere
A lore repugnant to thy parents' faith;
Ah, for my sake, this bold attempt forbear;
Put off these sable arms, appease thy wrath."
This said, he wept, she pensive stood and sad,
Because like dream herself but lately had.

XLI

With cheerful smile she answered him at last,
"I will this faith observe, it seems me true,
Which from my cradle age thou taught me hast;
I will not change it for religion new,
Nor with vain shows of fear and dread aghast
This enterprise forbear I to pursue,
No, not if death in his most dreadful face
Wherewith he scareth mankind, kept the place."

XLII

Approachen gan the time, while thus she spake,
Wherein they ought that dreadful hazard try;
She to Argantes went, who should partake
Of her renown and praise, or with her die.
Ismen with words more hasty still did make
Their virtue great, which by itself did fly,
Two balls he gave them made of hollow brass,
Wherein enclosed fire, pitch, and brimstone was.

XLIII

And forth they went, and over dale and hill
They hasted forward with a speedy pace,
Unseen, unmarked, undescried, until
Beside the engine close themselves they place,

303

New courage there their swelling hearts did fill,
Rage in their breasts, fury shown in their face,
They yearned to blow the fire, and draw the sword.
The watch descried them both, and gave the word.

XLIV
Silent they passed on, the watch begun
To rear a huge alarm with hideous cries,
Therewith the hardy couple forward run
To execute their valiant enterprise:
So from a cannon or a roaring gun
At once the noise, the flame, and bullet flies,
They run, they give the charge, begin the fray,
And all at once their foes break, spoil and slay.

XLV
They passed first through thousand thousand blows,
And then performed their designment bold,
A fiery ball each on the engine throws,
The stuff was dry, the fire took quickly hold,
Furious upon the timber–work it grows,
How it increased cannot well be told,
How it crept up the piece, and how to skies
The burning sparks and towering smoke upflies.

XLVI
A mass of solid fire burning bright
Rolled up in smouldering fumes, there bursteth out,
And there the blustering winds add strength and might
And gather close the sparsed flames about:
The Frenchmen trembled at the dreadful light,
To arms in haste and fear ran all the rout,
Down fell the piece dreaded so much in war,
Thus what long days do make one hour doth mar.

XLVII

Two Christian bands this while came to the place
With speedy haste, where they beheld the fire,
Argantes to them cried with scornful grace,
"Your blood shall quench these flames, and quench mine ire:"
This said, the maid and he with sober pace
Drew back, and to the banks themselves retire,
Faster than brooks which falling showers increase
Their foes augment, and faster on them press.

XLVIII
The gilden port was opened, and forth stepped
With all his soldiers bold, the Turkish king,
Ready to aid the two his force he kept,
When fortune should them home with conquest bring,
Over the bars the hardy couple leapt
And after them a band of Christians fling,
Whom Solyman drove back with courage stout,
And shut the gate, but shut Clorinda out.

XLIX
Alone was she shut forth, for in that hour
Wherein they closed the port, the virgin went,
And full of heat and wrath, her strength and power
Gainst Arimon, that struck her erst, she bent,
She slew the knight, nor Argant in that stowre
Wist of her parting, or her fierce intent,
The fight, the press, the night, and darksome skies
Care from his heart had ta'en, sight from his eyes.

L
But when appeased was her angry mood,
Her fury calmed, and settled was her head,
She saw the gates were shut, and how she stood
Amid her foes, she held herself for dead;
While none her marked at last she thought it good,
To save her life, some other path to tread,

305

She feigned her one of them, and close her drew
Amid the press that none her saw or knew:

LI
Then as a wolf guilty of some misdeed
Flies to some grove to hide himself from view,
So favored with the night, with secret speed
Dissevered from the press the damsel flew:
Tancred alone of her escape took heed,
He on that quarter was arrived new,
When Arimon she killed he thither came,
He saw it, marked it, and pursued the dame.

LII
He deemed she was some man of mickle might,
And on her person would he worship win,
Over the hills the nymph her journey dight
Toward another port, there to get in:
With hideous noise fast after spurred the knight,
She heard and stayed, and thus her words begin,
"What haste hast thou? ride softly, take thy breath,
What bringest thou?" He answered, "War and death."

LIII
"And war and death," quoth she, "here mayest thou get
If thou for battle come," with that she stayed:
Tancred to ground his foot in haste down set,
And left his steed, on foot he saw the maid,
Their courage hot, their ire and wrath they whet,
And either champion drew a trenchant blade,
Together ran they, and together stroke,
Like two fierce bulls whom rage and love provoke.

LIV
Worthy of royal lists and brightest day,
Worthy a golden trump and laurel crown,

The actions were and wonders of that fray
Which sable knight did in dark bosom drown:
Yet night, consent that I their acts display
And make their deeds to future ages known,
And in records of long enduring story
Enrol their praise, their fame, their worth and glory.

LV

They neither shrunk, nor vantage sought of ground,
They traverse not, nor skipped from part to part,
Their blows were neither false nor feigned found,
The night, their rage would let them use no art,
Their swords together clash with dreadful sound,
Their feet stand fast, and neither stir nor start,
They move their hands, steadfast their feet remain,
Nor blow nor loin they struck, or thrust in vain.

LVI

Shame bred desire a sharp revenge to take,
And vengeance taken gave new cause of shame:
So that with haste and little heed they strake,
Fuel enough they had to feed the flame;
At last so close their battle fierce they make,
They could not wield their swords, so nigh they came,
They used the hilts, and each on other rushed,
And helm to helm, and shield to shield they crushed.

LVII

Thrice his strong arms he folds about her waist,
And thrice was forced to let the virgin go,
For she disdained to be so embraced, .
No lover would have strained his mistress so:
They took their swords again, and each enchased
Deep wounds in the soft flesh of his strong foe,
Till weak and weary, faint, alive uneath,
They both retired at once, at once took breath.

307

Jerusalem Delivered

LVIII

Each other long beheld, and leaning stood
Upon their swords, whose points in earth were pight,
When day—break, rising from the eastern flood,
Put forth the thousand eyes of blindfold night;
Tancred beheld his foe's out—streaming blood,
And gaping wounds, and waxed proud with the sight,
Oh vanity of man's unstable mind,
Puffed up with every blast of friendly wind!

LIX

Why joy'st thou, wretch? Oh, what shall be thy gain?
What trophy for this conquest is't thou rears?
Thine eyes shall shed, in case thou be not slain,
For every drop of blood a sea of tears:
The bleeding warriors leaning thus remain,
Each one to speak one word long time forbears,
Tancred the silence broke at last, and said,
For he would know with whom this fight he made:

LX

"Evil is our chance and hard our fortune is
Who here in silence, and in shade debate,
Where light of sun and witness all we miss
That should our prowess and our praise dilate:
If words in arms find place, yet grant me this,
Tell me thy name, thy country, and estate;
That I may know, this dangerous combat done,
Whom I have conquered, or who hath me won."

LXI

"What I nill tell, you ask," quoth she, "in vain,
Nor moved by prayer, nor constrained by power,
But thus much know, I am one of those twain
Which late with kindled fire destroyed the tower."

Tancred at her proud words swelled with disdain,
"That hast thou said," quoth he, "in evil hour;
Thy vaunting speeches, and thy silence both,
Uncivil wretch, hath made my heart more wroth."

LXII
Ire in their chafed breasts renewed the fray,
Fierce was the fight, though feeble were their might,
Their strength was gone, their cunning was away,
And fury in their stead maintained the fight,
Their swords both points and edges sharp embay
In purple blood, whereso they hit or light,
And if weak life yet in their bosoms lie,
They lived because they both disdained to die.

LXIII
As Aegean seas when storms be calmed again
That rolled their tumbling waves with troublous blasts,
Do yet of tempests past some shows retain,
And here and there their swelling billows casts;
So, though their strength were gone and might were vain,
Of their first fierceness still the fury lasts,
Wherewith sustained, they to their tackling stood,
And heaped wound on wound, and blood on blood.

LXIV
But now, alas, the fatal hour arrives
That her sweet life must leave that tender hold,
His sword into her bosom deep he drives,
And bathed in lukewarm blood his iron cold,
Between her breasts the cruel weapon rives
Her curious square, embossed with swelling gold,
Her knees grow weak, the pains of death she feels,
And like a falling cedar bends and reels.

LXV

Jerusalem Delivered

The prince his hand upon her shield doth stretch,
And low on earth the wounded damsel layeth,
And while she fell, with weak and woful speech,
Her prayers last and last complaints she sayeth,
A spirit new did her those prayers teach,
Spirit of hope, of charity, and faith;
And though her life to Christ rebellious were,
Yet died she His child and handmaid dear.

LXVI

"Friend, thou hast won, I pardon thee, nor save
This body, that all torments can endure,
But save my soul, baptism I dying crave,
Come wash away my sins with waters pure:"
His heart relenting nigh in sunder rave,
With woful speech of that sweet creature,
So that his rage, his wrath, and anger died,
And on his cheeks salt tears for ruth down slide.

LXVII

With murmur loud down from the mountain's side
A little runnel tumbled near the place,
Thither he ran and filled his helmet wide,
And quick returned to do that work of grace,
With trembling hands her beaver he untied,
Which done he saw, and seeing, knew her face,
And lost therewith his speech and moving quite,
Oh woful knowledge, ah unhappy sight!

LXVIII

He died not, but all his strength unites,
And to his virtues gave his heart in guard,
Bridling his grief, with water he requites
The life that he bereft with iron hard,
And while the sacred words the knight recites,
The nymph to heaven with joy herself prepared;

310

And as her life decays her joys increase,
She smiled and said, "Farewell, I die in peace."

LXIX

As violets blue mongst lilies pure men throw,
So paleness midst her native white begun;
Her looks to heaven she cast, their eyes I trow
Downward for pity bent both heaven and sun,
Her naked hand she gave the knight, in show
Of love and peace, her speech, alas, was done,
And thus the virgin fell on endless sleep, —
Love, Beauty, Virtue, for your darling weep!

LXX

But when he saw her gentle soul was went,
His manly courage to relent began,
Grief, sorrow, anguish. sadness, discontent,
Free empire got and lordship on the man,
His life within his heart they close up pent,
Death through his senses and his visage ran:
Like his dead lady, dead seemed Tancred good,
In paleness, stillness, wounds and streams of blood.

LXXI

And his weak sprite, to be unbodied
From fleshly prison free that ceaseless strived,
Had followed her fair soul but lately fled
Had not a Christian squadron there arrived,
To seek fresh water thither haply led,
And found the princess dead, and him deprived
Of signs of life; yet did the knight remain
On live, nigh dead, for her himself had slain.

LXXII

Their guide far off the prince knew by his shield,
And thither hasted full of grief and fear,
Her dead, him seeming so, he there beheld,

311

And for that strange mishap shed many a tear;
He would not leave the corpses fair in field
For food to wolves, though she a Pagan were,
But in their arms the soldiers both uphent,
And both lamenting brought to Tancred's tent.

LXXIII
With those dear burdens to their camp they pass,
Yet would not that dead seeming knight awake,
At last he deeply groaned, which token was
His feeble soul had not her flight yet take:
The other lay a still and heavy mass,
Her spirit had that earthen cage forsake;
Thus were they brought, and thus they placed were
In sundry rooms, yet both adjoining near.

LXXIV
All skill and art his careful servants used
To life again their dying lord to bring,
At last his eyes unclosed, with tears suffused,
He felt their hands and heard their whispering,
But how he thither came long time he mused,
His mind astonished was with everything;
He gazed about, his squires in fine he knew,
Then weak and woful thus his plaints out threw:

LXXV
"What, live I yet? and do I breathe and see
Of this accursed day the hateful light?
This spiteful ray which still upbraideth me
With that accursed deed I did this night,
Ah, coward hand, afraid why should'st thou be;
Thou instrument of death, shame and despite,
Why should'st thou fear, with sharp and trenchant knife,
To cut the thread of this blood–guilty life?

Jerusalem Delivered

LXXVI

"Pierce through this bosom, and my cruel heart
In pieces cleave, break every string and vein;
But thou to slaughters vile which used art,
Think'st it were pity so to ease my pain:
Of luckless love therefore in torments' smart
A sad example must I still remain,
A woful monster of unhappy love,
Who still must live, lest death his comfort prove:

LXXVII

"Still must I live in anguish, grief, and care;
Furies my guilty conscience that torment,
The ugly shades, dark night, and troubled air
In grisly forms her slaughter still present,
Madness and death about my bed repair,
Hell gapeth wide to swallow up this tent;
Swift from myself I run, myself I fear,
Yet still my hell within myself I bear.

LXXVIII

"But where, alas, where be those relics sweet,
Wherein dwelt late all love, all joy, all good?
My fury left them cast in open street,
Some beast hath torn her flesh and licked her blood,
Ah noble prey! for savage beast unmeet,
Ah sweet! too sweet, and far too precious food,
Ah, seely nymph! whom night and darksome shade
To beasts, and me, far worse than beasts, betrayed.

LXXIX

"But where you be, if still you be, I wend
To gather up those relics dear at least,
But if some beast hath from the hills descend,
And on her tender bowels made his feast,
Let that fell monster me in pieces rend,

And deep entomb me in his hollow chest:
For where she buried is, there shall I have
A stately tomb, a rich and costly grave."

LXXX

Thus mourned the knight, his squires him told at last,
They had her there for whom those tears he shed;
A beam of comfort his dim eyes outcast,
Like lightning through thick clouds of darkness spread,
The heavy burden of his limbs in haste,
With mickle pain, he drew forth of his bed,
And scant of strength to stand, to move or go,
Thither he staggered, reeling to and fro.

LXXXI

When he came there, and in her breast espied
His handiwork, that deep and cruel wound,
And her sweet face with leaden paleness dyed,
Where beauty late spread forth her beams around,
He trembled so, that nere his squires beside
To hold him up, he had sunk down to ground,
And said, "O face in death still sweet and fair!
Thou canst not sweeten yet my grief and care:

LXXXII

"O fair right hand, the pledge of faith and love?
Given me but late, too late, in sign of peace,
How haps it now thou canst not stir nor move?
And you, dear limbs, now laid in rest and ease,
Through which my cruel blade this flood–gate rove,
Your pains have end, my torments never cease,
O hands, O cruel eyes, accursed alike!
You gave the wound, you gave them light to strike.

LXXXIII

"But thither now run forth my guilty blood,

Whither my plaints, my sorrows cannot wend."
He said no more, but, as his passion wood
Inforced him, he gan to tear and rend
His hair, his face, his wounds, a purple flood
Did from each side in rolling streams descend,
He had been slain, but that his pain and woe
Bereft his senses, and preserved him so.
LXXXIV
Cast on his bed his squires recalled his sprite
To execute again her hateful charge,
But tattling fame the sorrows of the knight
And hard mischance had told this while at large:
Godfrey and all his lords of worth and might,
Ran thither, and the duty would discharge
Of friendship true, and with sweet words the rage
Of bitter grief and woe they would assuage.

LXXXV
But as a mortal wound the more doth smart
The more it searched is, handled or sought;
So their sweet words to his afflicted heart
More grief, more anguish, pain and torment brought
But reverend Peter that would set apart
Care of his sheep, as a good shepherd ought,
His vanity with grave advice reproved
And told what mourning Christian knights behoved:

LXXXVI
"O Tancred, Tancred, how far different
From thy beginnings good these follies be?
What makes thee deaf? what hath thy eyesight blent?
What mist, what cloud thus overshadeth thee?
This is a warning good from heaven down sent,
Yet His advice thou canst not hear nor see
Who calleth and conducts thee to the way
From which thou willing dost and witting stray:

315

LXXXVII

"To worthy actions and achievements fit
For Christian knights He would thee home recall;
But thou hast left that course and changed it,
To make thyself a heathen damsel's thrall;
But see, thy grief and sorrow's painful fit
Is made the rod to scourge thy sins withal,
Of thine own good thyself the means He makes,
But thou His mercy, goodness, grace forsakes.

LXXXVIII

"Thou dost refuse of heaven the proffered
And gainst it still rebel with sinful ire,
Oh wretch! Oh whither doth thy rage thee chase?
Refrain thy grief, bridle thy fond desire,
At hell's wide gate vain sorrow doth thee place,
Sorrow, misfortune's son, despair's foul fire:
Oh see thine evil, thy plaint and woe refrain,
The guides to death, to hell, and endless pain."

LXXXIX

This said, his will to die the patient
Abandoned, that second death he feared,
These words of comfort to his heart down went,
And that dark night of sorrow somewhat cleared;
Yet now and then his grief deep sighs forth sent,
His voice shrill plaints and sad laments oft reared,
Now to himself, now to his murdered love,
He spoke, who heard perchance from heaven above.

XC

Till Phoebus' rising from his evening fall
To her, for her, he mourns, he calls, he cries;
The nightingale so when her children small
Some churl takes before their parents' eyes,

Jerusalem Delivered

Alone, dismayed, quite bare of comforts all,
Tires with complaints the seas, the shores, the skies,
Till in sweet sleep against the morning bright
She fall at last; so mourned, so slept the knight.

XCI
And clad in starry veil, amid his dream,
For whose sweet sake he mourned, appeared the maid,
Fairer than erst, yet with that heavenly beam.
Not out of knowledge was her lovely shade,
With looks of ruth her eyes celestial seem
To pity his sad plight, and thus she said,
"Behold how fair, how glad thy love appears,
And for my sake, my dear, forbear these tears.

XCII
"Thine be the thanks, my soul thou madest flit
At unawares out of her earthly nest,
Thine be the thanks, thou hast advanced it
In Abraham's dear bosom long to rest,
There still I love thee, there for Tancred fit
A seat prepared is among the blest;
There in eternal joy, eternal light,
Thou shalt thy love enjoy, and she her knight;

XCIII
"Unless thyself, thyself heaven's joys envy,
And thy vain sorrow thee of bliss deprive,
Live, know I love thee, that I nill deny,
As angels, men: as saints may wights on live:"
This said, of zeal and love forth of her eye
An hundred glorious beams bright shining drive,
Amid which rays herself she closed from sigh,
And with new joy, new comfort left her knight.

XCIV

Jerusalem Delivered

Thus comforted he waked, and men discreet
In surgery to cure his wounds were sought,
Meanwhile of his dear love the relics sweet,
As best he could, to grave with pomp he brought:
Her tomb was not of varied Spartan greet,
Nor yet by cunning hand of Scopas wrought,
But built of polished stone, and thereon laid
The lively shape and portrait of the maid.

XCV

With sacred burning lamps in order long
And mournful pomp the corpse was brought to ground
Her arms upon a leafless pine were hung,
The hearse, with cypress; arms, with laurel crowned:
Next day the prince, whose love and courage strong
Drew forth his limbs, weak, feeble, and unsound,
To visit went, with care and reverence meet,
The buried ashes of his mistress sweet:

XCVI

Before her new–made tomb at last arrived,
The woful prison of his living sprite,
Pale, cold, sad, comfortless, of sense deprived,
Upon the marble gray he fixed his sight,
Two streams of tears were from his eyes derived:
Thus with a sad "Alas!" began the knight,
"0 marble dear on my dear mistress placed!
My flames within, without my tears thou hast.

XCVII

"Not of dead bones art thou the mournful grave,
But of quick love the fortress and the hold,
Still in my heart thy wonted brands I have
More bitter far, alas! but not more cold;
Receive these sighs, these kisses sweet receive,
In liquid drops of melting tears enrolled,

And give them to that body pure and chaste,
Which in thy bosom cold entombed thou hast.

XCVIII
"For if her happy soul her eye doth bend
On that sweet body which it lately dressed,
My love, thy pity cannot her offend,
Anger and wrath is not in angels blessed,
She pardon will the trespass of her friend,
That hope relieves me with these griefs oppressed,
This hand she knows hath only sinned, not I,
Who living loved her, and for love now die:
XCIX
"And loving will I die, oh happy day
Whene'er it chanceth! but oh far more blessed
If as about thy polished sides I stray,
My bones within thy hollow grave might rest,
Together should in heaven our spirits stay,
Together should our bodies lie in chest;
So happy death should join what life doth sever,
0 Death, 0 Life! sweet both, both blessed ever."

C
Meanwhile the news in that besieged town
Of this mishap was whispered here and there,
Forthwith it spread, and for too true was known,
Her woful loss was talked everywhere,
Mingled with cries and plaints to heaven upthrown,
As if the city's self new taken were
With conquering foes, or as if flame and fire,
Nor house, nor church, nor street had left entire.

CI
But all men's eyes were on Arsetes bent,
His sighs were deep, his looks full of despair,
Out of his woful eyes no tear there went,

319

His heart was hardened with his too much care,
His silver locks with dust he foul besprent,
He knocked his breast, his face he rent and tare,
And while the press flocked to the eunuch old,
Thus to the people spake Argantes bold:

CII

"I would, when first I knew the hardy maid
Excluded was among her Christian foes,
Have followed her to give her timely aid,
Or by her side this breath and life to lose,
What did I not, or what left I unsaid
To make the king the gates again unclose?
But he denied, his power did aye restrain
My will, my suit was waste, my speech was vain:

CIII

"Ah, had I gone, I would from danger free
Have brought to Sion that sweet nymph again,
Or in the bloody fight, where killed was she,
In her defence there nobly have been slain:
But what could I do more? the counsels be
Of God and man gainst my designments plain,
Dead is Clorinda fair, laid in cold grave,
Let me revenge her whom I could not save.

CIV

"Jerusalem, hear what Argantes saith,
Hear Heaven, and if he break his oath and word,
Upon this head cast thunder in thy wrath:
I will destroy and kill that Christian lord
Who this fair dame by night thus murdered hath,
Nor from my side I will ungird this sword
Till Tancred's heart it cleave, and shed his blood,
And leave his corpse to wolves and crows for food."

CV
This said, the people with a joyful shout
Applaud his speeches and his words approve,
And calmed their grief in hope the boaster stout
Would kill the prince, who late had slain his love.
O promise vain! it otherwise fell out:
Men purpose, but high gods dispose above,
For underneath his sword this boaster died
Whom thus he scorned and threatened in his pride.

THIRTEENTH BOOK

THE ARGUMENT.
Ismeno sets to guard the forest old
The wicked sprites, whose ugly shapes affray
And put to flight the men, whose labor would
To their dark shades let in heaven's golden ray:
Thither goes Tancred hardy, faithful, bold,
But foolish pity lets him not assay
His strength and courage: heat the Christian power
Annoys, whom to refresh God sends a shower.

I
But scant, dissolved into ashes cold,
The smoking tower fell on the scorched grass,
When new device found out the enchanter old
By which the town besieged secured was,
Of timber fit his foes deprive he would,
Such terror bred that late consumed mass:
So that the strength of Sion's walls to shake,
They should no turrets, rams, nor engines make.

321

Jerusalem Delivered

II

From Godfrey's camp a grove a little way
Amid the valleys deep grows out of sight,
Thick with old trees whose horrid arms display
An ugly shade, like everlasting night;
There when the sun spreads forth his clearest ray,
Dim, thick, uncertain, gloomy seems the light;
As when in evening, day and darkness strive
Which should his foe from our horizon drive.

III

But when the sun his chair in seas doth steep,
Night, horror, darkness thick the place invade,
Which veil the mortal eyes with blindness deep
And with sad terror make weak hearts afraid,
Thither no groom drives forth his tender sheep
To browse, or ease their faint in cooling shade,
Nor traveller nor pilgrim there to enter,
So awful seems that forest old, dare venture.

IV

United there the ghosts and goblins meet
To frolic with their mates in silent night,
With dragons' wings some cleave the welkin fleet,
Some nimbly run o'er hills and valleys light,
A wicked troop, that with allurements sweet
Draws sinful man from that is good and right,
And there with hellish pomp their banquets brought
They solemnize, thus the vain Parians thought.

V

No twist, no twig, no bough nor branch, therefore,
The Saracens cut from that sacred spring;
But yet the Christians spared ne'er the more
The trees to earth with cutting steel to bring:

Jerusalem Delivered

Thither went Ismen old with tresses hoar,
When night on all this earth spread forth her wing,
And there in silence deaf and mirksome shade
His characters and circles vain he made:

VI
He in the circle set one foot unshod,
And whispered dreadful charms in ghastly wise,
Three times, for witchcraft loveth numbers odd,
Toward the east he gaped, westward thrice,
He struck the earth thrice with his charmed rod
Wherewith dead bones he makes from grave to rise,
And thrice the ground with naked foot he smote,
And thus he cried loud, with thundering note:

VII
"Hear, hear, you spirits all that whilom fell,
Cast down from heaven with dint of roaring thunder;
Hear, you amid the empty air that dwell
And storms and showers pour on these kingdoms under;
Hear, all you devils that lie in deepest hell
And rend with torments damned ghosts asunder,
And of those lands of death, of pain and fear,
Thou monarch great, great Dis, great Pluto, hear!

VIII
"Keep you this forest well, keep every tree,
Numbered I give you them and truly told;
As souls of men in bodies clothed be
So every plant a sprite shall hide and hold,
With trembling fear make all the Christians flee,
When they presume to cut these cedars old:"
This said, his charms he gan again repeat,
Which none can say but they that use like feat.

IX

At those strange speeches, still night's splendent fires
Quenched their lights, and shrunk away for doubt,
The feeble moon her silver beams retires,
And wrapt her horns with folding clouds about,
Ismen his sprites to come with speed requires,
"Why come you not, you ever damned rout?
Why tarry you so long? pardie you stay
Till stronger charms and greater words I say.

X
"I have not yet forgot for want of use,
What dreadful terms belong this sacred feat,
My tongue, if still your stubborn hearts refuse,
That so much dreaded name can well repeat,
Which heard, great Dis cannot himself excuse,
But hither run from his eternal seat,
O great and fearful!" — More he would have said,
But that he saw the sturdy sprites obeyed.

XI
Legions of devils by thousands thither come,
Such as in sparsed air their biding make,
And thousands also which by Heavenly doom
Condemned lie in deep Avernus lake,
But slow they came, displeased all and some
Because those woods they should in keeping take,
Yet they obeyed and took the charge in hand,
And under every branch and leaf they stand.

XII
When thus his cursed work performed was,
The wizard to his king declared the feat,
"My lord, let fear, let doubt and sorrow pass,
Henceforth in safety stands your regal seat,
Your foe, as he supposed, no mean now has
To build again his rams and engines great:"

And then he told at large from part to part,
All what he late performed by wondrous art.

XIII
"Besides this help, another hap," quoth he,
"Will shortly chance that brings not profit small.
Within few days Mars and the Sun I see
Their fiery beams unite in Leo shall;
And then extreme the scorching heat will be,
Which neither rain can quench nor dews that fall,
So placed are the planets high and low,
That heat, fire, burning all the heavens foreshow:

XIV
"So great with us will be the warmth therefore,
As with the Garamants or those of Inde;
Yet nill it grieve us in this town so sore,
We have sweet shade and waters cold by kind:
Our foes abroad will be tormented more,
What shield can they or what refreshing find?
Heaven will them vanquish first, then Egypt's crew
Destroy them quite, weak, weary, faint and few:

XV
"Thou shalt sit still and conquer; prove no more
The doubtful hazard of uncertain fight.
But if Argantes bold, that hates so sore
All cause of quiet peace, though just and right,
Provoke thee forth to battle, as before,
Find means to calm the rage of that fierce knight,
For shortly Heaven will send thee ease and peace,
And war and trouble mongst thy foes increase."

XVI
The king assured by these speeches fair,
Held Godfrey's power, his might and strength in scorn,

And now the walls he gan in part repair,
Which late the ram had bruised with iron horn,
With wise foresight and well advised care
He fortified each breach and bulwark torn,
And all his folk, men, women, children small,
With endless toil again repaired the wall.

XVII

But Godfrey nould this while bring forth his power
To give assault against that fort in vain,
Till he had builded new his dreadful tower,
And reared high his down–fallen rams again:
His workmen therefore he despatched that hour
To hew the trees out of the forest main,
They went, and scant the wood appeared in sight
When wonders new their fearful hearts affright:

XVIII

As silly children dare not bend their eye
Where they are told strange bugbears haunt the place,
Or as new monsters, while in bed they lie,
Their fearful thoughts present before their face;
So feared they, and fled, yet wist not why,
Nor what pursued them in that fearful chase.
Except their fear perchance while thus they fled,
New chimeras, sphinxes, or like monsters bred:

XIX

Swift to the camp they turned back dismayed,
With words confused uncertain tales they told,
That all which heard them scorned what they said
And those reports for lies and fables hold.
A chosen crew in shining arms arrayed
Duke Godfrey thither sent of soldiers bold,
To guard the men and their faint arms provoke
To cut the dreadful trees with hardy stroke:

XX

These drawing near the wood where close ypent
The wicked sprites in sylvan pinfolds were,
Their eyes upon those shades no sooner bent
But frozen dread pierced through their entrails dear;
Yet on they stalked still, and on they went,
Under bold semblance hiding coward fear,
And so far wandered forth with trembling pace,
Till they approached nigh that enchanted place:

XXI

When from the grove a fearful sound outbreaks,
As if some earthquake hill and mountain tore,
Wherein the southern wind a rumbling makes,
Or like sea waves against the scraggy shore;
There lions grumble, there hiss scaly snakes,
There howl the wolves, the rugged bears there roar,
There trumpets shrill are heard and thunders fell,
And all these sounds one sound expressed well.
XXII

Upon their faces pale well might you note
A thousand signs of heart–amating fear,
Their reason gone, by no device they wot
How to press nigh, or stay still where they were,
Against that sudden dread their breasts which smote,
Their courage weak no shield of proof could bear,
At last they fled, and one than all more bold,
Excused their flight, and thus the wonders told:

XXIII

"My lord, not one of us there is, I grant,
That dares cut down one branch in yonder spring,
I think there dwells a sprite in every plant,
There keeps his court great Dis infernal king,
He hath a heart of hardened adamant

That without trembling dares attempt the thing,
And sense he wanteth who so hardy is
To hear the forest thunder, roar and hiss."

XXIV

This said, Alcasto to his words gave heed,
Alcasto leader of the Switzers grim,
A man both void of wit and void of dreed,
Who feared not loss of life nor loss of limb.
No savage beasts in deserts wild that feed
Nor ugly monster could dishearten him,
Nor whirlwind, thunder, earthquake, storm, or aught
That in this world is strange or fearful thought.

XXV

He shook his head, and smiling thus gan say,
"The hardiness have I that wood to fell,
And those proud trees low in the dust to lay
Wherein such grisly fiends and monsters dwell;
No roaring ghost my courage can dismay,
No shriek of birds, beast's roar, or dragon's yell;
But through and through that forest will I wend,
Although to deepest hell the paths descend."

XXVI

Thus boasted he, and leave to go desired,
And forward went with joyful cheer and will,
He viewed the wood and those thick shades admired,
He heard the wondrous noise and rumbling shrill;
Yet not one foot the audacious man retired,
He scorned the peril, pressing forward still,
Till on the forest's outmost marge he stepped,
A flaming fire from entrance there him kept.

XXVII

The fire increased, and built a stately wall

Of burning coals, quick sparks, and embers hot,
And with bright flames the wood environed all,
That there no tree nor twist Alcasto got;
The higher stretched the flames seemed bulwarks tall,
Castles and turrets full of fiery shot,
With slings and engines strong of every sort; —
What mortal wight durst scale so strange a fort?

XXVIII
Oh what strange monsters on the battlement
In loathsome forms stood to defend the place?
Their frowning looks upon the knight they bent,
And threatened death with shot, with sword and mace:
At last he fled, and though but slow he went,
As lions do whom jolly hunters chase;
Yet fled the man and with sad fear withdrew,
Though fear till then he never felt nor knew.

XXIX
That he had fled long time he never wist,
But when far run he had discoverd it,
Himself for wonder with his hand he blist,
A bitter sorrow by the heart him bit,
Amazed, ashamed, disgraced, sad, silent, trist,
Alone he would all day in darkness sit,
Nor durst he look on man of worth or fame,
His pride late great, now greater made his shame.

XXX
Godfredo called him, but he found delays
And causes why he should his cabin keep,
At length perforce he comes, but naught he says,
Or talks like those that babble in their sleep.
His shamefacedness to Godfrey plain bewrays
His flight, so does his sighs and sadness deep:
Whereat amazed, "What chance is this ?" quoth he.

"These witchcrafts strange or nature's wonders be.

XXXI

"But if his courage any champion move
To try the hazard of this dreadful spring,
I give him leave the adventure great to prove,
Some news he may report us of the thing:"
This said, his lords attempt the charmed grove,
Yet nothing back but fear and flight they bring,
For them inforced with trembling to retire,
The sight, the sound, the monsters and the fire.

XXXII

This happed when woful Tancred left his bed
To lay in marble cold his mistress dear,
The lively color from his cheek was fled,
His limbs were weak his helm or targe to bear;
Nathless when need to high attempts him led,
No labor would he shun, no danger fear,
His valor, boldness, heart and courage brave,
To his faint body strength and vigor gave.

XXXIII

To this exploit forth went the venturous knight,
Fearless, yet heedful; silent, well advised,
The terrors of that forest's dreadful sight,
Storms, earthquakes, thunders, cries, he all despised:
He feared nothing, yet a motion light,
That quickly vanished, in his heart arised
When lo, between him and the charmed wood,
A fiery city high as heaven up stood.

XXXIV

The knight stepped back and took a sudden pause,
And to himself, "What help these arms?" quoth he,
"If in this fire, or monster's gaping jaws

I headlong cast myself, what boots it me?
For common profit, or my country's cause,
To hazard life before me none should be:
But this exploit of no such weight I hold,
For it to lose a prince or champion bold.

XXXV

But if I fly, what will the Pagans say?
If I retire, who shall cut down this spring?
Godfredo will attempt it every day.
What if some other knight perform the thing?
These flames uprisen to forestall my way
Perchance more terror far than danger bring.
But hap what shall;" this said, he forward stepped,
And through the fire, oh wondrous boldness, leapt!

XXXVI

He bolted through, but neither warmth nor heat!
He felt, nor sign of fire or scorching flame;
Yet wist he not in his dismayed conceit,
If that were fire or no through which he came;
For at first touch vanished those monsters great,
And in their stead the clouds black night did frame
And hideous storms and showers of hail and rain;
Yet storms and tempests vanished straight again.

XXXVII

Amazed but not afraid the champion good
Stood still, but when the tempest passed he spied,
He entered boldly that forbidden wood,
And of the forest all the secrets eyed,
In all his walk no sprite or phantasm stood
That stopped his way or passage free denied,
Save that the growing trees so thick were set,
That oft his sight, and passage oft they let.

Jerusalem Delivered

XXXVIII

At length a fair and spacious green he spied,
Like calmest waters, plain, like velvet, soft,
Wherein a cypress clad in summer's pride,
Pyramid—wise, lift up his tops aloft;
In whose smooth bark upon the evenest side,
Strange characters he found, and viewed them oft,
Like those which priests of Egypt erst instead
Of letters used, which none but they could read.

XXXIX

Mongst them he picked out these words at last,
Writ in the Syriac tongue, which well he could,
"Oh hardy knight, who through these woods hast passed:
Where Death his palace and his court doth hold!
Oh trouble not these souls in quiet placed,
Oh be not cruel as thy heart is bold,
Pardon these ghosts deprived of heavenly light,
With spirits dead why should men living fight?"

XL

This found he graven in the tender rind,
And while he mused on this uncouth writ,
Him thought he heard the softly whistling wind
His blasts amid the leaves and branches knit
And frame a sound like speech of human kind,
But full of sorrow grief and woe was it,
Whereby his gentle thoughts all filled were
With pity, sadness, grief, compassion, fear.

XLI

He drew his sword at last, and gave the tree
A mighty blow, that made a gaping wound,
Out of the rift red streams he trickling see
That all bebled the verdant plain around,
His hair start up, yet once again stroke he,

He nould give over till the end he found
Of this adventure, when with plaint and moan,
As from some hollow grave, he heard one groan.

XLII
"Enough, enough!" the voice lamenting said,
"Tancred, thou hast me hurt, thou didst me drive
Out of the body of a noble maid
Who with me lived, whom late I kept on live,
And now within this woful cypress laid,
My tender rind thy weapon sharp doth rive,
Cruel, is't not enough thy foes to kill,
But in their graves wilt thou torment them still?
XLIII
"I was Clorinda, now imprisoned here,
Yet not alone within this plant I dwell,
For every Pagan lord and Christian peer,
Before the city's walls last day that fell,
In bodies new or graves I wot not clear,
But here they are confined by magic's spell,
So that each tree hath life, and sense each bough,
A murderer if thou cut one twist art thou."

XLIV
As the sick man that in his sleep doth see
Some ugly dragon, or some chimera new,
Though he suspect, or half persuaded be,
It is an idle dream, no monster true,
Yet still he fears, he quakes, and strives to flee,
So fearful is that wondrous form to view;
So feared the knight, yet he both knew and thought
All were illusions false by witchcraft wrought:
XLV
But cold and trembling waxed his frozen heart,
Such strange effects, such passions it torment,
Out of his feeble hand his weapon start,

Himself out of his wits nigh, after went:
Wounded he saw, he thought, for pain and smart,
His lady weep, complain, mourn, and lament,
Nor could he suffer her dear blood to see,
Or hear her sighs that deep far fetched be.

XLVI

Thus his fierce heart which death had scorned oft,
Whom no strange shape or monster could dismay,
With feigned shows of tender love made soft,
A spirit false did with vain plaints betray;
A whirling wind his sword heaved up aloft,
And through the forest bare it quite away.
O'ercome retired the prince, and as he came,
His sword he found, and repossessed the same,

XLVII

Yet nould return, he had no mind to try
His courage further in those forests green;
But when to Godfrey's tent he proached nigh,
His spirits waked, his thoughts composed been,
"My Lord." quoth he, "a witness true am I
Of wonders strange, believe it scant though seen,
What of the fire, the shades, the dreadful sound
You heard, all true by proof myself have found;

XLVIII

"A burning fire, so are those deserts charmed,
Built like a battled wall to heaven was reared;
Whereon with darts and dreadful weapons armed,
Of monsters foul mis–shaped whole bands appeared;
But through them all I passed, unhurt, unharmed,
No flame or threatened blow I felt or feared,
Then rain and night I found, but straight again
To day, the night, to sunshine turned the rain.

XLIX

"What would you more? each tree through all that wood
Hath sense, hath life, hath speech, like human kind,
I heard their words as in that grove I stood,
That mournful voice still, still I bear in mind:
And, as they were of flesh, the purple blood
At every blow streams from the wounded rind;
No, no, not I, nor any else, I trow,
Hath power to cut one leaf, one branch, one bough."

L

While thus he said, the Christian's noble guide
Felt uncouth strife in his contentious thought,
He thought, what if himself in perzon tried
Those witchcrafts strange, and bring those charms to naught,
For such he deemed them, or elsewhere provide
For timber easier got though further sought,
But from his study he at last abraid,
Called by the hermit old that to him said:

LI

"Leave off thy hardy thought, another's hands
Of these her plants the wood dispoilen shall,
Now, now the fatal ship of conquest lands,
Her sails are struck, her silver anchors fall,
Our champion broken hath his worthless bands,
And looseth from the soil which held him thrall,
The time draws nigh when our proud foes in field
Shall slaughtered lie, and Sion's fort shall yield."

LII

This said, his visage shone with beams divine,
And more than mortal was his voice's sound,
Godfredo's thought to other acts incline,
His working brain was never idle found.
But in the Crab now did bright Titan shine,
And scorched with scalding beams the parched ground,

Jerusalem Delivered

And made unfit for toil or warlike feat
His soldiers, weak with labor, faint with sweat:

LIII
The planets mild their lamps benign quenched out,
And cruel stars in heaven did signorize,
Whose influence cast fiery flames about
And hot impressions through the earth and skies,
The growing heat still gathered deeper rout,
The noisome warmth through lands and kingdoms flies,
A harmful night a hurtful day succeeds,
And worse than both next morn her light outspreads.

LIV
When Phoebus rose he left his golden weed,
And donned a gite in deepest purple dyed,
His sanguine beams about his forehead spread,
A sad presage of ill that should betide,
With vermeil drops at even his tresses bleed,
Foreshows of future heat, from the ocean wide
When next he rose, and thus increased still
Their present harms with dread of future ill,

LV
While thus he bent gainst earth his scorching rays,
He burnt the flowers, burnt his Clytie dear,
The leaves grew wan upon the withered sprays,
The grass and growing herbs all parched were,
Earth cleft in rifts, in floods their streams decays,
The barren clouds with lightning bright appear,
And mankind feared lest Climenes' child again
Had driven awry his sire's ill−guided wain.

LVI
As from a furnace flew the smoke to skies,
Such smoke as that when damned Sodom brent,

Within his caves sweet Zephyr silent lies,
Still was the air, the rack nor came nor went,
But o'er the lands with lukewarm breathing flies
The southern wind, from sunburnt Afric sent,
Which thick and warm his interrupted blasts
Upon their bosoms, throats, and faces casts.

LVII
Nor yet more comfort brought the gloomy night,
In her thick shades was burning heat uprolled,
Her sable mantle was embroidered bright
With blazing stars and gliding fires for gold,
Nor to refresh, sad earth, thy thirsty sprite,
The niggard moon let fall her May dews cold,
And dried up the vital moisture was,
In trees, in plants, in herbs, in flowers, in grass.

LVIII
Sleep to his quiet dales exiled fled
From these unquiet nights, and oft in vain
The soldiers restless sought the god in bed,
But most for thirst they mourned and most complain;
For Juda's tyrant had strong poison shed,
Poison that breeds more woe and deadly pain,
Than Acheron or Stygian waters bring,
In every fountain, cistern, well and spring:

LIX
And little Siloe that his store bestows
Of purest crystal on the Christian bands,
The pebbles naked in his channel shows
And scantly glides above the scorched sands,
Nor Po in May when o'er his banks he flows,
Nor Ganges, waterer of the Indian lands,
Nor seven–mouthed Nile that yields all Egypt drink,
To quench their thirst the men sufficient think.

337

LX

He that the gliding rivers erst had seen
Adown their verdant channels gently rolled,
Or falling streams which to the valleys green
Distilled from tops of Alpine mountains cold,
Those he desired in vain, new torments been,
Augmented thus with wish of comforts old,
Those waters cool he drank in vain conceit,
Which more increased his thirst, increased his heat.

LXI

The sturdy bodies of the warriors strong,
Whom neither marching far, nor tedious way,
Nor weighty arms which on their shoulders hung,
Could weary make, nor death itself dismay;
Now weak and feeble cast their limbs along,
Unwieldly burdens, on the burned clay,
And in each vein a smouldering fire there dwelt,
Which dried their flesh and solid bones did melt.

LXII

Languished the steed late fierce, and proffered grass,
His fodder erst, despised and from him cast,
Each step he stumbled, and which lofty was
And high advanced before now fell his crest,
His conquests gotten all forgotten pass,
Nor with desire of glory swelled his breast,
The spoils won from his foe, his late rewards,
He now neglects, despiseth, naught regards.

LXIII

Languished the faithful dog, and wonted care
Of his dear lord and cabin both forgot,
Panting he laid, and gathered fresher air
To cool the burning in his entrails hot:

But breathing, which wise nature did prepare
To suage the stomach's heat, now booted not,
For little ease, alas, small help, they win
That breathe forth air and scalding fire suck in.

LXIV
Thus languished the earth, in this estate
Lay woful thousands of the Christians stout,
The faithful people grew nigh desperate
Of hoped conquest, shameful death they doubt,
Of their distress they talk and oft debate,
These sad complaints were heard the camp throughout:
"What hope hath Godfrey? shall we still here lie
Till all his soldiers, all our armies die?

LXV
"Alas, with what device, what strength, thinks he
To scale these walls, or this strong fort to get?
Whence hath he engines new? doth he not see,
How wrathful Heaven gainst us his sword doth whet?
These tokens shown true signs and witness be
Our angry God our proud attempts doth let,
And scorching sun so hot his beams outspreads,
That not more cooling Inde nor Aethiop needs.

LXVI
"Or thinks he it an eath or little thing
That us despised, neglected, and disdained,
Like abjects vile, to death he thus should bring,
That so his empire may be still maintained?
Is it so great a bliss to be a king,
When he that wears the crown with blood is stained
And buys his sceptre with his people's lives?
See whither glory vain, fond mankind drives.

LXVII

"See, see the man, called holy, just, and good,
That courteous, meek, and humble would be thought,
Yet never cared in what distress we stood
If his vain honor were diminished naught,
When dried up from us his spring and flood
His water must from Jordan streams be brought,
And how he sits at feasts and banquets sweet
And mingleth waters fresh with wines of Crete."

LXVIII

The French thus murmured, but the Greekish knight
Tatine, that of this war was weary grown:
"Why die we here," quoth he, "slain without fight,
Killed, not subdued, murdered, not overthrown?
Upon the Frenchmen let the penance light
Of Godfrey's folly, let me save mine own,"
And as he said, without farewell, the knight
And all his comet stole away by night.

LXIX

His bad example many a troop prepares
To imitate, when his escape they know,
Clotharius his band, and Ademare's,
And all whose guides in dust were buried low,
Discharged of duty's chains and bondage snares,
Free from their oath, to none they service owe,
But now concluded all on secret flight,
And shrunk away by thousands every night.

LXX

Godfredo this both heard, and saw, and knew,
Yet nould with death them chastise though he mought,
But with that faith wherewith he could renew
The steadfast hills and seas dry up to naught
He prayed the Lord upon his flock to rue,
To ope the springs of grace and ease this drought,
Out of his looks shone zeal, devotion, faith,

Jerusalem Delivered

His hands and eyes to heaven he heaves, and saith:

LXXI

"Father and Lord, if in the deserts waste
Thou hadst compassion on thy children dear,
The craggy rock when Moses cleft and brast,
And drew forth flowing streams of waters clear,
Like mercy, Lord, like grace on us down cast;
And though our merits less than theirs appear,
Thy grace supply that want, for though they be
Thy first–born son, thy children yet are we."

LXXII

These prayers just, from humble hearts forth sent,
Were nothing slow to climb the starry sky,
But swift as winged bird themselves present
Before the Father of the heavens high:
The Lord accepted them, and gently bent
Upon the faithful host His gracious eye,
And in what pain and what distress it laid,
He saw, and grieved to see, and thus He said:

LXXIII

"Mine armies dear till now have suffered woe,
Distress and danger, hell's infernal power
Their enemy hath been, the world their foe,
But happy be their actions from this hour:
What they begin to blessed end shall go,
I will refresh them with a gentle shower;
Rinaldo shall return, the Egyptian crew
They shall encounter, conquer, and subdue."

LXXIV

At these high words great heaven began to shake,
The fixed stars, the planets wandering still,
Trembled the air, the earth and ocean quake,

Spring, fountain, river, forest, dale and hill;
From north to east, a lightning flash outbrake,
And coming drops presaged with thunders shrill:
With joyful shouts the soldiers on the plain,
These tokens bless of long–desired rain.

LXXV

A sudden cloud, as when Helias prayed,
Not from dry earth exhaled by Phoebus' beams,
Arose, moist heaven his windows open laid,
Whence clouds by heaps out rush, and watery streams,
The world o'erspread was with a gloomy shade,
That like a dark mirksome even it seems;
The crashing rain from molten skies down fell,
And o'er their banks the brooks and fountains swell.

LXXVI

In summer season, when the cloudy sky
Upon the parched ground doth rain down send,
As duck and mallard in the furrows dry
With merry noise the promised showers attend,
And spreading broad their wings displayed lie
To keep the drops that on their plumes descend,
And where the streams swell to a gathered lake,
Therein they dive, and sweet refreshing take:

LXXVII

So they the streaming showers with shouts and cries
Salute, which heaven shed on the thirsty lands,
The falling liquor from the dropping skies
He catcheth in his lap, he barehead stands,
And his bright helm to drink therein unties,
In the fresh streams he dives his sweaty hands,
Their faces some, and some their temples wet,
And some to keep the drops large vessels set.
LXXVIII

Nor man alone to ease his burning sore,
Herein doth dive and wash, and hereof drinks,
But earth itself weak, feeble, faint before,
Whose solid limbs were cleft with rifts and chinks,
Received the falling showers and gathered store
Of liquor sweet, that through her veins down sinks,
And moisture new infused largely was
In trees, in plants, in herbs, in flowers, in grass.

LXXIX
Earth, like the patient was, whose lively blood
Hath overcome at last some sickness strong,
Whose feeble limbs had been the bait and food
Whereon this strange disease depastured long,
But now restored, in health and welfare stood,
As sound as erst, as fresh, as fair, as young;
So that forgetting all his grief and pain,
His pleasant robes and crowns he takes again.

LXXX
Ceased the rain, the sun began to shine,
With fruitful, sweet, benign, and gentle ray,
Full of strong power and vigor masculine,
As be his beams in April or in May.
0 happy zeal! who trusts in help divine
The world's afflictions thus can drive away,
Can storms appease, and times and seasons change,
And conquer fortune, fate, and destiny strange.

FOURTEENTH BOOK

THE ARGUMENT.

Jerusalem Delivered

The Lord to Godfrey in a dream doth show
His will; Rinaldo must return at last;
They have their asking who for pardon sue:
Two knights to find the prince are sent in haste,
But Peter, who by vision all foreknew,
Sendeth the searchers to a wizard, placed
Deep in a vault, who first at large declares
Armida's trains, then how to shun those snares.

I

Now from the fresh, the soft and tender bed
Of her still mother, gentle night out flew,
The fleeting balm on hills and dales she shed,
With honey drops of pure and precious dew,
And on the verdure of green forests spread
The virgin primrose and the violet blue,
And sweet–breathed Zephyr on his spreading wings,
Sleep, ease, repose, rest, peace and quiet brings.

II

The thoughts and troubles of broad–waking day,
They softly dipped in mild Oblivion's lake;
But he whose Godhead heaven and earth doth sway,
In his eternal light did watch and wake,
And bent on Godfrey down the gracious ray
Of his bright eye, still ope for Godfrey's sake,
To whom a silent dream the Lord down sent.
Which told his will, his pleasure and intent.

III

Far in the east, the golden gate beside
Whence Phoebus comes, a crystal port there is,
And ere the sun his broad doors open wide
The beam of springing day uncloseth this,
Hence comes the dreams, by which heaven's sacred guide
Reveals to man those high degrees of his,

Jerusalem Delivered

Hence toward Godfrey ere he left his bed
A vision strange his golden plumes bespread.

IV
Such semblances, such shapes, such portraits fair,
Did never yet in dream or sleep appear,
For all the forms in sea, in earth or air,
The signs in heaven, the stars in every sphere
All that was wondrous, uncouth, strange and rare,
All in that vision well presented were.
His dream had placed him in a crystal wide,
Beset with golden fires, top, bottom, side,

V
There while he wondereth on the circles vast,
The stars, their motions, course and harmony,
A knight, with shining rays and fire embraced,
Presents himself unwares before his eye,
Who with a voice that far for sweetness passed
All human speech, thus said, approaching nigh:
"What, Godfrey, knowest thou not thy Hugo here?
Come and embrace thy friend and fellow dear!"

VI
He answered him, "Thy glorious shining light
Which in thine eyes his glistering beams doth place,
Estranged hath from my foreknowledge quite
Thy countenance, thy favor, and thy face:"
This said, three times he stretched his hands outright
And would in friendly arms the knight embrace,
And thrice the spirit fled, that thrice he twined
Naught in his folded arms but air and wind.

VII
Lord Hugo smiled, "Not as you think," quoth he,
"I clothed am in flesh and earthly mould,

Jerusalem Delivered

My spirit pure, and naked soul, you see,
A citizen of this celestial hold:
This place is heaven, and here a room for thee
Prepared is among Christ's champions bold:"
"Ah when," quoth he, "these mortal bonds unknit,
Shall I in peace, in ease and rest there sit?"

VIII

Hugo replied, "Ere many years shall run,
Amid the saints in bliss here shalt thou reign;
But first great wars must by thy hand be done,
Much blood be shed, and many Pagans slain,
The holy city by assault be won,
The land set free from servile yoke again,
Wherein thou shalt a Christian empire frame,
And after thee shall Baldwin rule the same.

IX

"But to increase thy love and great desire
To heavenward, this blessed place behold,
These shining lamps, these globes of living fire,
How they are turned, guided, moved and rolled;
The angels' singing hear, and all their choir;
Then bend thine eyes on yonder earth and mould,
All in that mass, that globe and compass see,
Land, sea, spring, fountain, man, beast, grass and tree.

X

"How vile, how small, and of how slender price,
Is their reward of goodness, virtue's gain!
A narrow room our glory vain upties,
A little circle doth our pride contain,
Earth like an isle amid the water lies,
Which sea sometime is called, sometime the main,
Yet naught therein responds a name so great,
It's but a lake, a pond, a marish strait."

Jerusalem Delivered

XI

Thus said the one, the other bended down
His looks to ground, and half in scorn he smiled,
He saw at once earth, sea, flood, castle, town,
Strangely divided, strangely all compiled,
And wondered folly man so far should drown,
To set his heart on things so base and vild,
That servile empire searcheth and dumb fame,
And scorns heaven's bliss, yet proffereth heaven the same.

XII

Wherefore he answered, "Since the Lord not yet
Will free my spirit from this cage of clay,
Lest worldly error vain my voyage let,
Teach me to heaven the best and surest way:"
Hugo replied, "Thy happy foot is set
In the true path, nor from this passage stray,
Only from exile young Rinaldo call,
This give I thee in charge, else naught at all.

XIII

"For as the Lord of hosts, the King of bliss,
Hath chosen thee to rule the faithful band;
So he thy stratagems appointed is
To execute, so both shall win this land:
The first is thine, the second place is his,
Thou art this army's head, and he the hand,
No other champion can his place supply,
And that thou do it doth thy state deny.

XIV

"The enchanted forest, and her charmed treen,
With cutting steel shall he to earth down hew,
And thy weak armies which too feeble been
To scale again these walls reinforced new,
And fainting lie dispersed on the green,

347

Shall take new strength new courage at his view,
The high–built towers, the eastern squadrons all,
Shall conquered be, shall fly, shall die, shall fall."

XV

He held his peace; and Godfrey answered so:
"Oh, how his presence would recomfort me!
You that man's hidden thoughts perceive and know:
If I say truth, or if I love him, see.
But say, what messengers shall for him go?
What shall their speeches, what their errand be?
Shall I entreat, or else command the man?
With credit neither well perform I can."

XVI

"The eternal Lord," the other knight replied,
"That with so many graces hath thee blest,
Will, that among the troops thou hast to guide,
Thou honored be and feared of most and least:
Then speak not thou lest blemish some betide
Thy sacred empire if thou make request;
But when by suit thou moved art to ruth,
Then yield, forgive, and home recall the youth.

XVII

"Guelpho shall pray thee, God shall him inspire,
To pardon this offence, this fault commit
By hasty wrath, by rash and headstrong ire,
To call the knight again; yield thou to it:
And though the youth, enwrapped in fond desire,
Far hence in love and looseness idle sit,
Year fear it not, he shall return with speed,
When most you wish him and when most you need.

XVIII

"Your hermit Peter, to whose sapient heart

High Heaven his secrets opens, tells and shews,
Your messengers direct can to that part,
Where of the prince they shall hear certain news,
And learn the way, the manner, and the art
To bring him back to these thy warlike crews,
That all thy soldiers, wandered and misgone,
Heaven may unite again and join in one.

XIX
"But this conclusion shall my speeches end:
Know that his blood shall mixed be with thine,
Whence barons bold and worthies shall descend,
That many great exploits shall bring to fine."
This said, he vanished from his sleeping friend,
Like smoke in wind, or mist in Titan's shine;
Sleep fled likewise, and in his troubled thought,
With wonder, pleasure; joy, with marvel fought.
XX
The duke looked up, and saw the azure sky
With argent beams of silver morning spread,
And started up, for praise axed virtue lie
In toil and travel, sin and shame in bed:
His arms he took, his sword girt to his thigh,
To his pavilion all his lords them sped,
And there in council grave the princes sit,
For strength by wisdom, war is ruled by wit.

XXI
Lord Guelpho there, within whose gentle breast
Heaven had infused that new and sudden thought,
His pleasing words thus to the duke addressed:
"Good prince, mild, though unasked, kind, unbesought,
Oh let thy mercy grant my just request,
Pardon this fault by rage not malice wrought;
For great offence, I grant, so late commit,
My suit too hasty is, perchance unfit.

Jerusalem Delivered

XXII

But since to Godfrey meek benign and kind,
For Prince Rinaldo bold, I humbly sue,
And that the suitor's self is not behind
Thy greatest friends in state or friendship true;
I trust I shall thy grace and mercy find
Acceptable to me and all this crew;
Oh call him home, this trespass to amend,
He shall his blood in Godfrey's service spend.

XXIII

"And if not he, who else dares undertake
Of this enchanted wood to cut one tree?
Gainst death and danger who dares battle make,
With so bold face, so fearless heart as he?
Beat down these walls, these gates in pieces break,
Leap o'er these rampires high, thou shalt him see,
Restore therefore to this desirous band
Their wish, their hope, their strength, their shield, their hand;

XXIV

"To me my nephew, to thyself restore
A trusty help, when strength of hand thou needs,
In idleness let him consume no more,
Recall him to his noble acts and deeds!
Known be his worth as was his strength of yore
Wher'er thy standard broad her cross outspreads,
Oh, let his fame and praise spread far and wide,
Be thou his lord, his teacher and his guidel"

XXV

Thus he entreated, and the rest approve
His words, with friendly murmurs whispered low.
Godfrey as though their suit his mind did move
To that whereon he never thought tell now,

"How can my heart," quoth he, "if you I love,
To your request and suit but bend and bow?
Let rigor go, that right and justice be
Wherein you all consent and all agree.

XXVI
"Rinaldo shall return; let him restrain
Henceforth his headstrong wrath and hasty ire,
And with his hardy deeds let him take pain
To correspond your hope and my desire:
Guelpho, thou must call home the knight again,
See that with speed he to these tents retire,
The messengers appoint as likes thy mind,
And teach them where they should the young man find."

XXVII
Up start the Dane that bare Prince Sweno's brand,
"I will," quoth he, "that message undertake,
I will refuse no pains by sea or land,
To give the knight this sword, kept for his sake."
This man was bold of courage, strong of hand,
Guelpho was glad he did the proffer make:
"Thou shalt," quoth he, "Ubaldo shalt thou have
To go with thee, a knight, stout, wise, and grave."

XXVIII
Ubaldo in his youth had known and seen
The fashions strange of many an uncouth land,
And travelled over all the realms between
The Arctic circle and hot Meroe's strand,
And as a man whose wit his guide had been,
Their customs use he could, tongues understand,
Forthy when spent his youthful seasons were
Lord Guelpho entertained and held him dear.

XXIX

351

To these committed was the charge and care
To find and bring again the champion bold,
Guelpho commands them to the fort repair,
Where Boemond doth his seat and sceptre hold,
For public fame said that Bertoldo's heir
There lived, there dwelt, there stayed; the hermit old,
That knew they were misled by false report,
Among them came, and parleyed in this sort:

XXX

"Sir knights," quoth he, "if you intend to ride,
And follow each report fond people say,
You follow but a rash and truthless guide
That leads vain men amiss and makes them stray;
Near Ascalon go to the salt seaside,
Where a swift brook fails in with hideous sway,
An aged sire, our friend, there shall you find,
All what he saith, that do, that keep in mind.

XXXI

"Of this great voyage which you undertake,
Much by his skill, and much by mine advise
Hath he foreknown, and welcome for my sake
You both shall be, the man is kind and wise."
Instructed thus no further question make
The twain elected for this enterprise,
But humbly yielded to obey his word,
For what the hermit said, that said the Lord.

XXXII

They took their leave, and on their journey went,
Their will could brook no stay, their zeal, no let;
To Ascalon their voyage straight they bent,
Whose broken shores with brackish waves are wet,
And there they heard how gainst the cliffs, besprent
With bitter foam, the roaring surges bet,

Jerusalem Delivered

A tumbling brook their passage stopped and stayed,
Which late–fall'n rain had proud and puissant made,

XXXIII
So proud that over all his banks he grew,
And through the fields ran swift as shaft from bow,
While here they stopped and stood, before them drew
An aged sire, grave and benign in show,
Crowned with a beechen garland gathered new,
Clad in a linen robe that raught down low,
In his right hand a rod, and on the flood
Against the stream he marched, and dry shod yode.

XXXIV
As on the Rhene, when winter's freezing cold
Congeals the streams to thick and hardened glass,
The beauties fair of shepherds' daughters bold
With wanton windlays run, turn, play and pass;
So on this river passed the wizard old,
Although unfrozen soft and swift it was,
And thither stalked where the warriors stayed,
To whom, their greetings done, he spoke and said:

XXXV
"Great pains, great travel, lords, you have begun,
And of a cunning guide great need you stand,
Far off, alas! is great Bertoldo's son,
Imprisoned in a waste and desert land,
What soil remains by which you must not run,
What promontory, rock, sea, shore or sand
Your search must stretch before the prince be found,
Beyond our world, beyond our half of ground!

XXXVI
But yet vouchsafe to see my cell I pray,
In hidden caves and vaults though builded low,

353

Great wonders there, strange things I will bewray,
Things good for you to hear, and fit to know:"
This said, he bids the river make them way,
The flood retired, backward gan to flow,
And here and there two crystal mountains rise,
So fled the Red Sea once, and Jordan thrice.

XXXVII

He took their hands, and led them headlong down
Under the flood, through vast and hollow deeps,
Such light they had as when through shadows brown
Of thickest deserts feeble Cynthia peeps,
Their spacious caves they saw all overflown,
There all his waters pure great Neptune keeps,
And thence to moisten all the earth he brings
Seas, rivers, floods, lakes, fountains, wells and springs:
XXXVIII

Whence Ganges, Indus, Volga, Ister, Po,
Whence Euphrates, whence Tigris' spring they view,
Whence Tanais, whence Nilus comes also,
Although his head till then no creature knew,
But under these a wealthy stream doth go,
That sulphur yields and ore, rich, quick and new,
Which the sunbeams doth polish, purge and fine,
And makes it silver pure, and gold divine.

XXXIX

And all his banks the rich and wealthy stream
Hath fair beset with pearl and precious stone
Like stars in sky or lamps on stage that seem,
The darkness there was day, the night was gone,
There sparkled, clothed in his azure–beam,
The heavenly sapphire, there the jacinth shone,
The carbuncle there flamed, the diamond sheen,
There glistered bright, there smiled the emerald green.

XL

Amazed the knights amid these wonders passed,
And fixed so deep the marvels in their thought,
That not one word they uttered, till at last
Ubaldo spake, and thus his guide besought:
"O father, tell me by what skill thou hast
These wonders done? and to what place us brought?
For well I know not if I wake or sleep,
My heart is drowned in such amazement deep."

XLI

"You are within the hollow womb," quoth he,
"Of fertile earth, the nurse of all things made,
And but you brought and guided are by me,
Her sacred entrails could no wight invade;
My palace shortly shall you splendent see,
With glorious light, though built in night and shade.
A Pagan was I born, but yet the Lord
To grace, by baptism, hath my soul restored.

XLII

"Nor yet by help of devil, or aid from hell,
I do this uncouth work and wondrous feat,
The Lord forbid I use or charm or spell
To raise foul Dis from his infernal seat:
But of all herbs, of every spring and well,
The hidden power I know and virtue great,
And all that kind hath hid from mortal sight,
And all the stars, their motions, and their might.

XLIII

"For in these caves I dwell not buried still
From sight of Heaven. but often I resort
To tops of Lebanon or Carmel hill,
And there in liquid air myself disport,
There Mars and Venus I behold at will!

Jerusalem Delivered

As bare as erst when Vulcan took them short,
And how the rest roll, glide and move, I see,
How their aspects benign or froward be."

XLIV

"And underneath my feet the clouds I view,
Now thick, now thin, now bright with Iris' bow,
The frost and snow, the rain, the hail, the dew,
The winds, from whence they come and whence they blow,
How Jove his thunder makes and lightning new,
How with the bolt he strikes the earth below,
How comate, crinite, caudate stars are framed
I knew; my skill with pride my heart inflamed.

XLV

"So learned, cunning, wise, myself I thought,
That I supposed my wit so high might climb
To know all things that God had framed or wrought,
Fire, air, sea, earth, man, beast, sprite, place and time;
But when your hermit me to baptism brought,
And from my soul had washed the sin and crime,
Then I perceived my sight was blindness still,
My wit was folly, ignorance my skill.

XLVI

"Then saw I, that like owls in shining sun,
So gainst the beams of truth our souls are blind,
And at myself to smile I then begun,
And at my heart, puffed up with folly's wind,
Yet still these arts, as I before had done,
I practised, such was the hermit's mind:
Thus hath he changed my thoughts, my heart, my will,
And rules mine art, my knowledge, and my skill.

XLVII

"In him I rest, on him my thoughts depend,
My lord, my teacher, and my guide is he,

This noble work he strives to bring to end,
He is the architect, the workmen we,
The hardy youth home to this camp to send
From prison strong, my care, my charge shall be;
So He commands, and me ere this foretold
Your coming oft, to seek the champion bold."

XLVIII

While this he said, he brought the champions twain
Down to a vault, wherein he dwells and lies,
It was a cave, high, wide, large, ample, plain,
With goodly rooms, halls, chambers, galleries,
All what is bred in rich and precious vein
Of wealthy earth, and hid from mortal eyes,
There shines, and fair adorned was every part
With riches grown by kind, not framed by art:

XLIX

An hundred grooms, quick, diligent and neat,
Attendance gave about these strangers bold,
Against the wall there stood a cupboard great
Of massive plate, of silver, crystal, gold.
But when with precious wines and costly meat
They filled were, thus spake the wizard old:
"Now fits the time, sir knights, I tell and show
What you desire to hear, and long to know.

L

"Armida's craft, her sleight and hidden guile
You partly wot, her acts and arts untrue,
How to your camp she came, and by what wile
The greatest lords and princes thence she drew;
You know she turned them first to monsters vile,
And kept them since closed up in secret mew,
Lastly, to Gaza–ward in bonds them sent,
Whom young Rinaldo rescued as they went.

Jerusalem Delivered

LI

"What chanced since I will at large declare,
To you unknown, a story strange and true.
When first her prey, got with such pain and care,
Escaped and gone the witch perceived and knew,
Her hands she wrung for grief, her clothes she tare,
And full of woe these heavy words outthrew:
`Alas! my knights are slain, my prisoners free,
Yet of that conquest never boast shall he,

LII

" `He in their place shall serve me, and sustain
Their plagues, their torments suffer, sorrows bear,
And they his absence shall lament in vain,
And wail his loss and theirs with many a tear:'
Thus talking to herself she did ordain
A false and wicked guile, as you shall hear;
Thither she hasted where the valiant knight
Had overcome and slain her men in fight.

LIII

"Rinaldo there had dolt and left his own,
And on his back a Pagan's harness tied,
Perchance he deemed so to pass unknown,
And in those arms less noted false to ride.
A headless corse in fight late overthrown,
The witch in his forsaken arms did hide,
And by a brook exposed it on the sand
Whither she wished would come a Christian band:

LIV

"Their coming might the dame foreknow right well,
For secret spies she sent forth thousand ways,
Which every day news from the camp might tell,
Who parted thence, booties to search or preys:

Beside, the sprites conjured by sacred spell,
All what she asks or doubts, reveals and says,
The body therefore placed she in that part
That furthered best her sleight, her craft. and art;

LV
"And near the corpse a varlet false and sly
She left, attired in shepherd's homely weed,
And taught him how to counterfeit and lie
As time required, and he performed the deed;
With him your soldiers spoke, of jealousy
And false suspect mongst them he strewed the seed,
That since brought forth the fruit of strife and jar,
Of civil brawls, contention, discord, war.

LVI
"And as she wished so the soldiers thought
By Godfrey's practice that the prince was slain,
Yet vanished that suspicion false to naught
When truth spread forth her silver wings again
Her false devices thus Armida wrought,
This was her first deceit, her foremost train;
What next she practised, shall you hear me tell,
Against our knight, and what thereof befell.

LVII
"Armida hunted him through wood and plain,
Till on Orontes' flowery banks he stayed,
There, where the stream did part and meet again
And in the midst a gentle island made,
A pillar fair was pight beside the main,
Near which a little frigate floating laid,
The marble white the prince did long behold,
And this inscription read, there writ in gold:

LVIII

" `Whoso thou art whom will or chance doth bring
With happy steps to flood Orontes' sides,
Know that the world hath not so strange a thing,
Twixt east and west, as this small island hides,
Then pass and see, without more tarrying.'
The hasty youth to pass the stream provides,
And for the cogs was narrow, small and strait,
Alone he rowed, and bade his squires there wait;

LIX
"Landed he stalks about, yet naught he sees
But verdant groves, sweet shades, and mossy rocks
With caves and fountains, flowers, herbs and trees,
So that the words he read he takes for mocks:
But that green isle was sweet at all degrees,
Wherewith enticed down sits he and unlocks
His closed helm, and bares his visage fair,
To take sweet breath from cool and gentle air.

LX
"A rumbling sound amid the waters deep
Meanwhile he heard, and thither turned his sight,
And tumbling in the troubled stream took keep
How the strong waves together rush and fight,
Whence first he saw, with golden tresses, peep
The rising visage of a virgin bright,
And then her neck, her breasts, and all, as low
As he for shame could see, or she could show.

LXI
"So in the twilight does sometimes appear
A nymph, a goddess, or a fairy queen,
And though no siren but a sprite this were
Yet by her beauty seemed it she had been
One of those sisters false which haunted near
The Tyrrhene shores and kept those waters sheen,

360

Like theirs her face, her voice was, and her sound,
And thus she sung, and pleased both skies and ground:

LXII
" `Ye happy youths, who April fresh and May
Attire in flowering green of lusty age,
For glory vain, or virtue's idle ray,
Do not your tender limbs to toil engage;
In calm streams, fishes; birds, in sunshine play,
Who followeth pleasure he is only sage,
So nature saith, yet gainst her sacred will
Why still rebel you, and why strive you still?

LXIII
" `O fools who youth possess, yet scorn the same,
A precious, but a short–abiding treasure,
Virtue itself is but an idle name,
Prized by the world 'bove reason all and measure,
And honor, glory, praise, renown and fame,
That men's proud harts bewitch with tickling pleasure,
An echo is, a shade, a dream, a flower,
With each wind blasted, spoiled with every shower.

LXIV
" `But let your happy souls in joy possess
The ivory castles of your bodies fair,
Your passed harms salve with forgetfulness,
Haste not your coming evils with thought and care,
Regard no blazing star with burning tress,
Nor storm, nor threatening sky, nor thundering air,
This wisdom is, good life, and worldly bliss,
Kind teacheth us, nature commands us this.'
LXV
"Thus sung the spirit false, and stealing sleep,
To which her tunes enticed his heavy eyes,
By step and step did on his senses creep,

361

Still every limb therein unmoved lies,
Not thunders loud could from this slumber deep,
Of quiet death true image, make him rise:
Then from her ambush forth Armida start,
Swearing revenge, and threatening torments smart.
LXVI
"But when she looked on his face awhile,
And saw how sweet he breathed, how still he lay,
How his fair eyes though closed seemed to smile,
At first she stayed, astound with great dismay,
Then sat her down, so love can art beguile,
And as she sat and looked, fled fast away
Her wrath, that on his forehead gazed the maid,
As in his spring Narcissus tooting laid;

LXVII
"And with a veil she wiped now and then
From his fair cheeks the globes of silver sweat,
And cool air gathered with a trembling fan,
To mitigate the rage of melting heat,
Thus, who would think it, his hot eye–glance can
Of that cold frost dissolve the hardness great
Which late congealed the heart of that fair dame,
Who late a foe, a lover now became.

LXVIII
"Of woodbines, lilies, and of roses sweet,
Which proudly flowered through that wanton plain,
All platted fast, well knit, and joined meet,
She framed a soft but surely holding chain,
Wherewith she bound his neck his hands and feet;
Thus bound, thus taken, did the prince remain,
And in a coach which two old dragons drew,
She laid the sleeping knight, and thence she flew:

LXIX

"Nor turned she to Damascus' kingdoms large,
Nor to the fort built in Asphalte's lake,
But jealous of her dear and precious charge,
And of her love ashamed, the way did take,
To the wide ocean whither skiff or barge
From us doth seld or never voyage make,
And there to frolic with her love awhile,
She chose a waste, a sole and desert isle.

LXX

"An isle that with her fellows bears the name
Of Fortunate, for temperate air and mould,
There in a mountain high alight the dame,
A hill obscured with shades of forests old,
Upon whose sides the witch by art did frame
Continual snow, sharp frost and winter cold,
But on the top, fresh, pleasant, sweet and green,
Beside a lake a palace built this queen.

LXXI

"There in perpetual sweet and flowering spring,
She lives at ease, and joys her lord at will;
The hardy youth from this strange prison bring
Your valors must, directed by my skill,
And overcome each monster and each thing,
That guards the palace or that keeps the hill,
Nor shall you want a guide, or engines fit,
To bring you to the mount, or conquer it.

LXXII

"Beside the stream, yparted shall you find
A dame, in visage young, but old in years,
Her curled locks about her front are twined,
A party–colored robe of silk she wears:
This shall conduct you swift as air or wind,
Or that flit bird that Jove's hot weapon bears,

363

A faithful pilot, cunning, trusty, sure,
As Tiphys was, or skilful Palinure.

LXXIII
"At the hill's foot, whereon the witch doth dwell,
The serpents hiss, and cast their poison vilde,
The ugly boars do rear their bristles fell,
There gape the bears, and roar the lions wild;
But yet a rod I have can easily quell
Their rage and wrath, and make them meek and mild.
Yet on the top and height of all the hill,
The greatest danger lies, and greatest ill:

LXXIV
"There welleth out a fair, clear, bubbling spring,
Whose waters pure the thirsty guests entice,
But in those liquors cold the secret sting
Of strange and deadly poison closed lies,
One sup thereof the drinker's heart doth bring
To sudden joy, whence laughter vain doth rise,
Nor that strange merriment once stops or stays,
Till, with his laughter's end, he end his days:

LXXV
"Then from those deadly, wicked streams refrain
Your thirsty lips, despise the dainty cheer
You find exposed upon the grassy plain,
Nor those false damsels once vouchsafe to hear,
That in melodious tunes their voices strain,
Whose faces lovely, smiling, sweet, appear;
But you their looks, their voice, their songs despise,
And enter fair Armida's paradise.

LXXVI
"The house is builded like a maze within,
With turning stairs, false doors and winding ways,

364

The shape whereof plotted in vellum thin
I will you give, that all those sleights bewrays,
In midst a garden lies, where many a gin
And net to catch frail hearts, false Cupid lays;
There in the verdure of the arbors green,
With your brave champion lies the wanton queen.

LXXVII

"But when she haply riseth from the knight,
And hath withdrawn her presence from the place,
Then take a shield I have of diamonds bright,
And hold the same before the young man's face,
That he may glass therein his garments light,
And wanton soft attire, and view his case,
That with the sight shame and disdain may move
His heart to leave that base and servile love.

LXXVIII

"Now resteth naught that needful is to tell,
But that you go secure, safe, sure and bold,
Unseen the palace may you enter well,
And pass the dangers all I have foretold,
For neither art, nor charm, nor magic spell,
Can stop your passage or your steps withhold,
Nor shall Armida, so you guarded be,
Your coming aught foreknow or once foresee:

LXXIX

"And eke as safe from that enchanted fort
You shall return and scape unhurt away;
But now the time doth us to rest exhort,
And you must rise by peep of springing day."
This said, he led them through a narrow port,
Into a lodging fair wherein they lay,
There glad and full of thoughts he left his guests,
And in his wonted bed the old man rests.

FIFTEENTH BOOK

THE ARGUMENT.
The well instructed knights forsake their host,
And come where their strange bark in harbor lay,
And setting sail behold on Egypt's coast
The monarch's ships and armies in array:
Their wind and pilot good, the seas in post
They pass, and of long journeys make short way:
The far—sought isle they find; Armida's charms
They scorn, they shun her sleights, despise her arms.

I
The rosy—fingered morn with gladsome ray
Rose to her task from old Tithonus' lap
When their grave host came where the warriors lay,
And with him brought the shield, the rod, the map.
"Arise," quoth he, "ere lately broken day,
In his bright arms the round world fold or wrap,
All what I promised, here I have them brought,
Enough to bring Armida's charms to naught."

II
They started up, and every tender limb
In sturdy steel and stubborn plate they dight,
Before the old man stalked, they followed him
Through gloomy shades of sad and sable night,
Through vaults obscure again and entries dim,
The way they came their steps remeasured right;
But at the flood arrived, "Farewell," quoth he,

366

Jerusalem Delivered

"Good luck your aid, your guide good fortune be."

III
The flood received them in his bottom low
And lilt them up above his billows thin;
The waters so east up a branch or bough,
By violence first plunged and dived therein:
But when upon the shore the waves them throw,
The knights for their fair guide to look begin,
And gazing round a little bark they spied,
Wherein a damsel sate the stern to guide.

IV
Upon her front her locks were curled new,
Her eyes were courteous, full of peace and love;
In look a saint, an angel bright in show,
So in her visage grace and virtue strove;
Her robe seemed sometimes red and sometimes blue,
And changed still as she did stir or move;
That look how oft man's eye beheld the same
So oft the colors changed, went and came.

V
The feathers so, that tender, soft, and plain,
About the dove's smooth neck close couched been,
Do in one color never long remain,
But change their hue gainst glimpse of Phoebus' sheen;
And now of rubies bright a vermeil chain,
Now make a carknet rich of emeralds green;
Now mingle both, now alter, turn and change
To thousand colors, rich, pure, fair, and strange.

VI
"Enter this boat, you happy men," she says,
"Wherein through raging waves secure I ride,
To which all tempest, storm, and wind obeys,

Jerusalem Delivered

All burdens light, benign is stream and tide:
My lord, that rules your journeys and your ways,
Hath sent me here, your servant and your guide."
This said, her shallop drove she gainst the sand,
And anchor cast amid the steadfast land.

VII

They entered in, her anchors she upwound,
And launched forth to sea her pinnace flit,
Spread to the wind her sails she broad unbound,
And at the helm sat down to govern it,
Swelled the flood that all his banks he drowned
To bear the greatest ship of burthen fit;
Yet was her fatigue little, swift and light,
That at his lowest ebb bear it he might.

VIII

Swifter than thought the friendly wind forth bore
The sliding boat upon the rolling wave,
With curded foam and froth the billows hoar
About the cable murmur roar and rave;
At last they came where all his watery store
The flood in one deep channel did engrave,
And forth to greedy seas his streams he sent,
And so his waves, his name, himself he spent.

IX

The wondrous boat scant touched the troubled main
But all the sea still, hushed and quiet was,
Vanished the clouds, ceased the wind and rain,
The tempests threatened overblow and pass,
A gentle breathing air made even and plain
The azure face of heaven's smooth looking–glass,
And heaven itself smiled from the skies above
With a calm clearness on the earth his love.

X

Jerusalem Delivered

By Ascalon they sailed, and forth drived,
Toward the west their speedy course they frame,
In sight of Gaza till the bark arrived,
A little port when first it took that name;
But since, by others' loss so well it thrived
A city great and rich that it became,
And there the shores and borders of the land
They found as full of armed men as sand.

XI
The passengers to landward turned their sight,
And there saw pitched many a stately tent,
Soldier and footman, captain, lord and knight,
Between the shore and city, came and went:
Huge elephants, strong camels, coursers light,
With horned hoofs the sandy ways outrent,
And in the haven many a ship and boat,
With mighty anchors fastened, swim and float;

XII
Some spread their sails, some with strong oars sweep
The waters smooth, and brush the buxom wave,
Their breasts in sunder cleave the yielding deep,
The broken seas for anger foam and rave,
When thus their guide began, "Sir knights, take keep
How all these shores are spread with squadrons brave
And troops of hardy knights, yet on these sands
The monarch scant hath gathered half his bands.

XIII
"Of Egypt only these the forces are,
And aid from other lands they here attend,
For twixt the noon–day sun and morning star,
All realms at his command do bow and bend;
So that I trust we shall return from far,
And bring our journey long to wished end,

369

Before this king or his lieutenant shall
These armies bring to Zion's conquered wall."

XIV
While thus she said, as soaring eagles fly
Mongst other birds securely through the air,
And mounting up behold with wakeful eye,
The radiant beams of old Hyperion's hair,
Her gondola so passed swiftly by
Twixt ship and ship, withouten fear or care
Who should her follow, trouble, stop or stay,
And forth to sea made lucky speed and way.

XV
Themselves fornenst old Raffia's town they fand,
A town that first to sailors doth appear
As they from Syria pass to Egypt land:
The sterile coasts of barren Rhinocere
They passed, and seas where Casius hill doth stand
That with his trees o'erspreads the waters near,
Against whose roots breaketh the brackish wave
Where Jove his temple, Pompey hath his grave:
XVI
Then Damiata next, where they behold
How to the sea his tribute Nilus pays
By his seven mouths renowned in stories old,
And by an hundred more ignoble ways:
They pass the town built by the Grecian bold,
Of him called Alexandria till our days,
And Pharaoh's tower and isle removed of yore
Far from the land, now joined to the shore:

XVII
Both Crete and Rhodes they left by north unseen,
And sailed along the coasts of Afric lands,
Whose sea towns fair, but realms more inward been

370

All full of monsters and of desert sands:
With her five cities then they left Cyrene,
Where that old temple of false Hammon stands:
Next Ptolemais, and that sacred wood
Whence spring the silent streams of Lethe flood.

XVIII
The greater Syrte, that sailors often cast
In peril great of death and loss extreme,
They compassed round about, and safely passed,
The Cape Judeca and flood Magra's stream;
Then Tripoli, gainst which is Malta placed,
That low and hid, to lurk in seas doth seem:
The little Syrte then, and Alzerhes isle,
Where dwelt the folk that Lotos ate erewhile.

XIX
Next Tunis on the crooked shore they spied,
Whose bay a rock on either side defends,
Tunis all towns in beauty, wealth and pride
Above, as far as Libya's bounds extends;
Gainst which, from fair Sicilia's fertile side,
His rugged front great Lilybaeum bends.
The dame there pointed out where sometime stood
Rome's stately rival whilom, Carthage proud;

XX
Great Carthage low in ashes cold doth lie,
Her ruins poor the herbs in height scant pass,
So cities fall, so perish kingdoms high,
Their pride and pomp lies hid in sand and grass:
Then why should mortal man repine to die,
Whose life, is air; breath, wind; and body, glass?
From thence the seas next Bisert's walls they cleft,
And far Sardinia on their right hand left.

XXI

Numidia's mighty plains they coasted then,
Where wandering shepherds used their flocks to feed,
Then Bugia and Argier, the infamous den
Of pirates false, Oran they left with speed,
All Tingitan they swiftly overren,
Where elephants and angry lions breed,
Where now the realms of Fez and Maroc be,
Gainst which Granada's shores and coasts they see.

XXII

Now are they there, where first the sea brake in
By great Alcides' help, as stories feign,
True may it be that where those floods begin
It whilom was a firm and solid main
Before the sea there through did passage win
And parted Afric from the land of Spain,
Abila hence, thence Calpe great upsprings,
Such power hath time to change the face of things.

XXIII

Four times the sun had spread his morning ray
Since first the dame launched forth her wondrous barge
And never yet took port in creek or bay,
But fairly forward bore the knights her charge;
Now through the strait her jolly ship made way,
And boldly sailed upon the ocean large;
But if the sea in midst of earth was great,
Oh what was this, wherein earth hath her seat?

XXIV

Now deep engulphed in the mighty flood
They saw not Gades, nor the mountains near,
Fled was the land, and towns on land that stood,
Heaven covered sea, sea seemed the heavens to bear.
"At last, fair lady," quoth Ubaldo good,

"That in this endless main dost guide us here,
If ever man before here sailed tell,
Or other lands here be wherein men dwell."

XXV

"Great Hercules," quoth she, "when he had quailed
The monsters fierce in Afric and in Spain,
And all along your coasts and countries sailed,
Yet durst he not assay the ocean main,
Within his pillars would he have impaled
The overdaring wit of mankind vain,
Till Lord Ulysses did those bounders pass,
To see and know he so desirous was.

XXVI

"He passed those pillars, and in open wave
Of the broad sea first his bold sails untwined,
But yet the greedy ocean was his grave,
Naught helped him his skill gainst tide and wind;
With him all witness of his voyage brave
Lies buried there, no truth thereof we find,
And they whom storm hath forced that way since,
Are drowned all, or unreturned from thence:

XXVII

"So that this mighty sea is yet unsought,
Where thousand isles and kingdoms lie unknown,
Not void of men as some have vainly thought,
But peopled well, and wonned like your own;
The land is fertile ground, but scant well wrought,
Air wholesome, temperate sun, grass proudly grown."
"But," quoth Ubaldo, "dame, I pray thee teach
Of that hid world, what be the laws and speech?"
XXVIII
"As diverse be their nations," answered she,
"Their tongues, their rites, their laws so different are;

Some pray to beasts, some to a stone or tree,
Some to the earth, the sun, or morning star;
Their meats unwholesome, vile, and hateful be,
Some eat man's flesh, and captives ta'en in war,
And all from Calpe's mountain west that dwell,
In faith profane, in life are rude and fell."

XXIX

"But will our gracious God," the knight replied,
"That with his blood all sinful men hath bought,
His truth forever and his gospel hide
From all those lands, as yet unknown, unsought?"
"Oh no," quoth she, "his name both far and wide
Shall there be known, all learning thither brought,
Nor shall these long and tedious ways forever
Your world and theirs, their lands, your kingdoms sever.

XXX

"The time shall come that sailors shall disdain
To talk or argue of Alcides' streat,
And lands and seas that nameless yet remain,
Shall well be known, their boundaries, site and seat,
The ships encompass shall the solid main,
As far as seas outstretch their waters great,
And measure all the world, and with the sun
About this earth, this globe, this compass, run.

XXXI

"A knight of Genes shall have the hardiment
Upon this wondrous voyage first to wend,
Nor winds nor waves, that ships in sunder rent,
Nor seas unused, strange clime, or pool unkenned,
Nor other peril nor astonishment
That makes frail hearts of men to bow and bend,
Within Abilas' strait shall keep and hold
The noble spirit of this sailor bold.

Jerusalem Delivered

XXXII

"Thy ship, Columbus, shall her canvas wing
Spread o'er that world that yet concealed lies,
That scant swift fame her looks shall after bring,
Though thousand plumes she have, and thousand eyes;
Let her of Bacchus and Alcides sing,
Of thee to future age let this suffice,
That of thine acts she some forewarning give,
Which shall in verse and noble story live."

XXXIII

Thus talking, swift twixt south and west they run,
And sliced out twixt froth and foam their way;
At once they saw before, the setting sun;
Behind, the rising beam of springing day;
And when the morn her drops and dews begun
To scatter broad upon the flowering lay,
Far off a hill and mountain high they spied,
Whose top the clouds environ, clothe and hide;

XXXIV

And drawing near, the hill at ease they view,
When all the clouds were molten, fallen and fled,
Whose top pyramid–wise did pointed show,
High, narrow, sharp, the sides yet more outspread,
Thence now and then fire, flame and smoke outflew,
As from that hill, whereunder lies in bed
Enceladus, whence with imperious sway
Bright fire breaks out by night, black smoke by day.

XXXV

About the hill lay other islands small,
Where other rocks, crags, cliffs, and mountains stood,
The Isles Fortunate these elder time did call,
To which high Heaven they reigned so kind and good,

And of his blessings rich so liberal,
That without tillage earth gives corn for food,
And grapes that swell with sweet and precious wine
There without pruning yields the fertile vine.
XXXVI
The olive fat there ever buds and flowers,
The honey–drops from hollow oaks distil,
The falling brook her silver streams downpours
With gentle murmur from their native hill,
The western blast tempereth with dews and showers
The sunny rays, lest heat the blossoms kill,
The fields Elysian, as fond heathen sain,
Were there, where souls of men in bliss remain.

XXXVII
To these their pilot steered, "And now," quoth she,
"Your voyage long to end is brought well–near,
The happy Isles of Fortune now you see,
Of which great fame, and little truth, you hear,
Sweet, wholesome, pleasant, fertile, fat they be,
Yet not so rich as fame reports they were."
This said, toward an island fresh she bore,
The first of ten, that lies next Afric's shore;

XXXVIII
When Charles thus, "If, worthy governess,
To our good speed such tarriance be no let,
Upon this isle that Heaven so fair doth bless,
To view the place, on land awhile us set,
To know the folk and what God they confess,
And all whereby man's heart may knowledge get,
That I may tell the wonders therein seen
Another day, and say, there have I been."

XXXIX
She answered him, "Well fits this high desire

Thy noble heart, yet cannot I consent;
For Heaven's decree, firm, stable, and entire,
Thy wish repugns, and gainst thy will is bent,
Nor yet the time hath Titan's gliding fire
Met forth, prefixed for this discoverment,
Nor is it lawful of the ocean main
That you the secrets know, or known explain.

XL

"To you withouten needle, map or card
It's given to pass these seas, and there arrive
Where in strong prison lies your knight imbarred,
And of her prey you must the witch deprive:
If further to aspire you be prepared,
In vain gainst fate and Heaven's decree you strive."
While thus she said, the first seen isle gave place,
And high and rough the second showed his face.

XLI

They saw how eastward stretched in order long,
The happy islands sweetly flowering lay;
And how the seas betwixt those isles enthrong,
And how they shouldered land from land away:
In seven of them the people rude among
The shady trees their sheds had built of clay,
The rest lay waste, unless wild beasts unseen,
Or wanton nymphs, roamed on the mountains green.

XLII

A secret place they found in one of those,
Where the cleft shore sea in his bosom takes,
And 'twixt his stretched arms doth fold and close
An ample bay, a rock the haven makes,
Which to the main doth his broad back oppose,
Whereon the roaring billow cleaves and breaks,
And here and there two crags like turrets high,

377

Point forth a port to all that sail thereby:

XLIII
The quiet seas below lie safe and still,
The green wood like a garland grows aloft,
Sweet caves within, cool shades and waters shrill,
Where lie the nymphs on moss and ivy soft;
No anchor there needs hold her frigate still,
Nor cable twisted sure, though breaking oft:
Into this desert, silent, quiet, glad,
Entered the dame, and there her haven made.

XLIV
"The palace proudly built," quoth she, "behold,
That sits on top of yonder mountain's height,
Of Christ's true faith there lies the champion bold
In idleness, love, fancy, folly light;
When Phoebus shall his rising beams unfold,
Prepare you gainst the hill to mount upright,
Nor let this stay in your bold hearts breed care,
For, save that one, all hours unlucky are;

XLV
"But yet this evening, if you make good speed,
To that hill's foot with daylight might you pass."
Thus said the dame their guide, and they agreed,
And took their leave and leaped forth on the grass;
They found the way that to the hill doth lead,
And softly went that neither tired was,
But at the mountain's foot they both arrived,
Before the sun his team in waters dived.

XLVI
They saw how from the crags and clefts below
His proud and stately pleasant top grew out,
And how his sides were clad with frost and snow,

The height was green with herbs and flowerets sout,
Like hairy locks the trees about him grow,
The rocks of ice keep watch and ward about,
The tender roses and the lilies new,
Thus art can nature change, and kind subdue.

XLVII
Within a thick, a dark and shady plot,
At the hill's foot that night the warriors dwell,
But when the sun his rays bright, shining, hot,
Dispread of golden light the eternal well,
"Up, up," they cried, and fiercely up they got,
And climbed boldly gainst the mountain fell;
But forth there crept, from whence I cannot say,
An ugly serpent which forestalled their way.

XLVIII
Armed with golden scales his head and crest
He lifted high, his neck swelled great with ire,
Flamed his eyes, and hiding with his breast
All the broad path, he poison breathed and fire,
Now reached he forth in folds and forward pressed,
Now would he back in rolls and heaps retire,
Thus he presents himself to guard the place,
The knights pressed forward with assured pace:

XLIX
Charles drew forth his brand to strike the snake;
Ubaldo cried, "Stay, my companion dear,
Will you with sword or weapon battle make
Against this monster that affronts us here?"
This said, he gan his charmed rod to shake,
So that the serpent durst not hiss for fear,
But fled, and dead for dread fell on the grass,
And so the passage plain, eath, open was.

Jerusalem Delivered

L

A little higher on the way they met
A lion fierce that hugely roared and cried,
His crest he reared high, and open set
Of his broad–gaping jaws the furnace wide,
His stern his back oft smote, his rage to whet,
But when the sacred staff he once espied
A trembling fear through his bold heart was spread,
His native wrath was gone, and swift he fled.

LI

The hardy couple on their way forth wend,
And met a host that on them roar and gape,
Of savage beasts, tofore unseen, unkend,
Differing in voice, in semblance, and in shape;
All monsters which hot Afric doth forthsend,
Twixt Nilus, Atlas, and the southern cape,
Were all there met, and all wild beasts besides
Hyrcania breeds, or Hyrcane forest hides.

LII

But yet that fierce, that strange and savage host
Could not in presence of those worthies stand,
But fled away, their heart and courage lost,
When Lord Ubaldo shook his charming wand.
No other let their passage stopped or crossed;
Till on the mountain's top themselves they land,
Save that the ice, the frost, and drifted snow,
Oft made them feeble, weary, faint and slow.

LIII

But having passed all that frozen ground,
And overgone that winter sharp and keen,
A warm, mild, pleasant, gentle sky they found,
That overspread a large and ample green,
The winds breathed spikenard, myrrh, and balm around,

The blasts were firm, unchanged, stable been,
Not as elsewhere the winds now rise now fall,
And Phoebus there aye shines, sets not at all.

LIV

Not as elsewhere now sunshine bright now showers,
Now heat now cold, there interchanged were,
But everlasting spring mild heaven down pours, —
In which nor rain, nor storm, nor clouds appear, —
Nursing to fields, their grass; to grass, his flowers;
To flowers their smell; to trees, the leaves they bear:
There by a lake a stately palace stands,
That overlooks all mountains, seas and lands:

LV

The passage hard against the mountain steep
These travellers had faint and weary made,
That through those grassy plains they scantly creep;
They walked, they rested oft, they went, they stayed,
When from the rocks, that seemed for joy to weep,
Before their feet a dropping crystal played
Enticing them to drink, and on the flowers
The plenteous spring a thousand streams down pours,
LVI
All which, united in the springing grass,
Ate forth a channel through the tender green
And underneath eternal shade did pass,
With murmur shrill, cold, pure, and scantly seen;
Yet so transparent, that perceived was
The bottom rich, and sands that golden been,
And on the brims the silken grass aloft
Proffered them seats, sweet, easy, fresh and soft.

LVII

"See here the stream of laughter, see the spring,"
Quoth they, "of danger and of deadly pain,

Here fond desire must by fair governing
Be ruled, our lust bridled with wisdom's rein,
Our ears be stopped while these Sirens sing,
Their notes enticing man to pleasure vain."
Thus passed they forward where the stream did make
An ample pond, a large and spacious lake.

LVIII
There on a table was all dainty food
That sea, that earth, or liquid air could give,
And in the crystal of the laughing flood
They saw two naked virgins bathe and dive,
That sometimes toying, sometimes wrestling stood,
Sometimes for speed and skill in swimming strive,
Now underneath they dived, now rose above,
And ticing baits laid forth of lust and love.

LIX
These naked wantons, tender, fair and white,
Moved so far the warriors' stubborn hearts,
That on their shapes they gazed with delight;
The nymphs applied their sweet alluring arts,
And one of them above the waters quite,
Lift up her head, her breasts and higher parts,
And all that might weak eyes subdue and take,
Her lower beauties veiled the gentle lake.

LX
As when the morning star, escaped and fled
From greedy waves, with dewy beams up flies,
Or as the Queen of Love, new born and bred
Of the Ocean's fruitful froth, did first arise:
So vented she her golden locks forth shed
Round pearls and crystal moist therein which lies:
But when her eyes upon the knights she cast,
She start, and feigned her of their sight aghast.

LXI

And her fair locks, that in a knot were tied
High on her crown, she 'gan at large unfold;
Which falling long and thick and spreading wide,
The ivory soft and white mantled in gold:
Thus her fair skin the dame would clothe and hide,
And that which hid it no less fair was hold;
Thus clad in waves and locks, her eyes divine,
From them ashamed did she turn and twine.

LXII

Withal she smiled and she blushed withal,
Her blush, her smilings, smiles her blushing graced:
Over her face her amber tresses fall,
Whereunder Love himself in ambush placed:
At last she warbled forth a treble small,
And with sweet looks her sweet songs interlaced;
"Oh happy men I that have the grace," quoth she,
"This bliss, this heaven, this paradise to see.

LXIII

"This is the place wherein you may assuage
Your sorrows past, here is that joy and bliss
That flourished in the antique golden age,
Here needs no law, here none doth aught amiss:
Put off those arms and fear not Mars his rage,
Your sword, your shield, your helmet needless is;
Then consecrate them here to endless rest,
You shall love's champions be, and soldiers blest.

LXIV

"The fields for combat here are beds of down,
Or heaped lilies under shady brakes;
But come and see our queen with golden crown,
That all her servants blest and happy makes,

She will admit you gently for her own,
Numbered with those that of her joy partakes:
But first within this lake your dust and sweat
Wash off, and at that table sit and eat."

LXV

While thus she sung, her sister lured them nigh
With many a gesture kind and loving show,
To music's sound as dames in court apply
Their cunning feet, and dance now swift now slow:
But still the knights unmoved passed by,
These vain delights for wicked charms they know,
Nor could their heavenly voice or angel's look,
Surprise their hearts, if eye or ear they took.

LXVI

For if that sweetness once but touched their hearts,
And proffered there to kindle Cupid's fire,
Straight armed Reason to his charge up starts,
And quencheth Lust, and killeth fond Desire;
Thus scorned were the dames, their wiles and arts
And to the palace gates the knights retire,
While in their stream the damsels dived sad,
Ashamed, disgraced, for that repulse they had.

SIXTEENTH BOOK

THE ARGUMENT.
The searchers pass through all the palace bright
Where in sweet prison lies Rinaldo pent,
And do so much, that full of rage and spite,
With them he goes sad, shamed, discontent:

Jerusalem Delivered

With plaints and prayers to retain her knight
Armida strives; he hears, but thence he went,
And she forlorn her palace great and fair
Destroys for grief, and flies thence through the air.

I
The palace great is builded rich and round,
And in the centre of the inmost hold
There lies a garden sweet, on fertile ground,
Fairer than that where grew the trees of gold:
The cunning sprites had buildings reared around
With doors and entries false a thousandfold,
A labyrinth they made that fortress brave,
Like Daedal's prison, or Porsenna's grave.

II
The knights passed through the castle's largest gate,
Though round about an hundred ports there shine,
The door–leaves framed of carved silver–plate,
Upon their golden hinges turn and twine.
They stayed to view this work of wit and state.
The workmanship excelled the substance fine,
For all the shapes in that rich metal wrought,
Save speech, of living bodies wanted naught.

III
Alcides there sat telling tales, and spun
Among the feeble troops of damsels mild,
He that the fiery gates of hell had won
And heaven upheld; false Love stood by and smiled:
Armed with his club fair Iole forth run,
His club with blood of monsters foul defiled,
And on her back his lion's skin had she,
Too rough a bark for such a tender tree.

Jerusalem Delivered

IV

Beyond was made a sea, whose azure flood
The hoary froth crushed from the surges blue,
Wherein two navies great well ranged stood
Of warlike ships, fire from their arms outflew,
The waters burned about their vessels good,
Such flames the gold therein enchased threw,
Caesar his Romans hence, the Asian kings
Thence Antony and Indian princes brings.

V

The Cyclades seemed to swim amid the main,
And hill gainst hill, and mount gainst mountain smote,
With such great fury met those armies twain;
Here burnt a ship, there sunk a bark or boat,
Here darts and wild–fire flew, there drowned or slain
Of princes dead the bodies fleet and float;
Here Caesar wins, and yonder conquered been
The Eastern ships, there fled the Egyptian queen:

VI

Antonius eke himself to flight betook,
The empire lost to which he would aspire,
Yet fled not he nor fight for fear forsook,
But followed her, drawn on by fond desire:
Well might you see within his troubled look,
Strive and contend, love, courage, shame and ire;
Oft looked he back, oft gazed he on the fight,
But oftener on his mistress and her flight.

VII

Then in the secret creeks of fruitful Nile,
Cast in her lap, he would sad death await,
And in the pleasure of her lovely smile
Sweeten the bitter stroke of cursed fate:
All this did art with curious hand compile

Jerusalem Delivered

In the rich metal of that princely gate.
The knights these stories viewed first and last,
Which seen, they forward pressed, and in they passed:

VIII
As through his channel crooked Meander glides
With turns and twines, and rolls now to, now fro,
Whose streams run forth there to the salt sea sides
Here back return and to their springward go:
Such crooked paths, such ways this palace hides;
Yet all the maze their map described so,
That through the labyrinth they got in fine,
As Theseus did by Ariadne's line.

IX
When they had passed all those troubled ways,
The garden sweet spread forth her green to show,
The moving crystal from the fountains plays,
Fair trees, high plants, strange herbs and flowerets new,
Sunshiny hills, dales hid from Phoebus' rays,
Groves, arbors, mossy caves, at once they view,
And that which beauty moat, most wonder brought,
Nowhere appeared the art which all this wrought.

X
So with the rude the polished mingled was
That natural seemed all and every part,
Nature would craft in counterfeiting pass,
And imitate her imitator art:
Mild was the air, the skies were clear as glass,
The trees no whirlwind felt, nor tempest smart,
But ere the fruit drop off, the blossom comes,
This springs, that falls, that ripeneth and this blooms.

XI
The leaves upon the self–same bough did hide

Jerusalem Delivered

Beside the young the old and ripened fig,
Here fruit was green, there ripe with vermeil side,
The apples new and old grew on one twig,
The fruitful vine her arms spread high and wide
That bended underneath their clusters big,
The grapes were tender here, hard, young and sour,
There purple ripe, and nectar sweet forth pour.

XII

The joyous birds, hid under greenwood shade,
Sung merry notes on every branch and bough,
The wind that in the leaves and waters played
With murmur sweet, now sung, and whistled now;
Ceased the birds, the wind loud answer made,
And while they sung, it rumbled soft and low;
Thus were it hap or cunning, chance or art,
The wind in this strange music bore his part.

XIII

With party–colored plumes' and purple bill,
A wondrous bird among the rest there flew,
That in plain speech sung love–lays loud and shrill,
Her leden was like human language true;
So much she talked, and with such wit and skill,
That strange it seemed how much good she knew,
Her feathered fellows all stood hush to hear,
Dumb was the wind, the waters silent were.

XIV

"The gently budding rose," quoth she, "behold,
That first scant peeping forth with virgin beams,
Half ope, half shut, her beauties doth upfold
In their dear leaves, and less seen, fairer seems,
And after spreads them forth more broad and bold,
Then languisheth and dies in last extremes,
Nor seems the same, that decked bed and bower

388

Jerusalem Delivered

Of many a lady late, and paramour;

XV
"So, in the passing of a day, doth pass
The bud and blossom of the life of man,
Nor e'er doth flourish more, but like the grass
Cut down, becometh withered, pale and wan:
Oh gather then the rose while time thou hast
Short is the day, done when it scant began,
Gather the rose of love, while yet thou mayest,
Loving, be loved; embracing, be embraced."
XVI
He ceased, and as approving all he spoke,
The choir of birds their heavenly tunes renew,
The turtles sighed, and sighs with kisses broke,
The fowls to shades unseen by pairs withdrew;
It seemed the laurel chaste, and stubborn oak,
And all the gentle trees on earth that grew,
It seemed the land, the sea, and heaven above,
All breathed out fancy sweet, and sighed out love.

XVII
Through all this music rare, and strong consent
Of strange allurements, sweet bove mean and measure,
Severe, firm, constant, still the knights forthwent,
Hardening their hearts gainst false enticing pleasure,
Twixt leaf and leaf their sight before they sent,
And after crept themselves at ease and leisure,
Till they beheld the queen, set with their knight
Besides the lake, shaded with boughs from sight:

XVIII
Her breasts were naked, for the day was hot,
Her locks unbound waved in the wanton wind;
Some deal she sweat, tired with the game you wot,
Her sweat–drops bright, white, round, like pearls of Ind;

389

Jerusalem Delivered

Her humid eyes a fiery smile forthshot
That like sunbeams in silver fountains shined,
O'er him her looks she hung, and her soft breast
The pillow was, where he and love took rest.
XIX
His hungry eyes upon her face he fed,
And feeding them so, pined himself away;
And she, declining often down her head,
His lips, his cheeks, his eyes kissed, as he lay,
Wherewith he sighed, as if his soul had fled
From his frail breast to hers, and there would stay
With her beloved sprite: the armed pair
These follies all beheld and this hot fare.

XX
Down by the lovers' side there pendent was
A crystal mirror, bright, pure, smooth, and neat,
He rose, and to his mistress held the glass,
A noble page, graced with that service great;
She, with glad looks, he with inflamed, alas,
Beauty and love beheld, both in one seat;
Yet them in sundry objects each espies,
She, in the glass, he saw them in her eyes:

XXI
Her, to command; to serve, it pleased the knight;
He proud of bondage; of her empire, she;
"My dear," he said, "that blessest with thy sight
Even blessed angels, turn thine eyes to me,
For painted in my heart and portrayed right
Thy worth, thy beauties and perfections be,
Of which the form; the shape and fashion best,
Not in this glass is seen, but in my breast.

XXII
"And if thou me disdain, yet be content

390

Jerusalem Delivered

At least so to behold thy lovely hue,
That while thereon thy looks are fixed and bent
Thy happy eyes themselves may see and view;
So rare a shape no crystal can present,
No glass contain that heaven of beauties true;
Oh let the skies thy worthy mirror be!
And in dear stars try shape and image see."

XXIII
And with that word she smiled, and ne'ertheless
Her love–toys still she used, and pleasures bold!
Her hair, that done, she twisted up in tress,
And looser locks in silken laces rolled,
Her curles garlandwise she did up–dress,
Wherein, like rich enamel laid on gold,
The twisted flowers smiled, and her white breast
The lilies there that spring with roses dressed.

XXIV
The jolly peacock spreads not half so fair
The eyed feathers of his pompous train;
Nor golden Iris so bends in the air
Her twenty–colored bow, through clouds of rain;
Yet all her ornaments, strange, rich and rare,
Her girdle did in price and beauty stain,
Nor that, with scorn, which Tuscan Guilla lost,
Igor Venus Ceston, could match this for cost.

XXV
Of mild denays, of tender scorns, of sweet
Repulses, war, peace, hope, despair, joy, fear,
Of smiles, jests, mirth, woe, grief, and sad regreet,
Sighs, sorrows, tears, embracements, kisses dear,
That mixed first by weight and measure meet,
Then at an easy fire attempered were,
This wondrous girdle did Armida frame,

And, when she would be loved, wore the same.

XXVI

But when her wooing fit was brought to end,
She congee took, kissed him, and went her way;
For once she used every day to wend
Bout her affairs, her spells and charms to say:
The youth remained, yet had no power to bend
One step from thence, but used there to stray
Mongst the sweet birds, through every walk and grove
Alone, save for an hermit false called Love.

XXVII

And when the silence deep and friendly shade
Recalled the lovers to their wonted sport,
In a fair room for pleasure built, they laid,
And longest nights with joys made sweet and short.
Now while the queen her household things surveyed,
And left her lord her garden and disport,
The twain that hidden in the bushes were
Before the prince in glistering arms appear:

XXVIII

As the fierce steed for age withdrawn from war
Wherein the glorious beast had always wone,
That in vile rest from fight sequestered far,
Feeds with the mares at large, his service done,
If arms he see, or hear the trumpet's jar,
He neigheth loud and thither fast doth run,
And wiseth on his back the armed knight,
Longing for jousts, for tournament and fight:

XXIX

So fared Rinaldo when the glorious light
Of their bright harness glistered in his eyes,
His noble sprite awaked at that sight

His blood began to warm, his heart to rise,
Though, drunk with ease, devoid of wonted might
On sleep till then his weakened virtue lies.
Ubaldo forward stepped, and to him hield
Of diamonds clear that pure and precious shield.

XXX
Upon the targe his looks amazed he bent,
And therein all his wanton habit spied,
His civet, balm, and perfumes redolent,
How from his locks they smoked and mantle wide,
His sword that many a Pagan stout had shent,
Bewrapped with flowers, hung idly by his side,
So nicely decked that it seemed the knight
Wore it for fashion's sake but not for fight.

XXXI
As when, from sleep and idle dreams abraid,
A man awaked calls home his wits again;
So in beholding his attire he played,
But yet to view himself could not sustain,
His looks he downward cast and naught he said,
Grieved, shamed, sad, he would have died fain,
And oft he wished the earth or ocean wide
Would swallow him, and so his errors hide.

XXXII
Ubaldo took the time, and thus begun,
"All Europe now and Asia be in war,
And all that Christ adore and fame have won,
In battle strong, in Syria fighting are;
But thee alone, Bertoldo's noble son,
This little corner keeps, exiled far
From all the world, buried in sloth and shame,
A carpet champion for a wanton dame.

XXXIII

"What letharge hath in drowsiness up–penned
Thy courage thus? what sloth doth thee infect?
Up, up, our camp and Godfrey for thee send,
Thee fortune, praise and victory expect,
Come, fatal champion, bring to happy end
This enterprise begun, all that sect
Which oft thou shaken hast to earth full low
With thy sharp brand strike down, kill, overthrow."

XXXIV

This said, the noble infant stood a space
Confused, speechless, senseless, ill–ashamed;
But when that shame to just disdain gave place,
To fierce disdain, from courage sprung untamed,
Another redness blushed through his face,
Whence worthy anger shone, displeasure flamed,
His nice attire in scorn he rent and tore,
For of his bondage vile that witness bore;

XXXV

That done, he hasted from the charmed fort,
And through the maze passed with his searchers twain.
Armida of her mount and chiefest port
Wondered to find the furious keeper slain,
Awhile she feared, but she knew in short,
That her dear lord was fled, then saw she plain,
Ah, woful sight! how from her gates the man
In haste, in fear, in wrath, in anger ran.

XXXVI

"Whither, O cruel! leavest thou me alone?"
She would have cried, her grief her speeches stayed,
So that her woful words are backward gone,
And in her heart a bitter echo made;
Poor soul, of greater skill than she was one

Whose knowledge from her thus her joy conveyed,
This wist she well, yet had desire to prove
If art could keep, if charms recall her love.

XXXVII
All what the witches of Thessalia land,
With lips unpure yet ever said or spake,
Words that could make heaven's rolling circles stand,
And draw the damned ghosts from Limbo lake,
All well she knew, but yet no time she fand
To use her knowledge or her charms to make,
But left her arts, and forth she ran to prove
If single beauty were best charm for love.

XXXVIII
She ran, nor of her honor took regard,
Oh where be all her vaunts and triumphs now?
Love's empire great of late she made or marred,
To her his subjects humbly bend and bow,
And with her pride mixed was a scorn so hard,
That to be loved she loved, yet whilst they woo
Her lovers all she hates; that pleased her will
To conquer men, and conquered so, to kill.

XXXIX
But now herself disdained, abandoned,
Ran after him; that from her fled in scorn,
And her despised beauty labored
With humble plaints and prayers to adorn:
She ran and hasted after him that fled,
Through frost and snow, through brier, bush and thorn,
And sent her cries on message her before,
That reached not him till he had reached the shore.

XL
"Oh thou that leav'st but half behind," quoth she,

"Of my poor heart, and half with thee dost carry,
Oh take this part, or render that to me,
Else kill them both at once, ah tarry, tarry:
Hear my last words, no parting kiss of thee
I crave, for some more fit with thee to marry
Keep them, unkind; what fear'st thou if thou stay?
Thou may'st deny, as well as run away."

XLI

At this Rinaldo stopped, stood still, and stayed,
She came, sad, breathless, weary, faint and weak,
So woe–begone was never nymph or maid
And yet her beauty's pride grief could not break,
On him she looked, she gazed, but naught she said,
She would not, could not, or she durst not speak,
At her he looked not, glanced not, if he did,
Those glances shamefaced were, close, secret, hid.

XLII

As cunning singers, ere they strain on high,
In loud melodious tunes, their gentle voice,
Prepare the hearers' ears to harmony
With feignings sweet, low notes and warbles choice:
So she, not having yet forgot pardie
Her wonted shifts and sleights in Cupid's toys,
A sequence first of sighs and sobs forthcast,
To breed compassion dear, then spake at last:

XLIII

"Suppose not, cruel, that I come to vow
Or pray, as ladies do their loves and lords;
Such were we late, if thou disdain it now,
Or scorn to grant such grace as love affords,
At least yet as an enemy listen thou:
Sworn foes sometimes will talk and chaffer words,
For what I ask thee, may'st thou grant right well,

And lessen naught thy wrath and anger fell.

XLIV
"If me thou hate, and in that hate delight,
I come not to appease thee, hate me still,
It's like for like; I bore great hate and spite
Gainst Christians all, chiefly I wish thee ill:
I was a Pagan born, and all my might
Against Godfredo bent, mine art and skill:
I followed thee, took thee, and bore thee far,
To this strange isle, and kept thee safe from war.

XLV
"And more, which more thy hate may justly move,
More to thy loss, more to thy shame and grief,
I thee inchanted, and allured to love,
Wicked deceit, craft worthy sharp reprief;
Mine honor gave I thee all gifts above,
And of my beauties made thee lord and chief,
And to my suitors old what I denayed,
That gave I thee, my lover new, unprayed.

XLVI
"But reckon that among, my faults, and let
Those many wrongs provoke thee so to wrath,
That hence thou run, and that at naught thou set
This pleasant house, so many joys which hath;
Go, travel, pass the seas, fight, conquest get,
Destroy our faith, what shall I say, our faith?
Ah no! no longer ours; before thy shrine
Alone I pray, thou cruel saint of mine;
XLVII
"All only let me go with thee, unkind,
A small request although I were thy foe,
The spoiler seldom leaves the prey behind,
Who triumphs lets his captives with him go;

397

Among thy prisoners poor Armida bind,
And let the camp increase thy praises so,
That thy beguiler so thou couldst beguile,
And point at me, thy thrall and bondslave vile.

XLVIII
"Despised bondslave, since my lord doth hate
These locks, why keep I them or hold them dear?
Come cut them off, that to my servile state
My habit answer may, and all my gear:
I follow thee in spite of death and fate,
Through battles fierce where dangers most appear,
Courage I have, and strength enough perchance,
To lead thy courser spare, and bear thy lance:

XLIX
"I will or bear, or be myself, thy shield,
And to defend thy life. will lose mine own:
This breast, this bosom soft shall be thy bield
Gainst storms of arrows, darts and weapons thrown;
Thy foes, pardie, encountering thee in field,
Will spare to strike thee, mine affection known,
Lest me they wound, nor will sharp vengeance take
On thee, for this despised beauty's sake.

L
"O wretch! dare I still vaunt, or help invoke
From this poor beauty, scorned and disdained?"
She said no more, her tears her speeches broke,
Which from her eyes like streams from springs down rained:
She would have caught him by the hand or cloak,
But he stepped backward, and himself restrained,
Conquered his will, his heart ruth softened not,
There plaints no issue, love no entrance got.

LI

Jerusalem Delivered

Love entered not to kindle in his breast,
Which Reason late had quenched, his wonted flame;
Yet entered Pity in the place at least,
Love's sister, but a chaste and sober dame,
And stirred him so, that hardly he suppressed
The springing tears that to his eyes up came;
But yet even there his plaints repressed were,
And, as he could, he looked, and feigned cheer.

LII
"Madam," quoth he, "for your distress I grieve,
And would amend it, if I might or could.
From your wise heart that fond affection drive:
I cannot hate nor scorn you though I would,
I seek no vengeance, wrongs I all forgive,
Nor you my servant nor my foe I hold,
Truth is, you erred, and your estate forgot,
Too great your hate was, and your love too hot.

LIII
"But those are common faults, and faults of kind,
Excused by nature, by your sex and years;
I erred likewise, if I pardon find
None can condemn you, that our trespass hears;
Your dear remembrance will I keep in mind,
In joys, in woes, in comforts, hopes and fears,
Call me your soldier and your knight, as far
As Christian faith permits, and Asia's war.

LIV
"Ah, let our faults and follies here take end,
And let our errors past you satisfy,
And in this angle of the world ypend,
Let both the fame and shame thereof now die,
From all the earth where I am known and kenned,
I wish this fact should still concealed lie:

Nor yet in following me, poor knight, disgrace
Your worth, your beauty, and your princely race.

LV

"Stay here in peace, I go, nor wend you may
With me, my guide your fellowship denies,
Stay here or hence depart some better way,
And calm your thoughts, you are both sage and wise."
While thus he spoke, her passions found no stay,
But here and there she turned and rolled her eyes,
And staring on his face awhile, at last
Thus in foul terms, her bitter wrath forth brast:

LVI

"Of Sophia fair thou never wert the child,
Nor of the Azzain race ysprung thou art,
The mad sea—waves thee hare, some tigress wild
On Caucasus' cold crags nursed thee apart;
Ah, cruel man l in whom no token mild
Appears, of pity, ruth, or tender heart,
Could not my griefs, my woes, my plaints, and all
One sigh strain from thy breast, one tear make fall?

LVII

"What shall I say, or how renew my speech?
He scorns me, leaves me, bids me call him mine:
The victor hath his foe within his reach;
Yet pardons her, that merits death and pine;
Hear how he counsels me; how he can preach,
Like chaste Xenocrates, gainst love divine;
O heavens, O gods! why do these men of shame,
Thus spoil your temples and blaspheme your name?

LVIII

"Go cruel, go, go with such peace, such rest,
Such joy, such comfort, as thou leavest me here:

400

My angry soul discharged from this weak breast,
Shall haunt thee ever, and attend thee near,
And fury–like in snakes and firebrands dressed,
Shall aye torment thee, whom it late held dear:
And if thou 'scape the seas, the rocks, and sands
And come to fight among the Pagan bands,

LIX

"There lying wounded, mongst the hurt and slain,
Of these my wrongs thou shalt the vengeance bear,
And oft Armida shalt thou call in vain,
At thy last gasp; this hope I soon to hear:"
Here fainted she, with sorrow, grief and pain,
Her latest words scant well expressed were,
But in a swoon on earth outstretched she lies,
Stiff were her frozen limbs, closed were her eyes.

LX

Thou closed thine eyes, Armida, heaven envied
Ease to thy grief, or comfort to thy woe;
Ah, open then again, see tears down slide
From his kind eyes, whom thou esteem'st thy foe,
If thou hadst heard, his sighs had mollified
Thine anger, hard he sighed and mourned so;
And as he could with sad and rueful look
His leave of thee and last farewell he took.

LXI

What should he do? leave on the naked sand
This woful lady half alive, half dead?
Kindness forbade, pity did that withstand;
But hard constraint, alas! did thence him lead;
Away he went, the west wind blew from land
Mongst the rich tresses of their pilot's head,
And with that golden sail the waves she cleft,
To land he looked, till land unseen he left.

LXII

Waked from her trance, foresaken, speechless, sad,
Armida wildly stared and gazed about,
"And is he gone," quoth she, "nor pity had
To leave me thus twixt life and death in doubt?
Could he not stay? could not the traitor—lad
From this last trance help or recall me out?
And do I love him still, and on this sand
Still unrevenged, still mourn, still weeping stand?

LXIII

"Fie no! complaints farewell! with arms and art
I will pursue to death this spiteful knight,
Not earth's low centre, nor sea's deepest part,
Not heaven, nor hell, can shield him from my might,
I will o'ertake him, take him, cleave his heart,
Such vengeance fits a wronged lover's spite,
In cruelty that cruel knight surpass
I will, but what avail vain words, alas?

LXIV

"O fool! thou shouldest have been cruel than,
For then this cruel well deserved thine ire,
When thou in prison hadst entrapped the man,
Now dead with cold, too late thou askest fire;
But though my wit, my cunning nothing can,
Some other means shall work my heart's desire,
To thee, my beauty, thine be all these wrongs,
Vengeance to thee, to thee revenge belongs.

LXV

"Thou shalt be his reward, with murdering brand
That dare this traitor of his head deprive,
O you my lovers, on this rock doth stand
The castle of her love for whom you strive,
I, the sole heir of all Damascus land,

402

For this revenge myself and kingdom give,
If by this price my will I cannot gain,
Nature gives beauty; fortune, wealth in vain.

LXVI
"But thee, vain gift, vain beauty, thee I scorn,
I hate the kingdom which I have to give,
I hate myself, and rue that I was born,
Only in hope of sweet revenge I live."
Thus raging with fell ire she gan return
From that bare shore in haste, and homeward drive,
And as true witness of her frantic ire,
Her locks waved loose, face shone, eyes sparkled fire.

LXVII
When she came home, she called with outcries shrill,
A thousand devils in Limbo deep that won,
Black clouds the skies with horrid darkness fill,
And pale for dread became the eclipsed sun,
The whirlwind blustered big on every hill,
And hell to roar under her feet begun,
You might have heard how through the palace wide,
Some spirits howled, some barked, some hissed, some cried.

LXVIII
A shadow, blacker than the mirkest night,
Environed all the place with darkness sad,
Wherein a firebrand gave a dreadful light,
Kindled in hell by Tisiphone the mad;
Vanished the shade, the sun appeared in sight,
Pale were his beams, the air was nothing glad,
And all the palace vanished was and gone,
Nor of so great a work was left one stone.

LXIX
As oft the clouds frame shapes of castles great

Amid the air, that little time do last,
But are dissolved by wind or Titan's heat,
Or like vain dreams soon made, and sooner past:
The palace vanished so, nor in his seat
Left aught but rocks and crags, by kind there placed;
She in her coach which two old serpents drew,
Sate down, and as she used, away she flew.

LXX

She broke the clouds, and cleft the yielding sky,
And bout her gathered tempest, storm and wind,
The lands that view the south pole flew she by,
And left those unknown countries far behind,
The Straits of Hercules she passed, which lie
Twixt Spain and Afric, nor her flight inclined
To north or south, but still did forward ride
O'er seas and streams, till Syria's coasts she spied.

LXXI

Now she went forward to Damascus fair,
But of her country dear she fled the sight,
And guided to Asphaltes' lake her chair,
Where stood her castle, there she ends her flight,
And from her damsels far, she made repair
To a deep vault, far from resort and light,
Where in sad thoughts a thousand doubts she cast,
Till grief and shame to wrath gave place at last.

LXXII

"I will not hence," quoth she, "till Egypt's lord
In aid of Zion's king his host shall move;
Then will I use all helps that charms afford,
And change my shape or sex if so behove:
Well can I handle bow, or lance, or sword,
The worthies all will aid me, for my love:
I seek revenge, and to obtain the same,

Farewell, regard of honor; farewell, shame.

LXXIII
"Nor let mine uncle and protector me
Reprove for this, he most deserves the blame,
My heart and sex, that weak and tender be,
He bent to deeds that maidens ill became;
His niece a wandering damsel first made he,
He spurred my youth, and I cast off my shame,
His be the fault, if aught gainst mine estate
I did for love, or shall commit for hate."

LXXIV
This said, her knights, her ladies, pages, squires
She all assembleth, and for journey fit
In such fair arms and vestures them attires
As showed her wealth, and well declared her wit;
And forward marched, full of strange desires,
Nor rested she by day or night one whit,
Till she came there, where all the eastern bands,
Their kings and princes, lay on Gaza's sands.

SEVENTEENTH BOOK

THE ARGUMENT.
Egypt's great host in battle–ray forth brought,
The Caliph sends with Godfrey's power to fight;
Armida, who Rinaldo's ruin sought,
To them adjoins herself and Syria's might.
To satisfy her cruel will and thought,
She gives herself to him that kills her knight:
He takes his fatal arms, and in his shield

His ancestors and their great deeds beheld.

I
Gaza the city on the frontier stands
Of Juda's realm, as men to Egypt ride,
Built near the sea, beside it of dry sands
Huge wildernesses lie and deserts wide
Which the strong winds lift from the parched lands
And toss like roaring waves in roughest tide,
That from those storms poor passengers almost
No refuge find, but there are drowned and lost.

II
Within this town, won from the Turks of yore
Strong garrison the king of Egypt placed,
And for it nearer was, and fitted more
That high emprise to which his thoughts he cast,
He left great Memphis, and to Gaza bore
His regal throne, and there, from countries vast
Of his huge empire all the puissant host
Assembled he, and mustered on the coast.

III
Come say, my Muse, what manner times these were,
And in those times how stood the state of things,
What power this monarch had, what arms they bear,
What nations subject, and what friends he brings;
From all lands the southern ocean near,
Or morning star, came princes, dukes and kings,
And only thou of half the world well–nigh
The armies, lords, and captains canst descry.

IV
When Egypt from the Greekish emperor
Rebelled first, and Christ's true faith denied,

Jerusalem Delivered

Of Mahomet's descent a warrior
There set his throne and ruled that kingdom wide,
Caliph he hight, and Caliphs since that hour
Are his successors named all beside:
So Nilus old his kings long time had seen
That Ptolemies and Pharaohs called had been.

V

Established was that kingdom in short while,
And grew so great, that over Asia's lands
And Lybia's realms it stretched many a mile,
From Syria's coasts as far as Cirene sands,
And southward passed gainst the course of Nile,
Through the hot clime where burnt Syene stands,
Hence bounded in with sandy deserts waste,
And thence with Euphrates' rich flood embraced.

VI

Maremma, myrrh and spices that doth bring,
And all the rich red sea it comprehends,
And to those lands, toward the morning spring
That lie beyond that gulf, it far extends;
Great is that empire, greater by the king
That rules it now, whose worth the land amends,
And makes more famous, lord thereof by blood,
By wisdom, valor, and all virtues good.

VII

With Turks and Persians war he oft did wage,
And oft he won, and sometimes lost the field,
Nor could his adverse fortune aught assuage
His valor's heat or make his proud heart yield,
But when he grew unfit for war through age,
He sheathed his sword and laid aside his shield:
But yet his warlike mind he laid not down,
Nor his great thirst of rule, praise and renown,

Jerusalem Delivered

VIII

But by his knights still cruel wars maintained.
So wise his words, so quick his wit appears,
That of the kingdom large o'er which he reigned,
The charge seemed not too weighty for his years;
His greatness Afric's lesser kings constrained
To tremble at his name, all Ind him fears,
And other realms that would his friendship hold;
Some armed soldiers sent, some gifts, some gold.

IX

This mighty prince assembled had the flower
Of all his realms, against the Frenchmen stout,
To break their rising empire and their power,
Nor of sure conquest had he fear or doubt:
To him Armida came, even at the hour
When in the plains, old Gaza's walls without,
The lords and leaders all their armies bring
In battle—ray, mustered before their king.

X

He on his throne was set, to which on height
Who clomb an hundred ivory stairs first told,
Under a pentise wrought of silver bright,
And trod on carpets made of silk and gold;
His robes were such as best beseemen might
A king, so great, so grave, so rich, so old,
And twined of sixty ells of lawn and more
A turban strange adorned his tresses hoar.

XI

His right hand did his precious sceptre wield,
His beard was gray, his looks severe and grave,
And from his eyes, not yet made dim with eild,
Sparkled his former worth and vigor brave,

Jerusalem Delivered

His gestures all the majesty upheild
And state, as his old age and empire crave,
So Phidias carved, Apelles so, pardie,
Erst painted Jove, Jove thundering down from sky.

XII

On either side him stood a noble lord,
Whereof the first held in his upright hand
Of severe justice the unpartial sword;
The other bare the seal, and causes scanned,
Keeping his folk in peace and good accord,
And termed was lord chancellor of the land;
But marshal was the first, and used to lead
His armies forth to war, oft with good speed.

XIII

Of bold Circassians with their halberts long,
About his throne his guards stood in a ring,
All richly armed in gilden corslets strong,
And by their sides their crooked swords down hing:
Thus set, thus seated, his grave lords among,
His hosts and armies great beheld the king,
And every band as by his throne it went,
Their ensigns low inclined, and arms down bent:

XIV

Their squadrons first the men of Egypt show,
In four troops, and each his several guide,
Of the high country two, two of the low
Which Nile had won out of the salt seaside,
His fertile slime first stopped the waters' flow,
Then hardened to firm land the plough to bide,
So Egypt still increased, within far placed
That part is now where ships erst anchor cast.

XV

Jerusalem Delivered

The foremost band the people were that dwelled
In Alexandria's rich and fertile plain,
Along the western shore, whence Nile expelled
The greedy billows of the swelling main;
Araspes was their guide, who more excelled
In wit and craft than strength or warlike pain,
To place an ambush close, or to devise
A treason false, was none so sly, so wise.

XVI

The people next that gainst the morning rays
Along the coasts of Asia have their seat,
Arontes led them, whom no warlike praise
Ennobled, but high birth and titles great,
His helm ne'er made him sweat in toilsome frays,
Nor was his sleep e'er broke with trumpet's threat,
But from soft ease to try the toil of fight
His fond ambition brought this carpet knight.

XVII

The third seemed not a troop or squadron small,
But an huge host; nor seemed it so much grain
In Egypt grew as to sustain them all;
Yet from one town thereof came all that train,
A town in people to huge shires equal,
That did a thousand streets and more contain,
Great Caire it hight, whose commons from each side
Came swarming out to war, Campson their guide.

XVIII

Next under Gazel marched they that plough
The fertile lands above that town which lie
Up to the place where Nilus tumbling low
Falls from his second cataract from high;
The Egyptians weaponed were with sword and bow,
No weight of helm or hauberk list they try,
And richly armed, in their strong foes no dreed

410

Of death but great desire of spoil they breed.

XIX

The naked folk of Barca these succeed,
Unarmed half, Alarcon led that band,
That long in deserts lived, in extreme need,
On spoils and preys purchased by strength of hand.
To battle strong unfit, their king did lead
His army next brought from Zumara land.
Then he of Tripoli, for sudden fight
And skirmish short, both ready, bold, and light.

XX

Two captains next brought forth their bands to show
Whom Stony sent and Happy Araby,
Which never felt the cold of frost and snow,
Or force of burning heat, unless fame lie,
Where incense pure and all sweet odors grow,
Where the sole phoenix doth revive, not die,
And midst the perfumes rich and flowerets brave
Both birth and burial, cradle hath and grave.

XXI

Their clothes not rich, their garments were not gay,
But weapons like the Egyptian troops they had,
The Arabians next that have no certain stay,
No house, no home, no mansion good or bad,
But ever, as the Scythian hordes stray,
From place to place their wandering cities gad:
These have both voice and stature feminine,
Hair long and black, black face, and fiery eyne.

XXII

Long Indian canes, with iron armed, they bear,
And as upon their nimble steeds they ride,
Like a swift storm their speedy troops appear,

If winds so fast bring storms from heavens wide:
By Syphax led the first Arabians were;
Aldine the second squadron had no guide,
And Abiazar proud, brought to the fight
The third, a thief, a murderer, not a knight.

XXIII
The islanders came then their prince before
Whose lands Arabia's gulf enclosed about,
Wherein they fish and gather oysters store,
Whose shells great pearls rich and round pour out;
The Red Sea sent with them from his left shore,
Of negroes grim a black and ugly rout;
These Agricalt and those Osmida brought,
A man that set law, faith and truth at naught.

XXIV
The Ethiops next which Meroe doth breed,
That sweet and gentle isle of Meroe,
Twixt Nile and Astrabore that far doth spread,
Where two religions are, and kingdoms three,
These Assimiro and Canario led,
Both kings, both Pagans, and both subjects be
To the great Caliph, but the third king kept
Christ's sacred faith, nor to these wars outstepped.
XXV
After two kings, both subjects also, ride,
And of two bands of archers had the charge,
The first Soldan of Ormus placed in the wide
Huge Persian Bay, a town rich, fair, and large:
The last of Boecan, which at every tide
The sea cuts off from Persia's southern marge,
And makes an isle; but when it ebbs again,
The passage there is sandy, dry and plain.

XXVI

Nor thee, great Altamore, in her chaste bed
Thy loving queen kept with her dear embrace,
She tore her locks, she smote her breast, and shed
Salt tears to make thee stay in that sweet place,
"Seem the rough seas more calm, cruel," she said,
"Than the mild looks of thy kind spouse's face?
Or is thy shield, with blood and dust defiled,
A dearer armful than thy tender child?"

XXVII
This was the mighty king of Samarcand,
A captain wise, well skilled in feats of war,
In courage fierce, matchless for strength of hand,
Great was his praise, his force was noised far;
His worth right well the Frenchmen understand,
By whom his virtues feared and loved are:
His men were armed with helms and hauberks strong,
And by their sides broad swords and maces hong.

XXVIII
Then from the mansions bright of fresh Aurore
Adrastus came, the glorious king of Ind,
A snake's green skin spotted with black he wore,
That was made rich by art and hard by kind,
An elephant this furious giant bore,
He fierce as fire, his mounture swift as wind;
Much people brought he from his kingdoms wide,
Twixt Indus, Ganges, and the salt seaside.

XXIX
The king's own troop come next, a chosen crew,
Of all the camp the strength, the crown, the flower,
Wherein each soldier had with honors due
Rewarded been, for service ere that hour;
Their arms were strong for need, and fair for show,
Upon fierce steeds well mounted rode this power,

And heaven itself with the clear splendor shone
Of their bright armor, purple, gold and stone.

XXX
Mongst these Alarco fierce, and Odemare
The muster master was, and Hidraort,
And Rimedon, whose rashness took no care
To shun death's bitter stroke, in field or fort,
Tigranes, Rapold stem, the men that fare
By sea, that robbed in each creek and port,
Ormond, and Marlabust the Arabian named,
Because that land rebellious he reclaimed.

XXXI
There Pirga, Arimon, Orindo are,
Brimarte the scaler, and with him Suifant
The breaker of wild horses brought from far;
Then the great wresteler strong Aridamant,
And Tisapherne, the thunderbolt of war,
Whom none surpassed, whom none to match durst vaunt
At tilt, at tourney, or in combat brave,
With spear or lance, with sword, with mace or glaive.

XXXII
A false Armenian did this squadron guide,
That in his youth from Christ's true faith and light
To the blind lore of Paganism did slide,
That Clement late, now Emireno, hight;
Yet to his king he faithful was, and tried
True in all causes, his in wrong and right:
A cunning leader and a soldier bold,
For strength and courage, young; for wisdom, old.

XXXIII
When all these regiments were passed and gone,
Appeared Armide, and came her troop to show;

Jerusalem Delivered

Set in a chariot bright with precious stone,
Her gown tucked up, and in her hand a bow;
In her sweet face her new displeasures shone,
Mixed with the native beauties there which grow,
And quickened so her looks that in sharp wise
It seems she threats and yet her threats entice.

XXXIV

Her chariot like Aurora's glorious wain,
With carbuncles and jacinths glistered round:
Her coachman guided with the golden rein
Four unicorns, by couples yoked and bound;
Of squires and lovely ladies hundreds twain,
Whose rattling quivers at their backs resound,
On milk–white steeds, wait on the chariot bright,
Their steeds to manage, ready; swift, to flight.

XXXV

Followed her troop led forth by Aradin,
Which Hidraort from Syria's kingdom sent,
As when the new–born phoenix doth begin
To fly to Ethiop–ward, at the fair bent
Of her rich wings strange plumes and feathers thin
Her crowns and chains with native gold besprent,
The world amazed stands; and with her fly
An host of wondering birds, that sing and cry:

XXXVI

So passed Armida, looked on, gazed on, so,
A wondrous dame in habit, gesture, face;
There lived no wight to love so great a foe
But wished and longed those beauties to embrace,
Scant seen, with anger sullen, sad for woe,
She conquered all the lords and knights in place,
What would she do, her sorrows passed, think you,
When her fair eyes, her looks and smiles shall woo?

XXXVII

She passed, the king commanded Emiren
Of his rich throne to mount the lofty stage,
To whom his host, his army, and his men,
He would commit, now in his graver age.
With stately grace the man approached then;
His looks his coming honor did presage:
The guard asunder cleft and passage made,
He to the throne up went, and there he stayed.

XXXVIII

To earth he cast his eyes, and bent his knee:
To whom the king thus gan his will explain,
"To thee this sceptre, Emiren, to thee
These armies I commit, my place sustain
Mongst them, go set the king of Judah free,
And let the Frenchmen feel my just disdain,
Go meet them, conquer them, leave none alive;
Or those that scape from battle, bring captive."

XXXIX

Thus spake the tyrant. and the sceptre laid
With all his sovereign power upon the knight:
"I take this sceptre at your hand," he said,
"And with your happy fortune go to fight,
And trust, my lord, in your great virtue's aid
To venge all Asia's harms, her wrongs to right,
Nor e'er but victor will I see your face;
Our overthrow shall bring death, not disgrace.

XL

"Heavens grant if evil, yet no mishap I dread,
Or harm they threaten against this camp of thine,
That all that mischief fall upon my head,
Theirs be the conquest, and the danger mine;
And let them safe bring home their captain dead,

Buried in pomp of triumph's glorious shine."
He ceased, and then a murmur loud up went,
With noise of joy and sound of instrument.

XLI

Amid the noise and shout uprose the king,
Environed with many a noble peer
That to his royal tent the monarch bring,
And there he feasted them and made them cheer,
To him and him he talked, and carved each thing,
The greatest honored, meanest graced were;
And while this mirth, this joy and feast doth last,
Armida found fit time her nets to cast:

XLII

But when the feast was done, she, that espied
All eyes on her fair visage fixed and bent,
And by new notes and certain signs described,
How love's empoisoned fire their entrails brent,
Arose, and where the king sate in his pride,
With stately pace and humble gestures, went;
And as she could in looks in voice she strove
Fierce, stern, bold, angry, and severe to prove.

XLIII

"Great Emperor, behold me here," she said.
"For thee, my country, and my faith to fight,
A dame, a virgin, but a royal maid;
And worthy seems this war a princess hight,
For by the sword the sceptre is upstayed,
This hand can use them both with skill and might,
This hand of mine can strike, and at each blow
Thy foes and ours kill, wound, and overthrow.

XLIV

"Nor yet suppose this is the foremost day

417

Wherein to war I bent my noble thought,
But for the surety of thy realms, and stay
Of our religion true, ere this I wrought:
Yourself best know if this be true I say,
Or if my former deeds rejoiced you aught,
When Godfrey's hardy knights and princes strong
I captive took, and held in bondage long.

XLV

"I took them, bound them, and so sent them bound
To thee, a noble gift, with whom they had
Condemned low in dungeon under ground
Forever dwelt, in woe and torment sad:
So might thine host an easy way have found
To end this doubtful war, with conquest glad,
Had not Rinaldo fierce my knights all slain,
And set those lords, his friends, at large again.

XLVI

"Rinaldo is well known," and there a long
And true rehearsal made she of his deeds,
"This is the knight that since hath done me wrong,
Wrong yet untold, that sharp revengement needs:
Displeasure therefore, mixed with reason strong,
This thirst of war in me, this courage breeds;
Nor how he injured me time serves to tell,
Let this suffice, I seek revengement fell,

XLVII

"And will procure it, for all shafts that fly
Light not in vain; some work the shooter's will,
And Jove's right hand with thunders cast from sky
Takes open vengeance oft for secret ill:
But if some champion dare this knight defy
To mortal battle, and by fight him kill,
And with his hateful head will me present,

That gift my soul shall please, my heart content:

XLVIII
"So please, that for reward enjoy he shall,
The greatest gift I can or may afford,
Myself, my beauty, wealth, and kingdoms all,
To marry him, and take him for my lord,
This promise will I keep whate'er befall,
And thereto bind myself by oath and word:
Now he that deems this purchase worth his pain,
Let him step forth and speak, I none disdain."

XLIX
While thus the princess said, his hungry eyne
Adrastus fed on her sweet beauty's light,
"The gods forbid," quoth he, "one shaft of thine
Should be discharged gainst that discourteous knight,
His heart unworthy is, shootress divine,
Of thine artillery to feel the might;
To wreak thine ire behold me prest and fit,
I will his head cut off, and bring thee it.
L
"I will his heart with this sharp sword divide,
And to the vultures cast his carcass out."
Thus threatened he, but Tisapherne envied
To hear his glorious vaunt and boasting stout,
And said, "But who art thou, that so great pride
Thou showest before the king, me, and this rout?
Pardie here are some such, whose worth exceeds
Thy vaunting much yet boast not of their deeds."

LI
The Indian fierce replied, "I am the man
Whose acts his words and boasts have aye surpassed;
But if elsewhere the words thou now began
Had uttered been, that speech had been thy last."

Thus quarrelled they; the monarch stayed them than,
And 'twixt the angry knights his sceptre cast:
Then to Armida said, "Fair Queen, I see
Thy heart is stout, thy thoughts courageous be;

LII
"Thou worthy art that their disdain and ire
At thy commands these knights should both appease,
That gainst thy foe their courage hot as fire
Thou may'st employ, both when and where you please,
There all their power and force, and what desire
They have to serve thee, may they show at ease."
The monarch held his peace when this was said,
And they new proffer of their service made.
LIII
Nor they alone, but all that famous were
In feats of arms boast that he shall be dead,
All offer her their aid, all say and swear,
To take revenge on his condemned head:
So many arms moved she against her dear,
And swore her darling under foot to tread,
But he, since first the enchanted isle he left,
Safe in his barge the roaring waves still cleft.

LIV
By the same way returned the well−taught boat
By which it came, and made like haste, like speed;
The friendly wind, upon her sail that smote,
So turned as to return her ship had need:
The youth sometimes the Pole or Bear did note,
Or wandering stars which dearest nights forthspread:
Sometimes the floods, the hills, or mountains steep,
Whose woody fronts o'ershade the silent deep.

LV
Now of the camp the man the state inquires,

420

Jerusalem Delivered

Now asks the customs strange of sundry lands;
And sailed, till clad in beams and bright attires
The fourth day's sun on the eastern threshold stands:
But when the western seas had quenched those fires,
Their frigate struck against the shore and sands;
Then spoke their guide, "The land of Palestine
This is, here must your journey end and mine."

LVI

The knights she set upon the shore all three,
And vanished thence in twinkling of an eye,
Uprose the night in whose deep blackness be
All colors hid of things in earth or sky,
Nor could they house, or hold, or harbor see,
Or in that desert sign of dwelling spy,
Nor track of man or horse, or aught that might
Inform them of some path or passage right.

LVII

When they had mused what way they travel should,
From the west shore their steps at last they twined,
And lo, far off at last their eyes behold
Something, they wist not what, that clearly shined
With rays of silver and with beams of gold
Which the dark folds of night's black mantle lined.
Forward they went and marched against the light,
To see and find the thing that shone so bright.

LVIII

High on a tree they saw an armor new,
That glistered bright gainst Cynthia's silver ray,
Therein, like stars in skies, the diamonds show
Fret in the gilden helm and hauberk gay,
The mighty shield all scored full they view
Of pictures fair, ranged in meet array;
To keep them sate an aged man beside,

Who to salute them rose, when them he spied.

LIX

The twain who first were sent in this pursuit
Of their wise friend well knew the aged face:
But when the wizard sage their first salute
Received and quitted had with kind embrace,
To the young prince, that silent stood and mute,
He turned his speech, "In this unused place
For you alone I wait, my lord," quoth he,
"My chiefest care your state and welfare be.

LX

"For, though you wot it not, I am your friend,
And for your profit work, as these can tell,
I taught them how Armida's charms to end,
And bring you thither from love's hateful cell,
Now to my words, though sharp perchance, attend,
Nor be aggrieved although they seem too fell,
But keep them well in mind, till in the truth
A wise and holier man instruct thy youth.

LXI

"Not underneath sweet shades and fountains shrill,
Among the nymphs, the fairies, leaves and flowers;
But on the steep, the rough and craggy hill
Of virtue stands this bliss, this good of ours:
By toil and travel, not by sitting still
In pleasure's lap, we come to honor's bowers;
Why will you thus in sloth's deep valley lie?
The royal eagles on high mountains fly.

LXII

"Nature lifts up thy forehead to the skies,
And fills thy heart with high and noble thought,
That thou to heavenward aye shouldst lift thine eyes,

422

And purchase fame by deeds well done and wrought;
She gives thee ire, by which not courage flies
To conquests, not through brawls and battles fought
For civil jars, nor that thereby you might
Your wicked malice wreak and cursed spite.

LXIII
"But that your strength spurred forth with noble wrath,
With greater fury might Christ's foes assault,
And that your bridle should with lesser scath
Each secret vice, and kill each inward fault;
For so his godly anger ruled hath
Each righteous man beneath heaven's starry vault,
And at his will makes it now hot, now cold,
Now lets it run, now doth it fettered hold."

LXIV
Thus parleyed he; Rinaldo, hushed and still,
Great wisdom heard in those few words compiled,
He marked his speech, a purple blush did fill
His guilty checks, down went his eyesight mild.
The hermit by his bashful looks his will
Well understood, and said, "Look up, my child,
And painted in this precious shield behold
The glorious deeds of thy forefathers old.

LXV
"Thine elders' glory herein see and know,
In virtue's path how they trod all their days,
Whom thou art far behind, a runner slow
In this true course of honor, fame and praise:
Up, up, thyself incite by the fair show
Of knightly worth which this bright shield bewrays,
That be thy spur to praise!" At last the knight
Looked up, and on those portraits bent his sight.

Jerusalem Delivered

LXVI

The cunning workman had in little space
Infinite shapes of men there well expressed,
For there described was the worthy race
And pedigree of all of the house of Est:
Come from a Roman spring o'er all the place
Flowed pure streams of crystals east and west,
With laurel crowned stood the princes old,
Their wars the hermit and their battles told.

LXVII

He showed them Caius first, when first in prey
To people strange the falling empire went,
First Prince of Est, that did the sceptre sway
O'er such as chose him lord by tree consent;
His weaker neighbors to his rule obey,
Need made them stoop, constraint doth force content;
After, when Lord Honorius called the train
Of savage Goths into his land again,

LXVIII

And when all Italy did burn and flame
With bloody war, by this fierce people mad,
When Rome a captive and a slave became,
And to be quite destroyed was most afraid,
Aurelius, to his everlasting fame,
Preserved in peace the folk that him obeyed:
Next whom was Forest, who the rage withstood
Of the bold Huns, and of their tyrant proud.

LXIX

Known by his look was Attila the fell,
Whose dragon eyes shone bright with anger's spark,
Worse faced than a dog, who viewed him well
Supposed they saw him grin and heard him bark;
But when in single fight he lost the bell,

How through his troops he fled there might you mark,
And how Lord Forest after fortified
Aquilea's town, and how for it he died.

LXX

For there was wrought the fatal end and fine,
Both of himself and of the town he kept:
But his great son renowned Acarine,
Into his father's place and honor stepped:
To cruel fate, not to the Huns, Altine
Gave place, and when time served again forth leapt,
And in the vale of Po built for his seat
Of many a village a small city great;

LXXI

Against the swelling flood he banked it strong,
And thence uprose the fair and noble town
Where they of Est should by succession long
Command, and rule in bliss and high renown:
Gainst Odoacer then he fought, but wrong
Oft spoileth right, fortune treads courage down,
For there he died for his dear country's sake,
And of his father's praise did so partake.

LXXII

With him died Alforisio, Azzo was
With his dear brother into exile sent,
But homeward they in arms again repass —
The Herule king oppressed — from banishment.
His front through pierced with a dart, alas,
Next them, of Est the Epaminondas went,
That smiling seemed to cruel death to yield,
When Totila was fled, and safe his shield.

LXXIII

Of Boniface I speak; Valerian,

425

His son, in praise and power succeeded him,
Who durst sustain, in years though scant a man,
Of the proud Goths an hundred squadrons trim:
Then he that gainst the Sclaves much honor wan,
Ernesto, threatening stood with visage grim;
Before him Aldoard, the Lombard stout
Who from Monselce boldly erst shut out.

LXXIV

There Henry was and Berengare the bold
That served great Charles in his conquest high,
Who in each battle give the onset would,
A hardy soldier and a captain sly;
After, Prince Lewis did he well uphold
Against his nephew, King of Italy,
He won the field and took that king on live:
Next him stood Otho with his children five.

LXXV

Of Almeric the image next they view,
Lord Marquis of Ferrara first create,
Founder of many churches, that upthrew
His eyes, like one that used to contemplate;
Gainst him the second Azzo stood in rew,
With Berengarius that did long debate,
Till after often change of fortune stroke,
He won, and on all Italy laid the yoke.

LXXVI

Albert his son the Germans warred among,
And there his praise and fame was spread so wide,
That having foiled the Danes in battle strong,
His daughter young became great Otho's bride.
Behind him Hugo stood with warfare long,
That broke the horn of all the Romans' pride,
Who of all Italy the marquis hight,

And Tuscan whole possessed as his right.

LXXVII
After Tebaldo, puissant Boniface
And Beatrice his dear possessed the stage;
Nor was there left heir male of that great race,
To enjoy the sceptre, state and heritage;
The Princess Maud alone supplied the place,
Supplied the want in number, sex and age;
For far above each sceptre, throne and crown,
The noble dame advanced her veil and gown.

LXXVIII
With manlike vigor shone her noble look,
And more than manlike wrath her face o'erspread,
There the fell Normans, Guichard there forsook
The field, till then who never feared nor fled;
Henry the Fourth she beat, and from him took
His standard, and in Church it offered;
Which done, the Pope back to the Vatican
She brought, and placed in Peter's chair again.

LXXIX
As he that honored her and held her dear,
Azzo the Fifth stood by her lovely side;
But the fourth Azzo's offspring far and near
Spread forth, and through Germania fructified;
Sprung from the branch did Guelpho bold appear,
Guelpho his son by Cunigond his bride,
And in Bavaria's field transplanted new
The Roman graft flourished, increased and grew.

LXXX
A branch of Est there in the Guelfian tree
Engrafted was, which of itself was old,
Whereon you might the Guelfoes fairer see,
Renew their sceptres and their crowns of gold,

427

Of which Heaven's good aspects so bended be
That high and broad it spread and flourished bold,
Till underneath his glorious branches laid
Half Germany, and all under his shade.
LXXXI
This regal plant from his Italian rout
Sprung up as high, and blossomed fair above,
Fornenst Lord Guelpho, Bertold issued out,
With the sixth Azzo whom all virtues love;
This was the pedigree of worthies stout,
Who seemed in that bright shield to live and move.
Rinaldo waked up and cheered his face,
To see these worthies of his house and race.

LXXXII
To do like acts his courage wished and sought,
And with that wish transported him so far
That all those deeds which filled aye his thought,
Towns won, forts taken, armies killed in war,
As if they were things done indeed and wrought,
Before his eyes he thinks they present are,
He hastily arms him, and with hope and haste,
Sure conquest met, prevented and embraced.

LXXXIII
But Charles, who had told the death and fall
Of the young prince of Danes, his late dear lord,
Gave him the fatal weapon, and withal,
"Young knight," quoth he, "take with good luck this sword,
Your just, strong, valiant hand in battle shall
Employ it long, for Christ's true faith and word,
And of his former lord revenge the wrongs,
Who loved you so, that deed to you belongs."

LXXXIV
He answered, "God for his mercy's sake,

Grant that this hand which holds this weapon good
For thy dear master may sharp vengeance take,
May cleave the Pagan's heart, and shed his blood."
To this but short reply did Charles make,
And thanked him much, nor more on terms they stood:
For lo, the wizard sage that was their guide
On their dark journey hastes them forth to ride.

LXXXV

"High time it is," quoth he, "for you to wend
Where Godfrey you awaits, and many a knight,
There may we well arrive ere night doth end,
And through this darkness can I guide you right."
This said, up to his coach they all ascend,
On his swift wheels forth rolled the chariot light,
He gave his coursers fleet the rod and rein,
And galloped forth and eastward drove amain;

LXXXVI

While silent so through night's dark shade they fly,
The hermit thus bespake the young man stout:
"Of thy great house, thy race, thine offspring high,
Here hast thou seen the branch, the bole, the root,
And as these worthies born to chivalry
And deeds of arms it hath tofore brought out,
So is it, so it shall be fertile still,
Nor time shall end, nor age that seed shall kill.

LXXXVII

"Would God, as drawn from the forgetful lap
Of antique time, I have thine elders shown;
That so I could the catalogue unwrap
Of thy great nephews yet unborn, unknown,
That ere this light they view, their fate and hap
I might foretell, and how their chance is thrown,
That like thine elders so thou mightst behold

429

Thy children, many, famous, stout and bold.

LXXXVIII
"But not by art or skill, of things future
Can the plain truth revealed be and told,
Although some knowledge doubtful, dark, obscure
We have of coming haps in clouds uprolled;
Nor all which in this cause I know for sure
Dare I foretell: for of that father old,
The hermit Peter, learned I much, and he
Withouten veil heaven's secrets great doth see.

LXXXIX
"But this, to him revealed by grace divine,
By him to me declared, to thee I say,
Was never race Greek, barbarous, or Latine,
Great in times past, or famous at this day,
Richer in hardy knights than this of thine;
Such blessings Heaven shall on thy children lay
That they in fame shall pass, in praise o'ercome,
The worthies old of Sparta, Carthage, Rome.

XC
"But mongst the rest I chose Alphonsus bold,
In virtue first, second in place and name,
He shall be born when this frail world grows old,
Corrupted, poor, and bare of men of fame,
Better than he none shall, none can, or could,
The sword or sceptre use or guide the same,
To rule in peace or to command in fight,
Thine offspring's glory and thy house's light.

XCI
"His younger age foretokens true shall yield
Of future valor, puissance, force and might,
From him no rock the savage beast shall shield;

430

At tilt or tourney match him shall no knight:
After, he conquer shall in pitched field
Great armies and win spoils in single fight,
And on his locks, rewards for knightly praise,
Shall garlands wear of grass, of oak, of bays.

XCII

"His graver age, as well that eild it fits,
Shall happy peace preserve and quiet blest,
And from his neighbors strong mongst whom he sits
Shall keep his cities safe in wealth and rest,
Shall nourish arts and cherish pregnant wits,
Make triumphs great, and feast his subjects best,
Reward the good, the evil with pains torment,
Shall dangers all foresee, and seen, prevent.

XCIII

"But if it hap against those wicked bands
That sea and earth invest with blood and war,
And in these wretched times to noble lands
Give laws of peace false and unjust that are,
That he be sent, to drive their guilty hands
From Christ's pure altars and high temples far,
Oh, what revenge, what vengeance shall he bring
On that false sect, and their accursed king!

XCIV

"Too late the Moors, too late the Turkish king,
Gainst him should arm their troops and legions bold
For he beyond great Euphrates should bring,
Beyond the frozen tops of Taurus cold,
Beyond the land where is perpetual spring,
The cross, the eagle white, the lily of gold,
And by baptizing of the Ethiops brown
Of aged Nile reveal the springs unknown."
XCV

Thus said the hermit, and his prophecy
The prince accepted with content and pleasure,
The secret thought of his posterity
Of his concealed joys heaped up the measure.
Meanwhile the morning bright was mounted high,
And changed Heaven's silver wealth to golden treasure,
And high above the Christian tents they view
How the broad ensigns trembled, waved and blew,

XCVI
When thus again their leader sage begun,
"See how bright Phoebus clears the darksome skies,
See how with gentle beams the friendly sun
The tents, the towns, the hills and dales descries,
Through my well guiding is your voyage done,
From danger safe in travel off which lies,
Hence without fear of harm or doubt of foe
March to the camp, I may no nearer go."

XCVII
Thus took he leave, and made a quick return,
And forward went the champions three on foot,
And marching right against the rising morn
A ready passage to the camp found out,
Meanwhile had speedy fame the tidings borne
That to the tents approached these barons stout,
And starting from his throne and kingly seat
To entertain them, rose Godfredo great.

EIGHTEENTH BOOK

THE ARGUMENT.

Jerusalem Delivered

The charms and spirits false therein which lie
Rinaldo chaseth from the forest old;
The host of Egypt comes; Vafrin the spy
Entereth their camp, stout, crafty, wise and bold;
Sharp is the fight about the bulwarks high
And ports of Zion, to assault the hold:
Godfrey hath aid from Heaven, by force the town
Is won, the Pagans slain, walls beaten down.

I
Arrived where Godfrey to embrace him stood,
"My sovereign lord," Rinaldo meekly said,
"To venge my wrongs against Gernando proud
My honor's care provoked my wrath unstayed;
But that I you displeased, my chieftain good,
My thoughts yet grieve, my heart is still dismayed,
And here I come, prest all exploits to try
To make me gracious in your gracious eye."

II
To him that kneeled, folding his friendly arms
About his neck, the duke this answer gave:
"Let pass such speeches sad, of passed harms.
Remembrance is the life of grief; his grave,
Forgetfulness; and for amends, in arms
Your wonted valor use and courage brave;
For you alone to happy end must bring
The strong enchantments of the charmed spring.

III
"That aged wood whence heretofore we got,
To build our scaling engines, timber fit,
Is now the fearful seat, but how none wot,
Where ugly fiends and damned spirits sit;
To cut one twist thereof adventureth not

433

The boldest knight we have, nor without it
This wall can battered be: where others doubt
There venture thou, and show thy courage stout."

IV
Thus said he, and the knight in speeches few
Proffered his service to attempt the thing,
To hard assays his courage willing flew,
To him praise was no spur, words were no sting;
Of his dear friends then he embraced the crew
To welcome him which came; for in a ring
About him Guelpho, Tancred and the rest
Stood, of the camp the greatest, chief and best.

V
When with the prince these lords had iterate
Their welcomes oft, and oft their dear embrace,
Toward the rest of lesser worth and state,
He turned, and them received with gentle grace;
The merry soldiers bout him shout and prate,
With cries as joyful and as cheerful face
As if in triumph's chariot bright as sun,
He had returned Afric or Asia won.

VI
Thus marched to his tent the champion good,
And there sat down with all his friends around;
Now of the war he asked, now of the wood,
And answered each demand they list propound;
But when they left him to his ease, up stood
The hermit, and, fit time to speak once found,
"My lord," he said, "your travels wondrous are,
Far have you strayed, erred, wandered far.

VII
"Much are you bound to God above, who brought

Jerusalem Delivered

You safe from false Armida's charmed hold,
And thee a straying sheep whom once he bought
Hath now again reduced to his fold,
And gainst his heathen foes these men of naught
Hath chosen thee in place next Godfrey bold;
Yet mayest thou not, polluted thus with sin,
In his high service war or fight begin.

VIII

"The world, the flesh, with their infection vile
Pollute the thoughts impure, thy spirit stain;
Not Po, not Ganges, not seven-mouthed Nile,
Not the wide seas, can wash thee clean again,
Only to purge all faults which thee defile
His blood hath power who for thy sins was slain:
His help therefore invoke, to him bewray
Thy secret faults, mourn, weep, complain and pray."

IX

This said, the knight first with the witch unchaste
His idle loves and follies vain lamented;
Then kneeling low with heavy looks downcast,
His other sins confessed and all repented,
And meekly pardon craved for first and last.
The hermit with his zeal was well contented,
And said, "On yonder hill next morn go pray
That turns his forehead gainst the morning ray.

X

"That done, march to the wood, whence each one brings
Such news of furies, goblins, fiends, and sprites,
The giants, monsters, and all dreadful things
Thou shalt subdue, which that dark grove unites:
Let no strange voice that mourns or sweetly sings,
Nor beauty, whose glad smile frail hearts delights,
Within thy breast make ruth or pity rise,

But their false looks and prayers false despise."

XI
Thus he advised him, and the hardy knight
Prepared him gladly to this enterprise,
Thoughtful he passed the day, and sad the night;
And ere the silver morn began to rise,
His arms he took, and in a coat him dight
Of color strange, cut in the warlike guise;
And on his way sole, silent, forth he went
Alone, and left his friends, and left his tent.

XII
It was the time when gainst the breaking day
Rebellious night yet strove, and still repined,
For in the east appeared the morning gray
And yet some lamps in Jove's high palace shined,
When to Mount Olivet he took his way,
And saw, as round about his eyes he twined,
Night's shadows hence, from thence the morning's shine,
This bright, that dark; that earthly, this divine.

XIII
Thus to himself he thought, how many bright
And splendent lamps shine in heaven's temple high,
Day hath his golden sun, her moon the night,
Her fixed and wandering stars the azure sky,
So framed all by their Creator's might
That still they live and shine, and ne'er shall die
Till, in a moment, with the last day's brand
They burn, and with them burn sea, air, and land.

XIV
Thus as he mused, to the top he went,
And there kneeled down with reverence and fear,
His eyes upon heaven's eastern face he bent,

His thoughts above all heavens uplifted were:
"The sins and errors, which I now repent,
Of mine unbridled youth, O Father dear,
Remember not, but let thy mercy fall,
And purge my faults and mine offences all."

XV
Thus prayed he, with purple wings upflew
In golden weed the morning's lusty queen,
Begilding with the radiant beams she threw
His helm, his harness, and the mountain green;
Upon his breast and forehead gently blew
The air, that balm and nardus breathed unseen,
And o'er his head let down from clearest skies
A cloud of pure and precious clew there flies.

XVI
The heavenly dew was on his garments spread,
To which compared, his clothes pale ashes seem,
And sprinkled so, that all that paleness fled
And thence, of purest white, bright rays outstream;
So cheered are the flowers late withered
With the sweet comfort of the morning beam,
And so, returned to youth, a serpent old
Adorns herself in new and native gold.

XVII
The lovely whiteness of his changed weed,
The Prince perceived well, and long admired;
Toward the forest marched he on with speed,
Resolved, as such adventures great required;
Thither he came whence shrinking back for dread
Of that strange desert's sight the first retired,
But not to him fearful or loathsome made
That forest was, but sweet with pleasant shade:

Jerusalem Delivered

XVIII

Forward he passed, mid in the grove before
He heard a sound that strange, sweet, pleasing was;
There rolled a crystal brook with gentle roar,
There sighed the winds as through the leaves they pass,
There did the nightingale her wrongs deplore,
There sung the swan, and singing died, alas!
There lute, harp, cittern, human voice he heard,
And all these sounds one sound right well declared.

XIX

A dreadful thunder–clap at last he heard,
The aged trees and plants well–nigh that rent;
Yet heard the nymphs and sirens afterward,
Birds, winds, and waters, sing with sweet consent:
Whereat amazed he stayed, and well prepared
For his defence, heedful and slow forth went:
Nor in his way his passage aught withstood,
Except a quiet, still, transparent flood.

XX

On the green banks which that fair stream inbound,
Flowers and odors sweetly smiled and smelled,
Which reaching out his stretched arms around,
All the large desert in his bosom held,
And through the grove one channel passage found;
That in the wood; in that, the forest dwelled:
Trees clad the streams; streams green those trees aye made
And so exchanged their moisture and their shade.

XXI

The knight some way sought out the flood to pass,
And as he sought, a wondrous bridge appeared,
A bridge of gold, a huge and weighty mass,
On arches great of that rich metal reared;
When through that golden way he entered was,

Jerusalem Delivered

Down fell the bridge, swelled the stream, and weared
The work away, nor sign left where it stood,
And of a river calm became a flood.

XXII
He turned, amazed to see it troubled so,
Like sudden brooks increased with molten snow,
The billows fierce that tossed to and fro,
The whirlpools sucked down to their bosoms low;
But on he went to search for wonders mo,
Through the thick trees there high and broad which grow,
And in that forest huge and desert wide,
The more he sought, more wonders still he spied.

XXIII
Whereso he stepped, it seemed the joyful ground
Renewed the verdure of her flowery weed,
A fountain here, a wellspring there he found;
Here bud the roses, there the lilies spread
The aged wood o'er and about him round
Flourished with blossoms new, new leaves, new seed,
And on the boughs and branches of those treen,
The bark was softened, and renewed the green.

XXIV
The manna on each leaf did pearled lie,
The honey stilled from the tender rind;
Again he heard that wondrous harmony,
Of songs and sweet complaints of lovers kind,
The human voices sung a triple high,
To which respond the birds, the streams, the wind,
But yet unseen those nymphs, those singers were,
Unseen the lutes, harps, viols which they bear.

XXV
He looked, he listened, yet his thoughts denied

439

To think that true which he both heard and see,
A myrtle in an ample plain he spied,
And thither by a beaten path went he:
The myrtle spread her mighty branches wide,
Higher than pine or palm or cypress tree:
And far above all other plants was seen
That forest's lady and that desert's queen.

XXVI
Upon the trees his eyes Rinaldo bent,.
And there a marvel great and strange began;
An aged oak beside him cleft and rent,
And from his fertile hollow womb forth ran,
Clad in rare weeds and strange habiliment,
A nymph, for age able to go to man,
An hundred plants beside, even in his sight,
Childed an hundred nymphs, so great, so dight.

XXVII
Such as on stages play, such as we see
The Dryads painted whom wild Satyrs love,
Whose arms half–naked, locks untrussed be,
With buskins laced on their legs above,
And silken robes tucked short above their knee;
Such seemed the sylvan daughters of this grove,
Save that instead of shafts and boughs of tree,
She bore a lute, a harp, or cittern she.

XXVIII
And wantonly they cast them in a ring,
And sung and danced to move his weaker sense,
Rinaldo round about environing,
As centres are with their circumference;
The tree they compassed eke, and gan to sing,
That woods and streams admired their excellence;
"Welcome, dear lord, welcome to this sweet grove,

Jerusalem Delivered

Welcome our lady's hope, welcome her love.

XXIX

"Thou com'st to cure our princess, faint and sick
For love, for love of thee, faint, sick, distressed;
Late black, late dreadful was this forest thick,
Fit dwelling for sad folk with grief oppressed,
See with thy coming how the branches quick
Revived are, and in new blosoms dressed:"
This was their song, and after, from it went
First a sweet sound, and then the myrtle rent.

XXX

If antique times admired Silenus old
That oft appeared set on his lazy ass,
How would they wonder if they had behold
Such sights as from the myrtle high did pass?
Thence came a lady fair with locks of gold,
That like in shape, in face and beauty was
To sweet Armide; Rinaldo thinks he spies
Her gestures, smiles, and glances of her eyes.

XXXI

On him a sad and smiling look she cast,
Which twenty passions strange at once bewrays:
"And art thou come," quoth she, "returned at last
To her from whom but late thou ran'st thy ways?
Com'st thou to comfort me for sorrows past?
To ease my widow nights and careful days?
Or comest thou to work me grief and harm?
Why nilt thou speak? — why not thy face disarm?

XXXII

"Com'st thou a friend or foe? I did not frame
That golden bridge to entertain my foe,
Nor opened flowers and fountains as you came,

To welcome him with joy that brings me woe:
Put off thy helm, rejoice me with the flame
Of thy bright eyes, whence first my fires did grow.
Kiss me, embrace me, if you further venture,
Love keeps the gate, the fort is eath to enter."

XXXIII

Thus as she woos she rolls her rueful eyes
With piteous look, and changeth oft her cheer,
An hundred sighs from her false heart upflies,
She sobs, she mourns, it is great ruth to hear;
The hardest breast sweet pity mollifies,
What stony heart resists a woman's tear?
But yet the knight, wise, wary, not unkind,
Drew forth his sword and from her careless twined.

XXXIV

Toward the tree he marched, she thither start,
Before him stepped, embraced the plant and cried,
"Ah, never do me such a spiteful part,
To cut my tree, this forest's joy and pride,
Put up thy sword, else pierce therewith the heart
Of thy forsaken and despised Armide;
For through this breast, and through this heart unkind
To this fair tree thy sword shall passage find."

XXXV

He lift his brand, nor cared though oft she prayed,
And she her form to other shape did change;
Such monsters huge when men in dreams are laid
Oft in their idle fancies roam and range:
Her body swelled, her face obscure was made,
Vanished her garments, her face and vestures strange,
A giantess before him high she stands,
Like Briareus armed with an hundred hands.

Jerusalem Delivered

XXXVI

With fifty swords, and fifty targets bright,
She threatened death, she roared, cried and fought,
Each other nymph in armor likewise dight,
A Cyclops great became: he feared them naught,
But on the myrtle smote with all his might,
That groaned like living souls to death nigh brought,
The sky seemed Pluto's court, the air seemed hell,
Therein such monsters roar, such spirits yell.

XXXVII

Lightened the heavens above, the earth below
Roared loud, that thundered, and this shook;
Blustered the tempests strong, the whirlwinds blow,
The bitter storm drove hailstones in his look;
But yet his arm grew neither weak nor slow,
Nor of that fury heed or care he took,
Till low to earth the wounded tree down bended;
Then fled the spirits all, the charms all ended.

XXXVIII

The heavens grew clear, the air waxed calm and still,
The wood returned to his wonted state,
Of withcrafts free, quite void of spirits ill;
Of horror full, but horror there innate;
He further proved if aught withstood his will
To cut those trees as did the charms of late,
And finding naught to stop him, smiled, and said,
"O shadows vain! O fools, of shades afraid!"

XXXIX

From thence home to the campward turned the knight,
The hermit cried, upstarting from his seat,
"Now of the wood the charms have lost their might,
The sprites are conquered, ended is the feat,
See where he comes!" In glistering white all dight

Appeared the man, bold, stately, high and great,
His eagle's silver wings to shine begun
With wondrous splendor gainst the golden sun.

XL

The camp received him with a joyful cry,
A cry the dales and hills about that flied;
Then Godfrey welcomed him with honors high,
His glory quenched all spite, all envy killed:
"To yonder dreadful grove," quoth he, "went I,
And from the fearful wood, as me you willed,
Have driven the sprites away, thither let be
Your people sent, the way is safe and free."

XLI

Sent were the workmen thither, thence they brought
Timber enough, by good advice select,
And though by skilless builders framed and wrought
Their engines rude and rams were late elect,
Yet now the forts and towers from whence they fought
Were framed by a cunning architect,
William, of all the Genoese lord and guide,
Which late ruled all the seas from side to side;

XLII

But forced to retire from him at last,
The Pagan fleet the seas moist empire won,
His men with all their stuff and store in haste
Home to the camp with their commander run,
In skill, in wit, in cunning him surpassed
Yet never engineer beneath the sun,
Of carpenters an hundred large he brought,
That what their lord devised made and wrought.

XLIII

This man began with wondrous art to make,

Not rams, not mighty brakes, not slings alone,
Wherewith the firm and solid walls to shake,
To cast a dart, or throw a shaft or stone;
But framed of pines and firs, did undertake
To build a fortress huge, to which was none
Yet ever like, whereof he clothed the sides
Against the balls of fire with raw bull's hides.

XLIV

In mortices and sockets framed just,
The beams, the studs and puncheons joined he fast;
To beat the city's wall, beneath forth brust
A ram with horned front, about her waist
A bridge the engine from her side out thrust,
Which on the wall when need she cast;
And from her top a turret small up stood,
Strong, surely armed, and builded of like wood.

XLV

Set on an hundred wheels the rolling mass,
On the smooth lands went nimbly up and down,
Though full of arms and armed men it was,
Yet with small pains it ran, as it had flown:
Wondered the camp so quick to see it pass,
They praised the workmen and their skill unknown,
And on that day two towers they builded more,
Like that which sweet Clorinda burned before.

XLVI

Yet wholly were not from the Saracines
Their works concealed and their labors hid,
Upon that wall which next the camp confines
They placed spies, who marked all they did:
They saw the ashes wild and squared pines,
How to the tents, trailed from the grove, they slid:
And engines huge they saw, yet could not tell

How they were built, their forms they saw not well.

XLVII

Their engines eke they reared, and with great art
Repaired each bulwark, turret, port and tower,
And fortified the plain and easy part,
To bide the storm of every warlike stoure,
Till as they thought no sleight or force of Mart
To undermine or scale the same had power;
And false Ismeno gan new balls prepare
Of wicked fire, wild, wondrous, strange and rare.

XLVIII

He mingled brimstone with bitumen fell
Fetched from that lake where Sodom erst did sink,
And from that flood which nine times compassed hell
Some of the liquor hot he brought, I think,
Wherewith the quenchless fire he tempered well,
To make it smoke and flame and deadly stink:
And for his wood cut down, the aged sire
Would thus revengement take with flame and fire.

XLIX

While thus the camp, and thus the town were bent,
These to assault, these to defend the wall,
A speedy dove through the clear welkin went,
Straight o'er the tents, seen by the soldiers all;
With nimble fans the yielding air she rent,
Nor seemed it that she would alight or fall,
Till she arrived near that besieged town,
Then from the clouds at last she stooped down:

L

But lo, from whence I nolt, a falcon came,
Armed with crooked bill and talons long,
And twixt the camp and city crossed her game,

That durst nor bide her foe's encounter strong;
But right upon the royal tent down came,
And there, the lords and princes great among,
When the sharp hawk nigh touched her tender head
In Godfrey's lap she fell, with fear half dead:

LI
The duke received her, saved her, and spied,
As he beheld the bird, a wondrous thing,
About her neck a letter close was tied,
By a small thread, and thrust under her wing,
He loosed forth the writ and spread it wide,
And read the intent thereof, "To Judah's king,"
Thus said the schedule, "honors high increase,
The Egyptian chieftain wisheth health and peace:

LII
"Fear not, renowned prince, resist, endure
Till the third day, or till the fourth at most,
I come, and your deliverance will procure,
And kill your coward foes and all their host."
This secret in that brief was closed up sure,
Writ in strange language, to the winged post
Given to transport; for in their warlike need
The east such message used, oft with good speed.

LIII
The duke let go the captive dove at large,
And she that had his counsel close betrayed,
Traitress to her great Lord, touched not the marge
Of Salem's town, but fled far thence afraid.
The duke before all those which had or charge
Or office high, the letter read, and said:
"See how the goodness of the Lord foreshows
The secret purpose of our crafty foes.

LIV

"No longer then let us protract the time,
But scale the bulwark of this fortress high,
Through sweat and labor gainst those rocks sublime
Let us ascend, which to the southward lie;
Hard will it be that way in arms to climb,
But yet the place and passage both know I,
And that high wall by site strong on that part,
Is least defenced by arms, by work and art.

LV

"Thou, Raymond, on this side with all thy might
Assault the wall, and by those crags ascend,
My squadrons with mine engines huge shall fight
And gainst the northern gate my puissance bend,
That so our foes, beguiled with the sight,
Our greatest force and power shall there attend,
While my great tower from thence shall nimbly slide,
And batter down some worse defended side;

LVI

"Camillo, thou not far from me shalt rear
Another tower, close to the walls ybrought."
This spoken, Raymond old, that sate him near,
And while he talked great things tossed in his thought,
Said, "To Godfredo's counsel, given us here,
Naught can be added, from it taken naught:
Yet this I further wish, that some were sent
To spy their camp, their secret and intent,

LVII

"That may their number and their squadrons brave
Describe, and through their tents disguised mask."
Quoth Tancred, "Lo, a subtle squire I have,
A person fit to undertake this task,
A man quick, ready, bold, sly to deceive,

To answer, wise, and well advised to ask;
Well languaged, and that with time and place,
Can change his look, his voice, his gait, his grace."

LVIII
Sent for, he came, and when his lord him told
What Godfrey's pleasure was and what his own,
He smiled and said forthwith he gladly would.
"I go," quoth he, "careless what chance be thrown,
And where encamped be these Pagans bold,
Will walk in every tent a spy unknown,
Their camp even at noon–day I enter shall,
And number all their horse and footmen all;

LIX
"How great, how strong, how armed this army is,
And what their guide intends, I will declare,
To me the secrets of that heart of his
And hidden thoughts shall open lie and bare."
Thus Vafrine spoke, nor longer stayed on this,
But for a mantle changed the coat he ware,
Naked was his neck, and bout his forehead bold,
Of linen white full twenty yards he rolled.

LX
His weapons were a Syrian bow and quiver,
His gestures barbarous, like the Turkish train,
Wondered all they that heard his tongue deliver
Of every land the language true and plain:
In Tyre a born Phoenician, by the river
Of Nile a knight bred in the Egyptian main,
Both people would have thought him; forth he rides
On a swift steed, o'er hills and dales that glides.

LXI
But ere the third day came the French forth sent

449

Their pioneers to even the rougher ways,
And ready made each warlike instrument,
Nor aught their labor interrupts or stays;
The nights in busy toll they likewise spent
And with long evenings lengthened forth short days,
Till naught was left the hosts that hinder might
To use their utmost power and strength in fight.

LXII

That day, which of the assault the day forerun,
The godly duke in prayer spent well–nigh,
And all the rest, because they had misdone,
The sacrament receive and mercy cry;
Then oft the duke his engines great begun
To show where least he would their strength apply;
His foes rejoiced, deluded in that sort,
To see them bent against their surest port:

LXIII

But after, aided by the friendly night,
His greatest engine to that side he brought
Where plainest seemed the wall, where with their might
The flankers least could hurt them as they fought;
And to the southern mountain's greatest height
To raise his turret old Raymondo sought;
And thou Camillo on that part hadst thine,
Where from the north the walls did westward twine.

LXIV

But when amid the eastern heaven appeared
The rising morning bright as shining glass,
The troubled Pagans saw, and seeing feared,
How the great tower stood not where late it was,
And here and there tofore unseen was reared
Of timber strong a huge and fearful mass,
And numberless with beams, with ropes and strings,

They view the iron rams, the barks and slings.

LXV

The Syrian people now were no whit slow,
Their best defences to that side to bear,
Where Godfrey did his greatest engine show,
From thence where late in vain they placed were:
But he who at his back right well did know
The host of Egypt to be proaching near,
To him called Guelpho, and the Roberts twain,
And said, "On horseback look you still remain,

LXVI

"And have regard, while all our people strive
To scale this wall, where weak it seems and thin,
Lest unawares some sudden host arrive,
And at our backs unlooked–for war begin."
This said, three fierce assaults at once they give,
The hardy soldiers all would die or win,
And on three parts resistance makes the king,
And rage gainst strength, despair gainst hope doth bring.

LXVII

Himself upon his limbs with feeble eild
That shook, unwieldy with their proper weight,
His armor laid and long unused shield,
And marched gainst Raymond to the mountain's height;
Great Solyman gainst Godfrey took the field;
Fornenst Camillo stood Argantes straight
Where Tancred strong he found, so fortune will
That this good prince his wonted foe shall kill.

LXVIII

The archers shot their arrows sharp and keen,
Dipped in the bitter juice of poison strong,
The shady face of heaven was scantly seen,

Hid with the clouds of shafts and quarries long;
Yet weapons sharp with greater fury been
Cast from the towers the Pagan troops among,
For thence flew stones and clifts of marble rocks,
Trees shod with iron, timber, logs and blocks.

LXIX

A thunderbolt seemed every stone, it brake
His limbs and armors on whom so it light,
That life and soul it did not only take
But all his shape and face disfigured quite;
The lances stayed not in the wounds they make,
But through the gored body took their flight,
From side to side, through flesh, through skin and rind
They flew, and flying, left sad death behind.

LXX

But yet not all this force and fury drove
The Pagan people to forsake the wall,
But to revenge these deadly blows they strove,
With darts that fly, with stones and trees that fall;
For need so cowards oft courageous prove,
For liberty they fight, for life and all,
And oft with arrows, shafts, and stones that fly,
Give bitter answer to a sharp reply.

LXXI

This while the fierce assailants never cease,
But sternly still maintain a threefold charge,
And gainst the clouds of shafts draw nigh at ease,
Under a pentise made of many a targe,
The armed towers close to the bulwarks press,
And strive to grapple with the battled marge,
And launch their bridges out, meanwhile below
With iron fronts the rams the walls down throw.

LXXII
Yet still Rinaldo unresolved went,
And far unworthy him this service thought,
If mongst the common sort his pains he spent;
Renown so got the prince esteemed naught:
His angry looks on every side he bent,
And where most harm, most danger was, he fought,
And where the wall high, strong and surest was,
That part would he assault, and that way pass.

LXXIII
And turning to the worthies him behind,
All hardy knights, whom Dudon late did guide,
"Oh shame," quoth he, "this wall no war doth find,
When battered is elsewhere each part, each side;
All pain is safety to a valiant mind,
Each way is eath to him that dares abide,
Come let us scale this wall, though strong and high,
And with your shields keep off the darts that fly."

LXXIV
With him united all while thus he spake,
Their targets hard above their heads they threw,
Which joined in one an iron pentise make
That from the dreadful storm preserved the crew.
Defended thus their speedy course they take,
And to the wall without resistance drew,
For that strong penticle protected well
The knights, from all that flew and all that fell.

LXXV
Against the fort Rinaldo gan uprear
A ladder huge, an hundred steps of height,
And in his arm the same did easily bear
And move as winds do reeds or rushes light,
Sometimes a tree, a rock, a dart or spear,

Fell from above, yet forward clomb the knight,
And upward fearless pierced, careless still,
Though Mount Olympus fell, or Ossa hill:

LXXVI
A mount of ruins, and of shafts a wood
Upon his shoulders and his shield he bore,
One hand the ladder held whereon he stood,
The other bare his targe his face before;
His hardy troop, by his example good
Provoked, with him the place assaulted sore,
And ladders long against the wall they clap,
Unlike in courage yet, unlike in hap:

LXXVII
One died, another fell; he forward went,
And these he comforts, and he threateneth those,
Now with his hand outstretched the battlement
Well–nigh he reached, when all his armed foes
Ran thither, and their force and fury bent
To throw him headlong down, yet up he goes,
A wondrous thing, one knight whole armed bands
Alone, and hanging in the air, withstands:

LXXVIII
Withstands, and forceth his great strength so far,
That like a palm whereon huge weight doth rest,
His forces so resisted stronger are,
His virtues higher rise the more oppressed,
Till all that would his entrance bold debar,
He backward drove, upleaped and possessed
The wall, and safe and easy with his blade,
To all that after came, the passage made.

LXXIX
There killing such as durst and did withstand,

To noble Eustace that was like to fall
He reached forth his friendly conquering hand,
And next himself helped him to mount the wall.
This while Godfredo and his people land
Their lives to greater harms and dangers thrall,
For there not man with man, nor knight with knight
Contend, but engines there with engines fight.

LXXX

For in that place the Paynims reared a post,
Which late had served some gallant ship for mast,
And over it another beam they crossed,
Pointed with iron sharp, to it made fast
With ropes which as men would the dormant tossed,
Now out, now in, now back, now forward cast.
In his swift pulleys oft the men withdrew
The tree, and oft the riding–balk forth threw:

LXXXI

The mighty beam redoubted oft his blows,
And with such force the engine smote and hit,
That her broad side the tower wide open throws,
Her joints were broke, her rafters cleft and split;
But yet gainst every hap whence mischief grows,
Prepared the piece, gainst such extremes made fit,
Launch forth two scythes, sharp, cutting, long and broad
And cut the ropes whereon the engine rode:

LXXXII

As an old rock, which age or stormy wind
Tears from some craggy hill or mountain steep,
Doth break, doth bruise, and into dust doth grind
Woods, houses, hamlets, herds, and folds of sheep,
So fell the beam, and down with it all kind
Of arms, of weapons, and of men did sweep,
Wherewith the towers once or twice did shake,

Jerusalem Delivered

Trembled the walls, the hills and mountains quake.

LXXXIII

Victorious Godfrey boldly forward came,
And had great hope even then the place to win;
But lo, a fire, with stench, with smoke and flame
Withstood his passage, stopped his entrance in:
Such burning Aetna yet could never frame,
When from her entrails hot her fires begin,
Nor yet in summer on the Indian plain,
Such vapors warm from scorching air down rain.

LXXXIV

There balls of wildfire, there fly burning spears,
This flame was black, that blue, this red as blood;
Stench well–nigh choked them, noise deafs their ears,
Smoke blinds their eyes, fire kindleth on the wood;
Nor those raw hides which for defence it wears
Could save the tower, in such distress it stood;
For now they wrinkle, now it sweats and fries,
Now burns, unless some help come down from skies.

LXXXV

The hardy duke before his folk abides,
Nor changed he color, countenance or place,
But comforts those that from the scaldered hides
With water strove the approaching flames to chase:
In these extremes the prince and those he guides
Half roasted stood before fierce Vulcan's face,
When lo, a sudden and unlooked–for blast
The flames against the kindlers backward cast:

LXXXVI

The winds drove back the fire, where heaped lie
The Pagans' weapons, where their engines were,
Which kindling quickly in that substance dry,

Burnt all their store and all their warlike gear:
O glorious captain! whom the Lord from high
Defends, whom God preserves, and holds so dear;
For thee heaven fights, to thee the winds, from far,
Called with thy trumpet's blast, obedient are!

LXXXVII
But wicked Ismen to his harm that saw
How the fierce blast drove back the fire and flame,
By art would nature change, and thence withdraw
Those noisome winds, else calm and still the same;
'Twixt two false wizards without fear or awe
Upon the walls in open sight he came,
Black, grisly, loathsome, grim and ugly faced,
Like Pluto old, betwixt two furies placed;

LXXXVIII
And now the wretch those dreadful words begun,
Which trouble make deep hell and all her flock,
Now trembled is the air, the golden sun
His fearful beams in clouds did close and lock,
When from the tower, which Ismen could not shun,
Out fled a mighty stone, late half a rock,
Which light so just upon the wizards three,
That driven to dust their bones and bodies be.

LXXXIX
To less than naught their members old were torn,
And shivered were their heads to pieces small,
As small as are the bruised grains of corn
When from the mill dissolved to meal they fall;
Their damned souls, to deepest hell down borne
Far from the joy and light celestial,
The furies plunged in the infernal lake:
O mankind, at their ends ensample take!

Jerusalem Delivered

XC

This while the engine which the tempest cold
Had saved from burning with his friendly blast,
Approached had so near the battered hold
That on the walls her bridge at ease she cast:
But Solyman ran thither fierce and bold,
To cut the plank whereon the Christians passed.
And had performed his will, save that upreared
High in the skies a turret new appeared;

XCI

Far in the air up clomb the fortress tall,
Higher than house, than steeple, church or tower;
The Pagans trembled to behold the wall
And city subject to her shot and power;
Yet kept the Turk his stand, though on him fall
Of stones and darts a sharp and deadly shower,
And still to cut the bridge he hopes and strives,
And those that fear with cheerful speech revives.

XCII

The angel Michael, to all the rest
Unseen, appeared before Godfredo's eyes,
In pure and heavenly armor richly dressed,
Brighter than Titan's rays in clearest skies;
"Godfrey," quoth he, "this is the moment blest
To free this town that long in bondage lies,
See, see what legions in thine aid I bring,
For Heaven assists thee, and Heaven's glorious King:

XCIII

"Lift up thine eyes, and in the air behold
The sacred armies, how they mustered be,
That cloud of flesh in which for times of old
All mankind wrapped is, I take from thee,
And from thy senses their thick mist unfold,

458

That face to face thou mayest these spirits see,
And for a little space right well sustain
Their glorious light and view those angels plain.

XCIV
"Behold the souls of every lord and knight
That late bore arms and died for Christ's dear sake,
How on thy side against this town they fight,
And of thy joy and conquest will partake:
There where the dust and smoke blind all men's sight,
Where stones and ruins such an heap do make,
There Hugo fights, in thickest cloud imbarred,
And undermines that bulwark's groundwork hard.

XCV
"See Dudon yonder, who with sword and fire
Assails and helps to scale the northern port,
That with bold courage doth thy folk inspire
And rears their ladders gainst the assaulted fort:
He that high on the mount in grave attire
Is clad, and crowned stands in kingly sort,
Is Bishop Ademare, a blessed spirit,
Blest for his faith, crowned for his death and merit.

XCVI
"But higher lift thy happy eyes, and view
Where all the sacred hosts of Heaven appear."
He looked, and saw where winged armies flew,
Innumerable, pure, divine and clear;
A battle round of squadrons three they show
And all by threes those squadrons ranged were,
Which spreading wide in rings still wider go,
Moved with a stone calm water circleth so.

XCVII
With that he winked, and vanished was and gone;

Jerusalem Delivered

That wondrous vision when he looked again,
His worthies fighting viewed he one by one,
And on each side saw signs of conquest plain,
For with Rinaldo gainst his yielding lone,
His knights were entered and the Pagans slain,
This seen, the duke no longer stay could brook,
But from the bearer bold his ensign took:

XCVIII

And on the bridge he stepped, but there was stayed
By Solyman, who entrance all denied,
That narrow tree to virtue great was made,
The field as in few blows right soon was tried,
"Here will I give my life for Sion's aid,
Here will I end my days," the Soldan cried,
"Behind me cut or break this bridge, that I
May kill a thousand Christians first, then die."

XCIX

But thither fierce Rinaldo threatening went,
And at his sight fled all the Soldan's train,
"What shall I do? If here my life be spent,
I spend and spill," quoth he, "my blood in vain!"
With that his steps from Godfrey back he bent,
And to him let the passage free remain,
Who threatening followed as the Soldan fled,
And on the walls the purple Cross dispread:

C

About his head he tossed, he turned, he cast,
That glorious ensign, with a thousand twines,
Thereon the wind breathes with his sweetest blast,
Thereon with golden rays glad Phoebus shines,
Earth laughs for joy, the streams forbear their haste,
Floods clap their hands, on mountains dance the pines,
And Sion's towers and sacred temples smile

For their deliverance from that bondage vile.

CI

And now the armies reared the happy cry
Of victory, glad, joyful, loud, and shrill.
The hills resound, the echo showereth high,
And Tancred bold, that fights and combats still
With proud Argantes, brought his tower so nigh,
That on the wall, against the boaster's will,
In his despite, his bridge he also laid,
And won the place, and there the cross displayed.

CII

But on the southern hill, where Raymond fought
Against the townsmen and their aged king,
His hardy Gascoigns gained small or naught;
Their engine to the walls they could not bring,
For thither all his strength the prince had brought,
For life and safety sternly combating,
And for the wall was feeblest on that coast,
There were his soldiers best, and engines most.

CIII

Besides, the tower upon that quarter found
Unsure, uneasy, and uneven the way,
Nor art could help, but that the rougher ground
The rolling mass did often stop and stay;
But now of victory the joyful sound
The king and Raymond heard amid their fray;
And by the shout they and their soldiers know,
The town was entered on the plain below.

CIV

Which heard, Raymondo thus bespake this crew,
"The town is won, my friends, and doth it yet
Resist? are we kept out still by these few?

Shall we no share in this high conquest get?"
But from that part the king at last withdrew,
He strove in vain their entrance there to let,
And to a stronger place his folk he brought,
Where to sustain the assault awhile he thought.

CV
The conquerors at once now entered all,
The walls were won, the gates were opened wide,
Now bruised, broken down, destroyed fall
The ports and towers that battery durst abide;
Rageth the sword, death murdereth great and small,
And proud 'twixt woe and horror sad doth ride.
Here runs the blood, in ponds there stands the gore,
And drowns the knights in whom it lived before.

NINETEENTH BOOK

THE ARGUMENT.
Tancred in single combat kills his foe,
Argantes strong: the king and Soldan fly
To David's tower, and save their persons so;
Erminia well instructs Vafrine the spy,
With him she rides away, and as they go
Finds where her lord for dead on earth doth lie;
First she laments, then cures him: Godfrey hears
Ormondo's treason, and what marks he bears.

I
Now death or fear or care to save their lives
From their forsaken walls the Pagans chase:

Jerusalem Delivered

Yet neither force nor fear nor wisdom drives
The constant knight Argantes from his place;
Alone against ten thousand foes he strives,
Yet dreadless, doubtless, careless seemed his face,
Nor death, nor danger, but disgrace he fears,
And still unconquered, though o'erset, appears.

II

But mongst the rest upon his helmet gay
With his broad sword Tancredi came and smote:
The Pagan knew the prince by his array,
By his strong blows, his armor and his coat;
For once they fought, and when night stayed that fray,
New time they chose to end their combat hot,
But Tancred failed, wherefore the Pagan knight
Cried, "Tancred, com'st thou thus, thus late to fight?

III

"Too late thou com'st, and not alone to war,
But yet the fight I neither shun nor fear,
Although from knighthood true thou errest far,
Since like an engineer thou dost appear,
That tower, that troop, thy shield and safety are,
Strange kind of arms in single fight to bear;
Yet shalt thou not escape, O conqueror strong
Of ladies fair, sharp death, to avenge that wrong."

IV

Lord Tancred smiled, with disdain and scorn,
And answerd thus, "To end our strife," quoth he,
"Behold at last I come, and my return,
Though late, perchance will be too soon for thee;
For thou shalt wish, of hope and help forlorn,
Some sea or mountain placed twixt thee and me,
And well shalt know before we end this fray
No fear of cowardice hath caused my stay.

V

"But come aside, thou by whose prowess dies
The monsters, knights and giants in all lands,
The killer of weak women thee defies."
This said, he turned to his fighting bands,
And bids them all retire. "Forbear," he cries,
"To strike this knight, on him let none lay hands;
For mine he is, more than a common foe,
By challenge new and promise old also."

VI

"Descend," the fierce Circassian gan reply,
"Alone, or all this troop for succor take
To deserts waste, or place frequented high,
For vantage none I will the fight forsake:"
Thus given and taken was the bold defy,
And through the press, agreed so, they brake,
Their hatred made them one, and as they went,
Each knight his foe did for despite defend:

VII

Great was his thirst of praise, great the desire
That Tancred had the Pagan's blood to spill,
Nor could that quench his wrath or calm his ire
If other hand his foe should foil or kill.
He saved him with his shield, and cried "Retire!"
To all he met, "and do this knight none ill:"
And thus defending gainst his friends his foe,
Through thousand angry weapons safe they go.

VII

They left the city, and they left behind
Godfredo's camp, and far beyond it passed,
And came where into creeks and bosoms blind
A winding hill his corners turned and cast,
A valley small and shady dale they find

Jerusalem Delivered

Amid the mountains steep so laid and placed
As if some theatre or closed place
Had been for men to fight or beasts to chase.

IX

There stayed the champions both with rueful eyes,
Argantes gan the fortress won to view;
Tancred his foe withouten shield espies,
And said, "Whereon doth thy sad heart devise?
Think'st thou this hour must end thy life untrue?
If this thou fear, and dost foresee thy fate,
Thy fear is vain, thy foresight comes too late."

X

"I think," quoth he, "on this distressed town,
The aged Queen of Judah's ancient land,
Now lost, now sacked, spoiled and trodden down,
Whose fall in vain I strived to withstand,
A small revenge for Sion's fort o'erthrown,
That head can be, cut off by my strong hand."
This said, together with great heed they flew,
For each his foe for bold and hardy knew.

XI

Tancred of body active was and light,
Quick, nimble, ready both of hand and foot;
But higher by the head, the Pagan knight
Of limbs far greater was, of heart as stout:
Tancred laid low and traversed in his fight,
Now to his ward retired, now struck out,
Oft with his sword his foe's fierce blows he broke,
And rather chose to ward–than bear his stroke.

XII

But bold and bolt upright Argantes fought,
Unlike in gesture, like in skill and art,

465

Jerusalem Delivered

His sword outstretched before him far he brought,
Nor would his weapon touch, but pierce his heart,
To catch his point Prince Tancred strove and sought,
But at his breast or helm's unclosed part
He threatened death, and would with stretched−out brand
His entrance close, and fierce assaults withstand.

XIII
With a tall ship so doth a galley fight,
When the still winds stir not the unstable main;
Where this in nimbleness as that in might
Excels; that stands, this goes and comes again,
And shifts from prow to poop with turnings light;
Meanwhile the other doth unmoved remain,
And on her nimble foe approaching nigh,
Her weighty engines tumbleth down from high.

XIV
The Christian sought to enter on his foe,
Voiding his point, which at his breast was bent;
Argantes at his face a thrust did throw,
Which while the Prince awards and doth prevent,
His ready hand the Pagan turned so,
That all defence his quickness far o'erwent,
And pierced his side, which done, he said and smiled,
"The craftsman is in his own craft beguiled."

XV
Tancredi bit his lip for scorn and shame,
Nor longer stood on points of fence and skill,
But to revenge so fierce and fast he came
As if his hand could not o'ertake his will,
And at his visor aiming just, gan frame
To his proud boast an answer sharp, but still
Argantes broke the thrust; and at half−sword,
Swift, hardy, bold, in stepped the Christian lord.

XVI

With his left foot fast forward gan he stride,
And with his left the Pagan's right arm bent,
With his right hand meanwhile the man's right side
He cut, he wounded, mangled, tore and rent.
"To his victorious teacher," Tancred cried,
"His conquered scholar hath this answer sent;"
Argantes chafed, struggled, turned and twined,
Yet could not so his captive arm unbind:

XVII

His sword at last he let hang by the chain,
And griped his hardy foe in both his hands,
In his strong arms Tancred caught him again,
And thus each other held and wrapped in bands.
With greater might Alcides did not strain
The giant Antheus on the Lybian sands,
On holdfast knots their brawny arms they cast,
And whom he hateth most, each held embraced:

XVIII

Such was their wrestling, such their shocks and throws
That down at once they tumbled both to ground,
Argantes, — were it hap or skill, who knows,
His better hand loose and in freedom found;
But the good Prince, his hand more fit for blows,
With his huge weight the Pagan underbound;
But he, his disadvantage great that knew,
Let go his hold, and on his feet up flew:

XIX

Far slower rose the unwieldy Saracine,
And caught a rap ere he was reared upright.
But as against the blustering winds a pine
Now bends his top, now lifts his head on height,
His courage so, when it 'gan most decline,

The man reinforced, and advanced his might,
And with fierce change of blows renewed the fray,
Where rage for skill, horror for art, bore sway.

XX

The purple drops from Tancred's sides down railed,
But from the Pagan ran whole streams of blood,
Wherewith his force grew weak, his courage quailed
As fires die which fuel want or food.
Tancred that saw his feeble arm now failed
To strike his blows, that scant he stirred or stood,
Assuaged his anger, and his wrath allayed,
And stepping back, thus gently spoke and said:

XXI

"Yield, hardy knight, and chance of war or me
Confess to have subdued thee in this fight,
I will no trophy, triumph, spoil of thee,
Nor glory wish, nor seek a victor's right
More terrible than erst;" herewith grew he
And all awaked his fury, rage and might,
And said, "Dar'st thou of vantage speak or think,
Or move Argantes once to yield or shrink?
XXII

"Use, use thy vantage, thee and fortune both
I scorn, and punish will thy foolish pride:"
As a hot brand flames most ere it forth go'th,
And dying blazeth bright on every side;
So he, when blood was lost, with anger wroth,
Revived his courage when his puissance died,
And would his latest hour which now drew nigh,
Illustrate with his end, and nobly die.

XXIII

He joined his left hand to her sister strong,
And with them both let fall his weighty blade.

Tancred to ward his blow his sword up slung,
But that it smote aside, nor there it stayed,
But from his shoulder to his side along
It glanced, and many wounds at once it made:
Yet Tancred feared naught, for in his heart
Found coward dread no place, fear had no part.

XXIV

His fearful blow he doubled, but he spent
His force in waste, and all his strength in vain;
For Tancred from the blow against him bent,
Leaped aside, the stroke fell on the plain.
With thine own weight o'erthrown to earth thou went,
Argantes stout, nor could'st thyself sustain,
Thyself thou threwest down, O happy man,
Upon whose fall none boast or triumph can!

XXV

His gaping wounds the fall set open wide,
The streams of blood about him made a lake,
Helped with his left hand, on one knee he tried
To rear himself, and new defence to make:
The courteous prince stepped back, and "Yield thee!" cried,
No hurt he proffered him, no blow he strake.
Meanwhile by stealth the Pagan false him gave
A sudden wound, threatening with speeches brave:

XXVI

Herewith Tancredi furious grew, and said,
"Villain, dost thou my mercy so despise?"
Therewith he thrust and thrust again his blade,
And through his ventil pierced his dazzled eyes,
Argantes died, yet no complaint he made,
But as he furious lived he careless dies;
Bold, proud, disdainful, fierce and void of fear
His motions last, last looks, last speeches were.

XXVII

Tancred put up his sword, and praises glad
Gave to his God that saved him in this fight;
But yet this bloody conquest feebled had
So much the conqueror's force, strength and might,
That through the way he feared which homeward led
He had not strength enough to walk upright;
Yet as he could his steps from thence he bent,
And foot by foot a heavy pace forth–went;

XXVIII

His legs could bear him but a little stound,
And more he hastes, more tired, less was his speed,
On his right hand, at last, laid on the ground
He leaned, his hand weak like a shaking reed,
Dazzled his eyes, the world on wheels ran round,
Day wrapped her brightness up in sable weed;
At length he swooned, and the victor knight
Naught differed from his conquered foe in fight.

XXIX

But while these lords their private fight pursue,
Made fierce and cruel through their secret hate,
The victor's ire destroyed the faithless crew
From street to street, and chased from gate to gate.
But of the sacked town the image true
Who can describe, or paint the woful state,
Or with fit words this spectacle express
Who can? or tell the city's great distress?

XXX

Blood, murder, death, each street, house, church defiled,
There heaps of slain appear, there mountains high;
There underneath the unburied hills up–piled
Of bodies dead, the living buried lie;

470

There the sad mother with her tender child
Doth tear her tresses loose, complain and fly,
And there the spoiler by her amber hair
Draws to his lust the virgin chaste and fair.

XXXI

But through the way that to the west–hill yood
Whereon the old and stately temple stands,
All soiled with gore and wet with lukewarm blood
Rinaldo ran, and chased the Pagan bands;
Above their heads he heaved his curtlax good,
Life in his grace, and death lay in his hands,
Nor helm nor target strong his blows off bears,
Best armed there seemed he no arms that wears;

XXXII

For gainst his armed foes he only bends
His force, and scorns the naked folk to wound;
Them whom no courage arms, no arms defends,
He chased with his looks and dreadful sound:
Oh, who can tell how far his force extends?
How these he scorns, threats those, lays them on ground?
How with unequal harm, with equal fear
Fled all, all that well armed or naked were:

XXXIII

Fast fled the people weak, and with the same
A squadron strong is to the temple gone
Which, burned and builded oft, still keeps the name
Of the first founder, wise King Solomon;
That prince this stately house did whilom frame
Of cedar trees, of gold and marble stone;
Now not so rich, yet strong and sure it was,
With turrets high, thick walls, and doors of brass.

XXXIV

The knight arrived where in warklike sort
The men that ample church had fortified.
And closed found each wicket, gate and port,
And on the top defences ready spied,
He left his frowning looks, and twice that fort
From his high top down to the groundwork eyed,
And entrance sought, and twice with his swift foot
The mighty place he measured about.

XXXV

Like as a wolf about the closed fold
Rangeth by night his hoped prey to get,
Enraged with hunger and with malice old
Which kind 'twixt him and harmless sheep hath set:
So searched he high and low about that hold,
Where he might enter without stop or let,
In the great court he stayed, his foes above
Attend the assault, and would their fortune prove.

XXXVI

There lay by chance a posted tree thereby,
Kept for some needful use, whate'er it were,
The armed galleys not so thick nor high
Their tall and lofty masts at Genes uprear;
This beam the knight against the gates made fly
From his strong hands all weights which lift and bear,
Like a light lance that tree he shook and tossed,
And bruised the gate, the threshold and the post.

XXXVII

No marble stone, no metal strong outbore
The wondrous might of that redoubled blow,
The brazen hinges from the wall it tore,
It broke the locks, and laid the doors down low,
No iron ram, no engine could do more,
Nor cannons great that thunderbolts forth throw,

His people like a flowing stream inthrong,
And after them entered the victor strong;

XXXVIII
The woful slaughter black and loathsome made
That house, sometime the sacred house of God,
O heavenly justice, if thou be delayed,
On wretched sinners sharper falls thy rod!
In them this place profaned which invade
Thou kindled ire, and mercy all forbode,
Until with their hearts' blood the Pagans vile
This temple washed which they did late defile.

XXXIX
But Solyman this while himself fast sped
Up to the fort which David's tower is named,
And with him all the soldiers left he led,
And gainst each entrance new defences framed:
The tyrant Aladine eke thither fled,
To whom the Soldan thus, far off, exclaimed,
Thyself, within this fortress safe uplock:

XL
"For well this fortress shall thee and thy crown
Defend, awhile here may we safe remain."
"Alas!" quoth he, "alas, for this fair town,
Which cruel war beats down even with the plain,
My life is done, mine empire trodden down,
I reigned, I lived, but now nor live nor reign;
For now, alas! behold the fatal hour
That ends our life, and ends our kingly power."

XLI
"Where is your virtue, where your wisdom grave,
And courage stout?" the angry Soldan said,
"Let chance our kingdoms take which erst she gave,

Yet in our hearts our kingly worth is laid;
But come, and in this fort your person save,
Refresh your weary limbs and strength decayed:"
Thus counselled he, and did to safety bring
Within that fort the weak and aged king.

XLII

His iron mace in both his hands he hent,
And on his thigh his trusty sword he tied,
And to the entrance fierce and fearless went,
And kept the strait, and all the French defied:
The blows were mortal which he gave or lent,
For whom he hit he slew, else by his side
Laid low on earth, that all fled from the place
Where they beheld that great and dreadful mace.

XLIII

But old Raymondo with his hardy crew
By chance came thither, to his great mishap;
To that defended path the old man flew,
And scorned his blows and him that kept the gap,
He struck his foe, his blow no blood forth drew,
But on the front with that he caught a rap,
Which in a swoon, low in the dust him laid,
Wide open, trembling, with his arms displayed.

XLIV

The Pagans gathered heart at last, though fear
Their courage weak had put to flight but late,
So that the conquerors repulsed were,
And beaten back, else slain before the Gate:
The Soldan, mongst the dead beside him near
That saw Lord Raymond lie in such estate,
Cried to his men, "Within these bars," quoth he,
"Come draw this knight, and let him captive be."

474

Jerusalem Delivered

XLV

Forward they rushed to execute his word,
But hard and dangerous that emprise they found,
For none of Raymond's men forsook their lord,
But to their guide's defence they flocked round,
Thence fury fights, hence pity draws the sword,
Nor strive they for vile cause or on light ground,
The life and freedom of that champion brave,
Those spoil, these would preserve, those kill, these save.

XLVI

But yet at last if they had longer fought
The hardy Soldan would have won the field;
For gainst his thundering mace availed naught
Or helm of temper fine or sevenfold shield:
But from each side great succor now was brought
To his weak foes, now fit to faint and yield,
And both at once to aid and help the same
The sovereign Duke and young Rinaldo came.

XLVII

As when a shepherd, raging round about
That sees a storm with wind, hail, thunder, rain,
When gloomy clouds have day's bright eye put out,
His tender flocks drives from the open plain
To some thick grove or mountain's shady foot,
Where Heaven's fierce wrath they may unhurt sustain,
And with his hook, his whistle and his cries
Drives forth his fleecy charge, and with them flies:

XLVIII

So fled the Soldan, when he gan descry
This tempest come from angry war forthcast,
The armor clashed and lightened gainst the sky,
And from each side swords, weapons, fire outbrast:
He sent his folk up to the fortress high,
To shun the furious storm, himself stayed last,

Jerusalem Delivered

Yet to the danger he gave place at length,
For wit, his courage; wisdom ruled his strength.

XLIX
But scant the knight was safe the gate within,
Scant closed were the doors, when having broke
The bars, Rinaldo doth assault begin
Against the port, and on the wicket stroke
His matchless might, his great desire to win,
His oath and promise, doth his wrath provoke,
For he had sworn, nor should his word be vain,
To kill the man that had Prince Sweno slain.

L
And now his armed hand that castle great
Would have assaulted, and had shortly won,
Nor safe pardie the Soldan there a seat
Had found his fatal foes' sharp wrath to shun,
Had not Godfredo sounded the retreat;
For now dark shades to shroud the earth begun,
Within the town the duke would lodge that night,
And with the morn renew the assault and fight.

LI
With cheerful look thus to his folk he said,
"High God hath holpen well his children dear,
This work is done, the rest this night delayed
Doth little labor bring, less doubt, no fear,
This tower, our foe's weak hope and latest aid,
We conquer will, when sun shall next appear:
Meanwhile with love and tender ruth go see
And comfort those which hurt and wounded be;

LII
"Go cure their wounds which boldly ventured
Their lives, and spilt their bloods to get this hold,

476

That fitteth more this host for Christ forth led,
Than thirst of vengeance, or desire of gold;
Too much, ah, too much blood this day is shed!
In some we too much haste to spoil behold,
But I command no more you spoil and kill,
And let a trumpet publish forth my will."

LIII
This said, he went where Raymond panting lay,
Waked from the swoon wherein he late had been.
Nor Solyman with countenance less gay
Bespake his troops, and kept his grief unseen;
"My friends, you are unconquered this day,
In spite of fortune still our hope is green,
For underneath great shows of harm and fear,
Our dangers small, our losses little were:

LIV
"Burnt are your houses, and your people slain,
Yet safe your town is, though your walls be gone,
For in yourselves and in your sovereign
Consists your city, not in lime and stone;
Your king is safe, and safe is all his train
In this strong fort defended from their fone,
And on this empty conquest let them boast,
Till with this town again, their lives be lost;

LV
"And on their heads the loss at last will light,
For with good fortune proud and insolent,
In spoil and murder spend they day and night,
In riot, drinking, lust and ravishment,
And may amid their preys with little fight
At ease be overthrown, killed, slain and spent,
If in this carelessness the Egyptian host
Upon them fall, which now draws near this coast.

LVI

"Meanwhile the highest buildings of this town
We may shake down with stones about their ears,
And with our darts and spears from engines thrown,
Command that hill Christ's sepulchre that bears:"
Thus comforts he their hopes and hearts cast down,
Awakes their valors, and exiles their fears.
But while the things hapt thus, Vafrino goes
Unknown, amid ten thousand armed foes.

LVII

The sun nigh set had brought to end the day,
When Vafrine went the Pagan host to spy,
He passed unknown a close and secret way;
A traveller, false, cunning, crafty, sly,
Past Ascalon he saw the morning gray
Step o'er the threshold of the eastern sky,
And ere bright Titan half his course had run,
That camp, that mighty host to show begun.

LVIII

Tents infinite, and standards broad he spies,
This red, that white, that blue, this purple was,
And hears strange tongues, and stranger harmonies
Of trumpets, clarions, and well–sounding brass:
The elephant there brays, the camel cries.
The horses neigh as to and fro they pass:
Which seen and heard, he said within his thought,
Hither all Asia is, all Afric, brought.

LIX

He viewed the camp awhile, her site and seat,
What ditch, what trench it had, what rampire strong,
Nor close, nor secret ways to work his feat
He longer sought, nor hid him from the throng;

But entered through the gates, broad, royal, great,
And oft he asked, and answered oft among,
In questions wise, in answers short and sly;
Bold was his look, eyes quick, front lifted high:

LX
On every side he pried here and there,
And marked each way, each passage and each tent:
The knights he notes, their steeds, and arms they bear,
Their names, their armor, and their government;
And greater secrets hopes to learn, and hear,
Their hidden purpose, and their close intent:
So long he walked and wandered, till he spied
The way to approach the great pavilions' side:
LXI
There as he looked he saw the canvas rent,
Through which the voice found eath and open way
From the close lodgings of the regal tent
And inmost closet where the captain lay;
So that if Emireno spake, forth went
The sound to them that listen what they say,
There Vafrine watched, and those that saw him thought
To mend the breach that there he stood and wrought.

LXII
The captain great within bare–headed stood,
His body armed and clad in purple weed,
Two pages bore his shield and helmet good,
He leaning on a bending lance gave heed
To a big man whose looks were fierce and proud,
With whom he parleyed of some haughty deed,
Godfredo's name as Vafrine watched he heard,
Which made him give more heed, take more regard:

LXIII
Thus spake the chieftain to that surly sir,

"Art thou so sure that Godfrey shall be slain?"
"I am," quoth he, "and swear ne'er to retire,
Except he first be killed, to court again.
I will prevent those that with me conspire:
Nor other guerdon ask I for my pain
But that I may hang up his harness brave
At Gair, and under them these words engrave:

LXIV

" `These arms Ormondo took in noble fight
From Godfrey proud, that spoiled all Asia's lands,
And with them took his life, and here on high,
In memory thereof, this trophy stands.' "
The duke replied, "Ne'er shall that deed, bold knight,
Pass unrewarded at our sovereign's hands,
What thou demandest shall he gladly grant,
Nor gold nor guerdon shalt thou wish or want.

LXV

"Those counterfeited armors then prepare,
Because the day of fight approacheth fast."
"They ready are," quoth he; then both forbare
From further talk, these speeches were the last.
Vafrine, these great things heard, with grief and care
Remained astound, and in his thoughts oft cast
What treason false this was, how feigned were
Those arms, but yet that doubt he could not clear.

LXVI

From thence he parted, and broad waking lay
All that long night, nor slumbered once nor slept:
But when the camp by peep of springing day
Their banner spread, and knights on horseback leapt,
With them he marched forth in meet array,
And where they pitched lodged, and with them kept,
And then from tent to tent he stalked about,

To hear and see, and learn this secret out;

LXVII

Searching about, on a rich throne he fand
Armida set with dames and knights around,
Sullen she sat, and sighed, it seemed she scanned
Some weighty matters in her thoughts profounds,
Her rosy cheek leaned on her lily hand,
Her eyes, love's twinkling stars, she bent to ground,
Weep she, or no, he knows not, yet appears
Her humid eyes even great with child with tears.

LXVIII

He saw before her set Adrastus grim,
That seemed scant to live, move, or respire,
So was he fixed on his mistress trim,
So gazed he, and fed his fond desire;
But Tisiphern beheld now her now him,
And quaked sometime for love, sometime for ire,
And in his cheeks the color went and came,
For there wrath's fire now burnt, now shone love's flame.

LXIX

Then from the garland fair of virgins bright,
Mongst whom he lay enclosed, rose Altamore,
His hot desire he hid and kept from sight,
His looks were ruled by Cupid's crafty lore,
His left eye viewed her hand, her face, his right
Both watched her beauties hid and secret store,
And entrance found where her thin veil bewrayed
The milken–way between her breasts that laid.

LXX

Her eyes Armida lift from earth at last,
And cleared again her front and visage sad,
Midst clouds of woe her looks which overcast

481

She lightened forth a smile, sweet, pleasant, glad;
"My lord," quoth she, "your oath and promise passed,
Hath freed my heart of all the griefs it had,
That now in hope of sweet revenge it lives,
Such joy, such ease, desired vengeance gives."

LXXI

"Cheer up thy looks," answered the Indian king,
"And for sweet beauty's sake, appease thy woe,
Cast at your feet ere you expect the thing,
I will present the head of thy strong foe;
Else shall this hand his person captive bring
And cast in prison deep;" he boasted so.
His rival heard him well, yet answered naught,
But bit his lips, and grieved in secret thought.

LXXII

To Tisipherne the damsel turning right,
"And what say you, my noble lord ?" quoth she.
He taunting said, "I that am slow to fight
Will follow far behind, the worth to see
Of this your terrible and puissant knight,"
In scornful words this bitter scoff gave he.
"Good reason," quoth the king, "thou come behind,
Nor e'er compare thee with the Prince of Ind."

LXXIII

Lord Tisiphernes shook his head, and said,
"Oh, had my power free like my courage been,
Or had I liberty to use this blade,
Who slow, who weakest is, soon should be seen,
Nor thou, nor thy great vaunts make me afraid,
But cruel love I fear, and this fair queen."
This said, to challenge him the king forth leapt,
But up their mistress start, and twixt them stepped:

LXXIV

"Will you thus rob me of that gift," quoth she,
"Which each hath vowed to give by word and oath?
You are my champions, let that title be
The bond of love and peace between you both;
He that displeased is, is displeased with me,
For which of you is grieved, and I not wroth?"
Thus warned she them, their hearts, for ire nigh broke,
In forced peace and rest thus bore love's yoke."

LXXV

All this heard Vafrine as he stood beside,
And having learned the truth, he left the tent,
That treason was against the Christian's guide
Contrived, he wist, yet wist not how it went,
By words and questions far off, he tried
To find the truth; more difficult, more bent
Was he to know it, and resolved to die,
Or of that secret close the intent to spy.

LXXVI

Of sly intelligence he proved all ways,
All crafts, all wiles, that in his thoughts abide,
Yet all in vain the man by wit assays,
To know that false compact and practice hid:
But chance, what wisdom could not tell, bewrays,
Fortune of all his doubt the knots undid,
So that prepared for Godfrey's last mishap
At ease he found the net, and spied the trap.

LXXVII

Thither he turned again where seated was,
The angry lover, 'twixt her friends and lords,
For in that troop much talk he thought would pass,
Each great assembly store of news affords,
He sided there a lusty lovely lass,

And with some courtly terms the wench he boards,
He feigns acquaintance, and as bold appears
As he had known that virgin twenty years.

LXXVIII
He said, "Would some sweet lady grace me so,
To chose me for her champion, friend and knight,
Proud Godfrey's or Rinaldo's head, I trow,
Should feel the sharpness of my curtlax bright;
Ask me the head, fair mistress, of some foe,
For to your beauty wooed is my might;"
So he began, and meant in speeches wise
Further to wade, but thus he broke the ice.

LXXIX
Therewith he smiled, and smiling gan to frame
His looks so to their old and native grace,
That towards him another virgin came,
Heard him, beheld him, and with bashful face
Said, "For thy mistress choose no other dame
But me, on me thy love and service place,
I take thee for my champion, and apart
Would reason with thee, if my knight thou art."

LXXX
Withdrawn, she thus began, "Vafrine, pardie,
I know thee well, and me thou knowest of old,"
To his last trump this drove the subtle spy,
But smiling towards her he turned him bold,
"Ne'er that I wot I saw thee erst with eye,
Yet for thy worth all eyes should thee behold,
Thus much I know right well, for from the same
Which erst you gave me different is my name.
LXXXI
"My mother bore me near Bisertus wall,
Her name was Lesbine, mine is Almansore!"

"I knew long since," quoth she, "what men thee call,
And thine estate, dissemble it no more,
From me thy friend hide not thyself at all,
If I betray thee let me die therefore,
I am Erminia, daughter to a prince,
But Tancred's slave, thy fellow–servant since;

LXXXII
"Two happy months within that prison kind,
Under thy guard rejoiced I to dwell,
And thee a keeper meek and good did find,
The same, the same I am; behold me well."
The squire her lovely beauty called to mind,
And marked her visage fair: "From thee expel
All fear," she says, "for me live safe and sure,
I will thy safety, not thy harm procure.

LXXXIII
"But yet I pray thee, when thou dost return,
To my dear prison lead me home again;
For in this hateful freedom even and morn
I sigh for sorrow, mourn and weep for pain:
But if to spy perchance thou here sojourn,
Great hap thou hast to know these secrets plain,
For I their treasons false, false trains can say,
Which few beside can tell, none will betray."

LXXXIV
On her he gazed, and silent stood this while,
Armida's sleights he knew, and trains unjust,
Women have tongues of craft, and hearts of guile,
They will, they will not, fools that on them trust,
For in their speech is death, hell in their smile;
At last he said, "If hence depart you lust,
I will you guide; on this conclude we here,
And further speech till fitter time forbear."

Jerusalem Delivered

LXXXV

Forthwith, ere thence the camp remove, to ride
They were resolved, their flight that season fits,
Vafrine departs, she to the dames beside
Returns, and there on thorns awhile she sits,
Of her new knight she talks, till time and tide
To scape unmarked she find, then forth she gets,
Thither where Vafrine her unseen abode,
There took she horse, and from the camp they rode.

LXXXVI

And now in deserts waste and wild arrived,
Far from the camp, far from resort and sight,
Vafrine began, "Gainst Godfrey's life contrived
The false compacts and trains unfold aright:"
Then she those treasons, from their spring derived,
Repeats, and brings their hid deceits to light,
"Eight knights," she says, "all courtiers brave, there are,
But Ormond strong the rest surpasseth far:

LXXXVII

"These, whether hate or hope of gain them move,
Conspired have, and framed their treason so,
That day when Emiren by fight shall prove
To win lost Asia from his Christian foe,
These, with the cross scored on their arms above,
And armed like Frenchmen will disguised go,
Like Godfrey's guard that gold and white do wear,
Such shall their habit be, and such their gear:

LXXXVIII

"Yet each will bear a token in his crest,
That so their friends for Pagans may them know:
But in close fight when all the soldiers best
Shall mingled be, to give the fatal blow

They will keep near, and pierce Godfredo's breast,
While of his faithful guard they bear false show,
And all their swords are dipped in poison strong,
Because each wound shall bring sad death ere long.

LXXXIX

"And for their chieftain wist I knew your guise,
What garments, ensigns, and what arms you carry,
Those feigned arms he forced me to devise,
So that from yours but small or naught they vary;
But these unjust commands my thoughts despise,
Within their camp therefore I list not tarry,
My heart abhors I should this hand defile
With spot of treason, or with act of guile.

XC

"This is the cause, but not the cause alone:"
And there she ceased, and blushed, and on the main
Cast down her eyes, these last words scant outgone,
She would have stopped, nor durst pronounce them plain.
The squire what she concealed would know, as one
That from her breast her secret thoughts could strain,
"Of little faith," quoth he, "why would'st thou hide
Those causes true, from me thy squire and guide?"

XCI

With that she fetched a sigh, sad, sore and deep,
And from her lips her words slow trembling came,
"Fruitless," she said, "untimely, hard to keep,
Vain modesty farewell, and farewell shame,
Why hope you restless love to bring on sleep?
Why strive you fires to quench, sweet Cupid's flame?
No, no, such cares, and such respects beseem
Great ladies, wandering maids them naught esteem.

XCII

"That night fatal to me and Antioch town,
Then made a prey to her commanding foe,

My loss was greater than was seen or known,
There ended not, but thence began my woe:
Light was the loss of friends, of realm or crown;
But with my state I lost myself also,
Ne'er to be found again, for then I lost
My wit, my sense, my heart, my soul almost.

XCIII

"Through fire and sword, through blood and death, Vafrine,
Which all my friends did burn, did kill, did chase,
Thou know'st I ran to thy dear lord and mine,
When first he entered had my father's place,
And kneeling with salt ears in my swollen eyne;
`Great prince,' quoth I, `grant mercy, pity, grace,
Save not my kingdom, not my life I said,
But save mine honor, let me die a maid.'

XCIV

"He lift me by the trembling hand from ground,
Nor stayed he till my humble speech was done;
But said, `A friend and keeper hast thou found,
Fair virgin, nor to me in vain you run:'
A sweetness strange from that sweet voice's sound
Pierced my heart, my breast's weak fortress won,
Which creeping through my bosom soft became
A wound, a sickness, and a quenchless flame.

XCV

"He visits me, with speeches kind and grave
He sought to ease my grief, and sorrows' smart.
He said, `I give thee liberty, receive
All that is thine, and at thy will depart:'
Alas, he robbed me when he thought he gave,
Free was Erminia, but captived her heart,
Mine was the body, his the soul and mind,
He gave the cage but kept the bird behind.

XCVI

"But who can hide desire, or love suppress?
Oft of his worth with thee in talk I strove,
Thou, by my trembling fit that well could'st guess
What fever held me, saidst, `Thou art in love;'
But I denied, for what can maids do less?
And yet my sighs thy sayings true did prove,
Instead of speech, my looks, my tears, mine eyes,
Told in what flame, what fire thy mistress fries.

XCVII

"Unhappy silence, well I might have told
My woes, and for my harms have sought relief,
Since now my pains and plaints I utter bold,
Where none that hears can help or ease my grief.
From him I parted, and did close upfold
My wounds within my bosom, death was chief
Of all my hopes and helps, till love's sweet flame
Plucked off the bridle of respect and shame,

XCVIII

"And caused me ride to seek my lord and knight,
For he that made me sick could make me sound:
But on an ambush I mischanced to light
Of cruel men, in armour clothed round,
Hardly I scaped their hand by mature flight.
And fled to wilderness and desert ground,
And there I lived in groves and forests wild,
With gentle grooms and shepherds' daughters mild.

XCIX

"But when hot love which fear had late suppressed,
Revived again, there nould I longer sit,
But rode the way I came, nor e'er took rest,
Till on like danger, like mishap I hit,
A troop to forage and to spoil addressed,

Jerusalem Delivered

Encountered me, nor could I fly from it:
Thus was I ta'en, and those that had me caught,
Egyptians were, and me to Gaza brought,

C
"And for a present to their captain gave,
Whom I entreated and besought so well,
That he mine honor had great care to save,
And since with fair Armida let me dwell.
Thus taken oft, escaped oft I have,
Ah, see what haps I passed, what dangers fell,
So often captive, free so oft again,
Still my first bands I keep, still my first chain.

CI
"And he that did this chain so surely bind
About my heart, which none can loose but he,
Let him not say, `Go, wandering damsel, find
Some other home, thou shalt not bide with me,'
But let him welcome me with speeches kind,
And in my wonted prison set me free:"
Thus spake the princess, thus she and her guide
Talked day and night, and on their journey ride.

CII
Through the highways Vafrino would not pass,
A path more secret, safe and short, he knew,
And now close by the city's wall he was,
When sun was set, night in the east upflew,
With drops of blood besmeared he found the grass,
And saw where lay a warrior murdered new,
That all be−bled the ground, his face to skies
He turns, and seems to threat, though dead he lies:

CIII
His harness and his habit both betrayed

490

Jerusalem Delivered

He was a Pagan; forward went the squire,
And saw whereas another champion laid
Dead on the land, all soiled with blood and mire,
"This was some Christian knight," Vafrino said:
And marking well his arms and rich attire,
He loosed his helm, and saw his visage plain,
And cried, "Alas, here lies Tancredi slain!"

CIV
The woful virgin tarried, and gave heed
To the fierce looks of that proud Saracine,
Till that high cry, full of sad fear and dread,
Pierced through her heart with sorrow, grief and pine,
At Tancred's name thither she ran with speed,
Like one half mad, or drunk with too much wine,
And when she saw his face, pale, bloodless, dead,
She lighted, nay, she stumbled from her steed:

CV
Her springs of tears she looseth forth, and cries,
"Hither why bring'st thou me, ah, Fortune blind?
Where dead, for whom I lived, my comfort lies,
Where war for peace, travail for rest I find;
Tancred, I have thee, see thee, yet thine eyes
Looked not upon thy love and handmaid kind,
Undo their doors, their lids fast closed sever,
Alas, I find thee for to lose thee ever.

CVI
"I never thought that to mine eyes, my dear,
Thou couldst have grievous or unpleasant been;
But now would blind or rather dead I were,
That thy sad plight might be unknown, unseen!
Alas! where is thy mirth and smiling cheer?
Where are thine eyes' clear beams and sparkles sheen?
Of thy fair cheek where is the purple red,

And forehead's whiteness? are all gone, all dead?

CVII

"Though gone, though dead, I love thee still, behold;
Death wounds, but kills not love; yet if thou live,
Sweet soul, still in his breast, my follies bold
Ah, pardon love's desires, and stealths forgive;
Grant me from his pale mouth some kisses cold,
Since death doth love of just reward deprive;
And of thy spoils sad death afford me this,
Let me his mouth, pale, cold and bloodless, kiss;

CVIII

"O gentle mouth! with speeches kind and sweet
Thou didst relieve my grief, my woe and pain,
Ere my weak soul from this frail body fleet,
Ah, comfort me with one dear kiss or twain!
Perchance if we alive had happed to meet,
They had been given which now are stolen, O vain,
O feeble life, betwixt his lips out fly,
Oh, let me kiss thee first, then let me die!

CIX

"Receive my yielding spirit, and with thine
Guide it to heaven, where all true love hath place:"
This said, she sighed, and tore her tresses fine,
And from her eyes two streams poured on his face,
The man revived, with those showers divine
Awaked, and opened his lips a space;
His lips were open; but fast shut his eyes,
And with her sighs, one sigh from him upflies.

CX

The dame perceived that Tancred breathed and sighed,
Which calmed her grief somedeal and eased her fears:
"Unclose thine eyes," she says, "my lord and knight,

See my last services, my plaints and tears,
See her that dies to see thy woful plight,
That of thy pain her part and portion bears;
Once look on me, small is the gift I crave,
The last which thou canst give, or I can have."

CXI
Tancred looked up, and closed his eyes again,
Heavy and dim, and she renewed her woe.
Quoth Vafrine, "Cure him first, and then complain,
Medicine is life's chief friend; plaint her most foe:"
They plucked his armor off, and she each vein,
Each joint, and sinew felt, and handled so,
And searched so well each thrust, each cut and wound,
That hope of life her love and skill soon found.

CXII
From weariness and loss of blood she spied
His greatest pains and anguish most proceed,
Naught but her veil amid those deserts wide
She had to bind his wounds, in so great need,
But love could other bands, though strange, provide,
And pity wept for joy to see that deed,
For with her amber locks cut off, each wound
She tied: O happy man, so cured so bound!

CXIII
For why her veil was short and thin, those deep
And cruel hurts to fasten, roll and blind,
Nor salve nor simple had she, yet to keep
Her knight on live, strong charms of wondrous kind
She said, and from him drove that deadly sleep,
That now his eyes he lifted, turned and twined,
And saw his squire, and saw that courteous dame
In habit strange, and wondered whence she came.

CXIV

He said, "O Vafrine, tell me, whence com'st thou?
And who this gentle surgeon is, disclose;"
She smiled, she sighed, she looked she wist not how,
She wept, rejoiced, she blushed as red as rose.
"You shall know all," she says, "your surgeon now
Commands you silence, rest and soft repose,
You shall be sound, prepare my guerdon meet,"
His head then laid she in her bosom sweet.

CXV

Vafrine devised this while how he might bear
His master home, ere night obscured the land,
When lo, a troop of soldiers did appear,
Whom he descried to be Tancredi's band,
With him when he and Argant met they were;
But when they went to combat hand for hand,
He bade them stay behind, and they obeyed,
But came to seek him now, so long he stayed.

CXVI

Besides them, many followed that enquest,
But these alone found out the rightest way,
Upon their friendly arms the men addressed
A seat whereon he sat, he leaned, he lay:
Quoth Tancred, "Shall the strong Circassian rest
In this broad field, for wolves and crows a prey?
Ah no, defraud not you that champion brave
Of his just praise, of his due tomb and grave:
CXVII
"With his dead bones no longer war have I,
Boldly he died and nobly was he slain,
Then let us not that honor him deny
Which after death alonely doth remain:"
The Pagan dead they lifted up on high,
And after Tancred bore him through the plain.

Close by the virgin chaste did Vafrine ride,
As he that was her squire, her guard, her guide.

CXVIII

"Not home," quoth Tancred, "to my wonted tent,
But bear me to this royal town, I pray,
That if cut short by human accident
I die, there I may see my latest day,
The place where Christ upon his cross was rent
To heaven perchance may easier make the way,
And ere I yield to Death's and Fortune's rage,
Performed shall be my vow and pilgrimage."

CXIX

Thus to the city was Tancredi borne,
And fell on sleep, laid on a bed of down.
Vafrino where the damsel might sojourn
A chamber got, close, secret, near his own;
That done he came the mighty duke beforn,
And entrance found, for till his news were known,
Naught was concluded mongst those knights and lords,
Their counsel hung on his report and words.

CXX

Where weak and weary wounded Raymond laid,
Godfrey was set upon his couch's side,
And round about the man a ring was made
Of lords and knights that filled the chamber wide;
There while the squire his late discovery said,
To break his talk, none answered, none replied,
"My lord," he said, "at your command I went
And viewed their camp, each cabin, booth and tent;

CXXI

"But of that mighty host the number true
Expect not that I can or should descry,

495

Jerusalem Delivered

All covered with their armies might you view
The fields, the plains, the dales and mountains high,
I saw what way soe'er they went and drew,
They spoiled the land, drunk floods and fountains dry,
For not whole Jordan could have given them drink,
Nor all the grain in Syria, bread, I think.

CXXII

"But yet amongst them many bands are found
Both horse and foot, of little force and might,
That keep no order, know no trumpet's sound,
That draw no sword, but far off shoot and fight,
But yet the Persian army doth abound
With many a footman strong and hardy knight,
So doth the King's own troop which all is framed
Of soldiers old, the Immortal Squadron named.

CXXIII

"Immortal called is that band of right,
For of that number never wanteth one,
But in his empty place some other knight
Steps in, when any man is dead or gone:
This army's leader Emireno hight,
Like whom in wit and strength are few or none,
Who hath in charge in plain and pitched field,
To fight with you, to make you fly or yield.

CXXIV

"And well I know their army and their host
Within a day or two will here arrive:
But thee Rinaldo it behoveth most
To keep thy noble head, for which they strive,
For all the chief in arms or courage boast
They will the same to Queen Armida give,
And for the same she gives herself in price,
Such hire will many hands to work entice.

CXXV

"The chief of these that have thy murder sworn,
Is Altamore, the king of Samarcand!
Adrastus then, whose realm lies near the morn,
A hardy giant, bold, and strong of hand,
This king upon an elephant is borne,
For under him no horse can stir or stand;
The third is Tisipherne, as brave a lord
As ever put on helm or girt on sword."

CXXVI

This said, from young Rinaldo's angry eyes,
Flew sparks of wrath, flames in his visage shined,
He longed to be amid those enemies,
Nor rest nor reason in his heart could find.
But to the Duke Vafrine his talk applies,
"The greatest news, my lord, are yet behind,
For all their thoughts, their crafts and counsels tend
By treason false to bring thy life to end."

CXXVII

Then all from point to point he gan expose
The false compact, how it was made and wrought,
The arms and ensigns feigned, poison close,
Ormondo's vaunt, what praise, what thank he sought,
And what reward, and satisfied all those
That would demand, inquire, or ask of aught.
Silence was made awhile, when Godfrey thus, —
"Raymondo, say, what counsel givest thou us?"

CXXVIII

"Not as we purposed late, next morn," quoth he,
"Let us not scale, but round besiege this tower,
That those within may have no issue free
To sally out, and hurt us with their power,

Our camp well rested and refreshed see,
Provided well gainst this last storm and shower,
And then in pitched field, fight, if you will;
If not, delay and keep this fortress still.
CXXIX
"But lest you be endangered, hurt, or slain,
Of all your cares take care yourself to save,
By you this camp doth live, doth win, doth reign,
Who else can rule or guide these squadrons brave?
And for the traitors shall be noted plain,
Command your guard to change the arms they have,
So shall their guile be known, in their own net
So shall they fall, caught in the snare they set."

CXXX
"As it hath ever," thus the Duke begun,
"Thy counsel shows thy wisdom and thy love,
And what you left in doubt shall thus be done,
We will their force in pitched battle prove;
Closed in this wall and trench, the fight to shun,
Doth ill this camp beseem, and worse behove,
But we their strength and manhood will assay,
And try, in open field and open day.

CXXXI
"The fame of our great conquests to sustain,
Or bide our looks and threats, they are not able,
And when this army is subdued and slain
Then is our empire settled, firm and stable,
The tower shall yield, or but resist in vain,
For fear her anchor is, despair her cable."
Thus he concludes, and rolling down the west
Fast set the stars, and called them all to rest.

TWENTIETH BOOK

THE ARGUMENT.

The Pagan host arrives, and cruel fight
Makes with the Christians and their faithful power;
The Soldan longs in field to prove his might,
With the old king quits the besieged tower;
Yet both are slain, and in eternal night
A famous hand gives each his fatal hour;
Rinald appeased Armida; first the field
The Christians win, then praise to God they yield.

I

The sun called up the world from idle sleep,
And of the day ten hours were gone and past
When the bold troop that had the tower to keep
Espied a sudden mist, that overcast
The earth with mirksome clouds and darkness deep,
And saw it was the Egyptian camp at last
Which raised the dust, for hills and valleys broad
That host did overspread and overload.

II

Therewith a merry shout and joyful cry
The Pagans reared from their besieged hold;
The cranes from Thrace with such a rumor fly,
His hoary frost and snow when Hyems old
Pours down, and fast to warmer regions hie,
From the sharp winds, fierce storms and tempests cold;
And quick, and ready this new hope and aid,
Their hands to shoot, their tongues to threaten made.

III

From whence their ire, their wrath and hardy threat

Proceeds, the French well knew, and plain espied,
For from the walls and ports the army great
They saw; her strength, her number, pomp, and pride,
Swelled their breasts with valor's noble heat;
Battle and fight they wished, "Arm, arm!" they cried;
The youth to give the sign of fight all prayed
Their Duke, and were displeased because delayed

IV

Till morning next, for he refused to fight;
Their haste and heat he bridled, but not brake,
Nor yet with sudden fray or skirmish light
Of these new foes would he vain trial make.
"After so many wars," he says, "good right
It is, that one day's rest at least you take,"
For thus in his vain foes he cherish would
The hope which in their strength they have and hold.

V

To see Aurora's gentle beam appear,
The soldiers armed, prest and ready lay,
The skies were never half so fair and clear
As in the breaking of that blessed day,
The merry morning smiled, and seemed to wear
Upon her silver crown sun's golden ray,
And without cloud heaven his redoubled light
Bent down to see this field, this fray, this fight.

VI

When first he saw the daybreak show and shine,
Godfrey his host in good array brought out,
And to besiege the tyrant Aladine
Raymond he left, and all the faithful rout
That from the towns was come of Palestine
To serve and succor their deliverer stout,
And with them left a hardy troop beside

Of Gascoigns strong, in arms well proved, oft tried.

VII
Such was Godfredo's countenance, such his cheer,
That from his eye sure conquest flames and streams,
Heaven's gracious favors in his looks appear,
And great and goodly more than erst he seems;
His face and forehead full of noblesse were,
And on his cheek smiled youth's purple beams,
And in his gait, his grace, his acts, his eyes,
Somewhat, far more than mortal, lives and lies.

VIII
He had not marched far ere he espied
Of his proud foes the mighty host draw nigh;
A hill at first he took and fortified
At his left hand which stood his army by,
Broad in the front behind more strait uptied
His army ready stood the fight to try,
And to the middle ward well armed he brings
His footmen strong, his horsemen served for wings.

IX
To the left wing, spread underneath the bent
Of the steep hill that saved their flank and side,
The Roberts twain, two leaders good, he sent;
His brother had the middle ward to guide;
To the right wing himself in person went
Down, where the plain was dangerous, broad and wide,
And where his foes with their great numbers would
Perchance environ round his squadrons bold.
X
There all his Lorrainers and men of might,
All his best armed he placed, and chosen bands,
And with those horse some footmen armed light,
That archers were, used to that service, stands;

The adventurers then, in battle and in fight
Well tried, a squadron famous through all lands,
On the right hand he set, somedeal aside,
Rinaldo was their leader, lord and guide.

XI

To whom the Duke, "In thee our hope is laid
Of victory, thou must the conquest gain,
Behind this mighty wing, so far displayed,
Thou with thy noble squadron close remain;
And when the Pagans would our backs invade,
Assail them then, and make their onset vain;
For if I guess aright, they have in mind
To compass us, and charge our troops behind."

XII

Then through his host, that took so large a scope,
He rode, and viewed them all, both horse and foot;
His face was bare, his helm unclosed and ope,
Lightened his eyes, his looks bright fire shot out;
He cheers the fearful, comforts them that hope,
And to the bold recounts his boasting stout,
And to the valiant his adventures hard,
These bids he look for praise, those for reward.

XIII

At last he stayed where of his squadrons bold
And noblest troops assembled was best part;
There from a rising bank his will he told,
And all that heard his speech thereat took heart:
And as the mountain snow from mountains cold
Runs down in streams with eloquence and art,
So from his lips his words and speeches fell,
Shrill, speedy, pleasant, sweet, and placed well.

XIV

Jerusalem Delivered

"My hardy host, you conquerors of the East,
You scourge wherewith Christ whips his heathen fone,
Of victory behold the latest feast,
See the last day for which you wished alone;
Not without cause the Saracens most and least
Our gracious Lord hath gathered here in one,
For all your foes and his assembled are,
That one day's fight may end seven years of war.

XV
"This fight shall bring us many victories,
The danger none, the labor will be small,
Let not the number of your enemies
Dismay your hearts, grant fear no place at all;
For strife and discord through their army flies,
Their bands ill ranked themselves entangle shall,
And few of them to strike or fight shall come,
For some want strength, some heart, some elbow–room.

XVI
"This host, with whom you must encounter now,
Are men half naked, without strength or skill,
From idleness, or following the plough,
Late pressed forth to war against their will,
Their swords are blunt, shields thin, soon pierced through,
Their banners shake, their bearers shrink, for ill
Their leaders heard, obeyed, or followed be,
Their loss, their flight, their death I will foresee.

XVII
"Their captain clad in purple, armed in gold,
That seems so fierce, so hardy, stout and strong,
The Moors or weak Arabians vanquish could,
Yet can he not resist your valors long.
What can he do, though wise, though sage, though bold,
In that confusion, trouble, thrust and throng?

503

Ill known he is, and worse he knows his host,
Strange lords ill feared are, ill obeyed of most.

XVIII
"But I am captain of this chosen crew,
With whom I oft have conquered, triumphed oft,
Your lands and lineages long since I knew,
Each knight obeys my rule, mild, easy, soft,
I know each sword, each dart, each shaft I view,
Although the quarrel fly in skies aloft,
Whether the same of Ireland be, or France,
And from what bow it comes, what hand perchance.
XIX
"I ask an easy and a usual thing,
As you have oft, this day, so win the field,
Let zeal and honor be your virtue's sting,
Your lives, my fame, Christ's faith defend and shield,
To earth these Pagans slain and wounded bring,
Tread on their necks, make them all die or yield, —
What need I more exhort you? from your eyes
I see how victory, how conquest flies."

XX
Upon the captain, when his speech was done,
It seemed a lamp and golden light down came,
As from night's azure mantle oft doth run
Or fall, a sliding star, or shining flame;
But from the bosom of the burning sun
Proceeded this, and garland–wise the same
Godfredo's noble head encompassed round,
And, as some thought, foreshowed he should be crowned.

XXI
Perchance, if man's proud thought or saucy tongue
Have leave to judge or guess at heavenly things,
This was the angel which had kept him long,

That now came down, and hid him with his wings.
While thus the Duke bespeaks his armies strong,
And every troop and band in order brings.
Lord Emiren his host disposed well,
And with bold words whet on their courage fell;

XXII

The man brought forth his army great with speed,
In order good, his foes at hand he spied,
Like the new moon his host two horns did spreed,
In midst the foot, the horse were on each side,
The right wing kept he for himself to lead,
Great Altamore received the left to guide,
The middle ward led Muleasses proud,
And in that battle fair Armida stood.

XXIII

On the right quarter stood the Indian grim,
With Tisipherne and all the king's own band;
But when the left wing spread her squadrons trim
O'er the large plain, did Altamoro stand,
With African and Persian kings with him,
And two that came from Meroe's hot sand,
And all his crossbows and his slings he placed,
Where room best served to shoot, to throw, to cast.

XXIV

Thus Emiren his host put in array,
And rode from band to band, from rank to rank,
His truchmen now, and now himself, doth say,
What spoil his folk shall gain, what praise, what thank.
To him that feared, "Look up, ours is the day,"
He says, "Vile fear to bold hearts never sank,
How dareth one against an hundred fight?
Our cry, our shade, will put them all to flight."

XXV

But to the bold, "Go, hardy knight," he says,
"His prey out of this lion's paws go tear:"
To some before his thoughts the shape he lays,
And makes therein the image true appear,
How his sad country him entreats and prays,
His house, his loving wife, and children dear:
"Suppose," quoth he, "thy country doth beseech
And pray thee thus, suppose this is her speech.

XXVI

"Defend my laws, uphold my temples brave,
My blood from washing of my streets withhold,
From ravishing my virgins keep, and save
Thine ancestors' dead bones and ashes cold!
To thee thy fathers dear and parents grave
Show their uncovered heads, white, hoary, old,
To thee thy wife — her breasts with tears o'erspread —
Thy sons, their cradles, shows, thy marriage bed."

XXVII

To all the rest, "You for her honor's sake
Whom Asia makes her champions, by your might
Upon these thieves, weak, feeble, few, must take
A sharp revenge, yet just, deserved and right."
Thus many words in several tongues he spake,
And all his sundry nations to sharp fight
Encouraged, but now the dukes had done
Their speeches all, the hosts together run.

XXVIII

It was a great, a strange and wondrous sight,
When front to front those noble armies met,
How every troop, how in each troop each knight
Stood prest to move, to fight, and praise to get,
Loose in the wind waved their ensigns light,

Trembled the plumes that on their crests were set;
Their arms, impresses, colors, gold and stone,
Against the sunbeams smiled, flamed, sparkled, shone.

XXIX
Of dry topped oaks they seemed two forests thick,
So did each host with spears and pikes abound,
Bent were their bows, in rests their lances stick,
Their hands shook swords, their slings held cobbles round:
Each steed to run was ready, prest and quick,
At his commander's spur, his hand, his sound,
He chafes, he stamps, careers, and turns about,
He foams, snorts, neighs, and fire and smoke breathes out.

XXX
Horror itself in that fair fight seemed fair,
And pleasure flew amid sad dread and fear;
The trumpets shrill, that thundered in the air,
Were music mild and sweet to every ear:
The faithful camp, though less, yet seemed more rare
In that strange noise, more warlike, shrill and clear,
In notes more sweet, the Pagan trumpets jar,
These sung, their armors shined, these glistered far.

XXXI
The Christian trumpets give the deadly call,
The Pagans answer, and the fight accept;
The godly Frenchmen on their knees down fall
To pray, and kissed the earth, and then up leapt
To fight, the land between was vanished all,
In combat close each host to other stepped;
For now the wings had skirmish hot begun,
And with their battles forth the footmen run.

XXXII
But who was first of all the Christian train,

That gave the onset first, first won renown?
Gildippes thou wert she, for by thee slain
The King of Orms, Hircano, tumbled down,
The man's breastbone thou clov'st and rent in twain,
So Heaven with honor would thee bless and crown,
Pierced through he fell, and falling hard withal
His foe praised for her strength and for his fall.

XXXIII

Her lance thus broke, the hardy dame forth drew
With her strong hand a fine and trenchant blade,
And gainst the Persians fierce and bold she flew,
And in their troop wide streets and lanes she made,
Even in the girdling−stead divided new
In pieces twain, Zopire on earth she laid;
And then Alarco's head she swept off clean,
Which like a football tumbled on the green.

XXXIV

A blow felled Artaxerxes, with a thrust
Was Argeus slain, the first lay in a trance,
Ismael's left hand cut off fell in the dust,
For on his wrist her sword fell down by chance:
The hand let go the bridle where it lust,
The blow upon the courser's ears did glance,
Who felt the reins at large. and with the stroke
Half mad, the ranks disordered, troubled, broke.

XXXV

All these, and many mo, by time forgot,
She slew and wounded, when against her came
The angry Persians all, cast on a knot,
For on her person would they purchase fame:
But her dear spouse and husband wanted not
In so great need, to aid the noble dame;
Thus joined, the haps of war unhurt they prove,

508

Their strength was double, double was their love.

XXXVI

The noble lovers use well might you see,
A wondrous guise, till then unseen, unheard,
To save themselves forgot both he and she,
Each other's life did keep, defend, and guard;
The strokes that gainst her lord discharged be,
The dame had care to bear, to break, to ward,
His shield kept off the blows bent on his dear,
Which, if need be, his naked head should bear.

XXXVII

So each saved other, each for other's wrong
Would vengeance take, but not revenge their own:
The valiant Soldan Artabano strong
Of Boecan Isle, by her was overthrown,
And by his hand, the bodies dead among,
Alvante, that durst his mistress wound, fell down,
And she between the eyes hit Arimont,
Who hurt her lord, and cleft in twain his front.

XXXVIII

But Altamore who had that wing to lead
Far greater slaughter on the Christians made;
For where he turned his sword, or twined his steed,
He slew, or man and beast on earth down laid,
Happy was he that was at first struck dead,
That fell not down on live, for whom his blade
Had speared, the same cast in the dusty street
His horse tore with his teeth, bruised with his feet.

XXXIX

By this brave Persian's valor, killed and slain
Were strong Brunello and Ardonia great;
The first his head and helm had cleft in twain,
The last in stranger–wise he did intreat,

For through his heart he pierced, and his seat,
Where laughter hath his fountain and his seat,
So that, a dreadful thing, believed uneath,
He laughed for pain, and laughed himself to death.

XL
Nor these alone with that accursed knife,
Of this sweet light and breath deprived lie;
But with that cruel weapon lost their life
Gentonio, Guascar, Rosimond, and Guy;
Who knows how many in that fatal strife
He slew? what knights his courser fierce made die?
The names and countries of the people slain
Who tells? their wounds and deaths who can explain?

XLI
With this fierce king encounter durst not one.
Not one durst combat him in equal field,
Gildippes undertook that task alone;
No doubt could make her shrink, no danger yield,
By Thermodont was never Amazone,
Who managed steeled axe, or carried shield,
That seemed so bold as she, so strong, so light,
When forth she run to meet that dreadful knight.

XLII
She hit him, where with gold and rich anmail,
His diadem did on his helmet flame,
She broke and cleft the crown, and caused him veil
His proud and lofty top, his crest down came,
Strong seemed her arm that could so well assail:
The Pagan shook for spite and blushed for shame,
Forward he rushed, and would at once requite
Shame with disgrace, and with revenge despite.

XLIII

Jerusalem Delivered

Right on the front he gave that lady kind
A blow so huge, so strong, so great, so sore,
That out of sense and feeling, down she twined:
But her dear knight his love from ground upbore,
Were it their fortune, or his noble mind,
He stayed his hand and strook the dame no more:
A lion so stalks by, and with proud eyes
Beholds, but scorns to hurt a man that lies.

XLIV

This while Ormondo false, whose cruel hand
Was armed and prest to give the trait'rous blow,
With all his fellows mongst Godfredo's band
Entered unseen, disguised that few them know:
The thievish wolves, when night o'ershades the land,
That seem like faithful dogs in shape and show,
So to the closed folds in secret creep,
And entrance seek; to kill some harmless sheep.

XLV

He proached nigh, and to Godfredo's side
The bloody Pagan now was placed near:
But when his colors gold and white he spied,
And saw the other signs that forged were,
"See, see, this traitor false!" the captain cried,
"That like a Frenchman would in show appear,
Behold how near his mates and he are crept!"
This said, upon the villain forth he leapt;

LXVI

Deadly he wounded him, and that false knight
Nor strikes nor wards nor striveth to be gone;
But, as Medusa's head were in his sight,
Stood like a man new turned to marble stone,
All lances broke, unsheathed all weapons bright,
All quivers emptied were on them alone,

511

In parts so many were the traitors cleft,
That those dead men had no dead bodies left.

LXVII
When Godfrey was with Pagan blood bespread,
He entered then the fight and that was past
Where the bold Persian fought and combated,
Where the close ranks he opened, cleft and brast;
Before the knight the troops and squadrons fled,
As Afric dust before the southern blast;
The Duke recalled them, in array them placed,
Stayed those that fled, and him assailed that chased.

LXVIII
The champions strong there fought a battle stout,
Troy never saw the like by Xanthus old:
A conflict sharp there was meanwhile on foot
Twixt Baldwin good and Muleasses bold:
The horsemen also near the mountains rout,
And in both wings, a furious skirmish hold,
And where the barbarous duke in person stood,
Twixt Tisiphernes and Adrastus proud;

XLIX
With Emiren Robert the Norman strove,
Long time they fought, yet neither lost nor won;
The other Robert's helm the Indian clove,
And broke his arms, their fight would soon be done:
From place to place did Tisiphernes rove,
And found no match, against him none dust run,
But where the press was thickest thither flew
The knight, and at each stroke felled, hurt, or slew.
L
Thus fought they long, yet neither shrink nor yield,
In equal balance hung their hope and fear:
All full of broken lances lay the field,

All full of arms that cloven and shattered were;
Of swords, some to the body nail the shield,
Some cut men's throats, and some their bellies tear;
Of bodies, some upright, some grovelling lay,
And for themselves eat graves out of the clay.

LI

Beside his lord slain lay the noble steed,
There friend with friend lay killed like lovers true,
There foe with foe, the live under the dead,
The victor under him whom late he slew:
A hoarse unperfect sound did eachwhere spread,
Whence neither silence, nor plain outcries flew:
There fury roars, ire threats, and woe complains,
One weeps, another cries, he sighs for pains.

LII

The arms that late so fair and glorious seem,
Now soiled and slubbered, sad and sullen grow,
The steel his brightness lost, the gold his beam;
The colors had no pride nor beauty's show;
The plumes and feathers on their crests that stream,
Are strowed wide upon the earth below:
The hosts both clad in blood, in dust and mire,
Had changed their cheer, their pride, their rich attire.

LIII

But now the Moors, Arabians, Ethiops black,
Of the left wing that held the utmost marge,
Spread forth their troops, and purposed at the back
And side their heedless foes to assail and charge:
Slingers and archers were not slow nor slack
To shoot and cast, when with his battle large
Rinaldo came, whose fury, haste and ire,
Seemed earthquake, thunder, tempest, storm and fire.

Jerusalem Delivered

LIV

The first he met was Asimire, his throne
That set in Meroe's hot sunburnt land,
He cut his neck in twain, flesh, skin and bone,
The sable head down tumbled on the sand;
But when by death of this black prince alone
The taste of blood and conquest once he fand,
Whole squadrons then, whole troops to earth he brought,
Things wondrous, strange, incredible he wrought.

LV

He gave more deaths than strokes, and yet his blows
Upon his feeble foes fell oft and thick,
To move three tongues as a fierce serpent shows,
Which rolls the one she hath swift, speedy, quick,
So thinks each Pagan; each Arabian trows
He wields three swords, all in one hilt that stick;
His readiness their eyes so blinded hath,
Their dread that wonder bred, fear gave it faith.

LVI

The Afric tyrants and the negro kings
Fell down on heaps, drowned each in other's blood,
Upon their people ran the knights he brings,
Pricked forward by their guide's example good,
Killed were the Pagans, broke their bows and slings:
Some died, some fell; some yielded, none withstood:
A massacre was this, no fight; these put
Their foes to death, those hold their throats to cut.

LVII

Small while they stood, with heart and hardy face,
On their bold breasts deep wounds and hurts to bear,
But fled away, and troubled in the chase
Their ranks disordered be with too much fear:
Rinaldo followed them from place to place,

Till quite discomfit and dispersed they were.
That done, he stays, and all his knights recalls,
And scorns to strike his foe that flies or falls.

LVIII

Like as the wind stopped by some wood or hill,
Grows strong and fierce, tears boughs and trees in twain,
But with mild blasts, more temperate, gentle, still,
Blows through the ample field or spacious plain;
Against the rocks as sea–waves murmur shrill,
But silent pass amid the open main:
Rinaldo so, when none his force withstood,
Assuaged his fury, calmed his angry mood;

LIX

He scorned upon their fearful backs that fled
To wreak his ire and spend his force in vain,
But gainst the footmen strong his troops he led,
Whose side the Moors had open left and plain,
The Africans that should have succored
That battle, all were run away or slain,
Upon their flank with force and courage stout
His men at arms assailed the bands on foot:

LX

He brake their pikes, and brake their close array,
Entered their battle, felled them down around,
So wind or tempest with impetuous sway
The ears of ripened corn strikes flat to ground:
With blood, arms, bodies dead, the hardened clay
Plastered the earth, no grass nor green was found;
The horsemen running through and through their bands,
Kill, murder, slay, few scape, not one withstands.

LXI

Rinaldo came where his forlorn Armide

Jerusalem Delivered

Sate on her golden chariot mounted high,
A noble guard she had on every side
Of lords, of lovers, and much chivalry:
She knew the man when first his arms she spied,
Love, hate, wrath, sweet desire strove in her eye,
He changed somedeal his look and countenance bold,
She changed from frost to fire, from heat to cold.

LXII

The prince passed by the chariot of his dear
Like one that did his thoughts elsewhere bestow,
Yet suffered not her knights and lovers near
Their rival so to scape withouten blow,
One drew his sword, another couched his spear,
Herself an arrow sharp set in her bow,
Disdain her ire new sharped and kindled hath,
But love appeased her, love assuaged her wrath.

LXIII

Love bridled fury, and revived of new
His fire, not dead, though buried in displeasure,
Three times her angry hand the bow updrew,
And thrice again let slack the string at leisure;
But wrath prevailed at last, the reed outflew,
For love finds mean, but hatred knows no measure,
Outflew the shaft, but with the shaft, this charm,
This wish she sent: Heaven grant it do no harm:

LXIV

She bids the reed return the way it went,
And pierce her heart which so unkind could prove,
Such force had love, though lost and vainly spent,
What strength hath happy, kind and mutual love?
But she that gentle thought did straight repent,
Wrath, fury, kindness, in her bosom strove,
She would, she would not, that it missed or hit,

Her eyes, her heart, her wishes followed it.

LXV

But yet in vain the quarrel lighted not,
For on his hauberk hard the knight it hit,
Too hard for woman's shaft or woman's shot,
Instead of piercing, there it broke and split;
He turned away, she burnt with fury hot,
And thought he scorned her power, and in that fit
Shot oft and oft, her shafts no entrance found,
And while she shot, love gave her wound on wound.
LXVI
"And is he then unpierceable," quoth she,
"That neither force nor foe he needs regard?
His limbs, perchance, armed with that hardness be,
Which makes his heart so cruel and so hard,
No shot that flies from eye or hand I see
Hurts him, such rigor doth his person guard,
Armed, or disarmed; his foe or mistress kind
Despised alike, like hate, like scorn I find.

LXVII

"But what new form is left, device or art,
By which, to which exchanged, I might find grace?
For in my knights, and all that take my part,
I see no help; no hope, no trust I place;
To his great prowess, might, and valiant heart,
All strength is weak, all courage vile and base."
This said she, for she saw how through the field
Her champions fly, faint, tremble, fall and yield.

LXVIII

Nor left alone can she her person save,
But to be slain or taken stands in fear,
Though with a bow a javelin long she have,
Yet weak was Phebe's bow, blunt Pallas' spear.

But, as the swan, that sees the eagle brave
Threatening her flesh and silver plumes to tear,
Falls down, to hide her mongst the shady brooks:
Such were her fearful motions, such her looks.

LXIX

But Altamore, this while that strove and sought
From shameful flight his Persian host to stay,
That was discomfit and destroyed to nought,
Whilst he alone maintained the fight and fray,
Seeing distressed the goddess of his thought,
To aid her ran, nay flew, and laid away
All care both of his honor and his host:
If she were safe, let all the world be lost.

LXX

To the ill−guarded chariot swift he flew,
His weapon made him way with bloody war:
Meanwhile Lord Godfrey and Rinaldo slew
His feeble bands, his people murdered are,
He saw their loss, but aided not his crew,
A better lover than a leader far,
He set Armida safe, then turned again
With tardy succor, for his folk were slain.

LXXI

And on that side the woful prince beheld
The battle lost, no help nor hope remained;
But on the other wing the Christians yield,
And fly, such vantage there the Egyptians gained,
One of the Roberts was nigh slain in field;
The other by the Indian strong constrained
To yield himself his captive and his slave;
Thus equal loss and equal foil they have.

LXXII

Godfredo took the time and season fit
To bring again his squadrons in array,
And either camp well ordered, ranged and knit,
Renewed the furious battle, fight and fray,
New streams of blood were shed, new swords them hit;
New combats fought, new spoils were borne away,
And unresolved and doubtful, on each side,
Did praise and conquest, Mars and Fortune ride.

LXXIII
Between the armies twain while thus the fight
Waxed sharp, hot, cruel, though renewed but late,
The Soldan clomb up to the tower's height,
And saw far off their strife and fell debate,
As from some stage or theatre the knight
Saw played the tragedy of human state,
Saw death, blood, murder, woe and horror strange,
And the great acts of fortune, chance, and change.

LXXIV
At first astonished and amazed he stood
Then burnt with wrath, and self−consuming ire,
Swelled his bosom like a raging flood,
To be amid that battle; such desire,
Such haste he had; he donned his helmet good,
His other arms he had before entire,
"Up, up!" he cried, "no more, no more, within
This fortress stay, come follow, die or win."

LXXV
Whether the same were Providence divine
That made him leave the fortress he possessed,
For that the empire proud of Palestine
This day should fall, to rise again more blessed;
Or that he breaking felt the fatal line
Of life, and would meet death with constant breast,

Furious and fierce he did the gates unbar,
And sudden rage brought forth, and sudden war.

LXXVI

Nor stayed he till the folk on whom he cried
Assemble might, but out alone he flies,
A thousand foes the man alone defied,
And ran among a thousand enemies:
But with his fury called from every side,
The rest run out, and Aladine forth hies,
The cowards had no fear, the wise no care,
This was not hope, nor courage, but despair.

LXXVII

The dreadful Turk with sudden blows down cast
The first he met, nor gave them time to plain
Or pray, in murdering them he made such haste
That dead they fell ere one could see them slain;
From mouth to mouth, from eye to eye forth passed
The fear and terror, that the faithful train
Of Syrian folk, not used to dangerous fight,
Were broken, scattered, and nigh put to flight.

LXXVIII

But with less terror, and disorder less,
The Gascoigns kept array, and kept their ground,
Though most the loss and peril them oppress,
Unwares assailed they were, unready found.
No ravening tooth or talon hard I guess
Of beast or eager hawk, doth slay and wound
So many sheep or fowls, weak, feeble, small,
As his sharp sword killed knights and soldiers tall.

LXXIX

It seemed his thirst and hunger 'suage he would
With their slain bodies, and their blood poured out,

With him his troops and Aladino old
Slew their besiegers, killed the Gascoign rout:
But Raymond ran to meet the Soldan bold,
Nor to encounter him had fear or doubt,
Though his right hand by proof too well he know,
Which laid him late for dead at one huge blow.

LXXX

They met, and Raymond fell amid the field,
This blow again upon his forehead light,
It was the fault and weakness of his eild,
Age is not fit to bear strokes of such might,
Each one lift up his sword, advanced his shield,
Those would destroy, and these defend the knight.
On went the Soldan, for the man he thought
Was slain, or easily might be captive brought.

LXXXI

Among the rest he ran, he raged, he smote,
And in small space, small time, great wonders wrought
And as his rage him led and fury hot,
To kill and murder, matter new he sought:
As from his supper poor with hungry throat
A peasant hastes, to a rich feast ybrought;
So from this skirmish to the battle great
He ran, and quenched with blood his fury's heat.

LXXXII

Where battered was the wall he sallied out,
And to the field in haste and heat he goes,
With him went rage and fury, fear and doubt
Remained behind, among his scattered foes:
To win the conquest strove his squadron stout,
Which he unperfect left; yet loth to lose
The day, the Christians fight, resist and die,
And ready were to yield, retire and fly.

Jerusalem Delivered

LXXXIII

The Gascoign bands retired, but kept array,
The Syrian people ran away outright,
The fight was near the place where Tancred lay,
His house was full of noise and great affright,
He rose and looked forth to see the fray,
Though every limb were weak, faint, void of might;
He saw the country lie, his men o'erthrown,
Some beaten back, some killed, some felled down.

LXXXIV

Courage in noble hearts that ne'er is spent,
Yet fainted not, though faint were every limb,
But reinforced each member cleft and rent,
And want of blood and strength supplied in him;
In his left hand his heavy shield he hent,
Nor seemed the weight too great, his curtlax trim
His right hand drew, nor for more arms he stood
Or stayed, he needs no more whose heart is good:

LXXXV

But coming forth, cried, "Whither will you run,
And leave your leader to his foes in prey?
What! shall these heathen of his armor won,
In their vile temples hang up trophies gay?
Go home to Gascoign then, and tell his son
That where his father died, you ran away:"
This said, against a thousand armed foes,
He did his breast weak, naked, sick, oppose.

LXXXVI

And with his heavy, strong and mighty targe,
That with seven hard bulls' hides was surely lined,
And strengthened with a cover thick and large
Of stiff and well-attempered steel behind,

He shielded Raymond from the furious charge,
From swords, from darts, from weapons of each kind,
And all his foes drove back with his sharp blade,
That sure and safe he lay, as in a shade.

LXXXVII

Thus saved, thus shielded, Raymond 'gan respire,
He rose and reared himself in little space,
And in his bosom burned the double fire
Of vengeance; wrath his heart; shame filled his face;
He looked around to spy, such was his ire,
The man whose stroke had laid him in that place,
Whom when he sees not, for disdain he quakes,
And on his people sharp revengement takes.

LXXXVIII

The Gascoigns turn again, their lord in haste
To venge their loss his hand recorded brings,
The troop that durst so much now stood aghast,
For where sad fear grew late, now boldness springs,
Now followed they that fled, fled they that chased;
So in one hour altereth the state of things,
Raymond requites his loss, shame, hurt and all,
And with an hundred deaths revenged one fall.

LXXXIX

Whilst Raymond wreaked thus his just disdain
On the proud–heads of captains, lords and peers,
He spies great Sion's king amid the train,
And to him leaps, and high his sword he rears,
And on his forehead strikes, and strikes again,
Till helm and head he breaks, he cleaves, he tears;
Down fell the king, the guiltless land he bit,
That now keeps him, because he kept not it.

XC

Their guides, one murdered thus, the other gone,
The troops divided were, in diverse thought,
Despair made some run headlong gainst their fone,
To seek sharp death that comes uncalled, unsought;
And some, that laid their hope on flight alone,
Fled to their fort again; yet chance so wrought,
That with the flyers in the victors pass,
And so the fortress won and conquered was.

XCI

The hold was won, slain were the men that fled,
In courts, halls, chambers high; above, below,
Old Raymond fast up to the leads him sped,
And there, of victory true sign and show,
His glorious standard to the wind he spread,
That so both armies his success might know.
But Solyman saw not the town was lost,
For far from thence he was. and near the host;
XCII

Into the field he came, the lukewarm blood
Did smoke and flow through all the purple field,
There of sad death the court and palace stood,
There did he triumphs lead, and trophies build;
An armed steed fast by the Soldan yood,
That had no guide, nor lord the reins to wield,
The tyrant took the bridle, and bestrode
The courser's empty back, and forth he rode.

XCIII

Great, yet but short and sudden was the aid
That to the Pagans, faint and weak, he brought,
A thunderbolt he was, you would have said,
Great, yet that comes and goes as swift as thought
And of his coming swift and flight unstayed
Eternal signs in hardest rocks hath wrought,
For by his hand a hundred knights were slain,

Jerusalem Delivered

But time forgot hath all their names but twain;

XCIV

Gildippes fair, and Edward thy dear lord,
Your noble death, sad end, and woful fate,
If so much power our vulgar tongue afford,
To all strange wits, strange ears let me dilate,
That ages all your love and sweet accord,
Your virtue, prowess, worth may imitate,
And some kind servant of true love that hears,
May grace your death, my verses, with some tears.

XCV

The noble lady thither boldly flew,
Where first the Soldan fought, and him defied,
Two mighty blows she gave the Turk untrue,
One cleft his shield, the other pierced his side;
The prince the damsel by her habit knew,
"See, see this mankind strumpet, see," he cried,
"This shameless whore, for thee fit weapons were
Thy neeld and spindle, not a sword and spear."

XCVI

This said, full of disdain, rage and despite,
A strong, a fierce, a deadly stroke he gave,
And pierced her armor, pierced her bosom white,
Worthy no blows, but blows of love to have:
Her dying hand let go the bridle quite,
She faints, she falls, 'twixt life and death she strave,
Her lord to help her came, but came too late,
Yet was not that his fault, it was his fate.

XCVII

What should he do? to diverse parts him call
Just ire and pity kind, one bids him go
And succor his dear lady, like to fall,
The other calls for vengeance on his foe;

525

Love biddeth both, love says he must do all,
And with his ire joins grief, with pity woe.
What did he then? with his left hand the knight
Would hold her up, revenge her with his right.

XCVIII
But to resist against a knight so bold
Too weak his will and power divided were;
So that he could not his fair love uphold,
Nor kill the cruel man that slew his dear.
His arm that did his mistress kind enfold,
The Turk cut off, pale grew his looks and cheer,
He let her fall, himself fell by her side,
And, for he could not save her, with her died.

XCIX
As the high elm, whom his dear vine hath twined
Fast in her hundred arms and holds embraced,
Bears down to earth his spouse and darling kind
If storm or cruel steel the tree down cast,
And her full grapes to naught doth bruise and grind,
Spoils his own leaves, faints, withers, dies at last,
And seems to mourn and die, not for his own,
But for her death, with him that lies o'erthrown:

C
So fell he mourning, mourning for the dame
Whom life and death had made forever his;
They would have spoke, but not one word could frame,
Deep sobs their speech, sweet sighs their language is,
Each gazed on other's eyes, and while the same
Is lawful, join their hands, embrace and kiss:
And thus sharp death their knot of life untied,
Together fainted they, together died.

CI

Jerusalem Delivered

But now swift fame her nimble wings dispread,
And told eachwhere their chance, their fate, their fall,
Rinaldo heard the case, by one that fled
From the fierce Turk and brought him news of all.
Disdain, good−will, woe, wrath the champion led
To take revenge; shame, grief, for vengeance call;
But as he went, Adrastus with his blade
Forestalled the way, and show of combat made.

CII

The giant cried, "By sundry signs I note
That whom I wish, I search, thou, thou art he,
I marked each worthy's shield, his helm, his coat,
And all this day have called and cried for thee,
To my sweet saint I have thy head devote,
Thou must my sacrifice, my offering be,
Come let us here our strength and courage try,
Thou art Armida's foe, her champion I."

CIII

Thus he defied him, on his front before,
And on his throat he struck him, yet the blow
His helmet neither bruised, cleft nor tore,
But in his saddle made him bend and bow;
Rinaldo hit him on the flank so sore,
That neither art nor herb could help him now;
Down fell the giant strong, one blow such power,
Such puissance had; so falls a thundered tower.

CIV

With horror, fear, amazedness and dread,
Cold were the hearts of all that saw the fray,
And Solyman, that viewed that noble deed,
Trembled, his paleness did his fear bewray;
For in that stroke he did his end areed,
He wist not what to think, to do, to say,

527

A thing in him unused, rare and strange,
But so doth heaven men's hearts turn, alter, change.

CV
As when the sick or frantic men oft dream
In their unquiet sleep and slumber short,
And think they run some speedy course, and seem
To move their legs and feet in hasty sort,
Yet feel their limbs far slower than the stream
Of their vain thoughts that bears them in this sport,
And oft would speak, would cry, would call or shout,
Yet neither sound, nor voice, nor word send out:

CVI
So run to fight the angry Soldan would,
And did enforce his strength, his might, his ire,
Yet felt not in himself his courage old,
His wonted force, his rage and hot desire,
His eyes, that sparkled wrath and fury bold,
Grew dim and feeble, fear had quenched that fire,
And in his heart an hundred passions fought,
Yet none on fear or base retire he thought.

CVII
While unresolved he stood, the victor knight
Arrived, and seemed in quickness, haste and speed,
In boldness, greatness, goodliness and might,
Above all princes born of human seed:
The Turk small while resists, not death nor fight
Made him forget his state or race, through dreed,
He fled no strokes, he fetched no groan nor sigh,
Bold were his motions last, proud, stately, high.

CVIII
Now when the Soldan, in these battles past
That Antheus–like oft fell oft rose again,

Evermore fierce, more fell, fell down at last
To lie forever, when this prince was slain,
Fortune, that seld is stable, firm or fast,
No longer durst resist the Christian train,
But ranged herself in row with Godfrey's knights,
With them she serves, she runs, she rides, she fights.

CIX

The Pagan troops, the king's own squadron fled,
Of all the east, the strength, the pride, the flower,
Late called Immortal, now discomfited,
It lost that title proud, and lost all power;
To him that with the royal standard fled,
Thus Emireno said, with speeches sour,
"Art not thou he to whom to bear I gave
My king's great banner, and his standard brave?

CX

"This ensign, Rimedon, I gave not thee
To be the witness of thy fear and flight,
Coward, dost thou thy lord and captain see
In battle strong, and runn'st thyself from fight?
What seek'st thou? safety? come, return with me,
The way to death is path to virtue right,
Here let him fight that would escape; for this
The way to honor, way to safety is."

CXI

The man returned and swelled with scorn and shame,
The duke with speeches grave exhorts the rest;
He threats, he strikes sometime, till back they came,
And rage gainst force, despair gainst death addressed.
Thus of his broken armies gan he frame
A battle now, some hope dwelt in his breast,
But Tisiphernes bold revived him most,
Who fought and seemed to win, when all was lost;

CXII

Wonders that day wrought noble Tisipherne,
The hardy Normans all he overthrew;
The Flemings fled before the champion stern,
Gernier, Rogero, Gerard bold he slew;
His glorious deeds to praise and fame etern
His life's short date prolonged, enlarged and drew,
And then, as he that set sweet life at nought,
The greatest peril, danger, most he sought.

CXIII

He spied Rinaldo, and although his field
Of azure purple now and sanguine shows,
And though the silver bird amid his shield
Were armed gules; yet he the champion knows.
And says, "Here greatest peril is, heavens yield
Strength to my courage, fortune to my blows,
That fair Armida her revenge may see,
Help, Macon, for his arms I vow to thee."

CXIV

Thus prayed he, but all his vows were vain,
Mahound was deaf, or slept in heavens above,
And as a lion strikes him with his train,
His native wrath to quicken and to move,
So he awaked his fury and disdain,
And sharped his courage on the whetstone love;
Himself he saved behind his mighty targe,
And forward spurred his steed and gave the charge.

CXV

The Christian saw the hardy warrior come,
And leaped forth to undertake the fight,
The people round about gave place and room,
And wondered on that fierce and cruel sight,

Some praised their strength, their skill and courage some,
Such and so desperate blows struck either knight,
That all that saw forgot both ire and strife,
Their wounds, their hurts, forgot both death and life.

CXVI

One struck, the other did both strike and wound,
His arms were surer, and his strength was more;
From Tisipheme the blood streamed down around;
His shield was deft, his helm was rent and tore.
The dame, that saw his blood besmear the ground,
His armor broke, limbs weak, wounds deep and sore,
And all her guard dead, fled, and overthrown,
Thought, now her field lay waste, her hedge lay down:

CXVII

Environed with so brave a troop but late,
Now stood she in her chariot all alone,
She feared bondage, and her life did hate,
All hope of conquest and revenge was gone,
Half mad and half amazed from where she sate,
She leaped down, and fled from friends' and fone,
On a swift horse she mounts, and forth she rides
Alone, save for disdain and love, her guides.

CXVIII

In days of old, Queen Cleopatra so
Alone fled from the fight and cruel fray,
Against Augustus great his happy foe,
Leaving her lord to loss and sure decay.
And as that lord for love let honor go,
Followed her flying sails and lost the day:
So Tisipherne the fair and fearful dame
Would follow, but his foe forbids the same.

CXIX

But when the Pagan's joy and comfort fled,
It seemed the sun was set, the day was night,
Gainst the brave prince with whom he combated
He turned, and on the forehead struck the knight:
When thunders forged are in Typhoius' bed,
Not Brontes' hammer falls so swift, so right;
The furious stroke fell on Rinaldo's crest,
And made him bend his head down to his breast.

CXX

The champion in his stirrups high upstart,
And cleft his hauberk hard and tender side,
And sheathed his weapon in the Pagan's heart,
The castle where man's life and soul do bide;
The cruel sword his breast and hinder part
With double wound unclosed, and opened wide;
And two large doors made for his life and breath,
Which passed, and cured hot love with frozen death.

CXXI

This done, Rinaldo stayed and looked around,
Where he should harm his foes, or help his friends;
Nor of the Pagans saw he squadron sound:
Each standard falls, ensign to earth descends;
His fury quiet then and calm he found,
There all his wrath, his rage, and rancor ends,
He called to mind how, far from help or aid,
Armida fled, alone, amazed, afraid:
CXXII
Well saw he when she fled, and with that sight
The prince had pity, courtesy and care;
He promised her to be her friend and knight
When erst he left her in the island bare:
The way she fled he ran and rode aright,
Her palfrey's feet signs in the grass outware:
But she this while found out an ugly shade,

Jerusalem Delivered

Fit place for death, where naught could life persuade.

CXXIII
Well pleased was she with those shadows brown,
And yet displeased with luck, with life, with love;
There from her steed she lighted, there laid down
Her bow and shafts, her arms that helpless prove.
"There lie with shame," she says, "disgraced, o'erthrown,
Blunt are the weapons, blunt the arms I move,
Weak to revenge my harms, or harm my foe,
My shafts are blunt, ah, love, would thine were so!

CXXIV
Alas, among so many, could not one,
Not one draw blood, one wound or rend his skin?
All other breasts to you are marble stone,
Dare you then pierce a woman's bosom thin?
See, see, my naked heart, on this alone
Employ your force this fort is eath to win,
And love will shoot you from his mighty bow,
Weak is the shot that dripile falls in snow.

CXXV
"I pardon will your fear and weakness past,
Be strong, mine arrows, cruel, sharp, gainst me,
Ah, wretch, how is thy chance and fortune cast,
If placed in these thy good and comfort be?
But since all hope is vain all help is waste,
Since hurts ease hurts, wounds must cure wounds in thee;
Then with thine arrow's stroke cure stroke of love,
Death for thy heart must salve and surgeon prove.

CXXVI
"And happy me if, being dead and slain,
I bear not with me this strange plague to hell:
Love, stay behind, come thou with me disdain,

And with my wronged soul forever dwell;
Or else with it turn to the world again
And vex that knight with dreams and visions fell,
And tell him, when twixt life and death I strove
My last wish, was revenge — last word, was love."

CXXVII
And with that word half mad, half dead, she seems,
An arrow, poignant, strong and sharp she took,
When her dear knight found her in these extremes,
Now fit to die, and pass the Stygian brook,
Now prest to quench her own and beauty's beams;
Now death sat on her eyes, death in her look,
When to her back he stepped, and stayed her arm
Stretched forth to do that service last, last harm.

CXXVIII
She turns and, ere she knows, her lord she spies,
Whose coming was unwished, unthought, unknown,
She shrieks, and twines away her sdainful eyes
From his sweet face, she falls dead in a swoon,
Falls as a flower half cut, that bending lies:
He held her up, and lest she tumble down,
Under her tender side his arm he placed,
His hand her girdle loosed, her gown unlaced;

CXXIX
And her fair face, fair bosom he bedews
With tears, tears of remorse, of ruth, of sorrow.
As the pale rose her color lost renews
With the fresh drops fallen from the silver morrow,
So she revives, and cheeks empurpled shows
Moist with their own tears and with tears they borrow;
Thrice looked she up, her eyes thrice closed she;
As who say, "Let me die, ere look on thee."

CXXX

And his strong arm, with weak and feeble hand
She would have thrust away, loosed and untwined:
Oft strove she, but in vain, to break that band,
For he the hold he got not yet resigned,
Herself fast bound in those dear knots she fand,
Dear, though she feigned scorn, strove and repined:
At last she speaks, she weeps, complains and cries;
Yet durst not, did not, would not see his eyes.

CXXXI

"Cruel at thy departure, at return
As cruel, say, what chance thee hither guideth,
Would'st thou prevent her death whose heart forlorn
For thee, for thee death's strokes each hour divideth?
Com'st thou to save my life? alas, what scorn,
What torment for Armida poor abideth?
No, no, thy crafts and sleights I well descry,
But she can little do that cannot die.

CXXXII

"Thy triumph is not great nor well arrayed
Unless in chains thou lead a captive dame:
A dame now ta'en by force, before betrayed,
This is thy greatest glory, greatest fame:
Time was that thee of love and life I prayed,
Let death now end my love. my life, my shame.
Yet let not thy false hand bereave this breath,
For if it were thy gift, hateful were death.

CXXXIII

"Cruel, myself an hundred ways can find,
To rid me from thy malice, from thy hate,
If weapons sharp, if poisons of all kind,
If fire, if strangling fail, in that estate,
Yet ways enough I know to stop this wind:

A thousand entries hath the house of fate.
Ah, leave these flatteries, leave weak hope to move,
Cease, cease, my hope is dead, dead is my love."

CXXXIV

Thus mourned she, and from her watery eyes
Disdain and love dropped down, rolled up in tears;
From his pure fountains ran two streams likewise,
Wherein chaste pity and mild ruth appears:
Thus with sweet words the queen he pacifies,
"Madam, appease your grief, your wrath, your fears,
For to be crowned, not scorned, your life I save;
Your foe nay, but your friend, your knight, your slave.

CXXXV

"But if you trust no speech. no oath, no word;
Yet in mine eyes, my zeal, my truth behold:
For to that throne, whereof thy sire was lord,
I will restore thee, crown thee with that gold,
And if high Heaven would so much grace afford
As from thy heart this cloud this veil unfold
Of Paganism, in all the east no dame
Should equalize thy fortune, state and fame."

CXXXVI

Thus plaineth he, thus prays, and his desire
Endears with sighs that fly and tears that fall;
That as against the warmth of Titan's fire,
Snowdrifts consume on tops of mountains tall,
So melts her wrath; but love remains entire.
"Behold," she says, "your handmaid and your thrall:
My life, my crown, my wealth use at your pleasure;"
Thus death her life became, loss proved her tensure.
CXXXVII

This while the captain of the Egyptian host, —
That saw his royal standard laid on ground,

Saw Rimedon, that ensign's prop and post,
By Godfrey's noble hand killed with one wound,
And all his folk discomfit, slain and lost,
No coward was in this last battle found,
But rode about and sought, nor sought in vain,
Some famous hand of which he might be slain;

CXXXVIII

Against Lord Godfrey boldly out he flew,
For nobler foe he wished not, could not spy,
Of desperate courage showed he tokens true,
Where'er he joined, or stayed, or passed by,
And cried to the Duke as near he drew,
"Behold of thy strong hand I come to die,
Yet trust to overthrow thee with my fall,
My castle's ruins shall break down thy wall."

CXXXIX

This said, forth spurred they both, both high advance
Their swords aloft, both struck at once, both hit,
His left arm wounded had the knight of France,
His shield was pierced, his vantbrace cleft and split,
The Pagan backward fell, half in a trance,
On his left ear his foe so hugely smit,
And as he sought to rise, Godfredo's sword
Pierced him through, so died that army's lord.

CXL

Of his great host, when Emiren was dead,
Fled the small remnant that alive remained;
Godfrey espied as he turned his steed,
Great Altamore on foot, with blood all stained,
With half a sword, half helm upon his head,
Gainst whom a hundred fought, yet not one gained.
"Cease, cease this strife," he cried: "and thou, brave knight,
Yield, I am Godfrey, yield thee to my might!"

Jerusalem Delivered

CXLI

He that till then his proud and haughty heart
To act of humbleness did never bend,
When that great name he heard, from the north part
Of our wide world renowned to Aethiop's end,
Answered, "I yield to thee, thou worthy art,
I am thy prisoner, fortune is thy friend:
On Altamoro great thy conquest bold
Of glory shall be rich, and rich of gold:

CXLII

"My loving queen, my wife and lady kind
Shall ransom me with jewels, gold and treasure."
"God shield," quoth Godfrey, "that my noble mind
Should praise and virtue so by profit measure,
All that thou hast from Persia and from Inde
Enjoy it still, therein I take no pleasure;
I set no rent on life, no price on blood,
I fight, and sell not war for gold or good."

CXLIII

This said, he gave him to his knights to keep
And after those that fled his course he bent;
They to their rampiers fled and trenches deep,
Yet could not so death's cruel stroke prevent:
The camp was won, and all in blood doth steep
The blood in rivers streamed from tent to tent,
It soiled, defiled, defaced all the prey,
Shields, helmets, armors, plumes and feathers gay.

CXLIV

Thus conquered Godfrey, and as yet the sun
Dived not in silver waves his golden wain,
But daylight served him to the fortress won
With his victorious host to turn again,

538

Jerusalem Delivered

His bloody coat he put not off, but run
To the high temple with his noble train,
And there hung up his arms, and there he bows
His knees, there prayed, and there performed his vows.

CPSIA information can be obtained
at www.ICGtesting.com
Printed in the USA
BVHW091931191219
567229BV00006B/100/P